HER BASEBORN SCOT

THE HIGHLAND WARRIOR CHRONICLES

CHRISTINA PHILLIPS

PHOENIX 18 PUBLISHING

Edited by Amanda Ashby
Cover Art by Kim Killion Publishing
10/2021

ISBN 978-0-6451584-2-7

For Mark
With all my love

CHAPTER 1

THE KINGDOM OF FOTLA, PICTLAND.
WINTER 843

Mairi, Princess Annella of Fortriu, sank onto the edge of the bed and grasped her aged husband's hand. The candles flickered in the incessant drafts from the ill-fitting window shutters, and black shadows loomed across the cold, stone, walls of the chamber.

She took a deep breath. It would do no good to show fear. "I will send for the royal physician from Fib. You must recover, Nechtan."

He squeezed her fingers, a gesture to convey comfort, but his grip was weak, and the black fear curled tighter in her chest. "It's too late for that, my jewel. The veil is parting. You know this."

Of course she knew it. She had known it for weeks, even before Nechtan had fallen sick, but had chosen to ignore the warnings. The sight she'd inherited from her foremothers was not, after all, always right.

Yes, it is.

She ignored that truth, also. Nechtan, quite simply, could not be allowed to die.

"Then I shall offer great sacrifice to the goddess and beseech her to delay your journey." Tenderly, she stroked his gray hair back

1

from his brow. She had never loved him as a husband, but she loved him, nevertheless. "Pictland needs your strength, my lord."

Pain flared in his faded eyes, and he struggled to pull himself upright. Faithful Bhaic, her husband's dearest friend and advisor, and their constant companion, emerged from the shadows and came to their side. With infinite care, he helped Nechtan to sit, before taking a respectful step backward.

"Mairi, listen to me." Nechtan tore his lingering gaze from Bhaic and focused on her. "When I'm gone, you must wed Bhaic. It's the only way to protect you from MacAlpin's poisoned web."

Her stomach knotted at the sound of the hated name. Kenneth MacAlpin, upstart king of the Scots who had so recently murdered nine Pictish nobles with matrilineal ties to the throne of the supreme kingdom of the Picts, Fortriu.

Her birthright.

He was the reason she'd been hiding like a common criminal, in her own beloved land, for the last six months. The reason she hadn't seen any of her royal relatives, for fear that her presence might endanger them.

She'd heard how MacAlpin was ensnaring the princesses of Pictland and binding them to his cursed Scots warriors through forced marriages. A political tactic so he could encroach ever further into their precious highlands and claim it for his own.

Vengeance burned deep within her heart. She would make him pay for everything that her people had lost, or die in the attempt.

With difficulty, she forced the image to the back of her mind. Nechtan knew nothing of her thirst for retribution, and he never would. In his last hours, she owed him his peace of mind, at least.

But his words could not be ignored. "I will not wed Bhaic. There is no need."

Nechtan sucked in a rasping breath. "If MacAlpin discovers you're still alive, he will kill you, Mairi. You're the only one who could challenge his claim for the throne of Fortriu. He must never discover who you are."

"He won't." *Until I plunge my sword through his corrupt heart.* It was a wild dream, but it had kept her focused during her exile. Goddess willing, she would achieve justice for her people.

MacAlpin's lies could not be allowed to taint the future of Pictland.

"Promise me." There was a fierce light in his eyes now, and his grip on her hand tightened. "Never reveal who you truly are. Mairi, Princess Annella of Fortriu died six months ago. You are my second wife, and you'll inherit my stronghold in Fib. You'll be safe, but only if you conceal your birthright."

"Nechtan." She knew he was only trying to protect her. But it hurt, having to pretend to be someone she wasn't. When they had fled the palace of Forteviot, six months ago, she had never imagined their ruse would fool anyone. And yet no one had questioned it.

But that didn't mean she wanted the rest of her life to be a lie. Her beloved grandfather, King Wrad, had united the seven kingdoms of Pictland. Sorrow squeezed her heart at his recent passing, but she could not afford the luxury of succumbing to her grief. As the last of his bloodline, when the time was right, it was her duty to bring the kingdoms together to stand against the Scots upstart. "I can't hide forever."

"You can. You must." His grip became painful, and his breath erratic. Bhaic stepped closer and grasped Nechtan's shoulder in silent support and she crushed the flare of resentment that burned through her. Always, they had protected her. She had to remember that, even though whenever there was dissent, they both sided against her. "Mairi. I will not rest easy unless you give me your word on this matter."

She drew in a shaky breath. She couldn't save his life, but she could save him from bearing this heavy burden when he passed through the veil. "I give you my word. I'll tell no one my true name."

He sank back onto the pillows, the strength seeming to drain from him now he had her promise. "You have been a good wife, my jewel. Better than I deserved." He kissed her fingers, the way he had so many times in the past. There was no passion in the action. Merely the regard a father might feel for a beloved daughter. Her smile was sad as his gaze locked with hers, for perhaps the last time. "I need to speak to Bhaic alone."

She inclined her head, stood, and bestowed a chaste kiss upon his brow, before making her way across the chamber. At the door she paused and glanced back at the bed. Bhaic had taken her place and his head was bowed, and he and Nechtan grasped hands.

Familiar sorrow weaved through her heart. Once, long ago, she had dreamed of finding a love so powerful that not even the veil would separate them. Her dreams had died five years ago on her wedding day, and perhaps that was for the best. She was no longer a naïve maid of fifteen, pining for her handsome Pictish prince.

High King Wrad's blood flowed in her veins. Not only was she the last of his line, she was also the last remaining princess of her royal foremothers of Fortriu.

The future of Pictland was at stake, and she would not allow their legacy to die.

~

The Kingdom of Dal Riada

THE WIND WAS BITTER, freezing his skin and whipping at his hair as Finn Braeson drew his horse to a halt. It was late afternoon and dark clouds hung low in the sky, obscuring the sun. As he dismounted, fierce pride and bone-deep relief surged through him as he drank in the sight of his hillfort, Duncarn.

Home.

It had been two years since he'd acquired the property but even now the knowledge that his family was safe was something he never took for granted.

It was small, compared to many of his compatriots' estates, but it more than served his purposes. And, most importantly, it was tucked into the north-eastern corner of Dal Riada, as far away as possible from the royal stronghold of Dunadd, without encroaching into the savage lands of the Picts.

His steward hurried towards him. "Welcome home, my lord."

Finn grasped his shoulder. Even though the man was his step-sister's husband, he refused to call Finn by his given name. But it was a small complaint. Norval was a good husband to Annis. "It's a fleeting visit. I need to leave at first light."

Because MacAlpin wanted him at his damn council meeting in Dunadd the following day. God alone knew why. He hadn't demanded Finn's presence at such an assembly before. Why the fuck would he? Finn meant nothing to the king.

He shoved the disagreeable notion of his king to the back of his mind. Time enough to think on such things the following day. Norval accompanied him into the great hall, bringing him up to date with the estate's management, even though it had been barely three weeks since he had last visited.

The door to his mother's private chambers swung open and his little niece, followed by her young brother, ran to him. He laughed and scooped the pair of them into his arms. "It's been too long since I've seen you, Nessa. You're bonnier than ever."

Nessa giggled and wound her arms around his neck. He dropped a kiss on her soft curls, and the tension that invariably knotted his shoulders eased, the way it always did when the wee ones were near.

She took a deep breath, excitement bubbling from her. "Iver has a new tooth!"

"Does he, now?" He turned to the boy, who obligingly opened his mouth. Finn inspected the array of teeth. He had no clue which was the new one, but they were all delightful. "Well done."

Their mother Annis approached, her smile lighting up the hall. "Brother, it's so good to see you again. I will ensure your chamber is made ready for you." She glanced over her shoulder. "Our lady mother awaits you."

He kissed Annis' cheek and she patted his arm. How confident and strong she was. So different from the terrified child of seven he'd first met fourteen years ago, when his mother had wed the tavern keeper.

His gut curdled at the memory of those dark years, and instinctively his grip tightened on the bairns. They were safe. No harm would befall any of them, not under this roof. Not on his watch.

He strode into his mother's chamber. She sat by the hearth, and the fire cast a welcoming glow, but it was the smile on her face and the exclaims of pleasure from his stepsister and young half-sister that warmed his heart.

"How long are you staying for?" His half-sister Rhona stood, and dropped her embroidery onto her stool. "It has been so *dull* here without you."

"Dull is good." He set the bairns down, nodded a greeting to his stepsister, Glenna, and tossed a grin at his mother. "Has Rhona's embroidery improved since my last visit?"

Rhona gave a disagreeable sniff. They were all well aware she would rather be on horseback than concentrating on her needle, but noble blood ran in her veins. He was resolved that she learned every art a gently bred lady possessed.

She would never toil in degradation, the way their mother had. He forced the simmering anger down and thrust it once more into its cage. True vengeance for the way she had been wronged would never be his to claim, but at least now she could enjoy a semblance of the life that should have been hers.

"Her diligence has been most enlightening." There was a teasing gleam in his mother's eyes as she glanced at the exasperated Rhona. "It seems the promise of her own mare has wrought a miracle."

He laughed, and ruffled Rhona's hair. She batted his hand away and sighed dramatically. "I'm not a bairn, Finn."

No, she wasn't, and it sobered his mood. She was twelve, and soon it would be his duty to find her a suitable husband.

But not yet. She could enjoy a few more years untroubled by such things.

He went over to Glenna, where she stood beside his mother's chair, and took her hands. "How are you faring?"

"Well enough. I'm more than ready for this babe to make its appearance."

"You have everything you need?"

She squeezed his fingers. "Aye. This bairn will be the most spoiled creature in Dal Riada—after Nessa and Iver."

"They're not spoiled." He offered her a mocking grin. "Who else should I provide for, but my family?"

She shook her head and released his hands. "I know."

"But, Finn." There was a worried note in Rhona's voice. "What will happen when you wed? Your bride will be your family, then."

"Duncarn is big enough for all."

Rhona frowned. "Your wife will want her own household. What will become of us?"

A noblewoman would expect nothing less. But the chances of him securing such a woman as his bride were remote. No influential father would give his daughter's hand to an unclaimed bastard, no matter how wealthy.

He wasn't wealthy yet. But in another year or two, when he'd firmly secured all their futures, he would look for a bride from those whose blood wasn't tainted by the nobility. A woman to cherish who wouldn't care about his past. A lass who would love him, the way Annis and Glenna loved their husbands. And God willing, she'd provide him with beloved bairns of his own.

"Nothing will become of you," he assured his young sister. "When I choose my bride, I'll ensure she knows Duncarn is the home of the lady Brae." He glanced at his mother, but her answering smile looked oddly strained.

"Come, Rhona." Glenna held out her hand to her half-sister. "Let's go and help Annis with all the preparations I'm sure she's making for Finn's arrival." Once they had ushered Nessa and Iver from the chamber and closed the door, Finn sat on a stool beside his mother.

"Are you well?" He knew she still suffered from the years she'd labored in the tavern, and from the fist of the piece of shit she'd wed, but she never complained. Her honor forbade it.

"I'm all the better for seeing you, my son. But enough of me. Are the Norsemen repelled from Iona?"

After leaving Duncarn three weeks ago, he'd been ordered to the sacred Isle, which the northern barbarians had, once again, invaded. By the time he and his fellow warriors had arrived, they had already fled. But not before ransacking yet another holy site in their quest for treasure.

"Aye. For now." But they would return. Of that he had no doubt.

"How long can you stay?"

He let out a frustrated breath between clenched teeth. He was overdue for time away from the battlefields, but MacAlpin appeared oblivious to such considerations. And he'd rather tear out his own tongue than ask the king for such a favor. He would never lower himself to ask the king for anything.

Finn was certain that as far as MacAlpin was concerned, the debt Finn owed him would take a lifetime of unquestioning acquiescence to repay. The prospect weighed heavy in his chest, but despite that, it was better than the alternative had been.

"I'm expected back at Dunadd tomorrow."

"Is the king at Dunadd? I thought he was in Fortriu."

"He was. But he met with two Pictish princesses at Dunadd, who are now wed to our warriors."

"Strategic alliances, to be sure."

He grunted. He had no doubt they were, but what kind of marriages could they be? It was just as well MacAlpin barely acknowledged his existence. There was no way he wanted to be used in such as manner as both Connor MacKenzie and Cameron MacNeil had been.

Unease snaked through him. He'd joined the ranks at the age of sixteen. Why, after six years of service, had he been summoned to MacAlpin's inner sanctum? Only his most trusted advisors were invited to his war chamber. Or warriors such as MacKenzie and MacNeil, whose fathers had enjoyed the friendship of their king.

"Did you see the king, Finn?"

He dragged his attention back to the present. He knew his mother dearly wished for MacAlpin to show him favor, but it would never happen. Finn might fight for his king and country but that didn't mean he had to respect the man. Or want anything more from him than he afforded any of his other warriors.

Although a few months respite would be appreciated.

"Only from a distance. He was busy with his machinations." He couldn't keep the contempt from his voice, although he certainly managed to do so when he was with his fellow warriors. Any hint of disapproval regarding MacAlpin was considered nothing less than treason.

But he could say anything to his mother. Even if there were some things he would never share with her.

"A strong king must make many unpleasant decisions." There was a wistful note in his mother's voice and Finn set his expression into a stone mask. It wasn't that he disagreed. There was no place for a weak king yet he still despised MacAlpin's schemes.

I have no proof of my suspicions.

No proof that his king had betrayed the alliance between Scot and Pict, except for the certainty in his gut. A certainty he would take with him to the grave.

CHAPTER 2

DUNADD, DAL RIADA

The westerly breeze from the sea whipped icy talons across Finn's face and the tang of salt was heavy in the air as he made his way to the heavily fortified southern face of Dunadd.

There was still an hour before he was expected in the king's presence, which gave him time to visit one of the royal Pictish hostages that MacAlpin had seized six months ago.

The warrior on guard let him pass without comment and he entered the fort. Two more warriors patrolled the passageway, where locked doors led to the chambers of the incarcerated. He halted outside one and rapped on the wooden door. It was common courtesy. Not merely because the hostage was a prince but because six months ago they had fought the Northumbrians side by side, and the prince had earned his respect.

One of the guards rolled his eyes in evident contempt. Finn ignored him. They'd known each other for years and had engaged in many bloody fights while growing up.

He lifted the deadbolt and opened the door. Talargan, Prince of Ce, acknowledged him with a sharp nod.

"My lord." Finn stepped back to allow Talargan to leave the

chamber and they made their way outside, the guard following at some distance. The prince drew in a deep breath and without a word they strode from the shadow of Dunadd.

"This existence is intolerable." Talargan came to a halt and rounded on Finn. They were far enough away from the guard that their conversation wouldn't be overheard, but not far enough so that a prized hostage could attempt to flee. "How much longer does your king intend to keep us from our land?"

"You know I don't have the king's ear." Even if he did, he wouldn't pass the information onto Talargan, despite his personal feelings, and the prince knew it. But he understood the other man's frustration. If their positions were reversed, he would be desperate to escape the confines of Dunadd.

"I should be in Ce, where I can protect my kin."

Finn grunted. They'd had this conversation the last time he'd seen the prince, more than two months ago. And again, he understood. Talargan wanted to provide for his widowed mother and his sisters, just as Finn did with his own family.

"My only consolation," Talargan said, bitterness threading through the words, "is my sister, the eldest Princess Devorgilla of Ce, is happy to be wedded to Connor MacKenzie."

Interesting. The notion that the princess might not loathe the situation she had been coerced into had never occurred to him.

"I'm glad for the princess." He spoke the truth. He'd never met her, but he knew Connor well enough and had no reason to wish the warrior a lifetime of marital misery.

Talargan shook his head. "She deserves such happiness."

They were silent, as from their elevated position they contemplated the distant firth of Lorn and where, across that stretch of water, lay the sacred Isle of Iona.

Finally, Talargan spoke. "Has there still been no further word on the fate of the Princess of Fortriu?"

While in Northumbria, Talargan had spoken of the princess and had confessed he harbored a hope that one day they might forge a future together. Finn couldn't see it, but he hadn't disputed the prince's words. It was obvious he cared about this princess and even though, after MacAlpin had claimed the throne of Fortriu, rumors had reached Dunadd of her untimely death, Talargan refused to believe it.

"I've heard nothing of her, my lord." In truth, it was just as well. If she was, indeed, still alive, she was wise to keep as far away from the political maelstrom that engulfed Fortriu.

"Or of her husband." It wasn't a question. More a curse. "Finn, if you discover anything about her, you must tell me."

He'd already given his word, six months ago, when the prince had first been taken hostage. Nothing had changed.

"You know I will."

FINN ENTERED the king's antechamber and swallowed a curse. The door to the inner sanctum was closed but Constantine, the king's eldest son, was pacing the floor of the antechamber and when he caught sight of Finn, he stopped dead.

"What the fuck are you doing here?"

"I was summoned." He gained a measure of grim satisfaction that Constantine had been unaware of that fact.

"Fuck that." Constantine stalked across the floor, menace blazing from him. Finn curled his lip. It had been many years since the prince had been able to beat him in a fight. Even as a child, Finn hadn't let the threat of spilling royal blood stop him from defending himself.

Or his mother.

The door to the war chamber swung open and MacAllister, the king's right-hand man, cast his speculative gaze over them. "The king will see you now."

Constantine marched inside, and Finn followed. MacAllister closed the door behind them. So this was where the strategies and plans were made that affected all their lives. The chamber was smaller than he'd imagined, with the king sitting behind a heavy timber desk and four of his closest confidents flanking his chair. Aedh, Constantine's younger brother by a mere eleven months, came from MacAlpin's side to stand next to the eldest prince.

It had never been a secret as to which son the king favored.

Constantine went onto one knee and bowed his head. "My liege."

Masking his unwillingness as best he could, Finn also dropped onto his knee. "My liege." He only hoped the words sounded as sincere as Constantine's had.

"Rise." MacAlpin waved his hand in an impatient gesture. Finn stood at Constantine's left, two paces behind, as protocol demanded. They were not, after all, equals.

Finn caught one of the king's advisers giving him an assessing look. As if he couldn't quite fathom why he was there. That made two of them. He wished the king would get on with it. The war chamber was oppressive, and not simply because it possessed no windows.

The king leaned back in his great, carved chair and the silence grew heavy. Did he always do this within these walls? Finn had only ever received the king's orders second hand. He knew which method he preferred.

Finally, MacAlpin spoke.

"News has reached us that the elusive Princess of Fortriu has been sighted in Fotla."

Awareness rippled around the chamber, and Finn sucked in a sharp breath. Talargan had been right to believe she was still alive. But how long would she now remain so?

"Is she to be eliminated?" There was uncertainty in Constantine's voice. Clearly, he had reservations in murdering a princess of Pictland, even if he had no compunction in murdering her countrymen.

Enough. He could not allow such treasonous thoughts to cross his mind when in the presence of his king.

"Would that be your decision, Constantine, were you king?"

"The princess has a strong claim to the throne of Fortriu."

"Indeed." MacAlpin turned to one of his advisers. "What of you, Donald. Would that be your advice?"

Malice glowed in Donald's eyes. He was the king's half-brother but had no matrilineal claim on the Pictish kingdom. "Aye. If you want to make her a martyr to her people."

"I have no wish to harm the princess." MacAlpin's voice rang around the chamber. It was obvious he had made this decision before even convening this meeting. Did he always throw rhetorical questions to his advisers? "She is, after all, of my blood."

Finn cast his gaze around the gathered men. Their faces were shuttered, concealing their true thoughts. Aedh appeared composed, but Constantine's shoulders were rigid as though he were on trial.

Maybe he was.

Still didn't explain why *he* had been summoned to witness this show.

"Her husband, however, is not," Donald said.

Silence once again echoed around the chamber, as the chilling implication sank in. A knot of dread settled in Finn's gut. Was this meeting to arrange the assassination of the princess' husband?

Had he been chosen for this godless task?

"It's imperative we secure the princess, for her own safety." MacAlpin's steady gaze drilled into Aedh, then Constantine, before coming to rest on Finn. "She is far too valuable to be at the mercy of a husband who seems intent to force her to traverse Pictland like a fugitive. It is our duty to find her and bring her back home."

Was the king waiting for his response? He had never learned the diplomacy required for the royal court and had no desire to lose his head by telling the king what he truly thought of his plans. Because MacAlpin still hadn't addressed the problem of the princess' husband.

"Well, boy?" The king's gaze never left him, and Finn didn't quite manage to hide his affront at the insult. "What say you? Do you disapprove of bringing my royal cousin under my protection? You have my permission to speak freely."

Why the fuck was he asking him? But since he had, he would respond, and voice the unspoken question. "The princess may not wish to leave her husband behind, sire."

The king smiled. Clearly, his candor pleased him. "You are correct. She may not. However, he is elderly and it's unlikely he'll survive another harsh winter. When she is widowed, she'll have little choice in the matter."

And here it was. His muscles tensed, waiting for the order to murder the husband of the woman Talargan loved. An old man, a minor royal of Fib, who had once been a fearsome warrior, but who, according to the Pictish prince, hadn't wielded a sword since his marriage.

There was no honor in obeying such an order. But if he did not, his own life would be forfeit and land confiscated. Who would then be left to provide for his mother and his sisters?

But he couldn't remain silent.

"There's no guarantee her husband will perish this winter. He's survived until now."

The king's advisers drew in a collective breath at his nerve, and Donald smirked, but MacAlpin didn't appear outraged by his not-so-subtle implication.

"Once again, you speak the truth. Perhaps I should have invited you into my inner circle before now."

Constantine slung him a glare of loathing over his shoulder, but Finn ignored him. After a lifetime of disregard, the king had him in his sights.

Nothing good could come of being caught in MacAlpin's web, no matter how his mother thought otherwise.

"Consider this, Finn. In all the years they've been wed, he has sired no heir for Fortriu. It's possible, of course, the princess is barren. Which would be a blessing but not something we can rely upon."

Heat flooded through his veins. It was wrong to speak of the princess in such a manner, but it appeared no one else in the chamber thought anything of it. He glowered at the king, unable to help himself, but the only indication MacAlpin acknowledged his discomfort was a fleeting smile.

"Let us also consider, for our purposes, that the princess is widowed." Finally, MacAlpin released him from his fierce gaze and arrowed his attention on his royal born sons. "Barren or not, it would be remiss of us not to secure her a royal marriage worthy of her status. One that unites Scot and Pict."

So that was the king's plan. To forge an alliance between a noble born Scot and the Princess of Fortriu. Not that he was surprised. It strengthened his conviction that the only reason he had been included in this conclave was as the intended widow maker.

One question remained. Would he be allowed to live after obeying the king's command, or would he be publicly executed as a show of justice?

He was damned whatever happened after the act. To kill in battle was one thing. In cold blood, it was something else. And whatever the rumors might whisper, he had never killed in cold blood.

"A royal match?" Constantine glanced at his brother before looking back at the king. "Do you mean for Aedh or me to take a second wife?"

MacAlpin laughed but there was little humor in the sound. "No. Your alliances will not be threatened by such a barbaric arrangement. I'm acknowledging my son Finn, formerly known as Braeson, into the royal House of Alpin."

The words thundered in his head, an ominous echo, as his gaze caught MacAlpin's. The king had a satisfied smile on his face, as though he waited for Finn's gratitude at the great honor he had bestowed.

His chest tightened, restricting his lungs, and pressing into his heart. As a child, he had often wished his father would admit to his existence. But later, when he understood how much his mother had lost, the desire to be accepted had corroded and twisted into a dark resentment of the man who had ruined her life.

MacAlpin only recognized him now because it suited his purposes. Not because it was the honorable thing to do.

Fuck.

Realization blasted through him, colder than the ice that spread across the lochs in the depths of winter. MacAlpin didn't want him to assassinate the Pictish royal. He intended him to wed the Princess of Fortriu.

Through a red haze, he became aware of the subtle shift in the advisers' stances, and their assessing glances as they recategorized his status in their minds. He didn't give a shit for their good opinion. His future had just been torn from him, warped beyond recognition, and thrust back in his face with careless disregard.

"Finn?" Constantine swung around, animosity glittering in his eyes. He returned the glare, measure for measure, daring the older man to raise his fist. God damn it, he wanted Constantine to start a fight, so he could smash his fist into his face. But it wouldn't be his half-brother he saw in his mind. It was the king.

I need to get out of here.

He clenched his hands, but Constantine held back, as a deadly silence wrapped around the chamber. Aedh turned to look at him but as always it was impossible to read his expression. MacAlpin rose and strode around his desk until he stood before the three of them.

"Finn has proved his loyalty to me these last six years. He has earned this right." MacAlpin grasped his shoulder and Finn clenched his jaw. *Don't react.* "Henceforth, you will be known and addressed as Lord Finn, Prince of the House of Alpin."

The hell he would. The denial slammed through him. Forever contained. He had no choice in the matter, but in his heart, he would remain his mother's son. Not the son of the man who had abandoned her.

"Welcome, brother." There was a thread of amusement in Aedh's voice. "Am I correct in assuming congratulations are in order?"

"You are," MacAlpin confirmed. "This marriage between the House of Alpin and the Princess of Fortriu will irretrievably bind Scot and Pict together. Whether the union produces issue or not is immaterial. The lineage will be secured."

Issue.

His closely held dreams of one day having his own family withered and died. This marriage was nothing but another alliance to strengthen MacAlpin's grip on Pictland. The fate thrust upon both MacKenzie and MacNeil, was now also his.

Arranged marriages were usual for royalty and the nobility, and while love was rarely a factor, at least the bride wasn't spoils of war. The contract benefited all concerned and bairns were a natural progression of that union.

He had royal blood, but he'd never had the name. Never imagined the question of his bride would concern anyone but himself and her family.

Despair rolled through him at the prospect of a lifetime tethered to a Pictish princess who had yet to be widowed. A woman who would undoubtedly despise everything connected to the Scots. How could she not?

The Princess of Fortriu would never willingly agree to wed a man related to Kenneth MacAlpin, and a bastard at that.

Too much blood had been spilled.

Bitterness blazed deep inside his heart, a futile grief. There would be no *issue* from their union. How fortunate the king didn't require such a duty from him.

"You will be well compensated, Finn, never fear." The king smiled at him. It was a chilling thing to behold. "The princess will inherit all of her husband's considerable wealth, including his stronghold in the Kingdom of Fib. Naturally, all she possesses will pass to you upon your marriage."

He had no interest in acquiring her property, but it was just as well the princess had her own household. She would never fit in with the life he'd once planned at Duncarn.

"And then there is the small matter of your own inheritance."

"I have no inheritance." Did he sound surly? The sharp glances from the king's advisers suggested he did. MacAlpin, conversely, appeared not to care for his belligerence.

Because for the first time, the king needed him. Even so, it was foolhardy to antagonize him. Yet he couldn't help himself.

"Your noble mother's relatives will, I'm sure, be eager to align themselves with such a fortuitous alliance. You won't enter this marriage a pauper, Finn."

His mother's relatives could go to hell. He'd accept nothing from them. Not after the way they had turned their backs when their daughter had needed them the most. "I have my own estate."

"And I have long admired your resourcefulness."

Finn refused to bow beneath MacAlpin's piercing gaze. He wasn't the only warrior who had smuggled spoils of war for his own purposes over the last six years. But unlike the others, who used their boons on drink and women, everything he'd taken had gone towards securing his future home. A sanctuary where his mother and sisters could live without fear.

It appeared his actions hadn't been as circumspect as he'd

hoped. If the king expected an apology, he would feel death's cold embrace before Finn did such a thing.

"What is the princess' name?"

MacAlpin raised his eyebrows as though such a mundane question was beneath considering. "Annella, I believe."

Not that her name mattered. He would scarcely use it. She would forever be the Princess of Fortriu in his mind.

"There is still the problem of locating the princess, sire," Aedh said and finally MacAlpin tore his attention from Finn.

"We will send a contingent to the Kingdom of Fotla and ensure they are aware that their assistance in this matter will be to their great benefit."

Once again, he couldn't hold his tongue. "I doubt any threat will induce them to betray the whereabouts of the Princess of Fortriu."

"You have a great deal to learn of diplomacy, Finn." The king slapped his shoulder, the way Finn had seen him do many times in the past with his two other sons. "We have no intention of threatening the royal house of Fotla. We have a far more agreeable strategy to offer them."

CHAPTER 3

THE KINGDOM OF FOTLA

*T*he dwelling where Nechtan had brought them belonged to the second cousin of an old friend of his. Blood oaths had been exchanged before her birth, for reasons Mairi was ignorant of, but the Fotla nobleman had welcomed them into his home more than a month ago, accepting without question the fabrication they had told him.

But Nechtan had passed through the veil, and she could no longer prevail upon his friend's hospitality. The debt the nobleman had owed her royal born husband had more than been repaid.

She stood by the narrow window in the bedchamber she had been allocated and pulled her thick woolen shawl more securely around her shoulders. Night had fallen, and the deep unease that had settled into her bones three days ago, coiled tighter.

It was not connected to Nechtan, yet linked inextricably to him, nevertheless.

But more than that, her unease was linked to Pictland herself.

She glanced at the beautiful medicine casket she had inherited from her mother on her eighth birthday, that sat upon a table by her side. It was one of her most cherished possessions and had accompanied her on her journey since leaving Fortriu.

But it contained something equally precious. The sacred broach of the Supreme Kingdom and as long as it remained securely hidden within the secret compartment, there was hope for Pictland's freedom.

The sacred broach could not be allowed to fall into the clutches of MacAlpin.

She swung around, the imperative to leave the confines of the dwelling thundering through her mind. Her two ladies, who had uncomplainingly accompanied her since her exile from Fortriu, hurried in her wake as she left the chamber.

"Madam, what ails you?" One of them whispered, as they descended the curved staircase.

"Bride calls." But not in any way she had before. There was simply the overriding need to go outside.

The moon.

She stumbled on the final step. Bride, her beloved goddess who she had worshipped all her life, had never before shown her the moon.

Uncertain, she paused, and Bhaic strode across the great hall to her, concern etched on his features. She was scarcely aware when he reached her side as foreboding rippled along her spine. The season of Bride was waning, and in her stead the shadow of Cailleach loomed, as she waited to cover the land in her frosty, white mantle.

Mairi turned and made her way to the great doors that led to the courtyard. The guards opened the doors and she stepped into the bitter night air. One of her ladies had brought their cloaks, and she draped one around her shoulders as she gazed at the silver swathed face of the luminous full moon.

Their host joined them, along with a dozen of her faithful warriors who had sworn fealty to her upon the death of the High King. But none of them spoke. It seemed even the very wind itself stilled and an unnatural silence enwrapped them all. Mairi hitched in a shallow breath as the mighty goddess Cailleach cast her fearsome shadow across the starry firmament, relentlessly swallowing the light from the moon.

Darkness shivered across the land. But it was not the dark of a cloud strewn night. The moon glowed copper.

Blood moon.

Her ladies huddled closer, one on either side, as though they tried to protect her from unspeakable portents. But as she gazed at the eerie glow, a chilling understanding rippled through her. There was no hiding from her destiny. There never had been, no matter how hard Nechtan had tried to shield her.

For six months she had avoided the Scot barbarians who had deceived her people. But that respite was over. The Goddess of Winter had given her a warning none could ignore.

The savage betrayers who knew no honor had picked up her trail.

The threat of bloodshed tainted the air like a curse, but she wouldn't be caught unaware by her enemies, or stalked like a hunted deer.

When she faced MacAlpin it would be on her terms. Not his.

It was time to leave this sanctuary.

THE FOLLOWING morning as her ladies packed their belongings in readiness, she and Bhaic sat on low stools by the fire in the antechamber and discussed their options.

It was not going well.

They'd exhausted Nechtan's contacts in the kingdoms of Fib, Ce and Fotla. The only possibility that remained was returning to his estate in Fib but how long would she be safe there? The Scots most likely already had a contingent of warriors there, waiting for her reckless arrival.

There was a knock on the door to the antechamber, and one of her ladies, Struana, answered it. A few moments later, she came to her side.

"Madam, you have a visitor who requests an audience with you."

A visitor? How could that be? No one knew she was here. A terrible thought gripped her. Perhaps the Scots had arrived already. The warning had come too late.

She took a deep breath. She would show no agitation in front of her ladies. But to greet the stranger was out of the question.

"Tell them I am indisposed and cannot receive visitors."

Struana hesitated. "The message was most strange. I had the servant repeat it twice, so there's no mistake. 'May the juniper flourish in the barren glens.' What can this mean? Our glens are far from barren."

Goddess. For an eternal moment, shock rendered her speechless. This was no message from an unknown stranger. Five years ago, when her marriage to Nechtan was imminent, there had been only one in whom she could confide her terror. To confess the fearful, bloodied dreams that came direct from her blessed foremothers, and had haunted her since she had turned thirteen.

Her beloved cousin, the younger princess of Fotla, who hadn't expressed disapproval of her closely guarded secret but instead reminded her of ancient wisdom.

Mae, the juniper flourishes in the glens.

If she wished to be considered barren, the choice was hers. She had never needed to use Bride's sacred berries, but no one knew that. Just as no one but her cousin knew of that whispered conversation.

She dearly longed to see her cousin, Briana, again. But it was too dangerous. Yet Briana was here. The message was too personal for her cousin to have entrusted it to a messenger.

She caught Bhaic's sharp gaze, and realized she was twisting her fingers together. A sure sign of disquiet. With difficulty, she forced her hands to still and turned to Struana. "I will see the visitor. Have them brought here to me."

After Struana left to relay the message, Bhaic leaned closer to her so his words would not be overheard. "Is this wise, Madam? I fear this could be a trick."

Bhaic had always treated her kindly and she appreciated his counsel. Truly, she did. But she was far from ignorant. Did he really think she'd put all their lives at risk on a careless whim?

"It's not a trick. But no one must speak of this."

The door opened and three ladies, with shawls concealing their heads and faces, and a bodyguard entered the antechamber. Mairi stood, her stomach churning with a combination of excitement and nerves. It had been so long since she'd seen any of her kin, but she hoped to the goddess Briana had been careful. Spies, after all, were everywhere in Pictland now.

Briana came forward, leaving her small contingent in the center of the chamber. "My lady."

Mairi inclined her head and led her into the bedchamber before closing the door, so they were alone. She exhaled a ragged breath and hugged her cousin, blinking back foolish tears. But it had been more than two years since they'd last seen each other.

"Briana. It's so good to see you. I've missed you."

Briana pulled back and grasped her hands. "Dearest Mae," she said, using the childhood name that no one else had ever used. "If I had known you were in Fotla, I would have sought you out sooner."

"Then it's as well you didn't. I would not put you in danger for anything."

Briana sighed. "We're all in danger, my love. If the royal houses of Pictland cannot help their own kin, then who can we rely upon?"

The chamber was basic and had no chairs, and so Mairi indicated they should sit on the bed. A bittersweet pain engulfed her heart when Briana tucked her legs beneath her, as though they were carefree ten-year-old maids again.

She mirrored her cousin, because why not? No one was here to frown at her lack of decorum.

The question that had hovered since receiving Briana's message could be silenced no longer. "How did you know where I was?"

Worry clouded her cousin's eyes. "Bride showed me last night, when Cailleach captured the Blood Moon. The goddess whispered the name of your husband's friend, a noble of deep regard. I knew then that you needed my help."

"I can't accept your help, Briana. The Scots hunt me. I need to get as far away from Fotla as possible."

"Bride told you this?"

"The Goddess of Winter showed me it was time to leave."

Briana was silent. Mairi wrapped her shawl tighter around her shoulders and took her cousin's hand. Finally, Briana caught her gaze.

"We know the goddesses are in constant conflict, but they cannot exist one without the other."

It was true. The winter months could be cruel, but without the stern hand of Cailleach, Bride could never be reborn in spring. What seemed to be an endless battle was, in fact, the very essence of survival.

She frowned, considering. "Cailleach warns me to leave. And Bride shows you I need a safe refuge. But I don't see how this can be. When the Scots arrive, they will surely go direct to Fotla-eviot. I cannot hide in the palace."

"Not as the Princess of Fortriu," Briana agreed. "But you can surely hide in plain sight if you accompany me as one of my treasured ladies. There's been so much turmoil over the last few years. Many of my ladies that you knew have left the palace. No one will know who you truly are."

She was sorely tempted. How wonderful it would be, to stay a while with Briana. Someone she had known all her life, and with whom she wouldn't need to pretend to be someone she wasn't.

It meant she still needed to conceal her true identity to outsiders, but it seemed there was no way around that. Not yet.

Bride, or perhaps Cailleach, would let her know when the time for confrontation was right.

"What of the queen?"

Briana drew in a deep breath. "Mamma will never succumb to the Scot barbarians. She will protect you with her life's blood. When I shared my vision with her, it made her only more determined to thwart whatever plans MacAlpin might devise to strengthen his grip on Fortriu."

"Have you received any word from your father?"

"Not directly. Only that he remains a hostage of the Scots, to ensure our compliance." Bitterness edged the words. MacAlpin held so many royal and noble born Picts. Including the prince Mairi had once, long ago, woven pretty dreams around.

"MacAlpin won't harm him, Briana." MacAlpin wouldn't harm any of his distinguished hostages. They were too important for his schemes.

"I know." Briana shook her head. "Goddess, I'm sorry. I understand your esteemed husband has recently passed through the veil?"

"Two nights ago." Mairi bowed her head in his memory. He hadn't been the husband she had dreamed of. But perhaps, all things considered, he had been the husband she needed.

After a few moments of respectful silence, Briana squeezed her fingers. "We must make haste. Mamma expects you to return with me this day."

FINN PROWLED the perimeter of Fotla-eviot's great hall, as servants pushed back the tables in readiness for the evening's entertainment. MacAlpin had been right. The peace offering they had given the royal house of Fotla when they'd arrived yesterday afternoon, had ensured a measure of congeniality that no manner of threats would have extracted.

They had even been invited to the feast this evening. Even MacAllister had been impressed by that. As if conjured by a foul curse, the man appeared by his side.

"Do you have your eye on any particular lady, my lord?"

The honorific grated along his nerves. MacAllister had never abused him in the past, the way so many others had. He was too clever for that. Perhaps he had always believed that one day the king might recognize him. But the new veneer of respect MacAllister bestowed upon him didn't erase the years of disdain, or his complicity in the shaming of his mother.

He'd accept this newfound esteem but by God it wouldn't change his opinion of any of them. He knew who he trusted, and they were the warriors who had stood by his side when he was nothing but a common bastard with no claim to his royal lineage.

"I don't." Not that he'd tell MacAllister even if he did.

MacAllister cast his gaze across the hall. "The queen and princess have many delectable ladies. Pictish noblewomen are generally eager to taste the delights of Scots warriors."

He'd heard plenty of tales of how Pictish noblewomen enjoyed tumbling Scots. Not that he had any personal observation of that. This was his first time in a Pictish court.

"I'm sure they'll find plenty of amusement this night, then." Did he sound scathing? Most likely. But this sudden interest in who he might bed irritated him. It was none of MacAllister—or MacAlpin's—concern.

"My lord." MacAllister smiled, but his eyes were cold. "You're not wed yet and are not expected to remain celibate until such time as the elusive princess is discovered. Our plans for her safety are known only to the king's intimates. Many noble born Pictish ladies will spill secrets in the dark of night to their lover, that would never pass their lips in the light of day."

"I'm aware," he ground out, but God alone knew how he managed to reply to MacAllister at all, when the overriding urge to punch him to the ground assailed him. Growing up, his ability to fight hard and fast had saved his skin many a time and earned him grudging respect among those who would have relished leaving him in a bloodied mess on the ground.

He might not have the diplomatic skills required when dealing with kings. But he understood MacAllister's implication all too well.

MacAllister could fuck himself if he thought Finn would degrade himself in such a manner. If secrets were to be spilled, they wouldn't be within a Pictish noblewoman's bedchamber. With difficulty, he managed to keep his mouth shut.

"Excellent." MacAllister appeared unaware of Finn's ire. "Our presence here must be seen as positive. We are allies with the Picts, after all."

"I've no intention of antagonizing our allies."

MacAllister gave a half-bow before taking his leave. Seething, Finn left the great hall, where his compatriots appeared eager to make the acquaintance of the Pictish noblewomen, and made his way outside.

Let the other warriors do MacAlpin's spying. He had already pledged the king the rest of his life.

The sharp northerly wind bit into him, but he inhaled the chilled air with relief. The mingled smells of man and beast within the hall, not to mention roasted meats and untold delicacies, had been stifling.

The knowledge they were there to uncover information about the missing princess hadn't helped, either.

He thrust her from his mind. There was no need to torture himself with the inevitable, until the inevitable arrived.

Aside from the warriors on guard, who each stood beside a

blazing torch, it was deserted outside. Clearly it was too early in the evening for clandestine meetings. Or maybe it was just too damn cold for such trysts.

He strode along the eastern wall, ignoring the fierce glares of the guards he passed by. He understood their distrust. At least they were honest and didn't hide behind insincere smiles and false promises of fealty.

MacAlpin played a dangerous game. The royal house of Fotla may have welcomed them but he would trust none of them not to thrust a sword in his back at the slightest opportunity.

He rounded the corner and all but collided into a noble-woman who was walking backwards, her head tilted to the heavens. As he hastily backed up a step, she swung around, the hood of her cloak concealing her face in shadows.

"Apologies." His grasp of the Pictish language wasn't extensive, but he could get by. "I trust I did not alarm you?"

"Not at all." She responded in Gaelic and her accent was enchanting. His blood stirred and interest flared, and he took another hasty step back before she could judge him on it. "It takes more than a misstep to alarm me."

"I'm relieved to hear it." He reverted to his own language since she spoke it so beautifully. "I didn't think anyone else was out here. It's a fresh night."

"Indeed. I was merely observing the cycle of the moon."

He was so enamored with her voice, it took a moment for her words to penetrate. She might mean nothing more than her words conveyed, but he wasn't convinced. He'd forgotten some Picts still worshipped pagan gods, and if rumors were true, the moon held significant power to them.

Not that it was any of his concern what she believed in. But he shot the moon a cautious glance, nevertheless. It looked perfectly normal to him. There was no lingering aftereffect of the blood-red glow that had blighted the first night of their journey to Fotla.

From the corner of his eye he saw a warrior edge closer, as though he doubted Finn's motives. Only then did the strangeness hit him.

He didn't know for sure whether Pictish noblewomen wandered around unaccompanied, but even if they did, surely the fact their palace was now hosting two dozen Scots was reason enough to take more care.

"Forgive me." He gave the lady a half-bow. "My name is Finn Braeson, at your service." The House of Alpin might be his future, but in his heart he was Braeson, and tonight the future was a distant duty.

She hesitated, as though uncertain whether to continue to acknowledge him or not. Finally, she inclined her head, and the shadows swallowed her face completely. "Welcome to Fotla, Finn Braeson."

It was intriguing that she did not reveal her own name. Had she escaped her husband for a few moments respite, and didn't want anyone to know?

Unaccountably, the possibility she was married didn't sit well with him. To honor his mother's many lessons on how a nobleman behaved when in the presence of a lady, he should offer to escort this noblewoman back to the great hall. Not keep her out in the cold night air, simply because he wanted to inhale the very sight of her.

What strange madness tainted the Pictish air? He couldn't even see her face. Yet she entranced him. Like a mythical fae princess.

He would share a few more stolen moments with this mysterious Pict before returning her to her people.

"We're honored by the warm welcome, my lady."

"Surely you expected nothing less." There was a thread of disdain in her voice. "It was a clever strategy, to return the king and his eldest son."

Aye. MacAlpin had been right. The Queen of Fotla had been

most accommodating when she learned who the Scots had brought with them from Dal Riada. Whether that would lead to confidential information as to the whereabouts of the Princess of Fortriu was another matter.

He pushed the unsavory notion aside.

"Politics is nothing without strategy."

"What, I wonder, does the King of Dal Riada expect in return?'

He didn't miss her snub towards MacAlpin's claim to Fortriu but couldn't blame her for it. Her forthright remarks were refreshing. And astonishing. Did all Pictish ladies speak of politics so freely? "Our people must be allies, my lady. It's the only way to repel the Norsemen."

She sighed, the sound an ethereal whisper in the frost-tinged air. "You are right. I fear the Vikings will never stop until they've conquered all of Pictland."

"Not if I have anything to do with it."

Her head tilted, and for one glorious moment the moon illuminated the delicate features of her face. It was not enough to see the color of her eyes, but his heart slammed against his chest and breath choked in his throat.

She was exquisite. Nothing like the monstrous, pagan, barbarians he'd been taught all Picts were from the tales of older warriors who'd fought them in the past. But then, he knew that already. He had stood shoulder to shoulder with Pictish warriors when they'd battled the Northumbrians, a mere six months ago.

Yet this noblewoman was still a revelation. How had he not seen her at the feast? Yet he knew the answer. He'd been so intent on brooding upon his future, he had scarcely looked at anyone at all.

"Are you such a mighty warrior, Finn Braeson, that you'll singlehandedly keep the savage Vikings from our shores?" There was a hint of laughter in her voice, and he responded with a smile. Damn, but he wanted to see her face without these cursed shadows. Here, with the ancient Pictish palace looming by his side, he could almost believe it was the heathen gods themselves that kept the moonlight from revealing her to him.

"I'll keep them from harming you, my lady." The gallant words were out before he even realized. He wasn't known for paying pretty compliments. Somehow, they came easily tonight. Yet they weren't simply empty words.

He'd fight to his last breath to keep the Norsemen from invading the fragile peace of this captivating noblewoman.

"Such a sweet talker."

He could hear the smile in her voice. Was such a thing even possible? God, his brain was addled tonight, and he couldn't blame the Pictish mead. He'd barely finished his first tankard at the feast.

This enigmatic lady had bewitched him.

"I speak only the truth." Dare he offer her his arm? They hadn't been formally introduced but such impropriety didn't appear to concern her. He didn't even know her name, yet he didn't wish this night to end.

MacAllister's words came back to haunt him. Was this noble-woman looking for an illicit assignation with a Scots warrior tonight?

His blood heated and cock thickened at the prospect of drawing her into his arms. Of sliding the hood of her cloak to her shoulders so he could finally reveal her hidden beauty. But she made no move to encourage such familiarity and he could hardly ask her such a thing.

He'd never been in such a situation before. The few Scots lasses he'd bedded had been openly eager for a tumble and there had been no misunderstandings between them. But one wrong move with this lady would shatter the tenuous connection between them.

"The truth? Can a Scot speak such a thing?"

Entranced by how little she cared for maintaining the brittle illusion that their people had reason to trust each other, he bowed his head in acknowledgement. "Trust must be earned. It's not a thing to be given lightly."

She shook her head, as though in wonder. "You're a strange one, Finn Braeson. Unlike any barbarous Scot I have imagined. I don't know what to make of you."

He laughed, couldn't help himself. No one had ever said such a thing to him before. Usually, people knew exactly what to make of him and he had the scars to prove it. "And you, mysterious lady of Pictland, are unlike any noblewoman I've encountered before."

Once again, she tilted her head and for a fleeting moment, the moonlight illuminated her smile. And then just as swiftly, it seemed dark clouds scudded across the heavens as her smile faded and the shadows descended.

She stepped away from him and a chill breeze tempered his heated blood. What had he said to make her retreat?

"I should return to the palace." There was a formal note in her voice that had not been present until now. "I've been absent too long."

"Allow me to accompany you." He knew she was safe enough, with the Pictish warriors guarding the palace, but it was wrong that she should walk alone in the night. Scots' noblewomen would never do so. But his offer had little to do with established Scots' etiquette and everything to do with spending every last moment he could with her.

She didn't respond. He fell into step beside her. Had he inadvertently offended her? He racked his brains but could find no answer.

Except the obvious. That he was a Scot, and she had momentarily forgotten that fact.

The entrance to the palace loomed ahead. The doors were open, and light spilled from the many torches within the hall. Already a few Scots emerged, their arms linked with Pictish noblewomen. He glanced at the woman by his side, but she appeared oblivious to the fact her countrywomen found nothing remiss in conversing with their erstwhile enemy.

And then she came to abrupt halt. "Thank you for your company, Finn Braeson. Forgive me, but it's best if we don't enter the palace together."

Disappointment burned through him, although he was not surprised by her words. She hadn't left the palace for an illicit assignation, after all. He bowed his head but couldn't even take her hand for a chaste kiss. They were hidden within the folds of her cloak. "As you wish, my lady."

She gave a ragged sigh. "My wishes have little to do with it."

A solitary Pictish nobleman stood in the shadows cast by the open doors. He didn't move, but Finn gave him a sharp glance, nevertheless. It was impossible to know for sure, yet he knew without doubt the older man's gaze was fixed on his now silent companion.

Without another word, she turned and walked over to the other man, who bowed his head in fleeting respect before leading her back into the palace.

Something dark and savage twisted deep inside Finn's gut, and he sucked in a sharp breath. The cold air did nothing to cool the unfamiliar sensation.

The lady was wed, there was no doubt. And her husband wasn't posted to a far-off corner of Pictland, either. He was here, in Fotla, and he kept her in his sights.

There would be no more stolen moments in the moonlight with his enchanting Pictish companion. Finn was certain in his gut that her husband would, from now on, keep her close.

Finn would do well to forget about her. He should take MacAllister's advice and find a willing Pictish lady with whom he could share the nights, until their duty here was done.

But the prospect didn't fire his blood. And it didn't stop him from knowing the only Pictish lady he wanted in his bed was the one who had just vanished within the ancient stone palace.

CHAPTER 4

As they walked through the great hall, Mairi kept her expression neutral as Bhaic murmured in her ear. "Madam, you must take care never to be alone. I swore to my lord Nechtan that I would always keep you within my sight."

"There were many brave Pictish warriors about. I was in no danger." Except she had been in danger. Of falling under the Scots warrior's charm.

A treacherous ripple of warmth flowed through her blood, and she was grateful for her cloak that hid her responsive shiver. Bhaic was too observant by far. She didn't want him to know just how much the Scot had affected her.

It was wrong. She knew that to the very marrow of her bones. Yet when he'd spoken, and when he had smiled, she had all but forgotten he was her bitterest enemy.

She would not forget it again. Although she wouldn't admit it, Bhaic was right. It *was* dangerous to escape the palace's walls when she wasn't surrounded by Briana and her ladies. There was anonymity in being simply one of many.

"If they should ever discover you are here…" Bhaic cast a surreptitious glance around the hall. The musicians were playing, and Pict and Scot danced together, while the king and queen looked on. It appeared to be such a benevolent scene, but it was nothing but a charade. Only the necessity to keep peace prevented the Fotla king from ordering his warriors to slaughter the Scots.

A weary sorrow weaved through her heart as she took Bhaic's hands. "I will be more circumspect in the future."

~

THE BLOOD-SOAKED dream visited her once again that night.

Unimaginable pain clawed through her vitals, and the air was a crimson mist. Unknown hands held her down, pulled her back, and heavy wooden doors with rusting iron bolts and hinges slammed in her face.

Ice-cold wind gusted across her burning flesh, and hushed whispers drifted through her ravaged mind.

There is no hope for the poor lady.

Goddess willing, we must save the babe, at least.

A tiny sliver of sanity fought against the insidious blanket of impending darkness. *This is not real.* During the years when these stark warnings from her foremothers had been a nightly visitation, she'd learned how to escape its deadly grip. She had to focus on returning to the daytime world.

The stone walls tumbled, the whispers receded, and on the far horizon the faintest glimmer of sunrise could be seen.

Soon, she would awaken. If she could just hold onto the one true reality and not sink into the phantom abyss that threatened to suck her into eternal oblivion. Long ago she had understood the warning her foremothers tormented her with.

She could not survive a pregnancy.

Another voice penetrated the maelstrom. One she'd never heard before in these terrors, yet somehow it was achingly familiar. Deep timbred and with an irresistible accent she could not immediately place. "My lady. Take my hand."

Blindly, she reached for him. Strong fingers wrapped around her hand, and as sunlight pierced the crumbling stone walls, she saw his face.

Finn Braeson.

Gasping, she lurched upright, heart pounding. No one she knew had ever entered this recurring nightmare, least of all a man.

And a Scot, at that.

"Hush, Mae," grumbled the noblewoman she shared the bed with. "It's not time to rise yet."

Mairi drew in a ragged breath and forcibly relaxed her grip on the furs that covered the bed. The palace of Fotla was smaller than Forteviot, and she shared the chamber with another of Briana's ladies, as well as the two who had been her constant companions from Fortriu. And as far as anyone was aware, she was the widowed Lady Mae from Fib.

She and her cousin had decided it would attract too much attention, if Mairi shared Briana's chamber. But how she wished they did. Her cousin was the only one she could confide in. The only one who knew of these dreams, the dreams that hadn't plagued her since her marriage.

Why had it returned now? And, perhaps more alarmingly, why had a Scottish warrior inexplicably invaded it?

She shivered, and not just because the fire had all but died in the night. Stealthily, she lay back down and pulled the furs up to her chin. Had she called out during the dream? Heat curled through her. But not because she might have inadvertently spilled life-threatening secrets.

It was in case she had called out *his* name.

Stop thinking of him.

Forcibly, she thrust him from her mind. But however hard she wished it, he wouldn't leave. It had been dark last night, but the waning moon had bestowed enough light for her to see his face, and by the goddess, he'd taken her breath away. Strong and rugged, with hair the color of midnight, and his voice would likely haunt her for all time.

She squeezed her eyes shut. She would not think how it would feel if he took her into his arms. Or brushed his lips against hers. Illicit thrills raced through her, colliding between her thighs in a pleasurable dance of danger.

No man had ever kissed her lips. The closest she had come to a lover's embrace had been the few times Lord Talargan had chastely kissed her knuckles, during that carefree summer before she had been promised to Nechtan.

But even then, Talargan's ardent restraint hadn't stirred her the way the mere thought of Finn Braeson's touch did.

She could only hope that now the Scots had returned the king and prince, they would be on their way.

But it was a foolish wish. She knew why they were here. It was to discover the whereabouts of the missing Princess of Fortriu.

THE FOLLOWING MORNING, Mairi sat with Briana, the queen, and all their ladies in the queen's antechamber, as they embroidered delicate flowers and fabulous birds on lengths of fine wool. It was the fourth day she had been occupied in the task, and while she was proficient with the needle, it had never been her favorite pastime. But in Fotla, when the wind howled and rain threatened, horse riding was out of the question for the noblewomen.

She shifted on her stool and let out an unintentional sigh of frustration. Goddess, she needed air. The chamber was stifling. Worse, she could not even suggest leaving, since she was masquerading as a noble in the service of royalty.

"My dear Lady Mae. Do you need to excuse yourself?" The queen's tone was dry.

"I…" Mairi hesitated. She had no need of the garderobe and was certain the queen knew it. Was she giving her the opportunity to grasp a few moments of freedom? It was hard to tell from her serene expression, but the possibility was too enticing to ignore. "If it does not offend, Madam."

The queen waved a regal finger. It was almost as though she found grim satisfaction in the reversal of their status. After all, Fortriu was the Supreme Kingdom of Pictland and as such, Mairi outranked all other royals in the land.

She shook the feeling aside. It was the close confines of the palace playing with her mind. While it wasn't easy maintaining a deferential façade to those with whom she was more than equal, it was far better than the alternative.

Her head impaled on a Scots forged pike.

She swallowed, unnerved by the image, before standing and dropping the queen a curtsey.

"I will accompany you." Briana also stood and together they left the chamber. Once the door was shut behind them, her cousin took her hand. "Do you long for a ride across the countryside as much as I, Mae?"

"Yes. But I was going to content myself by merely visiting the stables." And ensuring her beloved mare, Audra, was being well cared for. Although she'd visited her each day, there hadn't been the opportunity for a ride.

She hated not being able to look after Audra herself, but the queen had very specific ideas on how the ladies within her circle should behave. Even grooming their own horses caused the queen to raise her eyebrows. Considering how much she owed the queen, Mairi had no choice but to obey the restrictions.

Briana bid a nearby servant to collect their cloaks, before turning back to Mairi.

"Certainly, we will visit the stables first." There was a mischievous gleam in Briana's eyes. "Mamma cannot stop us if she doesn't know our plans."

Once they were wrapped in their cloaks, they went outside, followed by a couple of warriors who were Briana's personal guards. Mairi's own faithful warriors had been reassigned within the Fotla guard, so as not to draw undue attention. The ground was damp, and the scent of more impending rain spiced the air. Some distance from the palace, the Scots were camped. She was amazed they hadn't demanded to be lodged within the palace, but it seemed they were determined to cause as little offence as possible to their hosts.

She trudged through the mud, lifting her skirts so they wouldn't get covered, and refused to think about one particular Scots warrior. It was intolerable that he occupied her thoughts so. And she couldn't even confide in Briana, as it would mean confessing she had slipped out of the palace unaccompanied last night. Something that, considering the circumstances, was unforgivably foolhardy.

The comforting smell of horse and hay greeted her as they entered the royal stables, and Audra whickered as Mairi approached. She rubbed the mare's ears and Audra leaned against her, giving one of her loving neck hugs, as one of the stable lads saddled her.

As protocol demanded, once they were mounted, she followed a few paces behind Briana until they were out of sight of the palace chattels. Once they were beyond the village's ramparts, they raced each other across the countryside, the wind whipping through her hair, chilling her skin, and clearing out the cobwebs from her mind.

They drew to a halt on the peak of a mighty hill, their guards some distance from them allowing them a degree of privacy. As she gazed across the distant loch in the valley below, it was hard to reconcile the tranquil scene with the bloodshed Pictland had so recently endured.

"Thank you, Briana."

"Do not thank me. Mamma has barely allowed me out of her sight these last six months. If Father and my brother were still hostages, she would never have allowed us to leave her chamber."

"Did the king bring news from Dal Riada?" It was the first time she had been alone with Briana to ask such a question.

"The other royal hostages are being treated as their status demands." Briana glanced at her. "Talargan is well."

"Good."

"But it's unlikely he'll be released any time soon."

Despite his sister, Aila, having wed Connor MacKenzie, Talargan was too much of a threat to Kenneth MacAlpin. But she knew what Briana was really saying.

"Even if he were free, we could never be together. It would give Talargan too great a claim on Fortriu and we know what MacAlpin does to those he considers his rivals for the throne of the Supreme Kingdom."

Briana expelled a ragged breath. "What do you see for your future, Mae?"

It was something she had asked herself a thousand times since fleeing Fortriu. But she didn't have the answer. "Bride will show me the way. She always does."

THEY WERE ONCE AGAIN within the ramparts of Fotla-eviot, and the palace was in sight when Mairi gasped and pulled Audra to a halt. Briana circled back to her, as Mairi dismounted and gently ran her hand over the mare's foreleg before examining her hoof.

"She's thrown her shoe." She stood and stroked Audra's forehead. "I'll walk her to the farrier. It's not too far."

"One of the guards can take her. We've been absent too long. We must return to the palace."

"You go." She smiled at the concerned expression on her

cousin's face. "I'll be perfectly safe with one warrior to protect me. But you shouldn't risk the queen's wrath on my account."

"I shouldn't leave you alone."

"I won't be alone. Besides, how scandalous would it be for the Princess of Fotla to accompany her noblewoman to the farrier?"

Briana leaned close. "Not as scandalous as the truth." She straightened and gave the order to one of the guards to remain with Mairi. "I will see you later, Mae."

Mairi watched her cousin gallop away, before leading Audra to the village. The guard also dismounted and trudged beside her, a grim frown distorting his forehead. He clearly didn't relish accompanying her to undertake such a mundane task.

As they reached the village, thunder rumbled overhead, and the skies opened. Mairi pulled her hood over her head and cursed beneath her breath as she tried to avoid the rapidly spreading puddles. The farrier's workshop was just ahead, by the village square, and appeared to be busy, with several horses tethered outside.

How long would she need to wait? If her royal status was known, she would be attended to directly. But she wasn't sure how much consideration a noblewoman connected to the royal house of Fotla was given when it came to such things.

She narrowly avoided a pile of horse manure and landed ankle deep in a puddle. Curses. She gritted her teeth and forged onwards through the lashing rain. Despite the weather, villagers milled about, jostling her without a second glance and her guard was either oblivious or uncaring.

A couple of small lads careered into her before disappearing into the rain and she stumbled against Audra. Before she could catch her breath, a dark figure loomed out of the rainy mist.

"My lady, can I offer my assistance?"

What? Her pluses raced and heart slammed unforgivably against her ribs. Goddess, no. It was Finn Braeson standing before her, in all his glorious Scots savagery. His midnight hair was plastered against his head and aristocratic cheekbones, and raindrops glittered on his dark eyelashes. In the moonlight he had been enthralling. In the cold light of day, and positively drenched, he was the most magnificent man she had ever encountered.

Of all the people who might have seen her looking like a bedraggled rat, it had to be this one.

She summoned up every fragment of pride she possessed and offered him a remote smile. "I thank you, but no."

He leaned closer, a curious expression lighting his breath-taking green eyes. "You're the noblewoman I met last night."

It wasn't even a question. He had recognized her. It was a dangerous thing, and yet her heart thrilled at the knowledge.

She tightened her grip on Audra's reins in an attempt to refocus her errant thoughts. Should she deny it had been her last night? But since he was so certain, to contradict him would only arouse his curiosity. And she couldn't afford to arouse any Scots curiosity.

"I am." She blinked the rain from her eyes and battled the urge to wipe her wet hair from her face. It wouldn't make her look any less disheveled.

"May I escort you to shelter?"

Goddess, his manners were enchanting. Were all Scots so thoughtful? She had never imagined them to be so.

He's my enemy. She couldn't afford to forget it for a single moment. And yet his suggestion was entirely sensible. She ignored the low growl of outrage from the warrior who had been assigned to accompany her. After all, he hadn't even offered his arm to assist her when she'd stumbled just now. "Thank you. That would be most kind."

Finn fell into step beside her as they continued to the farrier. "It's a foul day to be outside. Are you on an errand for your mistress?"

As if Briana would send any of her ladies out in such weather.

But Finn didn't know that. "No. My horse threw her shoe while I was out riding. I hope we won't have to wait too long."

They had arrived at the farrier's, and more horses were tethered along the alley beside the stone dwelling. Their bridles and saddles were of Scots workmanship, but their riders were nowhere to be seen. Most likely they'd all sought refuge in the tavern, which was a small mercy. It hadn't occurred to her the foreign warriors would make use of this Pictish service. She would be here for *hours* before her horse was seen.

She'd take Audra back to the royal stables and ask Briana to send for the farrier instead. It was the sensible course of action and far safer than staying here, passing pleasantries with a beguiling Scots warrior.

Finn took the reins from her and tied them to a hitching post. She wasn't sure whether to be enchanted by his chivalrous action or annoyed by his presumption. But his smile was so engaging, it was hard to feel anything but spellbound.

Remember who I am.

She shook her head, and raindrops scattered. It didn't help to clarify her scrambled senses. They went inside, where two assistants were hard at work, and the farrier was in the covered courtyard out the back.

"Allow me to offer you my position in the queue, my lady. I do believe my horse is next to be shod."

"That's very kind of you, but I cannot accept. You must have been waiting a fair while already."

"It's no hardship. I insist."

Goddess, his smile was infectious. It was hard not to simply melt beneath the admiring heat in his green eyes. "You're quite persuasive."

"So we are agreed?"

"It appears we are."

He offered her a gallant bow, before striding over to the farrier. She bit her bottom lip in a vain effort to rein in her unruly smile but failed. It was dangerous to flirt with this Scots warrior, no matter how irresistible he was, but the circumstances were out of her hands.

She couldn't return to the palace until Audra was reshod. And surely it was better if the farrier attended to her earlier, rather than later? The longer she lingered in the village, the more chance there was of being accosted by other Scots, who would surely not possess the gracious manner of Finn Braeson.

Therefore, this encounter was not merely enjoyable banter. It was necessary.

Surreptitiously, she pushed the wet strands of hair that had escaped her braid off her face and pulled her hood more securely beneath her chin to hide her disheveled state. Not that she should care what a barbarous Scot thought of her appearance. But despite his unfortunate heritage, he didn't emanate evil in the way she'd always imagined Scots did.

It was disconcerting.

She took a deep breath, trying to dislodge the contradictory thoughts that swirled through her mind. It didn't matter how intriguing she found him. Last night they had met by pure chance. Today, a strange stroke of luck. She could never allow herself to be alone with him again.

The future of Pictland depended on her keeping a clear head, and she would not let her people down.

CHAPTER 5

*A*fter speaking the with the farrier, Finn returned to the Pictish noblewoman. She hadn't moved from the doorway, and her wet cloak clung to her, giving an elusive hint of sensuous curves, and heat flowed through his blood, stirring his cock.

Last night, he had merely imagined her beauty, but his fantasies had fallen far short of reality. The rich blue of her cloak was the same shade as her eyes and her damp hair curled against her cheek, like wisps of burnished copper. She was, quite simply, the most exquisite creature he had ever encountered.

He didn't care that she was likely married. Or that he was betrothed to a missing princess. Today, right now, all that mattered was he had been given a second chance to win her favor.

"It's all arranged." He gestured to the farrier. "I fear we may have to stay here until he's finished. The only other place I know where we could escape the weather is the tavern."

She smiled. How could so small a gesture be able to suck the air from his lungs?

"It would not be seemly. But there's no need to stay with me. I don't wish to distract you from your business. My guard is here."

"My business is here, protecting you." God, what was he saying? Yet he couldn't help himself. He wanted to see her smile. She didn't disappoint.

"Protecting me?" Despite her smile, there was a hint of mockery in her voice. "There are no Vikings here, Finn Braeson. Or do you pledge to protect me from your barbarous countrymen?"

"No Scot would dare touch you, my lady." And if they did, they would answer to him. "May I have the honor of knowing your name?"

Her smile faltered. Damn, had he taken an unforgivable liberty? He was too ignorant in the ways of how Pictish nobility interacted. Yet she didn't appear offended. Stealthily, he shifted his weight from one foot to the other, but it didn't help clear his brain. Should he offer her an apology for his unintended insolence?

"I am known as Mae." Her voice was oddly formal, and her dark lashes swept over her eyes, concealing her expression. A delightful blush highlighted her aristocratic cheekbones, and he was rendered all but mute at the sight.

At his prolonged silence, she raised her lashes and their gazes meshed. She was clearly waiting for his response, while he was slowly drowning in the guileless blue of her eyes.

"Lady Mae," he said, and offered her his hand. After a moment's hesitation, she took it and his fingers curved around hers. Such a light touch, and she was even wearing gloves, yet it seared his flesh and lust burned through his loins.

Christ. A simple touch had never affected him in such a manner. It was astounding. He hoped she didn't notice. He brushed his lips over her leather-clad fingers, and she gave a faint gasp.

With reluctance, he released her, but she didn't immediately withdraw her hand. Her eyes had darkened, and her breath was uneven, and she gazed at him as though she wasn't sure whether to kiss him back or slap his face.

Finally, she spoke. "This is an odd thing." There was a husky note in her voice that scrambled what was left of his good sense. "I never thought to find a Scots warrior anything but despicable."

Her candor, just like last night, was like a breath of fresh air. "Until this year, I believed all Picts were savages."

She laughed, before slapping her hand across her mouth, as though she wished to smother her mirth. "That's a highly unchivalrous remark to make to a lady."

"Aye." He smiled back at her. "But it's the truth. I believe you respect that above pretty words."

She shook her head, perhaps in wonder at his nerve. "How can you possibly know that about me?"

"From last night. You say out loud what others merely think. I also prefer to hear the truth."

A hint of sadness shadowed her eyes. "Sometimes the truth will do nothing but cause untold devastation."

Unease flickered through him. If she discovered his newly bestowed status, would it change her opinion of him? He was certain it would. A son of MacAlpin could be nothing but despicable in her eyes. And unlike the members of the royal house of Fotla, she would not hide her disdain.

He wanted her good opinion, for the short time they would know each other. Just because the king had finally acknowledged him, didn't change who he was.

Finn Braeson. The man that Lady Mae found unlike any Scot she had imagined.

There was no way she could find out about his polluted bloodline. Although MacAlpin had acknowledged him, he and his advisers had decided not to publicly reveal Finn's elevated status until the princess had been secured.

In Dunadd, after his future had been remade by the king's

command, he hadn't given a shit what they decided. Now, he was relieved.

"I believe," he said, "the only truth that matters is the one we hold within our hearts."

She tilted her head, and the shadows that had clouded her eyes faded. "Yes," she whispered, as if he had just shared a great revelation. "I believe this, too. Are you a seer who can see the secrets of others?"

The enchanting curve of her lips assured him she was jesting, but something in her eyes caused an uncanny prickle along his arms. As though a part of her wasn't jesting in the least.

"I fear not, Lady Mae. Dal Riada has no seers."

"Ah." She blinked, and the ethereal sensation that she was speaking of something he could not quite grasp, scattered like raindrops in the wind. "Of course. Your people have abandoned the old ways. That is sad."

She sounded as though that knowledge really did sadden her. He was intrigued. She might be a pagan, but he no longer believed all pagans were savages, the way he'd been taught all his life. That had been knocked out of him when he'd fought side by side with the Picts six months ago.

They were an honorable race. Just like the Scots. Even if some Picts were misguided in their beliefs.

"It's not sad. It's all I've ever known. But I'm curious. Christianity is spread across Pictland, just like Dal Riada. How can you still worship your old gods without causing offense?"

"We are free to worship whichever gods we choose. There is no one to offend. Unless you speak of the gods themselves."

There was only one God, but he had no wish to argue the point with her. Not when, in the past, he'd railed against the existence of a deity who allowed such a gentle soul as his mother to suffer contemptible indignities in his name.

It bordered on blasphemy to even discuss such things, but

Mae fascinated him, and he wanted to discover all her secrets. "Is it the goddess of the moon whom you worship?"

She didn't ask him what he meant. Instead, she smiled, and shook her head. "I've studied the skies each night since the Blood Moon, but I'm a daughter of Bride, the fiery arrow."

He'd heard of Bride from the teaching of the monks in Dal Riada, but she was no goddess. It was likely best if he didn't remark on that. "What portends does your goddess see in the Blood Moon?"

MacAllister swore it was a good omen, foretelling victory for the Scots. Finn had seen only bloodshed reflected in the eerie phenomenon.

"It is…" Mae bit her lip as though contemplating whether to confide in him. "Complicated." She sighed and avoided his eyes. "But you should know this. Pictland will never willingly succumb to the Scots invasion."

Her words pierced his chest, as sharp as the blade of a dagger. Because she was right. MacAlpin spoke of an alliance, but it was an alliance forged in Pictish blood.

"Invasion is a harsh word." Not that he blamed her for using it. But he could not openly agree with her. To do so would amount to nothing less than treason against his king.

"I had such hopes of the alliance," she said, as though she had read his thoughts, but she wasn't looking at him. She was gazing through the open doors at the village square. "Pict and Scot, shoulder to shoulder, defending our land against the cursed Vikings."

"The alliance lives, my lady." It might not be based on trust, but necessity was a strong enough reason. "Pictland will prevail."

She looked at him then, but her expression didn't convey gratitude or relief at his words, as a Scotswoman's might. It was oddly calculating, as if she didn't merely accept his remark in the way he'd intended. To assuage her concerns.

He hadn't eased her mind in the least. She knew, as well as he, that MacAlpin wouldn't rest until he'd claimed all of Pictland for his own.

For a fleeting, deadly moment, the urge to abandon caution flooded his mind. A suicidal imperative to agree with her unspoken accusations against his king. It thundered against his skull and burned his blood, but a lifetime of attempting to live up to the loyalty and honor that had been expected of him, prevailed.

He had little respect for his king. But he would not besmirch the integrity of his mother. His actions affected her, and his sisters, and he'd wrench out his tongue before he uttered treacherous words that could rip their security from them.

The farrier approached, and he exhaled a measured breath as the man concluded his business with Mae. What was it about this woman that caused him to think such things in her company, never mind almost speak them aloud?

He couldn't drag his eyes from her face as she discussed her mare's health with the farrier. She was beautiful and stoked a fire in his blood that he'd barely experienced before, and yet he'd spent the whole time with her discussing religion and politics, instead of discovering whether she was agreeable for an enjoyable liaison.

The image of Mae, naked and willing in his arms, caused his breath to tangle in his throat. How many hours could they steal together before he had to leave? The thought of indulging in uninhibited sex, of wrapping her fiery hair around his fist and hearing her scream his name as he possessed her, damn near made him groan aloud.

But it wasn't simply her body he wanted. He couldn't deny how deeply her conversation fascinated him. Once their lust was sated, and their limbs entwined, they could indulge in stimulating discussions, the like of which he'd never imagined a noblewoman might entertain.

How much longer was this fucking farrier going to ramble

on? Their business was concluded. The man was merely wasting time while he covetously raked his insolent gaze over her.

His patience unraveled and he took a step towards them, just as Mae bade the farrier good day and finally turned back to him. "Thank you once again for allowing me to take your allotted position in the queue."

"It was my pleasure." He glanced outside. The rain no longer pelted down and was now only a faint drizzle. Reality slammed into him. Where the hell could he offer to take a Pictish noble-woman for an hour or two of pleasure? All he possessed in Fotla was a tent, and he shared that with three other warriors.

"Alas, I must return to the palace." Regret threaded through her words, but she didn't immediately leave. Damn it, he should have taken more notice of his fellow Scots last night, to understand the subtleties of the Pictish court. Was Lady Mae inviting him to accompany her for an illicit liaison?

Her guard approached, a sullen glare etched into his features. He was obviously intent on leaving, now their business was done. "My lady."

"Thank you," she responded, sparing the man a brief glance, before returning her attention to him. "Our discussion has been most enlightening, Finn Braeson. I'm sorry it must end." Her smile was sad as she inclined her head in a regal manner, before stepping away.

She was leaving?

"Lady Mae." He came to her side, too close for propriety, but she didn't back away. Involuntarily, he breathed in deep, savoring her elusive scent of raindrops and leather. When had such everyday aromas been so provocative? "When might I see you again?"

"Doubtless we will see each other at the feast tonight."

The feast. Of course. That was when the ladies of the court picked their nighttime companions.

"I will make sure of it." He smiled, but she did not return it. "Perhaps you will do me the honor of saving me a dance."

"I should like that very much. But..." she hesitated before taking a deep breath. "But it cannot be."

She gazed at him, her blue eyes filled with such innocence and sorrow it was a struggle to keep from wrapping her in his arms and offering whatever comfort she needed. God, what strange spell did she weave around him? And yet she wasn't attempting to seduce him with her undeniable charms.

Despite the desire that sparked between them, she had given no indication that she wished to pursue a clandestine affair. Such a heady outcome had all been in his lust-drenched mind. There was one distasteful but inevitable answer.

She remained loyal to her husband. The man who had met her at the palace doors last night. Hell, maybe she even loved him. Even if he was old enough to be her grandfather.

He followed her to where her horse was tethered, ignored the hostility pulsing from her guard, and held the bridle as she effortlessly swung herself into the saddle. Unlike Scots noblewomen, she sat astride. It was disconcertingly arousing.

"Good day," she said, and with damning reluctance he relinquished his grip on the bridle. For an endless moment she remained motionless, their gazes locked, and he imagined she sent him a concealed message.

He frowned, uncertain. He'd never played courtly games before. Not that it would have helped if he had. The Picts were not Scots. Had he been wrong in believing she wasn't receptive to an assignation with him?

She drew in a deep breath as though she was about to confirm his tortured thoughts, but then just as swiftly pressed her lips together, as though locking down whatever secret she had almost spilled.

Had she been waiting for him to give a sign? But he'd shown

his interest by requesting to dance with her this night. And she'd refused.

She left the village square at a sedate pace, her guard riding by her side. Finn stood, arms folded, his gaze fixed on the vibrant blue of her cloak. Willing her to turn, just for a moment, a sign that he wasn't wrong, and this goodbye wasn't final.

Just when he'd given up hope that she would give him some small acknowledgment, she glanced over her shoulder at him. And smiled.

He expelled a ragged breath. Damn, but he needed a drink. He strode across the square and into the tavern. Several of his countrymen were there, those that were waiting for the farrier to see to their horses, but none were mixing with the locals. He ordered a tankard of ale and downed half the contents in one long gulp. It didn't help clear his thoughts.

Ewan MacKinnon appeared by his side, his own tankard in hand. "You have the look of a man who's been thwarted in love, Braeson."

"Do you ever think of anything but women?" He knocked his tankard against Ewan's and they both took another swig of their ale. MacKinnon's late father had been close to their king, but Ewan had never been one of Constantine's confidents, the group of boys when they'd all been children who had thought it great sport to spill Finn's blood.

"Not if I can help it." Ewan laughed and Finn shook his head. The man was a renowned seducer but there were few he'd trust more to have by his side in battle. "Did you find a willing noblewoman to pass the night with?"

"I wasn't looking for one."

"Then I must look for you. The Pictish ladies are delightful company. They'll help pass the time until MacAllister deems it time to depart."

Finn was well aware what Ewan thought of MacAllister. Certainly, Ewan was loyal to their king, but at heart he was

Connor MacKenzie's man. But since Connor's marriage to the Pictish princess, Aila, their king considered him too valuable to be sent on endless missions around the country.

"The Pictish ladies are most entertaining," he conceded, but there was only one he found so. Only one he wanted in his bed. He finished his ale. While he had never required assistance when it came to understanding a woman before, the truth was plain. Ewan had been posted in Pictland for months and knew their ways. Maybe there was something he could learn from the other man about the mysterious methods of seduction the noble-women employed.

"I've always found them to be so."

Finn waited, but it appeared that was all the insight Ewan cared to share. He decided to take a chance. "You've never misjudged and been rebuffed?"

Ewan shot him a shrewd glance. Fuck. He should have kept his damn mouth shut.

"If no offense is caused, a rebuff means little to either party." Ewan shrugged, as though it was no great hardship. "There are, after all, many willing ladies in the palace to choose from."

Finn grunted. He had no interest in the other ladies, but he wasn't inclined to share that with anyone. "I'm surprised they want to have anything to do with us at all."

Ewan's grin faded and he glanced across the tavern, where MacAllister and several of their warriors were at a table.

"Aye," he said at last, no hint of his previous amusement in his voice. "The bloodshed at Dunadd in the spring was," he paused, his gaze piercing into Finn. Ewan knew, of course, that MacAlpin was his father. But he had no idea the king had acknowledged him. They were friends and had spoken of many things over the years. But they'd never let a whisper of treason taint their words.

Until now, there had never been a reason to. But Ewan's reluctance to continue told him two things. His friend didn't believe the official report concerning the massacre of the Pictish nobles in the spring. Even thinking that their king had betrayed the alliance in such a manner amounted to treason. And secondly, he was unwilling to confide those suspicions to Finn.

Because of his connection to MacAlpin?

Finn casually glanced around the tavern. MacAllister was deep in conversation with his men. He returned his attention to Ewan. And said one word. "Unnecessary."

Ewan avoided his eyes. "Beware, Finn." His voice was low. "MacAllister will have your head if he hears you voice such things."

A week ago, Finn would never have broached the subject. But now, although he'd never openly confront his king—after all, what evidence did they have? —he'd speak his mind to his friends. MacAlpin needed his bastard son to forge yet another bloodied alliance with the Picts and because of that, Finn's position was now not so precarious.

"I don't confide in MacAllister." Contempt tinged his voice. "But you and I, Ewan, fought side by side with the Picts in Northumbria. Something happened in Dunadd while we were gone, but I doubt it's the story we've been told."

"Even if that's true, we still need this alliance. Only our combined strength will keep the cursed Norsemen from flooding this land."

Silence fell between them. Ewan ordered another two tankards and handed one to Finn. "Have you heard the rumors as to why we were really sent here?"

"Rumors?"

"Aye." Ewan leaned in closer. "The king has set his mind to hunt down the missing Princess of Fortriu."

How the fuck did Ewan know that? He'd thought their true mission was a tightly held secret. Same as his new royal status. His glare intensified. Did Ewan know of that, too?

"Who told you?"

Ewan tapped the side of his nose. "I have my sources. Clearly, the release of the Fotla king and his son was a tactic to loosen tongues. Although between you and me, I doubt the royal house will give up a member of their own blood."

"MacAlpin plans to sacrifice another Scots warrior in his quest to conquer this land." Bitterness seeped through the words, and he took a long swallow of his ale. It didn't dull the knowledge that he was the unlucky one.

"If the princess is anything like her royal cousins who wed Connor and Cam, then the Scots warrior chosen should count his blessings." Ewan grinned. "Not that I would wish to be in his shoes, but the princesses of Pictland are visions to behold."

"I wouldn't know." He sounded surly but couldn't help it. Mae's sweet face filled his mind. She was a vision, for sure. A man could willingly sacrifice his freedom for her.

"I know one thing, Braeson. It's clearly been too long since you've enjoyed a good fuck. Forget the one who refused you. Tonight, I'll find you a Pictish lady who will erase all thoughts of her from your head."

CHAPTER 6

I *should not have looked back.*

The mantra played inside Mairi's head as she reached the stables and dismounted. But the temptation to see whether Finn Braeson had watched her leave, or not, had been too great.

She buried her face in Audra's mane and smothered a groan. The fact she had been too weak-willed to refrain from glancing over her shoulder at him was insignificant compared to what she'd said to him.

That Pictland would never willingly succumb to the Scots invasion.

Thankfully, he hadn't taken offense. But just because he was so easy to talk to, didn't mean she could speak her mind to him. Goddess, she shouldn't be speaking to him *at all*.

"My lady." A serving girl approached and bobbed a curtsey. Clearly, she had been waiting in the stables for her return. "The queen wishes to see you directly."

Mairi nodded and bit back her curse. She had hoped to tend to Audra before returning to the palace, but it would not do to keep the queen waiting any longer. It was only when she reached the queen's private chambers that she noticed the mud on the hem of her gown. Heat flared in her cheeks. What must Finn have thought of her?

Stop thinking of him. She drew in a deep breath and entered the chamber. The queen lifted one finger, and her ladies all stood without a word and left the chamber, but not without giving her surreptitious glances. Even Briana said nothing, but as she passed by, she gave her fingers a quick squeeze in sympathy.

Wonderful.

Once the door closed and they were alone, she braced herself and curtseyed. "You wished to speak to me, Madam?"

"Indeed. We are taking a grave risk, concealing your presence here, Mairi. I am perturbed, to say the least, that you decide to behave so rashly when our enemies surround us. If you wish to continue to take advantage of our protection, you must remain within the palace walls and out of sight."

Resentment burned through her. How dare the queen speak to her in such a manner? Before she could stop herself, the accusation escaped. "You wish to keep me imprisoned?"

The queen gave a tight smile. "Not the words I would have used. But ask yourself this. Would you prefer the alternative, of having the Scots discover your whereabouts?"

Was the queen threatening her? Her breath stalled in her chest and ice trickled over her arms. Surely not. *Clear your mind.*

She *had* been foolish. She should have returned with Briana, and let the guard take her mare to the farrier. It didn't matter that before, and throughout her marriage until six months ago, she had enjoyed a degree of independence that the queen of Fotla had always found unbecoming.

Neither did it matter that by virtue of her birth her status outranked the queen's. She was a fugitive, as good as banished from her own kingdom, and while she was in Fotla she was compelled to obey the queen.

She squashed her pride as best she could and bowed her head.

"You are right. Please accept my apologies. I'm most grateful for your protection."

The queen sighed. "Mairi. This situation grieves me greatly. Your dear mamma was my third cousin and like a sister to me. I'll do all in my power to keep you safe. But you also must play your part."

"I understand." She kept her eyes downcast, while wings of panic fluttered within her breast. For six months she had hidden away from the world, but at least she'd managed to take a daily ride. But now even that small measure of freedom was to be curtailed.

The chamber wasn't small, but the walls closed in on her and it became hard to breath. She had to get out of here. Even if just to escape to her own bedchamber.

Which isn't even mine.

"With your leave, I will retire."

"Of course." The queen dismissed her. Mairi pressed her lips together and left the chamber. Thankfully, she managed to avoid the queen's ladies, but before she reached the staircase that led to the upper floor, Bhaic emerged from a passageway.

"Madam, you shouldn't be wandering the palace unaccompanied."

She battened down her frustration, but it wasn't easy. "I'm merely going to my chamber."

He indicated that she should follow him to a secluded corner. "I'm uneasy with this arrangement." His voice was so low, she had to strain her ears to hear him. "The Scots pollute the very air we breathe. We should leave and find refuge in Fib."

I'll never see Finn again.

Oh, dear goddess. What was wrong with her? She had already vowed to herself not to see him again. At least, not the way she had today. Or last night. There was nothing she could do if she happened to see him from a distance, such as at the nightly feasts, was there?

Finn Braeson was utterly unconnected to a decision as to whether she stayed in Fotla or departed.

"Madam?" Bhaic's voice held a thread of censure and she forcibly thrust Finn from her mind. Why did he keep invading her thoughts so? He was her enemy, and she could *not* afford to forget it.

"Both Bride and Cailleach led me here. We can't leave until they send me a sign that the time is right."

Bhaic didn't look convinced. "I still believe a marriage between us is your best chance of surviving. When the Scots cannot pick up the Princess of Fortriu's trail, they'll believe she is dead, and you'll be safe."

"No. I won't enter into another," she bit off her words. Her marriage had been false, and so would one to Bhaic. But she wouldn't sully Nechtan's memory, or Bhaic's honor by uttering such a thing. "Another marriage," she said, instead, but Bhaic's fleeting frown told her he understood her perfectly. She touched his arm in a brief gesture of affection. If they couldn't speak the truth between them, they were lost. "We both deserve more than that."

"In these troubled times, it's unlikely we'll find what we deserve." A thread of bitterness tainted his voice. "The Scots encroach into Pictland like a plague. Beware of the one who attempts to enchant you. No good will come from it."

Had the guard spread word of her encounter with Finn? It had never occurred to her he might do such a thing. Surely that kind of gossip was beneath a warrior. But then, he was not one of her own loyal men.

Yet even if he had, she had nothing to hide. It was not as though she and Finn had met through an illicit assignation. But guilt ate through her, just the same.

"No one is attempting to enchant me." She injected a measure of disdain in the words. Besides, it was the truth. Finn wasn't attempting to enchant her. If he was, then he'd seek her out for whatever nefarious purpose he had in mind. So far, their encounters had been quite by chance.

A sliver of doubt edged into her mind.

Had they, though?

"Maybe not." Bhaic didn't sound convinced. "But his air was possessive when you left him last night. I don't trust him."

Last night. Relief tumbled through her. "You're mistaken, Bhaic. He was merely escorting me back to the palace."

Possessive? A shiver skittered across her skin, and it wasn't at all unpleasant. How thrilling would it be, to indulge in a light-hearted affair with him, the way so many Pictish ladies appeared to enjoy fleeting liaisons with Scots' warriors?

She had heard rumors of such things happening in the kingdom of Ce, and last night had observed it with her own eyes. The memory of Finn's lips against her fingers—even though she had been wearing gloves—sent prickles of awareness dancing through her blood.

How she longed to feel his lips on hers. Her breath caught in her throat and heart hammered against her ribs, as though she had just galloped across the glens. It was an effort not to press her palm against her breast to slow the erratic thunder.

Focus. She would never take Finn as her lover.

She wasn't a noblewoman. She was of royal blood, and she couldn't forget the ties of duty that bound her. To engage with her enemy in so intimate a manner would be tantamount to treason.

"Madam." There was an edge in Bhaic's voice. Clearly, he had spoken, and she'd completely missed what he had said. "I will escort you to your chamber."

There was no point refusing. He had sworn a deathbed oath to Nechtan to protect her. He would most likely stand guard outside her chamber, until Briana's ladies joined her. As the door to the chamber swung shut behind her, she sent a desperate plea to her goddess.

Bride, what is to become of me?

IT WAS late afternoon and Mairi brushed Briana's hair, as her cousin sat on a stool in her chamber and her ladies helped each other dress and pick jewelry for the feast that evening.

Apparently, the Scots had been hunting and presented their spoils to the king, as thanks for their hospitality. Another strategy to win favor. Naturally, the king had then invited them to dine within the palace. When would the Scots reveal the true reason why they were in Fotla?

As if she didn't know perfectly well why they were here.

"I hear my lord Constantine is the finest archer of all the Scots." Nairne, one of Briana's noblewomen, gave a dramatic sigh. "He is by far the most handsome of their warriors. I do believe I will take up our beloved queen's edict and take it upon myself to seduce all of his secrets from him this night."

Mairi leaned close to her cousin and breathed against her ear. "The queen's edict?"

Briana glanced at Nairne, but she was too busy regaling the other ladies as to all of Constantine's physical delights.

"Indeed," Briana confirmed. "Mamma has let it be known that if our noblewomen wish to take a Scot as their lover, they're obliged to disclose any secrets that might be spilled in the bedchamber."

Finn's green eyes haunted her. Ruthlessly, she forced the memory aside. "I'm sure the Scots have the same order from their king."

"Yes, but our Pictish noblewomen will never reveal anything. It's the one strength we have against men, who with a little encouragement will say anything while in the throes of passion."

"Hmm." Her cousin's hair was perfect, but Mairi fiddled with it a little more, so she didn't have to face Briana. She knew nothing of how men behaved in the throes of passion and although Briana knew her marriage had been far from satisfactory, Mairi had never confided that she was still an untouched maid.

It wasn't something she'd ever tell anyone. However unfairly, the knowledge could potentially dimmish what little influence she still retained within the royal houses of Pictland.

"Naturally, *I've* been forbidden from taking a Scot as a lover." There was a dry note in Briana's voice.

"And I have been banished to my bedchamber." Despite her pleas, Bride had remained elusive during the solitary hours she'd spent pacing the floor, before being summoned to Briana's chamber.

"Not at all." Briana stood and took Mairi's hand. "You are to accompany us to the feast. It would be unseemly for you to be excluded."

Don't think about seeing Finn.

Too late. She would most likely think of him for the rest of her days. The charming warrior whose smile could be hiding a thousand lies.

She stifled a sigh. It was a sad reflection of her life that two brief meetings with him could affect her so. The sooner the Scots left Fotla, the better.

"The queen believes it prudent that I remain hidden from view." She tried not to sound bitter but wasn't sure she succeeded.

Briana cast another glance at the chattering ladies. "I spoke to her about this, Mae. She understands that if you're confined to the bedchamber, it will cause far more gossip to circulate. But I'm sorry, I could not change her mind on allowing you the freedom to ride again."

Frustration burned through her. "If I were a man, I wouldn't be forced to conceal my birthright."

"If you were a man, you would either be dead, or held hostage in Dunadd."

Mairi shook her head. "Your logic doesn't make me feel any better. I want MacAlpin to pay for what he's done."

Briana tugged her hand and with reluctance she met her gaze. Concern etched her cousin's face. "Promise me you won't do anything foolish, Mae. The Scots won't remain here forever. They'll soon move on with their search—if indeed they're searching for you. They may be engaged in another strategy entirely for all we know."

It was possible, but in her heart, she knew exactly why the Scots were in Fotla. "I won't do anything foolish," she promised. Goddess, how many times did she have to repeat herself? Struana, who had accompanied her from Fortriu, broke away from the others and came to her side, and Mairi forced a smile to her lips. Struana was loyal, but she would never burden the young noblewoman with her own frustrations. "I'd better get ready for tonight."

She needed to change from her mud-splattered gown, and she hadn't tidied her hair since arriving back in the palace. But just because she wanted to look her best, had nothing to do with the fact Finn Braeson would be there.

Keep telling yourself that, Mairi.

CHAPTER 7

The feast that night was another grand affair, but by God. How many times did Constantine have to brag about how he'd single-handedly brought down the red stag? Even MacAllister was looking irked by the story.

Finn could only imagine what the Pict warriors thought.

"It's a pity we were burdened with Constantine," Ewan, who sat by Finn's side, said under his breath. "At least Aedh possesses diplomacy."

Finn grunted. Aedh remained in Dunadd, and Constantine had been his usual boorish self since they'd arrived in Fotla. When it came to diplomacy, MacAlpin put his trust in MacAllister. Finn could only assume the king believed that by sending a royal prince of Dal Riada on this mission showed the Picts he was willing to trust them.

Despite himself, once again his gaze traveled to the other long table in the hall, which was occupied by the Pictish nobles and their ladies. Occasionally, he'd glimpsed a view of Mae's back, where she sat on the bench beside the old man. Her husband.

"Are you still obsessed by the lady who rejected you?" Amusement threaded through Ewan's voice and Finn turned to glare at him. Ewan laughed. "I see you are. You haven't taken your gaze from her the entire evening."

Ewan was prone to exaggeration, but this time Finn found nothing humorous in it. "I've been admiring all the ladies of the court. As you suggested I do earlier."

It was a blatant lie but no way in hell did he want Ewan to guess which lady had so ensnared him. If it weren't so damn inconvenient, it would be funny.

"And which exquisite creature has caught your eye?" Ewan's grin suggested he didn't believe Finn's retort, but was willing to play along. That was good enough for him.

"I'll see how the night progresses."

"Or you can trust me in this matter. I promise that you'll enjoy bed sport such as you have never before imagined."

It was galling that Ewan believed Finn needed his assistance in such basic matters, but it was his own fault. He should have kept his mouth shut in the tavern.

When the feast ended, the tables and benches were pushed back to the walls, to make space for the dancing, as the musicians gathered beside the high table where the royal family sat. He cast a glance across the crowded hall, but Mae had disappeared. Damn it, why couldn't he erase her from his mind?

"Stay close." Ewan clapped him on the shoulder. "I spy two ladies I wish to introduce you to."

Although he wasn't especially eager to accompany Ewan in this quest, it had been months since he'd last enjoyed the comfort of a woman. Maybe, once he slaked his lust, he wouldn't be so obsessed with the elusive Lady Mae.

He wasn't convinced, but what choice did he have? Unlike many of her noble born countrywomen, she was clearly not looking for an illicit affair.

They bypassed a group of Picts, and his heart damn near

slammed through his chest. Standing in front of them, as though conjured up from his frenzied mind, was Mae.

She appeared as startled as he and instead of greeting her with a witty acknowledgment, any coherent words lodged in his throat. She was a vision in a pale green gown with golden thread embroidered across the bodice and along her sleeves. A matching green veil draped over her head, secured by a plain gold circlet, but her rich copper hair glowed through the translucent material, and trailed over her breast in a sleek braid. Her eyes were bluer than he recalled, her lashes longer, and the faint sprinkle of freckles across her nose was utterly bewitching.

"Lady Briana." There was an uncharacteristically stilted note in Ewan's voice as he bowed to the ladies. Fuck, he hadn't even noticed Mae's companion. Feeling like an utter fool, Finn also bowed.

It was a struggle not to allow his gaze to slip back to Mae, but he couldn't afford to offend the Princess of Fotla.

"Ewan MacKinnon," the princess said, as though the words emitted a foul odor. She didn't offer her hand for him to kiss. "Who is the fine warrior by your side?"

Ewan's jaw flexed. "Lady Briana, may I present Finn Braeson."

What the hell was wrong with MacKinnon? He sounded as though he had a pike shoved down his throat. He risked glancing at Mae and was rewarded by a tiny smile. She clearly found the situation as excruciating as he.

"Finn Braeson," the princess said. Despite the fact she spoke in Gaelic and her accent mirrored Mae's, it held no enchantment for him. "How delightful." She offered him her hand. After a second's hesitation he took it and bestowed a fleeting kiss on her knuckles.

"Lady Briana. It's an honour."

A deathly silence fell between them. The princess shot an oddly furtive glance at Mae. Unease crawled along his spine. What was happening? Even he, as excluded at court as he'd often been, knew etiquette well enough to know the princess should introduce them to Mae. It wasn't as though she was a servant. She was clearly noble born. And while they were not in the court at Dal Riada, things couldn't be that different, surely.

"Lady Mae." There was a reluctant note in the princess' voice. "Ewan MacKinnon, Finn Braeson."

"It's an honor." MacKinnon wasted no time in taking Mae's hand and lavishing a kiss upon her. Finn struggled to contain his glare, until MacKinnon released her, and she offered her hand to him.

He drew in a deep breath. Obviously, like him, she had told no one of their previous encounters which reinforced his conviction she was not seeking a diversion outside of the marital bed. If he had any sense, he would make this formality as brief as possible.

His fingers clasped hers and lightning blazed along his arm and caused his gut to tighten, and cock thicken. It was both exhilarating and somewhat alarming. He brushed his lips over her bare knuckles, but instead of then immediately releasing her, he lingered, savoring her touch.

Madness.

Slowly, he raised his head and his gaze meshed with hers. Her lips parted and she drew in a ragged breath. Beneath the constraints of her bodice her breasts offered a delectable, forbidden promise.

Release her hand.

Never had an order been so hard to obey.

And then the moment shattered as Constantine shouldered his way in between him and Ewan.

"Lady Briana." Constantine spoke in Pictish and gave a lavish bow before taking her hand. "Your beauty illuminates the entire hall. I trust you enjoyed the venison this night?"

Finn braced his muscles but inside he still winced. Stealthily, he edged back from the prince which brought him closer to Mae. No hardship there. He glanced at her, and her face was as serene as her mistress', as Constantine regaled them with an embellished tale of his hunting prowess.

He took advantage of the distraction to lean a little closer to Mae. "You look radiant," he whispered in Gaelic. It was a delayed compliment, but heartfelt, nevertheless.

Her smile held that hint of mockery that was becoming so damnably familiar. He had to lower his head to hear her murmured response. "Does my radiance illuminate the entire hall, though, Finn Braeson?"

As always, her accent enchanted him. He shot her a grin at her teasing words. "Your radiance illuminates Pictland herself."

"I like that image."

"I thought you might."

She stole a glance at her mistress before returning her attention to him. "Your prince is a great hunter, then."

He didn't miss the thread of derision in her tone. The fact she felt no obligation to pretend respect for a prince of Dal Riada was utterly intriguing. Or was the only reason he detected her veiled contempt because of the other times they had spoken?

To hell with it. If she could confide, then so could he. "The prince has a high opinion of himself altogether."

She laughed and hastily turned it into a cough when the princess gave her a sharp glance. Constantine didn't appear to notice the interruption at all.

"I would be honored if you would dance with me, my lady." Constantine held out his hand. The princess did not take it.

"I thank you, but I cannot abandon Lady Mae."

Constantine appeared taken aback by her reply. Hardly surprising. In Dal Riada, no woman refused Constantine's command. But then, Pictish women were not Scots, and Constantine was not their prince.

Unfortunately, he recovered instantly, and waved a dismissive hand in Finn's direction. "Braeson will partner Lady Mae. I will accept no refusal in this matter."

The princess gave a tight smile. It was clear to him, if not Constantine, that the prince of Dal Riada had just severely insulted the daughter of their host. "Very well." Her voice was ice as she accepted Constantine's hand.

Finn bowed his head at Mae. It wouldn't do to show how much he wanted this, but he couldn't entirely hide his smile. "I fear we're destined to dance this night, my lady."

"I fear you are right." She took his hand and her thumb gently caressed him. Such sweet agony. "But we can hardly refuse, can we?"

He led her to the center of the hall, where several couples were already congregating. And only then did the obvious occur to him.

"I don't know any Pictish dances." Did any Scots? Several warriors beside him and Constantine had secured partners.

"I'm certain the musicians will play something simple."

"I hope you're right, or my countrymen will be sorely disgraced."

"I'm sure they'll survive." Her voice was dry. The harpists played an introduction, and the music was oddly familiar. "It seems Pictland has adopted some of Dal Riada's culture during these last six months."

She didn't sound impressed, although he was relieved he wouldn't trip over his own feet attempting to learn new steps. "Dal Riada is honored by Pictland's tolerant policies."

As their fingers touched and he bowed, her sigh shivered through him. "*You* are the only reason I believe there may be honor in Dal Riada. But this is survival, Finn. Nothing more."

She curtseyed and for endless moments they were parted as the dancers switched partners. The fact she believed him honorable warmed him deep inside, but unease stirred. Just because he enjoyed her candor, didn't mean he wanted her to endanger her safety by saying these things to any of his compatriots. When they finally came back together, he risked breaking the symmetry of the dance and whispered in her ear.

"We all want to survive, my lady. Believe me, honor still lives in Dal Riada." Just not in Dunadd.

"I shall have to take your word for it."

Even though she slighted his people by her words and the way she didn't hide her true feelings he couldn't help smiling at her response. But caution kicked in. He had to warn her. "Not all of my countrymen would take kindly to having their faults laid out so bluntly, Lady Mae."

This time her smile appeared almost pitying. "Indeed, I'm well aware. I do not usually speak so freely, especially with a perceived enemy. But you," she paused, considering, and he bit back a curse as once again the strictures of the dance tore them apart.

It was an effort to concentrate on the young woman who partnered him and asked him inconsequential questions concerning the hunt earlier that day. When he reclaimed Mae's hand, he had the wild urge to pull her from the hall so they could continue this exhilarating interlude uninterrupted.

She didn't instantly resume their conversation, and he tugged on her hand. The need to know what she had wanted to tell him consumed his reason. "What is it about me?"

Her teasing smile turned pensive, and she tilted her head. "I wish I knew. I shall have to ask my goddess why I confide in a man who could so easily destroy my peace of mind."

"Have no fear on that account. I'll never harm you by thought or deed."

"Pretty words, for which I thank you. But you're a warrior, and your fealty is to your king."

"Aye." He acknowledged she was right and was rewarded by the way she inclined her head, as though she appreciated his honesty. But while MacAlpin was many things, none of which he'd repeat to Mae, he was certain that terrorizing Pictish noblewomen wasn't among his sins. "My king would never order me to disrupt your life."

"His very existence disrupts the lives of every Pict." She swirled away and it was another few torturous moments before they were once again reunited. "As you well know."

"I can't answer for him. But should he intrude on the short time we share together?"

A shadow passed over her face. "We shouldn't spend any time together."

As though drawn by unseen forces, Finn glanced over her shoulder. Standing in the crowd, arms folded, his unblinking gaze upon them, stood Mae's husband.

Fuck. He had entirely forgotten about the man's existence, but it was a timely reminder. It didn't matter how intriguing he found Mae or how much he enjoyed being with her. She was married, a loyal wife, and had plainly told him by her actions that she wasn't interested in an illicit affair.

The dance ended, and he bowed, taking Mae's hand. "I fear your husband is about to steal you away." He injected a light note in his voice so she wouldn't guess his frustration.

Scot and Pict milled around them, as Mae took a step closer to him, an oddly furtive expression on her face. "I am widowed."

It was the last thing he'd expected her to say. He'd been so convinced the man was her husband, by his possessive air and how Mae had gone to him last night. Who the hell was he?

Her father?

"I'm sorry for your loss." Christ, he hoped the Pict hadn't been one killed by MacAlpin's order in the spring. Ruthlessly, he swept the notion aside. Only those of royal blood and with a claim to the kingdom of Fortriu had been ambushed. If Mae had been wed to one of them, MacAlpin would have secured her as a valuable hostage and married her to one of his most trusted warriors.

Distaste curdled his gut, even though she'd been spared such a fate.

"Thank you. He was a good man." She lowered her eyes. "My lord Bhaic is a family friend."

A friend? Then he had no authority over Mae, or the company she kept. Why then did she defer to him? Had her late husband made Bhaic her guardian? Or did he intend to wed her?

top trusting Finn with all your secrets.

But it wasn't a secret that she was widowed. He could easily have discovered that for himself if he had asked anyone at court.

The knowledge he hadn't spoken of her in such a manner warmed Mairi's heart, and dissolved the lingering sense of unease that she should be more careful with what she shared with him.

There were many things she would never tell him, but she didn't want there to be any more half-truths between them than absolutely necessary.

"He keeps you in his sights. Is there an understanding between you?"

Taken aback by his unvarnished question, and the obvious meaning behind it, she missed a step of the dance. Thankfully, no one noticed as the music finished and applause rippled around the hall, giving her a moment to collect herself.

His remark was only surprising because in the past no one would have presumed to ask her such a thing, due to her rank. But here, in Fotla, she was merely another noblewoman. And given Bhaic's unsubtle determination to track her every move, Finn's question was reasonable.

"No. We are not betrothed, if that's what you're asking."

"Good."

"Would it make so much difference, if we were?" It was a foolish question. She knew it, as well as he. Yet she craved to hear him say the words, even if, ultimately, it made no difference to their situation.

He took her hand and pulled her close. The breath caught in her throat at his careless disregard for etiquette, but she didn't protest. His touch was too exhilarating and the fierce determination in his eyes, as he focused his attention on her, was too thrilling to spoil the moment with a hollow rebuke.

"It would to me."

He led her to the side of the hall, where the sturdy time-candle on its plinth was set into the thickness of the wall, protecting its flame. For a breathtaking second, she thought he meant to take her into the nook itself, where they might be afforded a fanciful façade of privacy.

She would protest, of course. It would not be seemly. Why, then, did her heart flutter with anticipation?

He halted beside the nook, still holding her hand. Anyone could see them, if they cared to look, but it wasn't as though she was the only Pict indulging in such a pastime with a visiting Scots warrior. If she pulled away from Finn now, it would cause more speculation, not less.

She wouldn't end this magical moment just yet. It wasn't as though she was with a Scot whose very existence drew attention to him, like the oaf, Constantine, who had accosted her cousin.

For all she knew, Finn didn't have even a drop of noble blood in his veins. No one would care with whom he passed a few flirtatious moments. She could enjoy this brief respite from duty without guilt that she was being reckless.

"Lady Mae. You entrance me." Finn's voice dropped to a

husky whisper. A strange lightheadedness assailed her, rippling through her entire body and tremors of fiery delight collided low in her belly. Her bodice was too tight, the air too scarce to take a breath, and the noise in the hall seemed to fade with every erratic beat of her heart.

It was hard to remain still when every nerve she possessed screamed at her to close the distance between them, to wind her arms around his broad shoulders, and press herself against his hard, muscular chest.

Heat flared through her at the shameless image, but she couldn't drag her gaze from his mesmerizing green eyes.

"I fear you entrance me, too." The confession escaped before she could prevent it. But then, she didn't try too hard. What harm could come of telling him this small truth?

"You haunt my mind whenever we're apart." Even though she knew he jested, his words were as captivating as his smile. "It's most distracting."

"I'm sure I should apologize for this, but I find I cannot."

"Never apologize for being irresistible."

She laughed at that. "Now you are simply being outrageous."

"I've been called far worse. I can work with outrageous."

They were still holding hands. She dared to take a step closer to him, and the spark of lightning that flashed through her blood was intoxicating. "I find it hard to believe you've been called worse."

"It's in the past. None of it matters anymore."

"And yet our past defines us."

His grin was pure sin. "Only if we allow it to do so."

She exhaled a ragged breath and her besotted gaze trailed to his lips. So close. All she needed to do was lean closer and they would kiss. Her mouth dried and chest constricted. Dear goddess, this Scot bedazzled her.

"It's not always possible to disregard our past. Sometimes, that is all we have." Her voice was hoarse, as though she'd been in a smoke-filled chamber. How extraordinary that Finn's mere presence could ignite her passions so. She'd never quite believed the whispered confessions shared between ladies of how a man's touch could cause the flesh to burn with unrequited hunger.

Goddess, she believed it now. And Finn had scarcely touched her at all.

"Sweet Mae." His tender murmur fluttered through her like a forbidden caress. "I can't erase the past. All I can offer you is a brief interlude. If you are willing."

An illicit affair. Molten desire licked through her blood, causing her legs to shake and flesh prickle with untrammeled need. How tempting to cast aside all inhibitions and fall into his arms. If only she could.

"I..." The words locked in her throat, as tantalizing glimpses of how it could be if she agreed to Finn's proposal. If she weren't still a maid and if she weren't so mindful of possible consequences, how easy her response would be.

"Forgive me," he whispered, and his warm breath caressed her cheek. "You are still in mourning for your husband. I meant no disrespect."

She swallowed and tried to clear her mind, but her mind was filled with Finn and the promise of something wild and wonderful. She did miss Nechtan and mourn his loss. But not in the way a woman would mourn the passing of a beloved husband.

It wasn't fair to use his memory as a shield. Even if Finn expected her to.

"It was not a love match." She didn't betray his memory by admitting that. Necessity, due to an ever-dwindling pool of suitable partners, decreed that few royals or nobles married for love. She had heard it was similar within the court of Dunadd. "I enjoy your company, but I fear I'm not ready for anything... more."

She braced herself for his rejection. The Scots were, after all, merely passing through Fotla, and would be gone when they'd satisfied themselves that the missing princess was elsewhere. If all Finn wished for was a willing Pictish noblewoman in his bed, he now knew he was wasting his time flirting with her.

He didn't relinquish his hold on her hand. Had she imagined that his fingers tightened around hers?

"I don't seek you out simply because I want you in my bed. Although, I'd be lying if I said I haven't thought of it since the moment we met."

Enchanted, she gazed at him. "I may not change my mind before you leave the kingdom."

"Yet I shall live in hope that you will." He brushed a gentle kiss across her knuckles and his touch whispered through the essence of her soul. "Regardless, I must also confess your conversation bewitches me. For that alone, the journey to Fotla was worthwhile."

"I'm gratified you find my constant insults entertaining."

"I cherish each one, my lady."

"Then I promise to continue. It will be no hardship, I assure you."

"Lady Mae."

Startled, Mairi spun around. Briana stood there, a polite smile on her face, but Mairi knew her cousin well enough. Briana was furious.

With reluctance, she pulled her hand from Finn's grasp and then remembered to drop a curtsey to Briana, as befit the charade she was playing. "My lady?"

"Come. I am in need of you." Briana inclined her head to Finn before turning away. Clearly, she expected Mairi to follow her. She dug her nails into the palms of her hands and inhaled a deep breath before turning back to Finn.

If only she didn't have to hide who she truly was, she could spend the entire night speaking with him, without having to defer to anyone.

But if she revealed that truth, her life would surely be forfeit.

"I must go." She should say a final farewell, yet her heart

rebelled. "Perhaps we shall have another chance encounter where we can continue to trade insults."

"I look forward to it. Although I don't believe I've insulted you. If I have, it was unintentional."

"Indeed, you are most charming. My apologies."

"Mae." This time there was no mistaking the sharp note in Briana's voice and Mairi smothered the flare of resentment that burned through her. Her cousin was right. They had to leave the hall.

With a final smile at Finn, she turned, and Briana took her arm as they made their way around the perimeter of the hall. It took every shred of self-control she possessed not to glance over her shoulder. And this time, unlike this morning when she'd left him at the farrier's, she managed to maintain her restraint.

Was he watching her leave? She fancied she could feel his eyes upon her. When would she next see him?

Would he find a willing lady to spend this night with?

The warmth bubbling through her blood cooled and her smile slid from her face. It was possible. Goddess, it was likely. Who was she trying to fool?

"Insufferable egotistical barbarian."

She pulled her scattered thoughts together and shot her cousin a concerned glance. It was obvious the Scots prince had continued to offend Briana while they had danced. "I'm sorry I couldn't help you avoid his obnoxious company, my love."

Briana drew in a deep breath as they left the hall and, followed by a guard, made their way up the stairs to her cousin's chamber.

"There was nothing you could do," Briana said over her shoulder as she navigated the narrow stone steps. "I shouldn't let his uncouth manners affect me so."

They entered her small antechamber and went over to the fireplace to warm their hands, as a servant stoked the flames. "He is certainly an oaf. Like his father."

Briana frowned. "His father? What do you know of his father?"

Were they speaking at cross purposes? "No more than you, I'm sure. Any son of MacAlpin can be nothing but despicable."

The servant bobbed a curtsey and retired to the other side of the chamber. Briana sighed.

"You're right. Constantine is certainly despicable. But I'm referring to Ewan MacKinnon. Such an arrogant man I have never before encountered."

"Oh." Mairi raised her eyebrows. She'd found nothing especially arrogant about the other warrior's demeanor. Then again, she'd been quite besotted by Finn's presence and hadn't taken much notice of MacKinnon. But her cousin was obviously in need of comfort. "It's not that surprising. He *is* a Scot, after all."

Briana shook her head and took Mairi's hands. "Never mind about that. I'm more enraged that you were given no recourse but to dance with that other warrior. I hope the ordeal wasn't too distasteful."

"No, it…" she hesitated, uncertain. How she longed to confide in Briana. But it would mean admitting she'd met Finn on two previous occasions and hadn't shared that with her cousin. Briana would be right to question it, and Mairi wasn't sure she had a legitimate defense. "It wasn't an ordeal at all. Finn Braeson is most agreeable. For a Scot," she added.

Briana appeared unconvinced. "He seemed entirely too eager to escort you from the safety of the hall."

She knew her cousin was only concerned, but this was taking it too far. "We were only standing by the time-candle."

"And I'm sure he only wanted you for scintillating conversation." Derision dripped from each word.

"If I'd been agreeable, he made it plain he wanted more. But *scintillating conversation* had to suffice." She hoped Briana hadn't heard the trace of bitterness in her voice. Because was Finn even now enjoying the earthlier delights of another Pictish lady?

Briana shook her head. "It's an intolerable situation. You'll share my room from now on, Mae. We will let it be known that because of your recent widowhood, you have no inclination in seducing our enemy. The ladies will quite understand."

Mairi was sure they would. Even though their queen had indicated such liaisons were permitted, no one who shared the princess' chamber would dare bring back a lover to spend the night. Nairne, whom Mae was replacing, would likely be delighted at the prospect of the additional freedom.

"I'd much prefer to share with you. But I don't like using the memory of Nechtan in this manner."

"It was the first reason I thought of. Do you have a better suggestion?"

"No," she admitted. It was a solid reason and would certainly prevent anyone from probing further. Who would wish to insult a noblewoman who had been so recently widowed by questioning her motives?

"Then it's settled." Briana sighed. "How much longer will the Scots keep us waiting, before they admit to their true purpose for being here?"

She had no answer to that. The longer the Scots remained in Fotla, the greater the threat of her deception being discovered became. And yet, in her heart, she couldn't wish them gone.

Because Finn would go with them.

CHAPTER 9

*A*fter Mae vanished from view, Finn took a deep breath. He needed air to clear his head although he wasn't certain that even the sharp Highland wind could manage such a feat.

Mae's beautiful blue eyes haunted his mind, and he couldn't dislodge the sweetness of her smile from his thoughts. She'd told him plainly she wouldn't fall into his bed, but that knowledge didn't lessen the craving to see her again.

Speak with her again.

He swallowed a groan and flexed his fingers, as though that might help ease the pounding in his blood. His cock throbbed with frustrated need, and it seemed a rock lodged deep in his chest. He strode through the hall but before he reached the doors, Ewan appeared by his side, an uncharacteristically grim expression on his face.

"If you're not on your way to an assignation, I'll join you."

Finn shrugged and they walked outside in silence. Storm clouds obscured the moon, and they were the only two fools who had ventured out into the frigid night air.

It didn't stop them marching further from the doors, away

from the mingling Scots and Picts, and the light that spilled into the courtyard. Finally, when shadows swallowed them and the blazing torches gave only isolated patches of illumination, Ewan halted. Silence stretched between them, and Finn braced himself for the inevitable questions regarding Mae that were sure to come.

"I don't like this." The abrupt words pierced the night air, and Finn frowned at the other man.

"What's happened?" Had MacAllister pushed for answers with their hosts, while Finn had indulged in pleasantries with Mae? Damn it, he didn't want answers. He didn't want this impossible moment out of time to shatter. Not yet.

Not ever.

"Nothing. How much longer do you think the Fotla king will tolerate our presence in his lands? Does MacAllister think he'll offer the information on the Fortriu princess voluntarily? Most of the men have suspicions as to why we're here, Finn. You can't tell me the Picts are ignorant of the real reason MacAlpin released the royal hostages."

He agreed, but he didn't want to discuss it. Except he couldn't tell Ewan that without revealing the reasons *why* he didn't want to fucking talk about it.

He compromised by giving a disagreeable grunt. With luck, Ewan would understand the conversation was over.

Unfortunately, it appeared Ewan hadn't finished. "To further erode our honor, MacAllister expects us to interrogate any Pictish noblewoman we bed."

So he hadn't been the only one MacAllister had approached with the despicable order. It was little consolation. But at least it was something he could talk about.

"I doubt any Pictish noblewoman would betray their people in such a manner."

"Not the point."

"Yet MacAllister believes it a viable strategy."

Ewan rolled his shoulders and cast a savage glance over his shoulder. "I'm a warrior. There's honor on the battlefields, no matter how bloody. But these political maneuvers don't sit right with me."

"We're all nothing but pawns in MacAlpin's game." Bitterness dripped from each word. "He won't rest until all of Pictland is within his grasp."

"At least you and I are safe from his plan to wed every available Pictish princess to a high-born Scot."

Finn folded his arms, but it didn't prevent the dull ache that spread through his chest like a malignant blight. "Don't be so sure. You're a high-born noble."

"But I don't have the right connections, like Connor. Or the right blood, like Cam. MacAlpin once said to tempt a Pictish king to part with a daughter, he had to offer royal blood."

"We both know MacAlpin will do whatever it takes to achieve his aim."

God knows, he already had.

Another silence fell, punctuated by the distant sound of harps carried on the wind. A haunting melody that wrapped around him like a suffocating mantle.

He dragged in a bracing lungful of air, but it didn't clear the sense of impending disaster.

Nothing could do that. Except, maybe, the discovery that the Princess of Fortriu had, indeed, perished six months ago as they had originally been led to believe.

"What are you doing out here anyway?" Ewan gave him a friendly punch on the shoulder. Clearly, he no longer wanted to discuss the depressing subject of politics. "Were you rejected yet again by another beautiful Pictish noblewoman?"

He should never have confided in Ewan earlier this day. "No."

"Ah. You're meeting her later?"

It would be too easy to say he was, and end Ewan's light-hearted mockery, but even if he had arranged an assignation with Mae, that secret would have remained between the two of them.

He had no intention of discussing her with anyone.

"No."

Ewan laughed. "If this is how you converse with them, it's no wonder they refuse your advances."

"What of you?" he countered. "Where are the ladies you intended to spend this night with?"

Too late, he recalled Ewan had invited him to share in such delights. The prospect did nothing to fire his blood.

Although it was dark, he saw Ewan frown. "A change of plan."

"They refused you?" He found the idea macabrely amusing.

"They did not."

Finn shook his head. "MacAllister's decree has withered your cock."

"MacAllister has nothing to do with it." A thread of irritation heated Ewan's response and Finn grinned. Clearly, Ewan didn't find it nearly as humorous when he was the butt of the joke.

"Admit it. Your charm is fading, MacKinnon."

Instead of a scathing retort, Ewan remained silent. Finn heaved a sigh and stamped his feet to get the blood moving once again before he froze inside his boots. "Are you going back inside the hall?"

"No. I've had my fill of Pictish ale."

"Then I'll see you tomorrow."

He watched Ewan swing about and head off to their camp before he made his way back to the palace. Not that he wanted to spend the night drinking Pictish ale, but the hall was preferable for another hour or two than returning to the dank confines of his tent.

Where, no doubt, erotic visions of the Lady Mae would besiege him until sunrise.

~

THIS CANNOT BE HAPPENING AGAIN SO SOON.

Mairi fought against the suffocating confines of her mind, as the nightmarish dream sucked her deep into its grasping vortex. Voices echoed and doors slammed, and crimson splattered all around.

Wake. Up.

Her heartbeat reverberated in her ears, an ominous tattoo that mirrored the pounding through her blood. As the ancient stone walls tumbled around her, dawn broke, shedding ribbons of orange and red across the horizon.

Relief spiked. Soon, she would be free. Soon, she would—

But reality did not intrude. Instead, sunlight flooded the unknown landscape. Riveted, she watched as a circle of sacred standing stones in the distance held back the glowing rays.

The stones had never appeared in this nightmare before. But they were not the blessed stones near the palace of Forteviot, where she had often worshipped her beloved Bride. She'd never seen these before, so breathtakingly majestic, and unblemished by the passage of the ages.

As if they had been erected by her ancestors mere days ago, instead of thousands of years.

The earth shifted, and great cracks appeared in the mighty stones. Renewed terror burst through her. *I must get out of here.*

The stones coalesced, pressing in on her, creating a dark corridor. Flames danced in sconces and rain thundered, unseen. Lightning blazed from an unknown source and then *he* was there, in front of her, and this time she saw his face. Piercing green eyes, black hair whipping across his aristocratic cheekbones, but there was no familiar, teasing smile on his lips.

"Trust me, my lady," he said, and held out his hand. Without hesitation, she took it, and was plunged ruthlessly back into the waking world.

Gasping, she shot upright, clutching the furs to her breast. Fragments of the dream clung to the edges of her mind, the details fading, as they always did, leaving behind the sense of dread—as they always did.

But this time it was different. She had never remained within the dream beyond the falling of the walls before. Of that she was certain. The image of the sacred standing stones, with the sun rising behind them, was seared into her mind, like a revelation from the great goddess herself.

Yet that wasn't the only difference. Because this was the second time Finn Braeson had invaded her intangible world and dragged her from it.

"Mae." Briana's sleepy whisper thrust her back to the present. "What is it?"

"I must commune with Bride." Surely Bride would have an answer for her. Here, in the real world, where she would be able to make sense of it.

"Of course," Briana murmured, before giving a yawn. "I trust the goddess will be receptive. She has been elusive to me since the Blood Moon."

Mairi hadn't felt the goddess' presence since the Blood Moon, either. Except now, with the appearance of the magnificent standing stones, uncertainty glimmered. Surely, that was a sign from Bride. But did that mean all these nightmares came from her? Why would her beloved goddess send such terrifying visions to her, for so many years?

She threw back the furs and shivered as the chill hit her.

"What are you doing?"

Mairi hastily pulled on her gown before going to the fire, where embers glowed in the hearth. "I told you. I must commune with Bride, at the standing stones."

"Now?" Her cousin sounded incredulous. "It's not even light, Mae."

"The goddess calls me. I am sure of it." She found her sturdy boots and sat on a stool to tie the laces. They were not deemed suitable footwear for Pictish noblewomen in the court of Fotla, but she wasn't going to trek across the dew laden grass in delicate leather slippers. "I must discover what message she's trying to send me."

"I'll accompany you." Briana didn't sound delighted by the prospect.

"No. I must go alone. I'll take a guard with me," she amended, before her cousin could reprimand her. "You know where I'll be if you need to find me."

Although there was still another two hours until sunrise, when she descended the stairs, the palace was already astir with servants preparing for the day. Mairi pulled the hood of her cloak over her head and the guard grabbed a lantern to light their way. He didn't say a word on their journey to the standing stones, but his disapproval of his mission was evident with every disgruntled step.

She ignored his unspoken censure. Although she'd always been aware that her status afforded her privilege, it wasn't until she'd left Fortriu that she'd learned how great the chasm was between the power a princess of royal blood could wield, compared to that of a mere noblewoman. She'd needed to invoke Briana's name before the guard would even agree to accompany her.

Enough. She shook her head to dislodge the troubling thoughts. Her mind needed to be clear to commune with Bride. Through the darkness ahead, a dull glow flickered from the Christian church windows, illuminating the small, sacred circle barely a stone's throw from the usurper.

It was blasphemous, how close to the hallowed ground the church dedicated to the new religion had been built. In Fortriu she'd had a cordial relationship with the monks in the local church, but at least it wasn't in the shadow of the ancient stones, and she had most certainly never attended their services or confessed her sins.

She pressed her lips together and turned her back on the

unwelcome symbol of how too many of her people were drifting from the ancient beliefs that had sustained them for so long.

She sank to her knees before the largest standing stone and pressed her palm against its face.

Beloved Bride. Hear my prayer.

The wind rustled the grass and the distant lowing of cattle and bleating of sheep drifted across the land. Mairi breathed in deep, then exhaled slowly, willing the tension that knotted her muscles to fade.

Unease prickled across her flesh, even though she was protected from the weather by her thick cloak. But it wasn't the elements that caused a shiver to ripple through her. It was the uncanny sensation that unseen eyes watched her from the gloom.

Enemy eyes.

Focus.

The Scots were *not* spying on her. It was all in her imagination.

She needed to discover what Bride was telling her and that wouldn't happen if she allowed her concentration to wander.

The dampness on the ground seeped through her clothes and into her bones. Her neck ached and head throbbed, and a cockerel crowed as twilight brushed the clouds a delicate shade of pink. But despite every entreaty, the goddess remained elusive.

The guard grunted and extinguished the lamp. Mairi clasped her numb fingers together and bowed her head. Perhaps her wish that Bride had sent her a vision was merely a desperate delusion.

How certain she'd been that Bride would guide her when she reached Fotla-eviot. A terrible conviction pierced her heart. Had Bride turned her back, because Mairi had followed the will of Cailleach?

Had she misread the significance of the Blood Moon? Should she have returned to Fib, after Nechtan had continued his journey through the Veil? But if she had, she would never have met Finn.

She had to stop thinking about him. He was not only disrupting her peace of mind, but also affecting her reason. She squeezed her eyes shut and sent out a despairing prayer.

I beg you to send me a sign to show which path I must take.

"Lady Mae. Are you unwell?"

Mairi jerked upright, heart pounding. Crouching not an arm's length from her, was Finn Braeson, a concerned frown marring his brow. Goddess, what was he doing here at this hour? Did he always look so breathtakingly beautiful, no matter what the time of day?

Goddess...

Chills raced along her arms as the significance of his appearance slammed through her.

Bride had sent her the sign she had begged for.

CHAPTER 10

*F*inn held out his hand to Mae, but she appeared frozen to the spot, her shocked eyes wide as she gazed at him as though he were an apparition from hell itself.

And then it hit him. *Fuck.*

She hadn't collapsed. She'd been worshipping at the heathen shrine. Why had he instantly jumped to the most dramatic conclusion? For God's sake, a Pict warrior stood guard over her. If she had been in any distress, the man would have seen her back to the palace. He could feel the warrior's glare burning into his back at his presumption, but he could scarcely stand up while Mae still kneeled on the wet ground.

He offered her a pained grin but before his bewitched brain could come up with a believable reason as to why he had so rudely interrupted her, she smiled.

The breath caught in his throat. She had invaded his dreams throughout the night, and he'd awoken hard and hot for her. But even his fevered imagination had fallen far short of the reality.

With the Highland mist swirling about them, she was like a vision from ancient tales, when the fabled fae folk roamed the mountains and ensnared unwary humans. Aye, he was ensnared, but anything more than a fleeting affair with her was impossible.

She didn't want an affair. Yet even that knowledge didn't dampen his desire. He was as captivated with her as the moment they'd met.

"I'm quite well," she said, and it took him agonizing seconds to realize she was replying to his question. He offered her his hand, and she took it without hesitation. "Thank you."

She stood but didn't instantly release his hand. Unable to stop himself, he tightened his grasp around her leather clad fingers. Dawn had broken and they were in danger of being seen by anyone, Scot or Pict, yet Mae didn't appear concerned by that possibility.

Even in her thick cloak, she emanated an air of fragility, and fierce protectiveness surged through him. Even though she was accompanied by a guard she was still vulnerable in the shadows before daybreak, away from the safety of the palace.

He should escort her back. But he couldn't end this just yet.

"I trust I didn't interrupt you." What a fucking stupid thing to say. He had quite obviously interrupted her. Mae, however, didn't appear to think his comment was out of place.

"Not at all. I had just finished communing with Bride. Are you on your way to the church?"

It was a reasonable assumption, given that the church was just beyond the heathen stones. But although he abided by the faith, he wasn't a great believer. Not that he'd ever shared that with anyone. Growing up, it would have been yet another stick to beat him with.

"I wasn't. But it might be less damp inside."

She returned his smile, clearly understanding his meaning. He certainly wasn't inviting her into the church to pray. Were all Pictish noblewomen so perceptive? "I have no objection. I confess, I'm chilled to the marrow. I had no idea how long I'd spent in the sacred circle."

Curiosity got the better of him. He'd never encountered anyone who spoke so freely of such heathen rites, and the monks in Dal Riada never shared their secrets with the common masses. "Does your goddess speak to you within the sacred circle?"

"My goddess may send me a vision at any time, if it pleases her." She hesitated, as though considering her words. "I came to the circle this morn as it is the holiest place in Fotla. I hoped Bride might deign to bless me with an answer to my question."

"And did she?"

They paused at the church gate, and she turned to him. A handful of copper curls escaped her hood, framing her face, and a delicate rose brushed her cheeks from the wintry breeze. How easy it would be to kiss her tempting lips and taste her forbidden pleasures. Just one kiss. His blood thundered in his head at the mere thought of it.

Yet one brief kiss would never be enough.

"I believe she did," Mae said softly and for a wild, crazy moment he had the unassailable conviction that whatever she'd asked her goddess had concerned him.

Madness appeared to be his constant companion, whenever he was in Mae's company.

"I'm happy your goddess speaks to you whenever you need her advice."

"I wouldn't wish to give you the wrong impression. Bride is not a goddess to be trifled with. We may beg her advice, but she may not always bestow it."

Fascinating. He'd imagined the Picts would always believe their heathen gods had heard their prayers and responded to them favorably. It was likely blasphemy to speak of such things while standing outside the church, but he couldn't help himself. Mae's evident devotion to her deity was something he found inexplicably intriguing.

"Do you worship any other gods?"

Her smile was enigmatic. "Are you interrogating me, Finn Braeson?"

"I wouldn't call it an interrogation."

"I heard all Scots believed we Picts are heathens, for believing in the old ways."

He sighed. "I cannot deny it, my lady. It is what we're taught. But I'm no longer convinced of it."

"That's most pleasing to know."

She was laughing at him. It was exhilarating. "Scot and Pict are more alike than different."

"Hmm. I wouldn't go *that* far."

"Then you need to spend more time in my company, so I might convince you."

This time she laughed aloud, the carefree sound sending a strange warmth through his chest. "I think I may be agreeable to that."

Shock speared through the warmth engulfing him. Had she just agreed that she was willing to see him again? After telling him the opposite the night before? Did that also mean she'd changed her mind about an affair?

Don't jump to conclusions. For now, being able to meet by design rather than leaving it to an unfathomable fate was a great improvement.

"I'm most gratified." He offered her a half-bow and was rewarded when she gave him another breath-stealing smile.

"In return for your gratitude, I will answer your question."

He'd all but forgotten his question. In fact, he'd thought she had deliberately avoided responding, but clearly he was wrong.

"We worship many gods, but only a few are blessed to be called into their sacred service. I am honored that Bride chose me." She bowed her head and unease rippled through him. Her answer wasn't straightforward, as he'd assumed it would be. It was enigmatic. And, disturbingly, reminded him of how the monks in Dal Riada spoke of their calling into the service of God.

His unease magnified. Until now, he'd believed she merely followed the pagan religion. Surely, he had misunderstood her words, yet he needed to hear her refute his suspicions. "You are a priestess of the old ways?"

He had imagined those tales, when women were conduits from heathen gods, to be nothing more than rumors from a long ago past. And in those tales, the priestesses were decrepit hags, more like witches than anything remotely pure or holy.

Certainly, they were nothing like Mae.

She stole a glance at the church, and her lips thinned, as though the sight did not please her.

"There are so few of us now." She turned back to him, and sadness glowed in her eyes. "Thirteen generations ago, many were blessed in every royal and noble house in Pictland. But now..." Her voice trailed away, and her shiver seeped into his blood, as though her sorrow were a tangible thing.

Thirteen generations. Three hundred years. He knew what great event had occurred. It was a cornerstone of the history they were taught in Dal Riada.

"When Saint Columba brought Christianity to Pictland."

"Yes." Her disdain was palpable. "As the new religion spread, our gods retreated. But I won't allow them to be forgotten."

They had already been forgotten in Dal Riada. If they had ever been known there at all. It was blasphemous, but he didn't let that stop him. "I wish you well in this endeavor."

"I do believe you mean that."

"I do." Even if, in his heart, he was sure her mission was doomed. "A difference in beliefs shouldn't be a reason to drive us apart."

"You astonish me every time we speak, Finn." Admiration and a trace of awe threaded through her voice. "I didn't realize Scots were so accepting in such matters."

As much as he didn't want to crush her delusion, he had to

make her aware. "We're not. I regret that there are many in Dal Riada who would take great offense in your beliefs."

"But not you. Not only do my insults roll off your back like water, but you are willing to embrace the truth of the past."

Just because her faith fascinated him, didn't mean he accepted the pagan beliefs of the past. But her admiration was too entrancing to shatter. "You have my upbringing to thank for me being able to see two sides to a story. Not everything is so clear cut, when you're an outsider."

They had reached the entrance to the church, and he pushed open one of the heavy wooden doors. But Mae appeared transfixed as she gazed at him as they stood on the threshold.

"An outsider?" She was obviously enthralled by his unwary words, yet he didn't regret them. She was so very easy to talk to. There was no harm in it. "Were you not brought up to worship the new God?"

He ushered her inside, out of the cold. Candles flickered by the windows, but the place was deserted. A small mercy. He was certain the monks, even if they were Picts, wouldn't approve of the conversation he and Mae shared.

"My lady mother is devoted to God. She is blameless when it comes to the multitude of my sins."

Before Mae could reply, the door wrenched open, and her guard stamped in. He didn't say a word, but the way he folded his arms and glowered said enough. Finn had the distinct impression the Pict would love nothing more than to run him through with his sword.

After a quick glance in the guard's direction, Mae returned her attention to him. She didn't pull free of his grasp. He had the strongest suspicion she was waiting for him to decide their next move.

He wasn't ready to release her yet. With a conspiratorial smile, he led her further into the church, so the Pict couldn't eavesdrop. The church was small, and shadows clung to the stone walls. It was the last place anyone would choose for a clandestine rendezvous and yet his blood thundered in his veins as though the two of them had found a refuge deep in the mountains, where no one could ever discover them.

They stood by a tall, narrow window, that had a view of the standing stones. The juxtaposition of old and new was fitting.

"Do you see your lady mother often?"

Startled, he stared at her. In all his conversations with women, both noble born and commoner, not one had enquired after his mother. But then, none of them had ever spoken of the things Mae did.

Certainly, he'd brought the subject up, but only in passing and not for a second had he imagined she would pursue it. But here in Fotla, unlike in the court of Dunadd, his mother's past wasn't common knowledge.

"When my duties allow me." Should he enquire after hers? "Do you, Lady Mae?"

"Alas, my mother passed through the veil while giving birth to me."

Fuck. He should have kept his mouth shut. Yet it had seemed such the obvious response to make. There was but one thing he could say.

"I'm sorry for your loss."

She inclined her head, accepting his awkward words of sympathy.

"It was long ago, of course, and I never knew her in this world. But I draw comfort that at long last she and her mother, my grandmamma, are finally reunited."

"Aye." He acknowledged the truth of that, even though he knew she spoke of pagan things. "Do you have any brothers or sisters, Mae?"

She sighed. "No. I have many cousins, but it's not the same, I am sure. What of you?"

"Three sisters." He wouldn't trouble her with his complicated family ties. "The youngest is but twelve."

"No brothers?" A teasing smile lit her face. "Your father must be greatly relieved whenever you visit, then."

His father could go to hell. "My mother and sisters reside in my hillfort, Duncarn. It's their home as much as mine."

Her fingers flexed within his clasp. "And what of a wife, Finn Braeson? Do you possess a lady who awaits you back in Duncarn?"

Stark reality crashed around his ears. For a few blissful moments, in Mae's company, he had forgotten the bleak future ahead of him.

But he wouldn't spoil this stolen time with her by railing against what could not be changed.

"I don't."

"What of a lady love? A betrothed?"

He laughed, couldn't help himself, even though with every word she forced him to acknowledge he would never find the kind of love he had dreamed of for so long.

"There is no lady waiting for me back in Dal Riada." At least that was the truth, and he'd not lie to her if he could help it. "Why do you ask? Does it make any difference?"

"Indeed." For the first time since he'd met her, she sounded oddly prim, and it was enchanting. "I'm aware warriors are rarely faithful when away from their wives. It's a fact of life. Yet it would grieve me to know you were one of them."

He kissed her hand, his lips lingering, and imagined he could taste her skin even through the soft leather of her gloves. Their gazes meshed, and he was lost. "If I had a lady such as you waiting for me, I would scarcely even see another woman. They all fade into insignificance beside you."

"If only you were a Pict, Finn." Her sigh was soft, and full of sorrow. "Perhaps then I could understand this strange connection between us."

"What is there to understand? I desire you, Mae. But I'll never take more than you're willing to give."

"It is a strange thing." Her voice had dropped to a whisper, and he had to lean in close to hear her. Her warm breath dusted his jaw. It was a sweet torture such as he had never imagined could exist. "Our paths continually cross as though our destinies are entwined."

He pressed his forehead against hers. The soft silk of her curls and the damp wool of her hood brushed against him, a tantalizing caress. He breathed in deep, savoring her unique scent, and his blood stirred in fruitless need.

"I know nothing of entwined destinies. But if this phenomenon exists, I curse the fates that allowed us to meet, only to rip us apart."

"We are not ripped apart yet."

He could hear the smile in her voice although he wasn't certain how that could be possible. He drew back, so he could once again drink in the vision of her face. Aye, she was smiling. An odd pain twisted through his chest. He would remember Mae's smile until the day he died.

"Good morning." The Pict voice, with a touch of censure, cut through him and he turned to see a tall, skeletal man in a brightly colored tunic striding to them from the depths of the church. A large cross hung from a chain around the stranger's neck, but it was the only clue he was a monk. In Dal Riada, monks wore subdued clothing, and they certainly didn't allow their hair to grow in wild abandon below their shoulders. The monk's glance skated across him and rested on Mae. "I haven't seen you in the church before, my lady."

Mae inclined her head in a manner that was becoming achingly familiar. Had it really been only two days since they had met?

"I apologize for my tardiness in making your acquaintance. Forgive me, but I follow the ancient faith."

Admiration weaved through him. Her manner was so regal, as though she genuinely believed she should have made the effort to present herself to the monk.

"As do many, my lady," the monk said, apparently unconcerned by her remark. How differently the monks in Dal Riada would have reacted. "I am always available, should you wish to discuss your enlightenment."

"You are too kind."

"And what of you, Dal Riadan? Should I prepare the confessional for you?"

Finn tore his besotted gaze from Mae and faced the monk. It had been years since he'd confessed any of his sins and he'd be damned if he'd start again now. Especially with a foreign monk. "I have no wish to inconvenience you. We should leave." He turned to Mae. "My lady."

They left the church, the guard at their heels. The sun had risen, and mist obscured the peaks of the surrounding mountains. Too many people milled around, and he wanted to take Mae at her word and spirit her away, so they could spend the day together without interruption.

Would she agree, if he asked her?

In the distance, beyond the standing stones, he caught sight of Constantine with two of his close confidants. Damn it. Of all the warriors who had travelled into Pictland, they were the last ones he wanted to confront while in Mae's company. It didn't matter that Pictish noblewomen enjoyed flirtations and found nothing amiss with illicit assignations.

Constantine would be only too eager to spread rumors if he believed it might irk Finn. There was no way he'd allow a whisper of such things when it came to Mae's reputation.

With reluctance, he released her hand. "I shall accompany you back to the palace."

She glanced over her shoulder, in the direction where his

half-brother had accosted a serving girl. Bawdy laughter floated on the wind, as the girl made good her escape.

Mae gave him a small smile, understanding glinting in her eyes. "I am quite safe with my guard. But do not fear. We shall meet again."

"inn Braeson?" the queen repeated. "Mairi, surely you are mistaken. If, as you say, the goddess has instructed you to make the acquaintance of one of the Scots warriors, would it not be their prince, Constantine?"

Mairi suppressed a shudder at the mere idea of becoming more intimately acquainted with the arrogant prince.

"It's the second time Bride has shown me this warrior in a vision. There is no mistake, Madam."

"But perhaps the goddess is warning you to keep away from this warrior. Could that not be a possibility?"

The terror that always accompanied her nightmares—her visions— had faded when Finn entered them. Bride had her reasons for sending him to her, and it was her duty to discover why.

To be sure, the thought of spending more time with him thrilled her soul. But of course, she couldn't share *that* with the queen.

"There is no sense of danger when Bride shows me Finn. Only a sense of," she hesitated, unsure how to explain what she meant. "That it is the right thing to do."

The queen glanced at Briana. The three of them were alone in the queen's private chamber and Mairi held her breath as she waited for the permission she so desperately needed.

"I confess I'm most disturbed by this revelation." The queen smoothed her gown, a frown marring her brow. "It goes against my instincts. Yet one cannot dismiss an instruction from the goddess."

Mairi clasped her hands together and bit her tongue. She had to allow the queen time to process her thoughts, but it was hard not to press her advantage. All her life she had not simply been the Princess of the Supreme Kingdom of Fortriu, she had also been a Chosen One of Bride.

Within her own kingdom it had given her additional prestige. Even her beloved grandfather, King Wrad, had listened when she spoke of Bride's revelations. The sacred Sight had been elusive for four generations until Mairi's birth, and the fact she had inherited it from distant foremothers was a sign that the old gods had not abandoned Pictland.

Before today, she had never confided in a stranger outside of the old faith about her gift. But Bride had sanctified her tentative bond with Finn. She could trust him with her secrets. He would never betray her.

"Perhaps," Briana said, "the goddess knows that Braeson is the one who will reveal the true reason why the Scots are here, and that Mae is the only one he will confide in."

Resentment flared in Mairi's breast at her cousin's words. She made Finn sound like a traitor to his own people. And while she despised his people and wanted to witness the downfall of his upstart king, she didn't want Finn to be the one to betray them.

She didn't care that she was allowing her feelings to rule her head. In her heart, she knew Finn was honorable. He couldn't help having been born a Scot.

"We all know the real reason why the Scots are here." Disdain tinged the queen's words. "There must be more that Bride wishes

Mairi to discover." She inhaled a deep breath. "The ways of the goddess have always been beyond my understanding. Briana, have you not received any vision of this from her?"

"No, Mamma. The goddess is elusive."

"As you know, your father and I had decided we would host no more feasts for the Scots." She returned her attention to Mairi. "But I cannot see how you'll be able to fulfil the goddess' wishes unless we once again pledge to entertain our enemies this eve."

"Tell them it's a farewell feast," Briana suggested. "Surely, they cannot expect to remain here indefinitely. It's nothing less than an invasion."

"Indeed." Ice dripped from the queen's voice. "Yet we cannot afford to offend them. They still hold hostage too many of royal Pictish blood."

Silence descended, broken only by the crackle of the logs burning in the fireplace. Finally, the queen spoke once again.

"You have our blessing to pursue this liaison, Mairi. But we can only allow you this one night. The Scots have outstayed their welcome in Fotla-eviot."

LATER THAT MORNING, as the weather was fine, the queen gave permission for the ladies of the court to go riding. It was bliss to gallop across the land on Audra with the Highland wind whipping against her face. Not that it helped to cool the fever in her blood that hadn't left her since seeing the queen.

You have our blessing to pursue this liaison

The unspoken implication thundered in her head. The queen assumed she had requested permission to embark on an affair with Finn. Why wouldn't she draw that conclusion? Any other lady of the court would have meant exactly that.

Except no other lady of the court would have asked the

queen's permission beforehand. They had already been granted it, by the queen's edict.

An enthralling possibility shimmered through her mind.

Is this what Bride expects from me?

Illicit thrills collided between her thighs, sending tremors of pleasure through her sensitized clit. Her breath shortened and it was hard to suck air into her lungs. What a relief no one could see. And even if they did look her way, they'd think her discomposure was due to the ride.

Finn's face filled her mind, his smile entrapping her senses. Whether it was Bride's plan for her or not, she couldn't shift the tantalizing image of Finn holding her in a lover's embrace. How she longed to feel the heat of his body and the strength of his arms as he held her close.

How dearly she yearned for Finn to take her maidenhead.

She gasped and blinked; the visceral fantasy so real in her mind that it was a shock to fall back into reality. Their party had slowed to a walk, and Briana was already dismounting. The glen was starkly beautiful with a river running through it, and once she had dismounted, she led Audra to the water.

She crouched by the riverbank, pulled off her glove and splashed icy water onto her burning cheeks. Was she truly considering having an affair with Finn?

How do I even arrange such a thing?

The queen had given the Scots one more night of hospitality. If she truly wished to embark on this tempting adventure, she had little time to plan for it, and no time to spend fruitless hours in a solitary debate of the rights or wrongs of such an action.

The question was simple. Did she want Finn, or not?

I do.

The small contingent of warriors that had accompanied them, including half a dozen of her own men, remained in their saddles, keeping an eye out for danger. She made her way to a stand of silvery-bark birch trees where Briana was talking with Lady Nairne and the other noblewomen.

She drew in a calming breath, but it did nothing to ease the fluttering of her heart. Tonight, somehow, she would find a way for her and Finn to be alone.

It would be the wedding night she had never experienced. A romantic tryst she would keep locked in her memories forever more. A few hours of abandoned pleasure with the only man she'd ever wanted to take as her lover, and she would not think of tomorrow.

Nairne gave a dramatic sigh and pressed her hand against her heart. "I invited my lord Constantine into my bed last night. Let me assure you, archery is not his only admirable talent."

"You must share *all* the details," one of the ladies said, patting Nairne's arm. "I trust he didn't speak of his hunting prowess yet again."

Several of the ladies laughed, but Nairne did not appear to be offended.

"Indeed, he did not. His mind was most firmly on *me*."

Nairne proceeded to whisper scandalous details of her night with the Scots prince. Apparently, he was quite insatiable. Mairi fixed a polite smile on her face, but graphic images of Finn flooded her mind, and it was almost unbearable to remain still. *Goddess*. If Finn did such things to her with his mouth and tongue and fingers, she would likely die from delight.

"One could almost overlook his despicable heritage for such bed sport," one of the other ladies said with an exaggerated sigh, when Nairne finally paused for breath.

Nairne gave a satisfied smile and turned to Briana. "I have not yet shared the best. He was most accommodating afterwards, while we lay before the firelight. The Scots did not merely bring our king and prince back from the goodness of their hearts. They are searching for the missing Princess of Fortriu and believe she's in Fotla."

It took all her will power not to glance at her cousin. Nairne had confirmed what they already knew.

"Very admirable, Lady Nairne." Briana took Nairne's hand. "Although why would they think the Princess of Fortriu is here?"

"Rumors reached them in Dunadd." Nairne shrugged. "I told him I feared the princess had died months ago. You will never guess his reply."

Unease stirred and she couldn't keep quiet any longer. "What did he say?"

Nairne glanced at her. "He said that would be a great loss to both Dal Riada and Pictland, as MacAlpin had planned a magnificent future for her."

"Indeed." Derision dripped from Briana's voice. Thankfully, that was enough to divert Nairne's attention from Mairi, and she stealthily hitched in a ragged breath, as her cousin continued. "And what magnificent future would this be? The princess' head on a spike?"

Inwardly, Mairi winced, but managed not to otherwise react. Briana was handling this perfectly. All *she* had to do was keep her mouth shut.

"I don't believe so. Constantine appeared," Nairne hesitated as though trying to find the right words. "It was strange. He seemed oddly bitter about it. As though his father's interest in the princess was a thorn in his side."

"That is strange." Briana nodded, but Mairi knew her cousin didn't think it was strange at all. It was quite clear to them both that whatever future Constantine spoke about, would be anything but magnificent for Mairi herself.

"I hope to see him again tonight," Nairne said. "If so, I shall press him further on this matter."

"Don't put yourself in danger," Mairi said. She couldn't help herself, even though it was safer to remain silent.

"I won't." Nairne smiled at her. "You know how men are. I

doubt he recalls telling me half the things we spoke of while under the furs."

First Briana, and now Nairne. What happened to a man's senses while beneath the furs? Did passion truly cause him to lose his mind and say things he would never otherwise dream of sharing?

She refused to believe that Finn's tongue would loosen in such a manner. It all seemed quite undignified.

But there were more important issues to focus on, such as the question that had churned through her mind for the last few hours, and Nairne most certainly had the answer.

While some ladies of the court had their own chambers, Nairne was in Briana's service and until last night had shared her chamber. But now she shared with three other noblewomen. With studied casualness, Mairi said, "How did you and the prince find privacy to be together?"

One of the noblewomen tittered, and Mairi stiffened. She should not have said anything. She didn't want anyone to think her gauche or unsophisticated. Even if, in matters of seduction, she *was*.

"Hush," Nairne admonished the other young woman, before bestowing a smile in her direction. "It's a fair question, my lady. You are only recently widowed and clearly not experienced in conducting illicit rendezvous."

It was true, but having her inexperience laid out for all to hear was less than gratifying. She managed to give Nairne a tight smile.

"There are two small guest chambers in the east wing. It's a simple matter to arrange." Curiosity glowed in Nairne's eyes. "Are you planning a liaison with the wild-looking Braeson?"

"What?" Goddess, were her thoughts so transparent? It was mortifying that Nairne had guessed, while *she* was still grappling with the very notion of it.

"Pray, do not look so shocked." Nairne appeared amused by

Mairi's discomfiture. "I glimpsed you dancing with him last night. He is quite besotted by you."

"I think you exaggerate, Nairne," Briana said. "Mae had no choice but to dance with the Scot."

"He *is* an exciting diversion though, wouldn't you agree, Mae?" Nairne clasped her hands together. "I am happy to help you with any arrangements, if you wish."

"I—" The words lodged in her throat. Not that she had any idea what those words might be since her brain had frozen. How could she possibly ever see Finn again, when the entire court of Fotla-eviot would know what she had done?

"Lady Nairne." Briana didn't raise her voice, but it was a reprimand, nonetheless. "As you so rightly pointed out, Lady Mae is recently widowed. She has no interest in such clandestine meetings with any man, least of all a Scot."

"Forgive me." Nairne bowed her head. "I meant no disrespect, Lady Mae."

"It is quite all right." Mairi smiled and hoped it didn't look as strained as it felt. "I'm simply not used to these court intrigues."

Nairne sighed. "Neither are we, my lady. But the Scots do enliven things so."

Blessed Bride. Wasn't *that* the truth.

WHEN THEY ARRIVED BACK at the stables, Mairi remained in the stall, grooming Audra, while the others returned to the palace. She knew her cousin would find her and within a moment, Briana appeared.

This wasn't going to be an easy conversation, but she had no option. Here, in Fotla, she had no influence and no way of arranging a secret assignation. She pulled Briana closer, so they would not be overheard.

"I fear I need some advice," she whispered.

Briana took her hand. "Take no notice of Nairne, my love. She's always been a hopeless romantic and knows nothing of politics. She didn't mean anything by her words."

"I'm not concerned by Nairne's words. But I believe the queen..." she hesitated, unsure how to continue. She was certain the queen expected her to seduce answers from Finn. But if Briana hadn't guessed that from their previous conversation, was it all an illusion inside Mairi's head?

Because seducing Finn is what I want to do?

"Mamma would never speak of your vision. Nairne was merely gossiping, as she loves to do."

Mairi shook her head. Clearly, her cousin didn't have the faintest idea what she was really asking. "Of course I don't believe Nairne knows of my vision. Briana, I am speaking of arranging an assignation with him."

Briana's eyes widened in comprehension. "Surely you do not think Mamma expects this of you? She would never..." Her voice trailed away, and she bit her lip.

"I don't know." Mairi cast a glance along the stable, but thankfully they were still alone. "Perhaps I misunderstood."

Except the truth was, she didn't care what the queen expected. She wanted this, for *herself*. Why was it so hard to admit the truth to her beloved cousin?

"I'm sure you did. Mamma meant for you to spend tonight in Finn's company at the feast and dancing, not yielding to his base instincts."

"You are likely right." Even though she still wasn't entirely convinced. She took a deep breath. Time was running out. If she wanted this, without enlisting the assistance of Nairne and subsequently having every lady of the court knowing about her rendezvous, she needed Briana's help. "But I must spend the night with Finn. Beneath the furs," she added, just in case she hadn't been clear enough.

"Oh." Briana stared at her as though that possibility had never crossed her mind. "Oh, my *goddess.*" Inexplicably, a blush heated her cousin's cheeks. "I did not see that when you shared your vision with us. Are you certain that is Bride's wish, Mae?"

It would be easier to say *yes*, but the truth was she still wasn't sure exactly what her goddess expected from her. "I am not. But this is something *I* wish. Will you help me to arrange the details? The chamber that Nairne spoke of?"

Briana drew in a sharp breath. "Forgive me for not understanding. I didn't imagine for a moment you would want a Scots warrior in your bed."

Merely two days ago, she had thought the same.

"This is quite shocking to me, also," she confessed. "But Finn is unlike any man I've met before. It's just one night, Briana, and I will likely never see him again. I long for one night with him. Is that so wicked of me?"

"No." There was a fierce note in her cousin's whisper. "If this is what you desire, then you deserve it. I know you were fond of your husband, but why shouldn't you have a night of pleasure with a man your own age?"

Shivers of anticipation raced over her skin, and it was a struggle to keep her mind on their conversation. It was essential she worked out the practicalities, otherwise there would be no pleasurable rendezvous at all.

"You will help me?"

"I will. You shall have my chamber for yourself this night."

This was the last thing she'd expected. "I cannot possibly, Briana."

"You are the Princess of the Supreme Kingdom. You certainly cannot use either of the notorious guest chambers. It would be most unseemly."

Heat bloomed through her. She loved her cousin dearly, but she didn't want Briana to witness what would be, essentially, the first time she'd ever been with a man. Even if Briana retired to her antechamber, it would still be too close for comfort.

"It's very kind of you." How could she possibly explain without offending her?

Briana smiled, and squeezed her fingers. "I shall stay with Mamma tonight. She will understand."

Mairi was sure she would. The queen would also know what she was doing.

Stop. Just because she was obsessed by the notion of taking Finn as her lover, was no reason to suppose anyone else would give it a second thought. Affairs were commonplace occurrences at court. The queen likely believed Mairi had taken lovers in the past. Why wouldn't she? Most married noblewomen, and royal wives, did so, especially when wed to a man old enough to be their father.

"I trust you have the feminine precautions you need," Briana said.

"Yes. My supplies are plentiful." Her treasured medicine casket was stocked for all eventualities.

"Good. The last thing we need to worry about is the possibility of conception."

Before her marriage, she had accumulated a great deal of knowledge about a woman's moon cycle and the ways to prevent a pregnancy. The versatile juniper berries were but one ancient remedy at her disposal. Even without the years of bloodied nightmares, that she knew foreshadowed her untimely death should she ever attempt to give birth, falling pregnant tonight would be a political disaster.

Her façade as a noblewoman would mean nothing, then. She couldn't be hastily married off to an accommodating noble. Her royal lineage would be revealed, and the repercussions would ripple throughout Pictland.

Bride was a goddess of fertility but, as in all things, there was balance. Mairi had no intention of relying on just one method of prevention. There were others she could use after the event. In fact, she would return to the sacred stones instantly, to offer sacrifice to the great goddess and ask for her additional protection.

It was fortunate her moon cycle was predictable to the very hour. It meant that she—

A gasp escaped as the revelation slammed through her mind.

The Blood Moon.

Awe shivered through her, shattering the last doubt that this was, indeed, what her goddess wanted. For reasons Mairi could not imagine, Bride, *not Cailleach,* had sent her an incontrovertible sign, days before she had even known of Finn's existence.

A sign that Mairi should take Finn as her lover, and not worry about possible consequences. For in three days, her moon time would be upon her, and there would be no chance of conceiving the Scots warrior's child.

CHAPTER 12

Sweat dripped into his eyes and his heart thundered in his chest, but Finn barely noticed as he parried a mighty blow from Constantine's weapon. It was midafternoon and they had been practicing in a clearing by the side of their camp for nearly an hour. Although the swords were made of wood, so as not to cause lethal injury, every muscle in his body throbbed from the exertion.

He welcomed it. It kept him from thinking of Mae.

Constantine took immediate advantage of his lapse in concentration and landed a bone grinding thwack on his shoulder. He stumbled but recovered instantly and with a twist of his weapon, his half-brother's sword flew across the muddy ground.

The warriors who had surrounded them broke into cheers or jeers, depending on how tight their allegiance to Constantine was. With an insincere grin, the prince approached, his arm outstretched.

"Well played."

What the fuck? This tactic was new. Body tense against certain betrayal, Finn gripped the other man's forearm. But

Constantine merely gripped his in return, the classic gesture between two combatants who acknowledged each other as a worthy opponent.

Constantine had never considered him a worthy opponent before. Finn doubted his opinion had changed since arriving in Fotla.

"Likewise," he said, since that was the expected response.

He caught a few of the warriors casting baffled glances at Constantine's sportsmanship, but none of them said anything.

Ewan tossed him a waterbag, and he gulped down the cool liquid, keeping one eye on his half-brother. But Constantine appeared focused on quenching his own thirst.

Constantine slung his waterbag at a servant and rolled his shoulders. "It seems we are invited to a farewell feast tonight."

"Farewell?" Ewan said, echoing his own unspoken question. "Are we returning to Dal Riada tomorrow?"

"The Picts would like to think so." There was a grim note in Constantine's voice and for a second, his glance snagged on Finn. "We are not done in Fotla yet."

"We've returned their king and prince. Why else are we here?" Douglas, the warrior who spoke, was one of Constantine's right-hand men. They had been friends since childhood, and Finn could never decide who of the two he despised the most.

"Because our king commands it," Constantine retorted, which shut the other warrior up.

"I'm not averse to spending more time enjoying the company of the noblewomen of Fotla-eviot." Stuart MacGregor grinned as several others agreed with him. "Truly, Pictish ladies are a revelation beneath the furs."

Finn scowled and folded his arms. Generally, he had no quarrel with MacGregor, and the man had never insulted his lady mother even when they were children. But his loose tongue when it came to his conquests rubbed Finn up the wrong way.

Always had.

Constantine laughed and slapped MacGregor on the back. "Indeed, you are right. The lady I fucked last night was utterly bewitching."

Ewan visibly stiffened and Finn shot him a frowning glance. Ewan was glaring at Constantine as though he'd like to throttle him.

"The rumors are true," Douglas said. "Pictish noblewomen are insatiable."

"Insatiable for Scots cock," Constantine said, smirking at his own wit. "And who can blame them, when they've been shackled to old men for so many years? What a waste of succulent flesh. The king is right. Pictish noblewomen should be wed to our warriors, to strengthen their dying bloodlines."

It was the first he'd heard of that plan although he wasn't surprised. When all the royal princesses had been caught, it made strategic sense to hunt down the noblewomen next. Like a spider, MacAlpin schemed to snare all of Pictland in his web.

MacAllister appeared by Constantine's side, a silent warning to the prince to watch his tongue. Constantine's jaw flexed in clear irritation, but he didn't continue. Instead, he turned to Finn and the malicious gleam in his eyes sent a warning crawling along his spine.

"Who was the delectable creature you accosted outside the church, Braeson? She was no serving maid, I'll wager."

Damn it, he'd hoped Constantine hadn't noticed them this morning, since he'd been intent on terrorizing a serving wench. He smothered his inclination to tell the other man to go to hell, since that would only play straight into Constantine's hands.

"A lady from the court. We barely passed the time of day."

"Outside the church?" MacGregor laughed. "That's unlike you, Braeson. You're a borderline heathen."

Constantine slung MacGregor a glare at the interruption of

his sport. "Half the Picts are fucking heathens. Braeson is many things, but he is certainly no pagan."

What the fuck was happening? Constantine had never defended his bastard half-brother before. And then realization struck.

Sooner or later, MacAlpin would make his acknowledgement of Finn known. Whether Constantine liked it or not, Finn was now a member of the House of Alpin, a pillar of Christianity, and he was clearly under orders not to undermine Finn's position in the meantime.

Beside him, Ewan gave a disbelieving grunt under his breath, the only sign he found the prince's behavior incomprehensible.

"Aye, my lord." MacGregor backed off, as confusion flashed across his face. "I was merely jesting."

Constantine ignored him, his attention back on Finn. "What of the little redhead you danced with last night? Was she a fair distraction from duty, Braeson?"

Finn flexed his fingers. The prince was goading him under the guise of warrior banter. Except they both knew Constantine wasn't referring to his duty as a warrior. It was a direct taunt on the edict MacAlpin had given Finn on his future.

"My lord, a word, if I may," MacAllister said, and Constantine gave a curt nod, dismissing the rest of them. As he and Ewan turned away, MacAllister spoke again. "Braeson, remain where you are."

Ewan shot him a frowning glance and Finn shrugged. God knows what MacAllister wanted to impart. It was Constantine he needed to pull into line for his loose talk and Finn sure as hell didn't want to be around to witness the prince's reaction to that.

When the three of them were alone, MacAllister addressed Constantine. "You said earlier that you needed to speak to Finn and me. What information have you discovered, my lord?"

Constantine drew in an exaggerated deep breath. "According

to my source, the Picts believe that the Princess of Fortriu did indeed die six months ago. There hasn't been a whisper of her possible whereabouts in all my encounters with the ladies of the court. It appears we were misled with our information."

Wild hope flared. If they could prove the princess had died, he would be free once again.

Free to pursue Lady Mae? God, could that even be a possibility? She was noble born, but for her, if it would help his suit, he'd embrace his cursed royal blood.

"Yet no trace of her last resting place has been discovered in Forteviot," MacAllister said. "Nor any sign pointing to how she may have died after the Pictish nobles betrayed our alliance."

Annoyance flashed over Constantine's face. "You believe the Pictish noblewoman lied to me?"

"No. I believe few know the truth of the whereabouts of the Princess of Fortriu. If any information is to be had, it will come only from the royal family."

Constantine gave a snort of disgust. "You want me to fuck their princess? She is ice cold and aloof. I would need to render her insensible with wine before she parts her legs."

MacAllister gave a wintry smile. "No, my lord. I don't believe such a tactic would be in the Scots best interests."

Reluctant admiration for MacAllister stirred. It was no wonder the king trusted him to keep the peace. Finn would have told Constantine he was a piece of shit, but MacAllister turned it around and made it all about politics.

"What do you suggest, then?" Constantine's tone implied he wasn't as oblivious to the other man's gift of diplomacy as Finn imagined.

"From my observations, the princess is uncommonly close with one particular noblewoman. I suggest our strategy should center on discovering what this lady knows of the court intrigues."

"I've observed no such thing," Constantine retorted. Finn hadn't, either. Then again, the only noblewoman he was interested in observing was Mae.

"It's my responsibility to see what others do not," MacAllister said. "The princess favors this young woman above all others. I'd wager there are few secrets between them."

"Are you going to share this mysterious creature's name, so I might know who I am seducing tonight?" Acid dripped from each word.

"This onerous duty will not fall on your shoulders, my lord." MacAllister gave another of his smiles that never reached his eyes. "My lord Finn has already gained a measure of her trust."

Finn glared at the other man. He couldn't stop himself even though by doing so he was giving MacAllister far more information than any words might. But he had no words. Because denial thundered through his mind, blocking out everything but the realization that the king's man had been spying on him.

And he hadn't even known it.

"Finn?" Constantine shot him a blank look, before comprehension dawned. "The redhead from last night?"

God help him, if Constantine referred to Mae again as the redhead, he'd punch the prince in his disrespectful mouth and to hell with the consequences. "I won't seduce a woman to learn her secrets."

Constantine scoffed. "Is your technique in the bedchamber so uncouth that no woman would wish to whisper confidences in your ear?"

"If information is to be discovered, it won't be through betraying a noblewoman's trust."

"My lords," MacAllister said. "This discussion does us a disservice. How the information is extracted is unimportant. If my lord Finn can persuade his lady to share what she knows in a manner that cannot be perceived as betrayal, then that's all that matters."

Obviously, he and MacAllister had different ideas as to what betrayal meant. There was no way in this lifetime that he'd ever share with MacAllister anything that Mae confided in him.

But what if she knew of the whereabouts of the Princess of Fortriu?

He thrust the notion aside. Even if she did possess that knowledge, why would she share it with him unless he asked?

And he had no intention of asking. Once the princess was found, his life would irrevocably be chained to hers, and this interlude with Mae would end. For all he cared, the princess could remain elusive forever.

UNLIKE THE PREVIOUS TWO FEASTS, where the Scots had been relegated to a secondary table, tonight they were escorted to the one directly in front of the royal dais. He stood behind the bench, waiting for the arrival of the royal party, and cast his glance along the table.

They'd been instructed to spread out along the benches and anticipation hammered through his blood. Were the nobles sharing this table tonight as a show of solidarity, before expecting the Scots to be on their way?

Specifically, would Mae be sitting close by? Even if they couldn't speak, at least he'd be able to see her.

This obsession would be the end of him. He smothered a wry smile before Constantine, who unfortunately was directly opposite him, remarked on it.

The ladies of the court entered the hall, preceding the royal party as they always did. But this time, the Princess of Fotla was among them, and she bypassed the dais and instead sat on a chair at the head of the table, to his left. But the honor barely registered, as Mae, following her mistress, took her place on the bench beside him.

There was no time to do anything more than smile at her before the royal party made their way to the High Table, where the king proceeded to give a speech. It was eloquent, spoken in Gaelic, and despite the diplomatic words, made it clear that should the Scots remain in Fotla-eviot after this night, there would be no more hospitality within the palace walls.

He sat next to Mae and as the servants brought out the platters and the babble of conversation increased, he risked leaning closer to her. "This is an unexpected pleasure, my lady."

"Indeed." Her smile illuminated her face and the whole damn hall. "The pity is this will be the only time we share such a moment."

"Then we must make the most of it."

"I intend to treasure every second."

"As do I." He lifted his goblet. She mirrored his action, and silently they toasted each other. Unlike the previous two nights, tonight they hadn't been served common ale, and the wine flowed freely.

"You must meet many ladies in your travels." She didn't look at him, instead concentrating on cutting her food with her knife. Her beautiful copper hair trailed over her shoulder in its usual plait, but tonight tiny blue gems glittered along its length, the color enhancing the delicate shade of her gown. Sapphires in the shape of teardrops sparkled from her ears and the same plain gold circlet that she always wore kept her translucent veil in place.

"I don't," he confessed, and she turned to look at him, a questioning expression on her face. "This is my first diplomatic mission."

Her smile faded and concern clouded her bewitching blue eyes. Clearly, she had understood the words he'd left unsaid. "Have you seen many battles?"

"Too many." He attempted to make light of it, but knew he failed when she didn't smile once again. Surely such a grim topic wasn't acceptable conversation and yet Mae had asked. "I recently returned from Iona. The Norsemen are persistent and won't rest until they've plundered the entire Isle."

"They are utterly barbaric. I thank the goddess you survived to make the journey to Fotla."

He grinned at her evident concern, but he couldn't let her believe he had been in danger. "They had long gone with their stolen treasures by the time we arrived. It often happens that way. But to answer your question. Even when no battle is fought, I've never met any lady as enchanting as you."

"Your king should send you on more diplomatic missions. You have a talent for it."

"I confess I'm not sure whether that was a compliment or insult."

The ghost of a smile hovered, and he could barely tear his entrapped gaze from her tempting lips. "I'm amused you cannot immediately tell what I mean when I point out one of your admirable qualities."

"No one has ever accused me of diplomacy before."

"Scots are a strange people. I wasn't accusing you of anything."

"Then I accept your compliment and thank you for it."

She shook her head, her eyes sparkling with mirth. "I do believe your king underestimates your worth."

"I do believe you're right." The words slid from his tongue before he could stop them, but what did they matter? For the first time when anyone had mentioned the king to him in such a manner, his chest hadn't knotted in that old, familiar way that had plagued him since childhood.

It felt good. Hell, it was great, flirting with Mae who knew nothing of his past.

"Perhaps we should petition your king to keep you in Fotla as an ambassador of peace."

"If it meant I could see you every day, perhaps I would accept a lifetime in Fotla."

Her smile turned pensive, as though he had inadvertently struck a nerve. "Fotla is beautiful, to be sure. But I miss the kingdom of my birth."

Intrigued, he gave up the pretense of eating and focused fully on her. "Which kingdom are you from, Mae?"

Wariness flashed across her face. Hadn't she expected him to ask? But it was the most natural question. Why did she look so strangely haunted?

"Oh. My—my late husband is from the Kingdom of Fib." She lowered her gaze to her plate, in deference to her dead husband and he cursed his unruly tongue, and the damning need that pushed him to learn all he could about her.

He raked through his addled brain for an appropriate response but could find nothing. "I've never been to Fib," he offered at last, since it was clear Mae was unable to break the silence that had fallen between them. "I hear it is as beautiful as any kingdom in Pictland."

She smiled, before once again looking his way. There was a sadness in her eyes that hadn't been there before. For all that she hadn't loved her husband, it was clear she still missed him.

"Indeed. But I imagine Dal Riada has a savage charm of her own."

Relief speared through him. She had taken a moment to remember her husband, but she hadn't allowed it to overshadow their one and only feast together. He bowed his head in mock deference. "As savage as her people, you mean?"

"It is quite uncanny how well you know me."

Aye, he knew her a little. Perhaps better than he had ever known another woman. But his fierce desire for her had only magnified from the first night they had met, and even now it raged like a caged wolf deep in his chest. Craving escape.

Craving Mae.

They might never share more than a chaste kiss, but that didn't lessen his need. The memory of her smile and the way she so delightfully teased with every word she uttered would linger long after his brief stay in Fotla had been consigned to history.

The elusive Pictish noblewoman who was everything he wanted, and everything he could never have.

CHAPTER 13

Mairi gazed into Finn's admiring green eyes and the unease at having to, yet again, skate along the edges of the truth faded. It did not matter how dearly she wished she could confide in him as to her true birthright. Finn wouldn't betray her, of that she was certain, but it was too dangerous.

Not only did she need to keep her identity a secret to protect the royal house of Fotla. She had sworn a deathbed oath to Nechtan.

It was hard to remember that they were in the great hall where anyone might be watching them, when all she could see was Finn. They were sitting closer on the bench than propriety demanded and the seductive heat from his body wove a magical spell through her senses, but she scarcely cared if anyone noticed or disapproved.

This night was for her, to forget about her duty to her people or the knowledge that Finn, an enemy warrior, was the last man she should be planning to seduce. Soon, he would be gone and all that would remain would be memories.

She'd ensure those memories were worth any heartbreak their parting might bring.

Finn leaned closer until his breath dusted her cheek, an ethereal caress against her warm skin. "Do you think me a savage, Mae?"

Her gaze meshed with his and her breath caught in her throat. They were so close, she could see golden flecks in his green eyes, and a faint, ragged, scar that ran across his temple. All her life she'd considered the Scots were nothing less than savages, and MacAlpin's betrayal in the spring had fueled her conviction.

But nothing would persuade her that Finn shared those barbarous traits.

"I'm inclined to believe you may well have Pictish blood in your veins," she said. It was only when he offered her a faintly bemused smile that she realized he might not take her words as the compliment she intended. "That was not an insult," she added, just to clarify.

"I know." Amusement threaded through his response. "Believe me, my blood has caused me grief in the past. A Pict heritage wouldn't be so bad at all."

Curiosity burned through her. "How do you mean? I thought all Scots were inordinately proud of their lineage."

"Aye." He bowed his head in acknowledgement that she was right, but there was a strange tautness to his smile she'd never seen before. "And I'm proud of the noble blood of my lady mother. But of my father, I cannot speak."

Understanding flowed through her, and she dared to rest her hand on his forearm. It was the lightest of touches yet tingles of awareness danced across her palm, causing a thousand butterflies to collide within her breast.

Finn was obviously the product of an illicit affair. It was not uncommon among Pictish royalty or nobility, when marriages were invariably a contract to strengthen alliances between the houses. An unspoken understanding, as old as Pictland herself, ensured that so long as legitimate heirs had been conceived first to keep the bloodline pure, a blind eye was turned if a bastard was subsequently born.

Such secrets were shared in hushed whispers but rarely acknowledged in public. Perhaps things were done differently in Dal Riada. She was certain a Pictish warrior would never state so private a matter.

But she loved that Finn trusted her enough to tell her something so personal. She would treasure his confidence forever.

And she had learned another thing about him. He was, indeed, noble born.

Although in truth, that disclosure was irrelevant. No matter how noble his blood, there could never be anything lasting between them. Even if a tiny part of her longed for the chance to spend more time with him, to learn everything she could about him, she knew that wish was folly. A single night was all the goddess could grant them.

Tonight. Rose-hued images fluttered through her mind, of how it would be when Finn took her in his arms when they were in the bedchamber. *Naked* and alone…

Finn lowered his head to her. They were close enough to kiss. "Are you cold, my lady?"

"No." Her voice was husky. She could scarcely tell him she trembled with desire and anticipation of how this night would end. Unless he rebuked her advances? But surely he would not. Renewed nerves danced through her and even her fingertips prickled with need. "I fear I cannot help myself whenever you are near."

His smile caused a strange pain deep within her breast. As though her very heart was melting. *Don't fall, Mairi.* It would make leaving him in the morning even harder. Except she was fooling herself. She had fallen for him the night they'd met.

"And you, sweet Mae, have bewitched me. Should I confess you've haunted my dreams these last two nights?"

"Please do. It's only fair, since you have invaded mine."

"I'm honored. I hope." His grin was pure sin and the breath caught in her throat. "Tell me what we do in your dreams."

Her smile froze, as the tattered remnants of her dreams flooded through her mind. She had responded without thinking because Finn was always in her thoughts. But goddess, how could she tell him of the blood-splattered night terrors that plagued her?

"Mae?" The questioning note in his voice pulled her back to the present and she attempted to smile. For so long she had regarded her nightmares as a warning from her foremothers that if she conceived, her fate would be theirs. But Bride had sent Finn into those dreams. And both times he had dragged her from them.

It seemed the goddess was determined to entwine their fates. But how could that be? The only way was if she conceived his child and that would never happen tonight.

She would not try to untangle the threads now. When the time was right, Bride would reveal to Mairi Finn's place in her plan.

"It's a strange thing." Stealthily, she slid her hand from his arm. It would not do for anyone to think she was being too familiar with this Scot. Not when she and Briana had gone to such lengths to ensure her tryst with him tonight would remain undetected. Ribbons of heat swirled through her, and it was hard to recall what she had been saying. "You have lately entered a recurring dream I've experienced for years."

"I trust it wasn't an unpleasant invasion."

"Not entirely. But it was most unexpected."

His lips twitched with amusement. "I'm gratified my presence didn't cause you too much discomfort."

"Indeed, you did not. In fact, I saw more of the dream world when you were by my side than I ever have before."

For the first time, uncertainty flickered over his face, and she stifled a sigh. He had clearly linked her dream to her goddess and was not sure what to make of it. "What did you see?"

Maybe she shouldn't continue this conversation. She didn't want to give him any reason to lose interest. Yet he already knew she worshipped Bride and her faith didn't seem to unduly concern him.

She would tell him. It would help, in some small way, to alleviate the sorrow that there was so much of her life she could never share with him.

"A new dawn breaking on the horizon, beyond the sacred stones."

He was silent for a moment, as though contemplating her words. "I must admit, this dream of yours is nothing like I imagined it might be."

"Ah." She nodded, smothering a smile, and only just managed to stop herself from stroking his arm again. "I wager you imagined something far earthlier."

His glance was guarded. "A little."

"We did hold hands." *When you pulled me from the wreckage.* She shoved the memory to the darkest corners of her mind. She wasn't going to recall those half-forgotten shreds *now*.

"Aye, but did we kiss?" He raised his eyebrows and gave a lecherous grin. She bit her lip to smother a giggle. No man had ever flirted so outrageously with her before. Even before she was married, Pictish nobles had never been this familiar, in deference of her rank.

It was the one positive thing about hiding her identity from Finn. Aside from the fact his people were hunting her, if he knew she was the Princess of Fortriu, his manner would change. There was no doubt.

"We did not," she told him. "I am most grieved by the oversight."

He laughed, and from the corner of her eye she saw Constantine shoot a sharp glance their way. She ignored him. It had been

Briana's idea to seat them this way tonight, and she had promised to occupy the prince's attention, so no one would think it strange when Mairi consequently occupied Finn's.

She owed her dear cousin a great debt and could only hope Constantine wasn't being as boorish as the previous evening.

"I trust you'll allow me to make amends for such negligence. I wouldn't wish to grieve you for the world."

It was the perfect opening for her to invite him into her bed. Her mouth dried and heart hammered, and she all but forgot how to breathe.

Say it. Surely, it wasn't that hard. Clandestine assignations were frequently initiated, and it was nothing to obsess about. If her marriage hadn't been a sham, she wouldn't give this a second thought.

"Perhaps," she whispered, and Finn leaned closer to catch her words, and his unique scent of woodland glens tantalized her senses with illicit promise. *Please let him understand what I mean.* The thought of explaining her wishes in detail was daunting in the extreme.

She tightened her grip on her knife in a vain attempt to focus. "You may wish to make amends to me tonight."

SHE DOESN'T MEAN *what I wish she means.*

Finn kept the smile on his face and his hands to himself, although God alone knew how he managed it. Every fiber yearned to pull Mae into his arms and taste her sweet lips. The notion consumed him and being so close to her tormented his soul.

She was merely flirting, and he would *not* read more into it. Even if her beautiful eyes invited him to drown within their flawless blue depths, and her elusive scent of raindrops on leather scrambled his brain, he'd keep his distance even if it damn near killed him.

"I would do anything within my power to make amends to you, Mae." He bowed his head, so she wouldn't see the lust he was certain burned in his eyes. He inhaled a deep breath and forced the hunger back into its cage. "Should I invade your dreamworld once again, feel free to kiss me until I'm utterly at your mercy."

She gave a breathless laugh and he risked looking at her once again. Her copper hair glowed in the light from the torches and the fire that burned in the great hearth, and beyond the thudding of his heart, a despairing rebellion stirred.

Was this all there could ever be between them?

"I am hoping for more than a dream kiss tonight, Finn."

Her smile was gentle, almost shy, as though she wasn't certain of what his response might be. His gaze sharpened, but she didn't glance away.

There was no mistake. She was offering more than a chaste kiss this night.

Wasn't she?

His mouth dried and cock thickened as lascivious images from his graphic dreams thundered through his heated brain. For a reason he couldn't fathom, but had no intention of questioning, she'd changed her mind from when they'd spoken earlier.

Despite his resolve, the question escaped, regardless. "Are you certain, Mae?"

Her smile was tremulous. "I am." Her voice was so soft he scarcely heard her words, but he had no need of words. Not when her eyes said everything. "But I must request we keep our…" she hesitated, and a delicate blushed heated her cheeks. Gently, he squeezed her fingers. Whatever her request, he would gladly agree with it. She took a deep breath. "We must keep our liaison confidential from the court."

"You have my word." But even without her request, he would never have breathed a word about her. He never spoke of his conquests, the way some warriors did. And even though they would likely share only one night together, Mae would always be more than a fleeting encounter who had distracted him from an unpalatable future.

She was the light that would keep the darkness at bay.

"Thank you. I cannot risk being linked to any scandal."

Despite his arousal that burned the very blood in his veins, a wave of fierce protectiveness flashed through him. "No one will dare besmirch your name in my presence. Or they will answer to me for it."

"The truth is," she hesitated and toyed with her knife, before taking a deep breath. "I have never indulged in a clandestine affair before. You must forgive me if I appear to be unduly cautious."

Her confession was enchanting. "Would it help ease your mind to know this is my first clandestine affair also?"

She tilted her head and gave him an assessing look. "You've never enjoyed an affair?" She sounded disbelieving and it was an effort not to take her hand as a gesture of reassurance that he was telling her the truth. But she didn't want to rouse anyone's suspicions of their plans, and by sheer force of will he kept his distance.

"This is my first diplomatic mission, remember? I'm not usually included in courtly intrigues."

"Then it's just as well I've made all suitable arrangements for this night."

What had changed since the last time they'd spoken? She had been adamant there could be nothing more between them. The question gnawed the outer edges of his mind, but in the end, it was of no significance.

This was all he'd wanted since the moment he'd met her.

All too soon, although not soon enough for the fire in his blood, the feast ended. Like the previous night, after the tables were cleared, they were pushed back against the walls while the musicians tuned their instruments. Mae's whispered instructions thundered through his head, a tapestry of subterfuge that included the assistance of the princess herself.

Damn it, MacAllister had been right about the close friendship between Mae and her mistress. He didn't know what to make of MacAllister's shrewd observations, other than to redouble his efforts to make damn sure the other man remained in ignorance of tonight's tryst. There was no doubt he'd relay everything that happened in Fotla to the king, and Finn had no intention of allowing Mae's name to be sullied in any way.

All the king's man had so far was speculation, and that was how it would remain.

They lingered near the princess and Constantine, and a few ladies of the court joined them, along with several of his compatriots. He was acutely aware when Mae drifted to the edge of the group but managed to keep his attention fixed elsewhere.

And not only because Mae wished to keep their liaison from the rest of the court. MacAllister, across the hall, appeared in deep discussion with his second in command, but Finn wasn't fooled. The older man was tracking both Mae and him like a hawk.

He spied Lady Nairne, whom Mae had previously pointed out to him. While she remained oblivious to the plans unfolding, Mae had assured him the other lady would be delighted by the part she would unknowingly play. Because, inexplicably, Lady Nairne enjoyed Constantine's company.

Before any other warrior could claim her, he offered her a half bow. "May I have the honor of the first dance, my lady?"

Her eyes widened in apparent surprise, and she cast a furtive glance around the gathering. Since it was impossible to miss Constantine, he could only imagine she was searching for Mae. There was no contingency plan if Nairne refused him. Mae had clearly not believed the other noblewoman would do so, and he had been too focused on Mae and the coming night to see the flaws in her plan.

Before his lust infused brain could come up with an alternative, Nairne smiled. "I should be delighted."

He released a relieved breath, took her proffered hand, and followed Constantine and the princess where they took their places in the center of the hall. His half-brother appeared to be enjoying himself, despite his disparaging remarks about the princess earlier.

It was hard to concentrate on Lady Nairne's agreeable remarks on the talent of the musicians, and the excitement generated by the visiting Scots, when all he could think about was Mae. Waiting for him, alone in her chamber.

His chest tightened and the air thickened around him. Soon, he would see her. But first he had to ensure no one would connect him leaving the hall with her earlier departure.

When the dance ended, they were standing beside Constantine and the princess, and as they applauded the musicians, she caught his eye and inclined her head.

It was his cue to bow before her, and she responded by allowing him to take her hand.

"Finn Braeson," the princess said, after he'd kissed her knuckles and straightened.

"My lady."

"The next dance begins," Constantine said to her. "Or would you prefer more wine?"

"I am a little fatigued," she replied. "But I would not wish to interrupt your entertainment. Braeson can escort me across the hall. Perhaps you could honor Lady Nairne with a dance in my stead?"

"It would be my honor, indeed." Constantine sounded uncommonly gallant for once. Except he then cast a lascivious eye over Lady Nairne which ruined the effect.

"My lady." Nairne curtseyed. "If you are unwell, I will of course accompany you."

The princess waved her hand. "I would not dream of depriving you of a dance with the dashing Lord Constantine."

Nairne looked thrilled, before she dropped another curtsey and accepted Constantine's hand.

Finn accompanied the princess as she made her way to one of the tables, where goblets of wine were waiting. He ignored the speculative glance MacAllister threw his way, but as he handed the princess a goblet, could feel the other's man's eyes burning into his back.

The princess raised the goblet to her mouth but didn't take a sip. Her gaze remained fixed on the dancing couples. "This situation is highly irregular. But Lady Mae trusts you in this matter and therefore, so must I."

Since it was obvious the princess didn't wish anyone to know they were speaking, he also raised his goblet and cast his glance across the hall. "There is no cause for worry. I would protect Lady Mae's honor with my last breath."

"Let us hope it doesn't come to that." There was a trace of amusement in her voice as she placed her goblet on the table. "I shall take my leave of you. Goodbye, Braeson."

He bowed, and she disappeared into the crowd, accompanied by Mae's faithful friend, Bhaic. And now, all he needed to do was dance with another willing lady or two, before ensuring those that mattered witnessed him leaving the hall—alone.

CHAPTER 14

$\mathcal{T}$he night was bitterly cold when he left the hall, but he welcomed it, and sucked in great lungfuls of the frigid air, in a vain effort to clear his mind. But it didn't help cool the fire in his blood and in truth, he didn't want the images of Mae that filled his head to vanish.

He strode the same path where, mere nights ago, he had come upon Mae as she observed the moon. Tonight, no one else had ventured outside, and apart from the Pictish warriors who stood guard, and leveled suspicious glares his way, he was alone.

Storm clouds obscured the skies and darkness engulfed him as he left the light from the torches behind. He made his way along the palace's western wall, which Mae had assured him would be free of prying eyes.

From the gloom, a figure approached, wearing a cloak with a hood that concealed his appearance. Finn's senses went on red alert. Even though this was part of the plan, there was always the chance Mae had been betrayed. And if so, it would be the last act the traitor discharged.

The man halted before him. It was unmistakably Bhaic, and he was clearly deeply offended by the task he was undertaking.

Without a word, he thrust a heavy cloak at Finn. Mae hadn't mentioned a disguise, but he could see the benefit.

Yet as he swung the garment over his shoulders, a thread of disquiet gnawed at the back of his mind. He was committed to defending Mae's reputation, but this level of secrecy bordered on obsession.

Then again, what did he know of such things? Maybe even the warriors who bragged of their conquests went through a similar pre-seduction routine when their lover was a lady of the court.

Yet he doubted it.

Bhaic led him to a door set deep in the stone wall and he followed the man inside. A torch flickered in a sconce, and Bhaic grabbed it before locking the door with an iron key. The space was cramped, and the air musty, and an eerie shudder crawled along Finn's spine as he made his way through the narrow passageway that had been created between the inner and outer walls of the palace.

How many others knew of this unguarded entrance?

They came to an abrupt halt before a gate of latticed iron bars, which Bhaic unlocked with another key. This might be a secret passageway into the palace, but it was far from unprotected. For which he was relieved. Even if enemies did enter this way, they could be easily trapped and destroyed by the Picts.

A spiral staircase led upwards. The space was so confined his shoulders brushed against the curved wall, and all he could see was the glimmer from the torch that deepened the dark shadow of Bhaic above him.

Finally, Bhaic halted before yet another locked door, before stepping out of the cramped stairwell. Finn followed, and without a word, the other man secured the door before casting a black glare his way.

"Wait here." His voice was barely above a low growl. "I will summon you."

Bhaic strode along the passage, and Finn remained within the recess. His lip quirked at the absurdity of it all. Did Mae know the extent of this subterfuge? The secrecy couldn't be tighter if the queen of Fotla herself was embarking on an illicit affair.

Muted voices drifted along the passage, one unmistakably Lady Briana. How had MacAllister known of their close relationship? It was uncanny. Mae's heritage must be grand indeed, to have snared such loyal friendship from a royal princess.

Bhaic returned and gave a brusque wave, indicating Finn should follow him. The Pict led him to a partially opened door and as he flattened his hand on the wood, the older man leaned close.

"I shall remain here throughout the night."

It was an unsubtle warning, but Finn didn't care for the Pict's animosity. The door opened, and Mae stood in the center of the antechamber. Her beautiful hair flowed over her shoulders, and the firelight cast a translucent glow over her white gown that clung to her curves like a sensual caress.

His heart kicked against his ribs and the air thickened around him. She was a vision, a Pictish lady he had no hope of winning, but tonight she was his, and he would ensure he lived on in her memories forever.

He pushed the door shut and her tremulous smile caused something deep in his chest to contract, as though she had driven a spear through his heart. She'd never know how much this night meant to him. Or how he'd keep it locked inside, a shining glimpse of what might have been, had he not been burdened with cursed duty.

"Mae," he whispered, and held out his hand to her.

FINN STOOD BEFORE HER, a glorious Scots warrior, his wild black hair tamed into a semblance of civility by a black velvet ribbon. Although she had seen him scarcely an hour ago, now that he was in her bedchamber, he seemed different, somehow. Exotic. Foreign.

Dangerous.

The word thudded through her mind, an exhilarating counterpoint to the erratic thunder of her heart. Although she'd prepared for this, and it was something she wanted more than anything, her legs refused to move.

Finn smiled, and any hope she had of mastering her paralyzed limbs dissolved beneath his hypnotic gaze. He would think her a fool if she didn't at least say something. Feverishly, she attempted to pull her scattered wits together.

"I'm glad you are here."

He closed the distance between them, but didn't take her hand, as though he waited for her to make that move. "The journey was worth it, my lady."

"It's kind of you to say so. I know it's... unconventional."

"I would have climbed the walls of the palace and entered through your window, had you commanded it."

She laughed, and the twisting threads of nervousness that had haunted her all evening faded. She took his hand, and he gently squeezed her fingers. "I should never command you to do so foolhardy a thing on my account."

"I would do a great deal on your account, Mae."

He was smiling and she knew he spoke in jest, yet his words thrilled her, all the same. "Then it's fortunate I shall never ask you to undertake anything more treacherous than following my lord Bhaic through the hidden passageways of the palace."

"Are these passageways not common knowledge?"

She almost answered him before reluctant caution whispered through her mind. The ancient palaces in Pictland had all been constructed with many stairwells hidden within their walls. It had been a means of swift escape for the royal families during those turbulent times before the Scots had laid claim to Dal

Riada, when each Pict clan had fought the other in an endless cycle.

She trusted Finn not to betray her. But it was not her place to trust him with information on her people's strategies.

"Don't the palaces in Dal Riada possess such things?"

"If they do, I've never seen them. But I'm not privy to the inner workings of the royal court." He took another step, until he was so close that she could see the mysterious golden flecks in his green eyes, and warmth flowed through her like molten honey. "I've wanted to be alone with you since the moment we met. Do you truly wish to discuss the hillforts of Dal Riada?"

Goddess, no. Her stomach fluttered and she tightened her grip on his hand. "I most assuredly do not."

He traced calloused fingertips along her jaw, a tender caress that stole her breath and caused shivers of pleasure to dance over her flesh. "Tell me what you do want, Mae."

She swallowed, but her throat was dry, and her heart raced so fast she doubted she could speak if her life depended on it. Instead, she pressed her hand against his chest, and even through his linen shirt, his taut muscles imprinted upon her palm.

He gave a strangled groan and lowered his head. His breath scorched her lips. "You torment me with your slightest touch. What spell have you woven around me?"

"The same one you have ensnared me with." Her words were husky but thank the goddess she had at least found her voice. "I've never wanted any man the way I want you, Finn."

At last, his lips claimed hers, a featherlight touch that sent sparks of fire across her skin and primal waves of desire to unfurl between her thighs. It was everything she had dreamed it might be since the night they'd met, yet so much more. He broke the kiss, his breath uneven against her face, and her fingers clutched his shirt. How could so fleeting a kiss ignite such longing within her?

It was magical. She needed more.

She rose onto her toes and brushed her lips over his. He gave a low rumble that vibrated through his body and filled her mind, a primitive sound that thrilled her soul. She pressed closer, her hand sliding to his powerful shoulder, and he wound his arm around her, capturing her against his magnificent, hard body.

His tongue teased her lips and instinctively she opened to his unspoken command. He slid inside, and the sensation of delicious invasion was exquisite. Her low moan filled the heated air, and his hold around her tightened in blatant possession.

He released her hand and threaded his fingers through her hair, tugging on her curls as he cradled the back of her head. His kiss deepened, became less gentle, more demanding, and her eyes fluttered closed at the wonder of it all.

The kiss of a lover was truly nothing like she had imagined.

He tore his mouth from hers, his breath hot against her bruised lips. "I swore to take my time this night, Mae. To savor every second with you. But God help me, it's killing me."

She stroked her fingers along his aristocratic cheekbone, before cupping his roughened jaw. In her fantasy world, this was her wedding night and Finn was her bridegroom, and they would have a lifetime together. But in the real world, there was only tonight, there was perhaps only one time, and she needed—craved—for it to be perfect.

A frenzied coupling might be wonderful, but she knew a woman's first time was rarely as satisfactory as a man's. And while she had no intention of admitting her innocence to Finn, she would do everything possible to ensure this night with him would hold no regrets.

She didn't want to let him go. But perhaps it was the only way to prolong this illicit pleasure. It was hard to find her voice, never mind the words, but somehow, she pushed them out. "Would you care for some wine?"

"You're the only wine I need."

"I have no wish for your restraint to kill you."

His laugh warmed her heart. "Nor I, sweet Mae. If you wish for wine, then we shall drink wine."

She sighed and wound her arms around his neck. His plaid was between them, and she longed to feel his naked flesh but did not quite have the nerve to suggest he should strip. "All I wish is to stay in your arms forever."

He rested his cheek against the top of her head. Need rippled through her. It seemed even his simplest gesture was destined to arouse her beyond reason. "I wish I could offer more than a fleeting affair." There was a trace of bitterness in his voice she'd not noticed before, and she raised her head to look at him. He smiled, and her heart shivered at the desolation she glimpsed in his eyes. "Have you changed your mind, Mae? Tell me now, before I lose my senses and take you where you stand."

Once again, she rolled onto her toes so she could taste his lips. "Never," she breathed, and he crushed her in an embrace that seared the fabric of her being. When she could once again breathe, she whispered, "A fleeting affair is all there can ever be for us, Finn."

"Aye." He traced his fingertips along her face. "But the memory of you will be with me forever."

How she hoped that was true. It would be an intangible connection between them, at least.

"Come." She took his hand and led him into the bedchamber. The walls were thick, and she did not believe for a moment that Bhaic would listen at the door, but she wanted more privacy against the reality of the outside world. "We will not be disturbed tonight."

Without relinquishing her hand, he closed the door behind them. "You have powerful connections, my lady."

He was smiling, and it was clear he didn't expect her to answer, but a flicker of unease brushed through her, nevertheless. A Pictish warrior would never mistake the precautions she'd taken as being anything but extraordinary. No matter how close a princess was to her ladies, she would never give up her bedchamber so one might enjoy a clandestine night of love.

She could only play this dangerous game because Finn was a Scot, and unaware of their customs. To be sure, he found the subterfuge extreme, but he wasn't suspicious of her motives.

If only there was no need for secrets between them. But there was nothing she could do about it. Only enjoy what they *could* share.

It was enough. It had to be.

CHAPTER 15

*D*aringly, Mairi tugged the length of velvet ribbon that tamed his hair and dropped it to the floor. That was better. He looked more like the wild Scots warrior she had first seen beneath the light of the moon.

He lowered his head, and his silky hair brushed her cheek as he kissed the sensitive spot behind her ear. Goddess, how could that feel so wonderful? A shiver skimmed through her, and she tipped her head back and dug her fingers into his shoulders. It seemed he understood her silent command and trailed teasing kisses along the length of her throat.

His breath was hot, and his teeth grazed her flesh in a sensuous caress she had never imagined could be possible. When he pulled back and looked at her, his eyes were dark with passion and again the alluring notion swirled through her mind.

Dangerous.

Without breaking their gaze, he stepped back, and her hands slid from his shoulders. Slowly, he unwound his length of plaid. Unaccustomed tension wound tighter deep inside, in places she had barely known existed before meeting Finn. He was taking forever, and she clasped her fingers together to stop herself from losing all dignity and tearing the material from him herself.

He tossed his plaid onto a nearby stool and the air stalled in her lungs as he gripped his shirt and ripped it over his head. Firelight flickered over his bronzed chest, enhancing each taut muscle and mysterious shadow. And then her gaze slipped to his magnificent cock, and her mouth dried.

She had never seen a naked man before. Were they all so well endowed? Alarm collided with lust and damp heat bloomed between her thighs. It was unseemly to stare so, but she couldn't drag her eyes away.

He tilted her face up, his fingers sending sparks of lightning across her jaw and cheek. "I trust I don't disappoint." There was a thread of laughter in his voice. Should they be laughing when they were about to embark on a night of sex?

But it was impossible not to smile back at him. "You do not."

"I'm gratified."

Would he guess her inexperience if she stole another quick glance at his wondrous manhood? She wasn't sure but didn't want to risk it, so kept her gaze fixed on his face instead. But his expanse of naked flesh entranced her, and she trailed her fingertips over his biceps. Leashed power radiated from him, and the breath caught in her throat when he cradled her hips in a blatantly possessive gesture.

"Sweet Mae." His murmured endearment was as potent as a sensual caress and before she could stop herself, she dug her nails into his hard flesh. "I don't know if I'll be able to let you go when morning comes."

"There are many hours until the morning." But not nearly enough. There would never be enough.

"Aye. And we shouldn't waste them in idle talk."

She didn't want him to misunderstand.

"That's not what I meant. I enjoy our—" She sucked in a sharp gasp as he tugged her nightgown from her shoulder and pressed his lips against her skin. She swallowed and clung onto him as he loosened the ties at her bodice, his hot breath sending thrills racing across her exposed breasts.

He shackled her wrists and lowered her arms. Uncomprehending, she gazed at him, but his smile melted her flicker of unease. "I need to see you, Mae. I need to feel your beautiful body against mine."

"Yes," she whispered, barely aware she had even spoken. Without breaking eye-contact, he eased her nightgown over her arms and the delicate fabric floated to the floor and pooled at her feet.

Slowly, his gaze roved over her. Heat flooded through her blood, and she was paralyzed beneath his intense scrutiny. Goddess, it was exhilarating, and he wasn't even touching her.

Except his eyes held a magic of their own, and the way his jaw flexed, and chest rose and fell in shallow breaths, was as thrilling as his addictive kisses.

And then he cupped her face, and his kiss wasn't tender or gentle. It was hard and demanding, stealing her senses as he plundered her mouth. She wrapped her arms around him, and their bodies melded, his thick erection rigid and hot as he branded her flesh.

She moaned into his mouth and moved restlessly, his chest chafing her nipples in a seductive caress. Wild desire erupted low in her belly, and exquisite tendrils of need licked her sensitive bud. It was hard—no, it was impossible—to remain still within his arms when the overwhelming demand to crush herself against him thudded through her scrambled mind.

Before she realized his intentions, he scooped her into his powerful arms and strode across the chamber to the bed. She linked her fingers behind his neck and nibbled kisses along his aristocratic jaw. A growl rumbled in his throat, and a shudder chased through her at his response.

"Do you wish to unman me?" He turned his head and

ensnared her with his piercing gaze, his hold on her tightening as though he imagined she might flee. "Your slightest touch drives me to the edge of my control."

"Is that so bad?" She smiled at him, delighting in their game of words. "Do you wish me to stop touching you, Finn?"

"I don't believe I said that." He laid her on the bed and then straddled her, his knees bracketing her hips. "But I have plans for you, Mae, and they don't involve me losing control."

They were further from the fire now, and the shadows were deeper. If only she'd had the foresight to light one or two sconces. How dearly she wanted to see every expression on Finn's face. She trailed her hands along his rock-hard thighs, only to be stilled when he grasped her wrists. Before she could protest, he lowered his head, and his mouth ignited a fiery trail of pleasure across her breasts.

His tongue circled her nipple and she gasped, arching her back. His hair dusted her skin, a tantalizing whisper of sensation, that magnified the dark enchantment of his mouth upon her. As he continued to torment her with his lips and tongue, he released her wrists, and his hands played a magical caress along her waist and hips.

Her body melted, burning. Feverishly, she tangled her fingers in his glorious hair, loving how the silky tendrils were yet another sensuous slide across her flesh. And then he shifted position, easing her legs apart with his knees, until she opened before him. It was scandalous, and breathtaking, and when he glanced up and caught her gaze, his wicked smile turned her bones to liquid honey.

"You're more than I ever dared to dream." His voice was raw with lust and molten desire rippled through her. "How will I release you when morning comes?"

She knew many ladies who had shared the pretty compliments men murmured while intoxicated by passion. It meant nothing and a woman was foolish if she believed the honeyed declarations of devotion.

But they both knew nothing could come of this wondrous night. She could bask in his admiration without losing sight of the truth. There was nothing undignified in Finn's heated words and how dearly she would hold them deep in her heart when he was but a cherished memory.

His hot gaze raked over her body, leaving a fiery trail in his wake. It was dark, yet suddenly not quite dark enough, when his searing exploration halted at the juncture of her thighs.

She shifted, unsure how to react to his scrutiny. It was exhilarating, but did he expect her to *do* something?

He lowered his head and the breath caught in her throat. No, surely he was not going to…

She collapsed back onto the bed as his mouth captured her in a primal kiss that sucked every sane thought from her mind. His tongue probed her slit, penetrating with delectable restraint, before teasing her swollen clitoris.

Goddess.

Her fingers gripped his hair, her only anchor in a world surging with unimaginable sensation. Sparks of lightning collided; the pleasure so intense it shimmered on the edge of pain. Her breath rasped, a ragged sound in the mystical cocoon that ensnared them, but she didn't even care at the loss of her dignity.

Nothing mattered, except that Finn continued to weave this irresistible web of decadence inside her.

His hands roamed over her, cupping her breasts, and teasing her nipples. She writhed, mindless, as waves of ecstasy rocked her body and consumed her reason. Gasping, she dragged open her eyes as Finn raised his head. Her legs were shaking, and tremors still raced through her. She could scarcely breathe, her heart hammered like a wild creature, and goddess help her, but she didn't want him to stop.

He loomed over her, blocking out the light from the fire, and it was enthralling. "I need you, Mae." His voice was hoarse, and renewed quivers skated over her sensitized skin. "I need to feel you come while I'm buried deep inside you."

His potent words caused erotic images to fill her spinning mind.

"I want that, too." Her voice croaked, and any other time she'd be mortified. "I want you, Finn."

His jaw flexed, almost as though her whispered confession caused him pain. Then his mouth crashed down on hers, a searing kiss that tasted of her passion. She had never imagined such a thing. It was thrilling, and she wound her arms around his shoulders so he could not escape, before invading him with the tip of her tongue.

His groan filled her mouth, filled her head, until it was all she could hear. The sound reverberated through her blood, and she slid in further, their tongues tangling in a breath-stealing dance of seduction.

He shifted, his powerful shoulders tensing beneath her questing fingers, and his thick, hard, cock pushed inside her. She froze, her nails digging into him, her muscles locking in shock. Her heartbeat thundered in her ears as she desperately willed her body to relax.

She wanted this. More than anything. But although Finn had stilled, there was a burning pressure radiating from his possession, and she couldn't move. But she had to. Otherwise, he would guess her secret.

Panic fluttered and her legs started to shake. Goddess, why had he stopped? If he continued, surely this moment would pass?

"Mae?" Finn sounded agonized, but she didn't even have the breath to reassure him. "Did I hurt you?"

She managed to shake her head but even in the gloom she saw he didn't believe her. She gulped in an elusive wisp of air. It was imperative she answered him. "A little."

What? No, that was not what she had intended to say. Yet she couldn't lie to him. Not unless she had no choice. "It is nothing," she added hastily, and gave his shoulder a little pat, in the hope that would distract him.

It didn't.

He heaved himself up, bracing his weight on his fists. "Are you a maid?"

This conversation was most improper, and the last subject she wished to discuss with Finn, of all people, was her inexperience in such matters. And yet, absurdly, she had the alarming urge to laugh.

"I do not believe I am any longer."

It was obvious he found no humor in her attempt to lighten the mood. Indeed, her confession appeared to stun him speechless. Well, it was too late to take back her hasty words and pretend she had a cramp or something. She didn't regret any of this, and she certainly didn't want him to, either.

She patted his shoulder again, and then trailed her fingers down his back. He shuddered and gave a choked groan. Encouraged, she stroked his jaw, delighting in the way his stubble grazed her palm. "Finn, do you no longer want me?"

"How can you ask me that?" There was a fierce note in his voice. "I want you more than you'll ever know. But I didn't expect to take your maidenhead. I should have been more mindful."

At least he hadn't pulled out of her, and the moment of discomfort had faded. Truly, the way he stretched her untouched flesh, was the most exquisite sensation. Experimentally, she tightened around him, and his big body shook, as though he fought a mighty internal battle for control.

"You're the only man I've ever wanted to share my bed." The confession escaped before she could think better of it, but when Finn raked his fingers through her hair and cradled her head, any doubts that she'd done the right thing vanished like the morning mist.

"Sweet Mae. Forgive me. I should do the honorable thing, but I fear such sacrifice is beyond me."

Slowly, and with infinite tenderness, he pushed deeper into her, and her breath stalled in her chest. He filled her so completely, pinning her to the bed, and she was sure she could not move if her very life depended on it.

He cupped her face, and his kiss was restrained, chaste even, yet she could feel the ravening hunger he tried so hard to keep in check.

But she didn't want him to hold back.

She wrapped her legs around him and gasped at the sudden shift in his penetration as he sank even deeper within her.

"Mae?" His groan vibrated through every particle of her being and his regard for her comfort when he was clearly battling to retain control, was a heady aphrodisiac.

"Yes," she breathed, barely aware that she spoke, knowing only that she needed all of him, craved everything he could give her, and wanted no barriers between them. "Make me yours."

"You'll always be mine." His voice was savage, as though he stated a fact and not merely sweet words in the heat of the moment. It made no difference. In her heart, and in the safety of her memories, she would believe. But in the cold light of day, her head would always rule.

It was dark. They were alone. Her pledge would be forever between the two of them. "And you are mine."

He rocked against her, stealing her breath and scorching her soul. His harsh breath filled the air, and his fingers teased her breasts and waist in a sizzling trail of fiery sensation.

His muscles flexed and despite the lust that swirled through her blood and fogged her mind, she had the uncanny certainty he was about to withdraw from her. Instinctively, her legs tightened around him even as warmth flooded her heart at his concern. "No," she gasped. "It's safe, Finn. I shall not conceive this night."

His teeth bared in a feral grin and his breath was hot against her face. "Are you sure? I wouldn't tarnish your reputation for the world, my love."

My love. If only it were true. But she treasured his endearment, nevertheless.

"Fill me," she breathed against his lips.

Her words seemed to unlock his last restraint. He pounded into her, and the friction was unbearably exquisite as she fell, once again, into the starlit horizon.

CHAPTER 16

Finn rolled onto his back, bringing Mae with him. She snuggled against him, her hand on his chest, and he dragged in a ragged breath. In all but name, this was his wedding night, with the woman who, in his heart, would forever be his bride.

His virgin bride.

A protective wave of possessiveness surged through him, and he pulled her closer. Her satisfied sigh drifted across his naked chest, and he pressed his lips against her soft hair. The elusive fragrance of raindrops and leather perfumed the air. The scent of Mae.

He traced a finger along her cheek. "Are you all right?"

"I have never been better."

She sounded sincere but was she speaking the truth?

"Had I known you were a maid, I would have taken more time." God, what was he saying? If he'd known she'd never been with a man, the only honorable course of action he should have taken was to leave her alone.

He feared that, when it came to Mae, he was incapable of doing the honorable thing.

"Then I'm glad you didn't know. Had you taken any longer, I may have expired from the anticipation."

He laughed and couldn't resist stealing another kiss from her delectable lips. "I can't imagine how your husband left you untouched. Was he a monk?" He knew of the strange, passionless marriages that were endorsed by the church, but Mae wasn't of the church.

"No. But he was a good man."

He was silent as he contemplated her reply. She had already shared that her marriage hadn't been a love-match, but it was obvious she'd cared for her husband. Unless ordered by the church, it was inconceivable that any man would neglect to claim his rights with so charming a bride.

There was only one thing to conclude. Her husband had preferred the company of men.

"How long were you wed?"

"Five years, last summer."

It was none of his concern, yet he couldn't remain silent. "Has your father arranged another marriage for you yet?"

Even as he asked the question, it sickened him to think of Mae being given in marriage to another man and his muscles tensed as he waited for her response.

Finally, she gave a deep sigh. "My father died two winters ago."

Damn it. He'd shoved his boot in his mouth once again when it came to Mae and her parents. "I'm sorry. Were you close?"

Fuck, what was wrong with him? He didn't wish to speak of things that might upset her, and yet the concept of having any kind of relationship with one's father had always secretly intrigued him. Not that he could really fathom why. There were few men he knew who enjoyed a cordial relationship with their sire. And his stepsisters had been terrified of the brute his mother had wed.

"Yes." There was a wistful note in her voice. "I was his only living child. I've heard it said both he and my grandfather doted upon me. I don't think it was meant unkindly."

"How could they not dote upon you?" If he had a daughter, he would do the same. A dull ache gripped his vitals. He would never father a daughter. Not now. But he wouldn't tarnish these precious moments with Mae by recalling the barren future that stretched ahead.

She gave a silent laugh. "I was not an obedient daughter, Finn. I caused them much anguish with my love of riding in the mountains."

Yet she had married the man her father had chosen for her. When it counted, Mae had been dutiful.

"All noblewomen ride." If only he could see her face clearly, but the flames from the fire cast too many shadows. "How did this cause them anguish?"

"This is true. But they were certain my constitution was too delicate to withstand such rigors." She raised herself onto her elbow and gazed down at him, her beautiful hair tumbling over her shoulders. "I'm much stronger than I look, Finn. But alas, my reputation precedes me."

"I know nothing of this reputation." He wound his hand around her neck and stole another lingering kiss. "But I can't fault your father for his concern."

"I sometimes wonder…" she hesitated and then shook her head. "Goddess, what am I saying? I cannot share such thoughts with you."

Intrigued, he traced his fingers along her face. "You can share anything with me. It will go no further than this bedchamber."

"Oh." She gave a small laugh. "It's not a secret that will bring about the downfall of Pictland." She brushed a tender kiss across his lips and his cock stirred. It was an effort to remain still and not pin her beneath him once again. "But I've sometimes wondered if my father and grandfather chose my bridegroom because they knew he would never get me with child."

It wasn't a secret that might bring about the downfall of Pictland, but it was a startling revelation, nevertheless. What father would willingly wed his only daughter to a man he knew would never allow her to fulfil her destiny?

He had no idea how to respond to her, but he needed to say something. Especially since he'd encouraged her to confide. But instead of comforting words, he said what was on his mind.

"Why would they do such a thing?"

Her head drooped, and he slid his fingers beneath her chin and raised her face. She let out a long breath. "I can only surmise they didn't wish me to die in the same manner as both my grandmamma and mamma."

Hellfire. He'd never spoken of such intimate things with any woman and had never imagined a moment when he might. Childbirth was risky. It was a fact of life. But he had never dwelt on it before. Not even when it concerned his stepsisters, because what good would it do?

"But what of your wishes, Mae? Surely you wanted bairns of your own?"

"I…" she hesitated once again. "I am not certain I do."

He'd never heard such a thing before. It was, after all, a woman's primary fate to give birth. Surely, he had misunderstood her meaning.

"But all women want bairns."

Despite the gloom, and how he still captured her face in his hand, she managed to give him a regal look. "I am not *all women*."

That was true enough, but he was still stunned by her confession. "What if your husband had taken you in the marriage bed? It wouldn't always be safe."

The way she had assured him it was tonight.

Was it a trick of the light, or had her gaze turned pitying?

"There are ways known only to those who follow the goddess. We are not all at the mercy of a man's seed."

Speechless, he stared at her, this beautiful, Pictish noblewoman who had haunted his mind since the moment they had met. She was a heathen, it was true, but it had never occurred to him that any woman might possess the power to evade the inevitability of conception.

It edged into the realm of witchcraft.

He didn't believe in witches. And he didn't believe in her goddess. Mae spoke of the ancient lore of her people. That was all.

Of one thing he was certain. No Scotswoman possessed such knowledge.

She shifted, crossing her arms over his chest, and gazed into his face. "Have I shocked you, Finn Braeson?"

Maybe she had, but he'd never admit it. "Your ways intrigue me, Lady Mae. Everything you say is a revelation."

"I shall take that as a compliment, even if you didn't mean it as such."

His hands roamed down her naked back and cupped her luscious backside. Lust stirred, burning through his blood, and he fought to contain it. They only had tonight, and he'd intended to take Mae many times before dawn broke, but that was before he'd discovered she had been a virgin.

Regret that her innocence might prevent them from indulging in endless hours of raw pleasure warred with fierce satisfaction that he had been her first. He wanted her memories of this night to delight her whenever she recalled him, not have them marred by evidence of his unbridled lust. But damn, it was hard to keep his thoughts in check when her exquisite body molded his.

"It was an observation." His voice was hoarse, and he barely even knew what he said. Ruthlessly, he battened down the desire scorching through his blood but with Mae all but lying on top of him, it was a losing battle.

He'd lose his mind before he lost control and possessed her irresistible body once again.

"I have been undertaking some observations of my own." Her

breathy whisper ignited the rebellious flames that turned his resolve to ash, and he gritted his teeth. He would not succumb to his base nature.

Mae appeared oblivious to the war that raged within him, as she shifted her position and slid her knee between his thighs. He swallowed, his mouth dry, and attempted to recall why he couldn't take her again, right now.

She pressed her lips onto his shoulder and his fingers flexed against her rounded flesh. He should move his hands away from temptation but was incapable of following his own good advice.

"Are you not in the least bit curious?" Her warm breath dusted his flesh. He had no idea what she was asking him. He could scarcely recall his own damn name, never mind anything else.

"Aye." The word rumbled from the depths of his chest. He could only hope she made sense of it.

She wriggled against him, clearly making herself comfortable, while he suffered agonies of self-imposed restraint.

"Your shoulders are truly magnificent."

He grunted, incapable of uttering anything more coherent.

"And your biceps are surely a gift from the gods."

A pained laugh escaped. "Do you intend to itemize every part of my body?"

"Indeed." She wriggled a little more until she was kneeling between his thighs, her palms flat against his chest. His resolve cracked, and he cupped her breasts, his thumbs teasing her nipples, and her jagged gasps were the sweetest sounds he'd ever heard.

"Your hands," Mae said, her voice uneven, which served only to further stoke his lust, "are instruments of magical pleasure."

His grin felt feral, but he couldn't prevent it. "I commend your powers of observation."

"Your chest." She paused, and lightly scored her fingernails over his taut muscles. A tortured groan tore his throat, and primitive need rolled through him when she leaned closer and dropped a gentle kiss on his lips. "Could make a maiden weep."

"I'm staggered by the depth of your scrutiny."

She leaned into him, bracing her weight on his chest, as she eased her legs over his, bracketing his hips with her knees. "I have never seen a finer male specimen in my life."

"Specimen," he choked, unsure whether she meant it in admiration or as one of her enchanting insults. And in truth, he didn't care. Her candid words ensnared him as surely as her enticing body. "Your impressions are as fascinating as you."

"Do you promise to remember this night for all time?"

"Until the last breath leaves my body." He teased her nipples with the pad of his thumbs, and her shudder vibrated the very air around them.

"That is all I wish," she whispered, as the tips of her fingers left trails of fire across his skin.

He heaved himself up onto his elbows. Mae had stilled in her exploration and was gazing at his cock. She didn't say a word and she was no longer touching him, but her scrutiny was as potent as though she had taken him into her mouth.

The visual burned into his brain, and it took every shred of self-control he possessed not to bring his fantasy to glorious life.

She lowered her head, and her warm breath caressed his groin. His savage groan echoed around the chamber, and she glanced up at him, her hair tumbling around her face.

"Christ, Mae." He had no idea how he managed to say anything at all. "You're killing me."

"Forgive me." Her voice was breathy, and she didn't sound in the least contrite by his plight. "I wish to learn all I can about you. I may never have another chance to explore a man's body in such a manner."

Bracing his weight on one arm, he plunged his fingers through her hair, winding her long curls around his fist. "Don't say such things." His command was fierce, and his mind blurred with outrage at the mere possibility that she might touch any other man this way. Or that another man might ever dare take such liberties with her. "You're mine, do you hear me?"

"Always."

Her soft acceptance should be enough, but deep in his brain the disquiet lingered. Brutally, he shoved it deeper. The future had no place here. Yet he couldn't quite let it go. "Promise me."

"We shall always belong to each other," she said. "No matter what happens in all our tomorrows."

He kept his fingers tangled in her hair as she returned her gaze to his cock. He sucked in a harsh breath as she traced a finger along his length, before lavishing the same attention onto his throbbing balls. He squeezed his eyes shut and collapsed back onto the bed, as Mae continued to tease and tempt with her untrained fingers. His grasp tightened in her hair, but he couldn't help himself.

Keep it together. He would not disgrace himself.

It was a torturous pleasure such as he had never believed existed. But when her lips pressed against his hot erection, he could hold on no longer.

With a primal growl he wrapped her in his arms and rolled her onto her back. She was chilled, and in the sane sliver of his mind he cursed his lust that had allowed her to remain too long without the furs wrapped around her.

But she didn't need the furs. He would warm her until she burned like a furnace.

Despite the need that hammered through him to possess her once again, he held back. He'd not take her like an uncivilized barbarian from the north, but his kisses grew increasingly wild as her nails scored his shoulders, and her gasps filled his ears. He tore his mouth from hers and worshipped the perfection of her breasts, swirling his tongue around her ripe nipples.

"Finn." Desperation tinged her plea and primitive satisfaction blazed through him. He stroked his fingers across her belly and cupped her sex, before teasing her wet folds until she writhed beneath him.

He reined in the thundering imperative to thrust deep inside and gritted his teeth as he slowly pushed into her welcoming heat. She gasped, and he stilled, body shaking with the effort. For endless moments time hung, suspended, and then her tense muscles relaxed, and she wrapped her legs around him.

It was too much.

He pumped into her, her silken flesh a tight cocoon of inexpressible pleasure. Her hair spread across the pillows in tangled disarray, a visual feast, and he couldn't get enough. Harsh breaths filled the air, delicate shudders rippled through her, and when she convulsed around him, he fell with her over the edge of the earth.

As he spilled his seed deep within her, and she clung onto him as though her life depended on it, her name echoed through his soul.

Mae.

CHAPTER 17

*I*t was still dark when Mairi stirred and open her eyes. Languid contentment bathed her with a sense of completeness she had never experienced before. A small smiled tugged her lips. Finn had been everything she had dreamed, and so much more. She slowly stretched, and that was when the strangeness penetrated.

Curled on her side, she was chilled, despite the furs that covered her to her neck. Yet Finn had pulled her into his heat as she'd slipped into slumber. Cautiously, she reached behind her.

The bed was empty.

The warm glow in her chest fled and she sat up, clutching the furs to her breast. Surely, he hadn't left her while she was asleep? How could he—

From the corner of her eye, she saw a dark shadow crouching by the fire, stoking the embers. Relief tumbled through her. He hadn't disappeared without a word. Not that she had truly expected he would. He was too honorable for such a despicable act.

He stood and came back to the bed. Alas, he was dressed. But at least he had not left.

"I hope I didn't disturb you." He sat on the edge of the bed and took her hand.

She shook her head, as she interlaced her fingers with his. "Why are you up already? It is still night."

Except it wasn't, and she knew it. She just didn't want to admit it.

"Dawn is approaching." He heaved a sigh before brushing a tender kiss across her knuckles. "I must go before the palace awakes."

She knew this. She had, after all, planned it. But surely they could spend a little more time together?

"Finn, come back to bed. I just want to hold you one last time." A dull ache wrapped around her heart as she said the words. Saying goodbye was never going to be easy, but it was so much harder than she'd imagined.

He cradled her face, his thumb stroking her cheek. "If I get back in the bed, I fear I shall never leave it."

"Why did our fates entwine when we can never be together?" When the Scots left Fotla she would beg Bride for insight. But in a secret corner of her heart, she knew there was nothing her goddess could show her that would make parting from Finn worth the pain.

"I don't want to leave you, Mae." His voice was low, but there was a fierceness that warmed her heart. "If there was anything I could do, to keep you by my side, I would. But all I can offer is a clandestine affair. And you deserve so much more than that."

She gave a jagged sigh. "So do you."

"You wouldn't say that if you could read my thoughts. I dishonor you by even thinking such things."

"I do not believe that's possible. Tell me."

His fingers tightened around hers and once again his thumb stroked her cheek. "We could wed in secret. I'd carry you away in the dead of night to a remote hillfort and keep you all to myself."

She couldn't help a gentle laugh. "You would abduct me, like a barbaric Viking? I confess, the notion doesn't alarm me."

"The fatal flaw in the plan is that I don't possess a remote hill-fort." He pressed his forehead against hers and she closed her eyes and breathed in deep. It would be the last time she had the opportunity to savor the unique scent that was all Finn. *Do not weep in front of him.*

"That is unfortunate, to be sure." Her voice was husky and it hurt to clear her throat. "Although I'm certain I would be a most disagreeable captive for you."

His smile was crooked, and a sad inevitability washed through her. She had to let him go. The longer he lingered, the higher the possibility of him being seen when he returned to his camp.

Yet in this moment, she barely cared if the entire contingent of the Scots discovered their illicit assignation.

Finally, he pulled back. "There must be a way we can see each other again before I leave Fotla."

Hope flared. After all, just because the Scots were no longer welcome within the palace, didn't mean they intended to leave the kingdom immediately. It was highly likely they could meet again. Indeed, she would make certain of it.

"You are right." She grasped his hand and pressed it against her breast. "For as long as you remain in Fotla, we must do all we can to continue our liaison."

"And I shall work on my strategy of stealing you away from Pictland, and back to Dal Riada."

"I'll never live in Dal Riada. But you could make your home in Pictland."

He kissed her; a lingering kiss filled with promises that could never be. "I'll see you again soon," he whispered, before standing and striding across the chamber. At the door he paused and glanced back at her. "I wasn't jesting, Mae. About wanting to wed you."

With that, he swung about and left the chamber.

∽

HIS WORDS still echoed in her ears hours later, after Briana had returned to the bedchamber and dawn had broken. It was nothing but a pretty dream, but she cherished his declaration regardless.

And he hadn't said it in the heat of the moment, either, when a man might never recall such vows. He hadn't been attempting to flatter her or flirt the way so many men did with the ladies of the court.

He knew, as well as she, it was an impossible future. But oh, how she wished it weren't.

"Goddess, Mae, have you heard a word I've said to you?" There was a touch of exasperation in her cousin's voice, and she blinked, attempting without success to dispel Finn's face from her mind.

"Forgive me. Do you need help with your hair?" There was only the two of them, and the guard who had accompanied Briana back to the chamber had, she presumed, returned to the queen. And although she had pulled her nightgown on after Finn had left, it suddenly occurred to her that she must look most disheveled.

"I do not." Briana sat on the bed and tucked her legs beneath her. "And I'm not asking if you enjoyed the night since happiness fairly glows from you. I merely asked if you had learned anything of import."

Was she truly glowing? She would need to be more careful to hide her feelings. It would not do for anyone besides her cousin to remark upon it.

"Mae?"

Once again, she forcibly dragged her thoughts back into line. "I learned Finn is the most chivalrous of men."

But she had already known that. When Briana frowned, she tried again. "He is truly the most thoughtful of lovers."

Not that she had any experience to judge him by, but she didn't need to. He was all she had ever wanted. He would never know how much last night had meant to her.

"I am glad for you." There was an oddly constrained note in Briana's voice, and she appeared fascinated by her hands, entwined on her lap. "But what of the Scots' plans? Did he divulge anything of interest?"

Heat swept through her. It hadn't even occurred to her to question Finn in such matters. Even though it should have been her priority. But she hadn't taken him into her bed for the sake of Pictland. She had wanted him for herself, not for politics.

She hadn't wanted to tarnish their time together with a secret agenda.

In the past, she had kept few secrets from her cousin, but she couldn't share this. Because they both knew the queen had given her permission for this liaison with the expectation that Mairi would do her duty. "No."

Briana glanced at her. "Did he ask if you knew where the Princess of Fortriu might be?"

Mairi quelled the flare of anger. Briana didn't know Finn the way she did. "He did not."

He hadn't asked her anything even remotely political, and warmth squeezed her heart.

Briana exhaled a long breath. "Well then." She smoothed her gown and didn't look at Mairi. "We learned nothing, but at least you had a pleasant interlude."

DAWN HAD BROKEN, the sky was clear, and there was great excitement among the ladies as they gathered in the courtyard. The Scots, it seemed, were to embark on another hunt.

"The prince is determined to repay the royal hospitality

before leaving Fotla," Nairne confided as she and Briana joined them.

"So, their business here is concluded?" Briana said, and it took all Mairi's self-control not to let her feelings show on her face at cousin's question.

"Indeed." Nairne craned her neck, clearly searching for a glimpse of Constantine among the foreign warriors who milled about, attending to their horses. "I'm certain they believe the poor princess has passed through the veil."

Mairi cast a casual glance over the warriors, but Finn was not among them. And then she spied him leading his horse away from the crowd, towards the royal stables.

Butterflies cascaded in the pit of her stomach. They hadn't made eye-contact or arranged a clandestine meeting, but in her heart, she knew Finn had seen her. And that he trusted she would find a way to steal a few moments alone with him.

She turned to Briana and dropped a curtsey. "May I be excused? I wish to attend to Audra."

One of the ladies shot her a sharp glance, and it was true, her manner hadn't been sufficiently subservient. But it was hard to keep the smile from her face or eagerness from her voice, never mind remember that when in public, she was supposed to show deference to Briana.

"Of course. Lady Nairne may accompany you."

The last thing she wanted was a chaperone. "I wouldn't wish to deprive Lady Nairne of the pleasure of watching the prince."

"I wish to attend my own horse. We shall go together."

Mairi pressed her lips together and bowed her head, so none of the ladies might see her flash of resentment. She was certain Briana knew why Mairi wanted permission to leave, and while it was improper in Fotla-eviot for a lady to go to the stables by herself, it wasn't as though she'd be in any danger.

Since she could scarcely argue the point, they made their way around the perimeter of the courtyard and onward to the stables.

When they were out of sight of the ladies, Briana gave her a side-ways glance.

"I know you wanted to come alone. But it would be unseemly, and we both know Mamma would find out."

It was true, but even so. "I cannot bear to think he will soon leave Fotla. We'll never see each other again."

Briana sighed. "I shall give you all the privacy I can, my love."

It wasn't the same, but it was better than nothing.

They entered the stables, and Finn was waiting for her. His smile enveloped her in a cocoon of heat and her bodice felt too tight, too restrictive, as her skin prickled with awareness.

He took a step towards her, leading his horse, before he gave a formal bow. "My lady."

It took her a second to realize he was addressing Briana, not her. She drew in a shaky breath. Finn's presence addled her mind, but she would have it no other way.

If only the goddess could allow them to spend more time together.

"Finn Braeson." Briana's voice was neutral as she allowed Finn to kiss her hand. "I must attend to my mare." She swept into a nearby stall, presenting them with her back and Mairi returned her attention to Finn. His gaze was fixed on her, as though she was the only woman he could see.

"You look radiant," he whispered, and there was a wicked gleam in his eyes as though he recalled the other time he had complimented her so. Or maybe he was merely referring to the night they had shared. It seemed she hadn't managed to dull the glow after Briana's warning. But it wasn't something she wanted to hide from Finn, anyway.

She stepped closer to him, until they all but touched. "That may be so, but does my radiance illuminate the entire stables?"

He leaned closer and his warm breath caressed her ear. "You illuminate Pictland herself."

She gave a soft laugh and couldn't stop herself from cupping his jaw. "These have truly been the happiest days of my life."

Shadows darkened his eyes. "Mine, also. I've spent the hours since leaving you working on endless strategies to keep you by my side. But all of them would compromise your honor."

The honor of her foremothers was all she had left of the royal legacy that had been handed down by her ancestors for more than a thousand years. It wasn't something she could forsake, when Fortriu had lost so much already. She owed it to the people of Pictland to keep her integrity, even if her heart wished to be with Finn, no matter the consequences.

"Let us not speak of such things." She glanced over her shoulder, but Briana was intent on grooming her mare. She took Finn's hand and led him to Audra's stall. It wasn't much, but at least they would be momentarily hidden from sight, should anyone enter the stables.

He looped his horse's reins over a post and pulled her into his arms. "God, Mae. Why would the Fates allow me to find you, when we can have no future together?"

She hadn't known the Scots' religion allowed them to believe in Fate, and oddly, it soothed the ache in her heart. "The goddess' ways are not always for us to understand."

He shook his head, as if in wonder. "Do you never rail against the injustices of your gods?"

Unease sparked through her, and she fought to quell it. It was true that sometimes, deep in her heart, she raged at Bride for what had happened to her beloved land and people, and how she had lost her birthright to an upstart king. But it wasn't something she ever voiced. The goddess, all-powerful, would be sure to hear.

It was possible Bride saw into the deepest recesses of Mairi's heart, too, but she hoped not. Her goddess' personal wrath was not something she ever wished to experience.

"It does no good," she said, and went onto her toes and kissed his irresistible lips.

His groan echoed in her mouth and raw need rippled through her as he tugged her close. Silently, she cursed the thickness of her cloak that came between them. How she longed to wrap her naked body around his again, but at least she had the memories of the one glorious night they'd shared. Feverishly, she tangled her fingers in his hair and closed her eyes, reveling in the sensation of having him in her arms once again.

He wrapped his hand around the back of her neck. It was blatantly possessive, and her nipples chafed against her bodice, as damp heat bloomed between her thighs. The earthy aroma of hay and horse mingled with Finn's masculine scent of pine filled woodland glens, igniting her senses. Her breath caught in her throat and desire flooded her blood, and the threat of discovery faded with every erratic beat of her heart.

From a thousand miles away, Briana's startled voice pierced the sensual cocoon. Uncomprehending, Mairi broke the kiss at the same moment as Finn. Panting, they gazed at each other, and only when a frown slashed his brow, did the outside world truly penetrate.

"I wish you good hunting." Briana's voice was unnaturally loud but no less regal for that. It was a warning. Her cousin was trying to protect them and Mairi's heart slammed against her chest, but her fingers refused to release Finn from her grip.

"Mae," he whispered but before she could gather her wits to answer him, a shadow fell across them, and Lord Constantine stood at the entrance to the stall.

She snatched her hands from Finn and heat swept through her at the insolent way Constantine raked his glance over her. His accompanying smile was positively predatory, and indignation spiked through her, smothering the flare of embarrassment at having been caught in such a compromising situation.

"My lady." There was nothing respectful in his tone. "Fotla abounds with delightful intrigues. Forgive my intrusion."

"Constantine." There was a clear threat in Finn's voice as he moved between her and the prince, protecting her from the barbarian's gaze. But even as warmth flooded her at Finn's chivalrous action, concern burned. She didn't want him to suffer any punishment on her behalf, for his lack of respect to his oafish prince.

Constantine laughed. It was not a pleasant sound. "So we're on a first name basis now? I presume the reason you dare to speak to me in such a manner in public is because you have spilled a certain secret to your little redhead. Was disclosing your true bloodline the only way to gain her favor?"

Finn's jaw tightened and she clasped his arm in warning. To be sure, Constantine deserved to be called out on his insult, but she would rather him label her a *little redhead* a thousand times, than have Finn suffer any indignity at the hands of MacAlpin's ill-bred son.

"Enough," Finn growled, and apprehension shivered along her spine. Had he lost his senses? The little she knew of the Scots prince was enough for her to be certain he wouldn't suffer such insolence from a commoner, no matter how well deserved it was.

Briana stepped around the prince, her gaze locking with Mairi. "Lady Mae, if you please."

It was right and proper that she leave with Briana, but she couldn't abandon him to whatever punishment Constantine might deliver in response to Finn's noble defense of her honor. Even though it went against the grain, she dropped him a curtsey. "My lord Constantine, Finn Braeson was kind enough to escort us to the stables to check our horses. I trust his concern for the princess' safety has not caused offense."

"Not at all." Grim amusement threaded through the prince's words. "I merely hope my half-brother hasn't turned your pretty head with promises he has no way of keeping."

My half-brother.

The words echoed through her head. They were perfectly clear and unambiguous. And made no earthly sense at all.

Finn did not possess the tainted royal blood of MacAlpin. The very idea turned her stomach. She forgot about her masquerade as a noblewoman and gave Constantine a scathing glare. "You underestimate the women of Pictland if you believe our heads can be turned by such shallow assertations."

She scarcely realized Briana was by her side until her cousin gripped her arm. "Mae, we should leave." There was a brittle note in her voice, but Mairi had no intention of leaving yet. Why didn't Finn defend himself against such slander? She could think of nothing worse than being linked to that barbaric usurper.

Constantine smirked. It was obvious he was enjoying this enraging encounter. "Why don't you ask your lover for the truth, my lady? I'm sure he—"

"Shut your filthy mouth." Finn lunged at Constantine and for a terrifying second, Mairi was certain he was about to punch the prince in the face. "The Lady Mae and I are not lovers, and you won't tarnish her reputation by spreading such rumors."

Unease twisted through her. Finn's gallantry was touching and yet...

A man risked his very head for speaking in such a way to his royal master.

Constantine shrugged, but she didn't miss the anger that flashed in his eyes. "It's of no consequence to me either way. Douse your temper before it lands you in more trouble than even our father would be willing to extract you from. I came to tell you we're ready to start the hunt, so make haste, brother."

With that, he gave Briana a stiff bow, before marching from the stables.

A deathly silence descended. So thick, it seemed a fog had filled the stables making it hard to even see clearly, never mind breathe. She sucked in a sharp breath, but it didn't help ease the galloping of her heart or stop the frenzied spinning of her mind.

Finn had been eloquent in praise of his mother but had told her he couldn't speak of his father. She'd assumed he was the product of an illicit affair, and she was right. But she had never come close to guessing the truth.

Finn Braeson was the bastard son of Kenneth MacAlpin.

"Mae." He held out his hand and she recoiled. He froze as though she had mortally wounded him, but she was only seeing what she wanted to see. Everything about him was a lie, and bitter mockery at how easily she'd been duped thundered through her head.

But maybe there was a simple explanation. There had to be. Even if she couldn't imagine what it might be.

"Is it true?" Thank the goddess that she sounded cold and remote, when inside she was a seething mess. "Or does Constantine lie?"

It was the only thread of hope she had, but it withered when Finn flinched, as though her words had flayed his soul.

"MacAlpin is my sire." He sounded surly that his subterfuge had been uncovered but what had he hoped to gain by concealing such a thing from her?

He wasn't to know she would not have looked at him twice if she'd been aware of his bloodline.

Keep telling yourself that.

She ignored that tiny voice in the back of her mind. She would *not* have succumbed to Finn's charms, had she known. But why had he kept the truth from her?

A chilling answer pierced through her.

Because the Scots wanted information on the Princess of Fortriu, and he needed to gain my trust. A trust she would never have given, had she known he was really a prince of Dal Riada.

A horrified gasp escaped as another possibility whipped her

scrambled thoughts. Had Finn guessed her heritage, right from the start? Had this all been an elaborate trap?

"Mae," he said again, although this time he didn't attempt to touch her. "Let me explain. This isn't how it appears."

Did he think her an utter fool? He had played her once. She would not allow him to do so again. "There's nothing to explain. Now go. Your royal brother awaits."

The foul words burned her tongue, but she didn't wait for him to leave. She wasn't certain she would be able to maintain her calm façade for much longer, and she would rather die than let him witness her falling apart. Instead, she turned with Briana and walked out of the stables, head held high, even though all she wanted to do was find a nearby cave and crawl into it.

She half expected him to follow her, but he didn't. Her fingers were icy, and her stomach churned, and she refused to think of anything except for the need to return to the palace as swiftly as possible.

They skirted the milling crowd in the courtyard and in silence made their way to Briana's bedchamber. Mairi stood by the fire, gazing at the flames, but all she saw was Finn's face and how he had confirmed that MacAlpin was his sire.

"Sit." Briana brought a stood to the fire and firmly pushed her down upon it. "I don't know what to say to comfort you."

"There is nothing to say." She gripped her fingers together on her lap. "I have been a fool, Briana. The queen was right. I should have remained hidden within this chamber when the Scots descended upon us."

"No, you haven't been foolish." There was a fierce note in her cousin's voice. "The Scots' deception is not your fault."

Perhaps not. But the knowledge she had so easily tumbled into the arms of the son of her sworn enemy would haunt her forever. What now of those precious memories of the night she and Finn had shared? No longer would they warm her in the endless years that stretched ahead.

They would taunt her. A twisted mockery of everything she'd believed had blossomed between them.

Her head drooped and she squeezed her eyes shut. She had been so sure Bride had placed Finn in her path so she might enjoy a fleeting glimpse of a different life.

But she'd misread the signs. Her goddess hadn't wanted her to fall for Finn's charms.

Right from the start, Bride had been warning her against the Scot. And she had chosen not to see, because Finn had dazzled her.

Yet if that were true, why had he invaded her nightmares, and led her to safety?

Stop. She was making excuses for her foolishness. She needed to beg Bride for her forgiveness and beseech that the goddess give her clarity.

But first, she needed to get far away from Finn.

Her heart ached but there was nothing else for it. "I must leave Fotla-eviot."

Briana clasped her hand. "Do you truly believe you're in any more danger now than you were yesterday? To be sure, you must avoid Braeson, but there's no reason to suppose he knows your true identity."

Perhaps not. But she couldn't shake the overpowering urge to flee.

"I cannot risk it."

Briana squeezed her hand. "But the Scots are leaving after their hunt. There is no need for you to go."

She shook her head. "Just because they're no longer welcome in the palace, doesn't mean they intend to leave Fotla. We have no way of knowing how long it will be before they break camp."

Briana pressed her lips together before letting out a harsh breath. "This is intolerable. There must be another way."

"There isn't." And then, a terrible revelation crashed through her, and fear crushed her breast. "Goddess. Briana, Finn knows of our secret escape routes."

Nausea churned and she swallowed down the dread. He wouldn't betray such a thing. But he was the son of MacAlpin, and MacAlpin possessed no honor. Blood was everything, and if the Scots needed to breach the palace's fortifications, then she had given Finn the perfect map.

How many other secrets did I spill to him? Too many. Because she had trusted him.

The enemy of her people.

CHAPTER 18

To hell with etiquette. Finn gritted his teeth and broke ranks, galloping ahead of the hunting party. It wasn't enough to douse the rage thundering through his blood or ease the savage ache in his chest, but at least it meant he didn't need to engage with his fellow warriors.

The shock, *the betrayal*, on Mae's face when she had discovered his heritage ate into him like acid. He'd watched the fragile tendrils of trust that had grown between them shatter like shards of ice beneath an ax.

He hadn't wanted MacAlpin's acknowledgement. But he hadn't imagined making that connection known would be so devastating.

As soon as this damn hunt was over, he needed to see her. God alone knew how he'd manage it, since it was clear she wanted nothing more to do with him. But he couldn't leave Fotla without first speaking with her again.

To beg for her forgiveness, for keeping the truth from her. Even if it had been commanded of him by his king.

Constantine drew level with him. Finn refused to give the other man the satisfaction of glancing his way. But it was more than that. Finn wasn't certain that if he looked at the prince, he'd be able to keep himself from throttling his half-brother.

Oblivious to the danger, Constantine drew even closer. "You gave yourself away, brother." He appeared to take satisfaction in acknowledging the kinship between them, but Finn was under no illusion as to why. It had nothing to do with Constantine having accepted Finn's recent elevation in status. "No rank-and-file warrior speaks to his betters in such a manner and gets away with his life."

The ground was uneven, and the forest closed in, and there was no choice but to slow down. He still refused to glance at Constantine because, fuck it, he was right. Finn had laid the trap himself. If Constantine hadn't run him through with his sword back at the stables for Finn's insolence, the prince would have lost respect.

Yet, despite the fallout, he couldn't regret it. He would allow no man, prince or not, to besmirch the reputation of Lady Mae without repercussions.

MacAllister rode up alongside Constantine. "Is anything amiss, my lords?"

The honorific still grated, coming from the king's man, and Finn ignored him. Not that MacAllister was really asking for his opinion, in any case.

"There's nothing wrong with Finn that a good fuck wouldn't resolve. It appears his pretty little redhead is averse to parting her thighs for him."

Don't react. All Constantine wanted was to provoke him into a fight, and God damn it, he was sorely tempted. But he'd far rather accept this mockery of his inability to secure a noble-woman's favor than have anyone guess the truth.

Mae had trusted him, and the knowledge of their night together would go with him to the grave.

"Indeed." MacAllister's voice was neutral, but Finn shot him a sharp glance, for some reason not trusting the man's unquestioning acceptance. He gritted his teeth and once again concentrated ahead. What the hell was wrong with him? MacAllister could not possibly know of his night with Mae. "Then may I take it, my lord, that the lady in question could provide no answers to assist us on our quest?"

Since MacAllister was clearly now speaking to him, Finn took grim satisfaction in responding. "She most certainly could not."

"Lady Mae," Constantine remarked, "appears unable to do very much at all."

With difficulty, Finn relaxed his death grip on the reins. With no reaction to his jibes, the prince would lose interest and move onto another form of entertainment. But injustice burned through his chest. Mae deserved to be defended. Yet if he did, it would bring too much attention onto her.

He swung away from Constantine and raked his gaze at the surrounding forest. Up ahead, high in the trees, a flash of light caught his eye. It was wrong and unnatural, and primal warning streaked through him.

Instinctively, he lunged at Constantine, pushing him off balance, at the same moment as an arrow hissed through the air and embedded itself in the prince's shoulder. Constantine reeled, MacAllister yelled, and Finn took off after the would-be assassin.

He was soon joined by several other warriors, and they combed the area but found nothing. Ewan pulled up beside him. "What do you think? A lone peasant with a grudge, or something more sinister?"

"Why would the Fotla king order the assassination of Constantine on his own land? MacAlpin would burn the kingdom to the ground."

Ewan grunted. "Thanks to your quick reflexes, the prince still lives. You should receive a goodly boon from MacAlpin for such a service."

He'd received more than enough from MacAlpin to last him a lifetime. Nothing good ever came from being in the king's sights.

They made their way back to Constantine. MacAllister had broken the arrow, but the head remained embedded in the prince's shoulder.

"The Picts will pay for this outrage," Constantine said between his teeth as they rode back to Fotla-eviot.

"I'm certain the king of Fotla will do everything possible to hunt down those who sought to harm you, my lord," MacAllister said. "They have no wish to threaten this alliance between our people."

"Damn arrow missed my throat by mere inches."

"Thanks to Braeson, my lord." MacAllister shot Finn a glance he couldn't decipher, but it looked calculating. Let him think what he liked. Finn had acted on pure instinct, honed from endless hours of training and bloodied combat on the battle-fields. There had been no strategy behind it.

Constantine clenched his jaw. Clearly, he didn't relish being in Finn's debt.

On MacAllister's orders, they didn't return to their camp but instead approached the palace. It was obvious the king's man was going to milk this situation for as much as he could. Finn didn't care what MacAllister did, but if it gave them an extra day or two within Fotla-eviot, it meant there was more chance he could speak with Mae.

As if conjured by his thoughts, he saw Bhaic emerge from the stables. Finn's heart slammed against his chest as he waited for Mae to appear, but she did not. Instead, he caught the stony glare the old man leveled his way. It was clear that Mae and the princess were not the only Picts who now knew of his royal bloodline.

They remained mounted, while MacAllister sent a message to the king. As word got out, the courtyard filled with curious Picts, but Mae was not among them. He craned his neck, searching for Bhaic, but the man had disappeared.

It was unnerving, being the center of attention in this way. He glanced to his side, expecting to see Ewan, but it was Constantine. Behind the prince, was MacAllister. And behind him, the rest of the warriors.

How the fuck had he ended up at the head of the party with Constantine? It couldn't have happened without MacAllister's aid. He twisted around and caught Ewan's quizzical glance. And he wasn't the only one. Shit. Had MacAllister decided to let Finn's newly bestowed rank become common knowledge?

No. Why would he? It wasn't up to the king's man to make such decisions. Constantine's growl penetrated his thoughts. "I could fucking die out here."

"Not unless the arrowhead is poisoned."

Constantine grunted, apparently not appreciating his retort. "They're all fucking barbarians. Do not leave my side when their physician attends to me."

That got his attention. "But that's MacAllister's duty. He'll ensure no harm befalls you."

Constantine leaned forward. Sweat streaked his face and his eyes were glazed. "Aye. He does his job well enough. But MacAllister isn't of my blood."

Finn didn't respond. There was nothing to say. He and Constantine had always shared the same blood, but until MacAlpin had acknowledged him, it had meant nothing.

It would always mean nothing to him. It was the reason he had no chance of a future with Mae.

BHAIC ENTERED BRIANA'S ANTECHAMBER, where Mairi and the two ladies who had accompanied her during her exile were packing her belongings. She had made the decision to leave, and it needed to be done quickly, before the Scots returned from their hunt.

"Are the horses ready?" she asked, although she couldn't think how. Bhaic had only left her a short time ago. And she was still waiting for an audience with the queen, to let her know of her plans.

"The Dal Riadans have returned, Madam."

"What?" She clutched his arm as her heart pounded in her chest and her mind filled with the image of Finn. No. She couldn't think of him. Not ever, but most especially not now when she needed all her wits about her.

A terrible certainty gripped her. There was only one reason why a hunt would be abandoned. "Was someone injured?"

And by *someone*, she meant *Finn*. But surely not. He had deceived her, but she didn't wish harm to befall him. Even if he deserved it.

"Their eldest prince." The contempt in Bhaic's voice conveyed his opinion on that.

Relief streaked through her. At least Finn had suffered no broken bones and as for Constantine...

"No doubt his arrogance finally caught up with him." Bitterness seeped into the last words. How could she escape Fotla-eviot now, without the Scots knowledge? Even if they had no idea who she was, a noblewoman leaving the palace with heavily laden wagons and several dozen warriors would be sure to capture their attention.

"Indeed. But their prince didn't fall from his horse. They were ambushed in the forest and there was an attempted assassination."

"Goddess." She spun about, so she was no longer facing Bhaic. He had only mentioned the prince. Which meant Finn was unharmed. She sucked in a jagged breath and briefly closed her eyes.

Focus.

It was imperative she leave the Kingdom of Fotla as quickly as possible. She simply needed to come up with an adjusted plan on how to evade the Scots' prying eyes. Decision made, she once again faced the older man.

"We must split the contingent. Three quarters will accompany the wagons to the border of Fotla, and we will meet them there later. It will draw less attention if I ride with only a small band of warriors."

Bhaic frowned. He clearly disapproved of the plan but before he could voice his dissent, there was a knock on the door. Struana answered, and a few moments later came over to Mairi.

"Madam." She dropped a curtsey but there was a worried note in her voice. "The king has ordered additional guards be posted to protect you. There are two new ones outside the door, and we have been commanded to remain within this chamber until further notice."

Mairi battened down her panic and inclined her head. It wouldn't do to show her disquiet to her loyal companion. Whatever the king's motives, she was now effectively a prisoner in the palace. "Thank you. We shall simply have to wait a little longer before leaving."

Once Struana had returned to her tasks, Mairi faced Bhaic. He gave a single nod, understanding her unspoken command.

"I'll find out all that I can," he murmured, before giving her a bow and leaving the chamber.

MAIRI PEERED through the narrow window of the bedchamber. The sun had passed its zenith, and Bhaic had been gone for hours. She twisted her fingers together, unable to help herself, but not knowing what was happening was driving her to distraction.

Why hadn't Briana come to her? Or was she, also, forbidden to freely navigate the palace?

A chilling thought occurred to her. Had Constantine died of his injuries? Was the court of Fotla effectively now under siege from the vengeful Scots?

Inevitably, Finn filled her mind and pain stabbed through her breast. She had thought him so honorable. A commoner, with noble blood, and integrity that would not have disgraced the highest born Pict.

But he had entered Fotla under false pretenses. Her foolish heart might not wish any harm to come to him, but she would do well to remember that she could no longer trust him.

After all, betrayal ran in his blood. Six months ago, his own father had slaughtered nine Pictish nobles who could claim matrilineal lineage to the throne of Fortriu.

She wrapped her arms around her waist and exhaled a shaky breath. There had never been any doubt in her mind that the Scots were hunting her. But she couldn't work out the strategy behind their decision to conceal Finn's royal heritage.

Except the kernel of dread that had cracked open when she'd first discovered who he was, would not die. Had Finn deliberately followed her outside the night they'd met, because he knew who she really was?

Yet if the Scots knew she was the missing princess, why hadn't they killed her already? It made no sense. She would *not* believe Finn had deceived her so utterly.

Struana entered the bedchamber and came to her side. "Madam, the queen requests an audience with you."

Finally. But as she tugged her shawl more securely around her, unease flickered. Too much had happened since she had made that request. As she and Struana followed the guard who had come to collect them, a question gnawed in her mind, no matter how she tried to quell it.

Why was the queen truly sending for her?

CHAPTER 19

*M*airi was ushered into the queen's inner sanctum, leaving Struana and the queen's own ladies in the antechamber. Briana rose from her stool beside her mamma and came to greet her.

"Did you hear the news? Lord Constantine was shot and is now ensconced within the palace with our healer."

"I heard."

The queen stood and paced the floor. "There was nothing else to be done. That odious MacAllister made it clear that should the prince die from this attack, his king would personally hold the Royal House of Fotla responsible."

"That is outrageous." Mairi glanced at her cousin, before adding, "It was not a sanctioned attempt at assassination, I am sure."

"Certainly not." The queen's voice was cool, as though the mere suggestion offended her. "However, that fact barely signifies. We have been assured by the royal healer that his wound will mend without complications, but nevertheless, this attack puts us in a vulnerable position."

Yes, it did. Mairi had been so wrapped up in her own

heartache, and the desperate need to flee, that she hadn't given the political ramifications much thought.

The oversight was unforgiveable. She could not allow her personal feelings to blind her to the security of Pictland.

"Father has sent word to the local villages," Briana said, "but it's doubtful the culprit will be found. No one would mourn the death of the foreign prince. Too much Pictish blood has been spilled by the Scots."

"The reward offered might loosen some tongues." The queen drew in a deep breath before sighing. "Our personal feelings do not matter. We cannot afford another war with the Scots, and they know it."

It was true. Too many hostages were still held in Dal Riada, MacAlpin's insurance to keep the Pictish kingdoms in line.

Mairi forced the familiar, futile, anger back into its cage. One day she might face the upstart king, but today she needed to leave Fotla. Not just for her own safety, but for the royal family's, too.

"Madam, I request your leave to depart the court as soon as possible. I fear it's no longer safe for me to remain within the Kingdom of Fotla."

The queen inclined her head but didn't meet her eyes. "You are correct. This shift in dynamics has put us all in danger. Even if the prince recovers without any consequences, the brittle trust between the Scots king and Fotla has been irreparably damaged."

"Then it's imperative the would-be assassin is found." Briana didn't sound happy about it.

"Indeed." The queen finally ceased pacing the chamber and stood in front of her chair. "However, there is another way to ensure lasting peace, whether or not the failed assassin is brought to justice."

Unease skittered along Mairi's senses, and it seemed the very air thickened around her. She resisted the overwhelming urge to twist her fingers together and instead clutched her shawl more tightly. There was no need for this alarm, and yet her stomach churned, regardless.

"What other way?" Briana asked and Mairi held her breath. Her jagged thoughts were madness. Her suspicions were wrong.

Let me be wrong.

With seeming reluctance, the queen caught her gaze. "The Scots are eager to forge an alliance between their king's bloodline and the missing Princess of Fortriu. Should the princess surrender to the Scots, Fotla's fortunes would be reversed and the insult against their prince eliminated."

No. *No.*

A wild buzzing filled her head and her heart thundered so fiercely it hurt her chest. In the far distance she heard Briana's shocked exclamation.

"You cannot be serious, Mamma. Mae cannot possibly sacrifice herself to the Scots."

"We speak of marriage into the House of Alpin, not execution."

There was no difference. If she wed the Scots' king, she might as well be dead. And likely would be, before the next full moon.

How wrong she had been to imagine Bride had set her on this path. She should have taken heed of the warning from Cailleach, when the Blood Moon had filled the winter skies. Whatever message Briana had received from Bride had not been meant for Mairi.

And now, because she had been so desperate for a respite from the burden of being a fugitive, and because she'd wanted to be with her kin, she was trapped in MacAlpin's deadly web.

"No." The denial burst from her before she could prevent it. "Tell them Mairi, Princess Annella of Fortriu is dead. Tell them you saw her lifeless body with your own eyes."

"Yes, Mamma." Briana came to her side and took her chilled hand. "How can they prove otherwise? We cannot allow Mae to enter Dal Riada."

The queen closed her eyes for a brief moment before once again focusing on Mairi. "Think what you're saying, Mairi. You can unite the supreme royal house of Pictland with the royal lineage of Dal Riada. This alliance will prevent more bloodshed between our people and strengthen our force against the Vikings."

Mairi couldn't remain silent. "The Scots need us as much as we need them to keep the Vikings at bay. They will not risk war with us, when the Vikings take every opportunity to plunder their sacred Isle of Iona."

"Perhaps." There was an edge in the queen's voice now. "But is this a risk we should take? Your new elevated status will ensure you can negotiate from within the inner circle itself, for the liberation of the Picts that remain hostage in Dunadd."

Mairi's breath caught in her throat. How could the queen be so naive? She wasn't ignorant of the barbaric ways of the Scots. Unlike in Pictland, where royal wives held a great deal of power behind the throne, they both knew women had no voice in the Dal Riadan political sphere.

"Madam, if I agree to this farce of a marriage to the king of the Scots, I shall be dead before the sun rises the following morning."

"MacAlpin?" Distaste dripped from the word and the queen shook her head. "No, Mairi. That is not the alliance he proposes. He wishes to unite the Princess of Fortriu with his son, Finn Braeson."

Her throat closed and chest tightened, and she struggled to suck air into her starved lungs. Shadows darkened in the corners of the chamber, and the walls themselves seemed to close in on her.

Finn.

The upstart king wanted her to wed his bastard son.

Knife sharp pain plunged through her heart, and it took every particle of her strength not to crumple to the floor. She was the reason they had come to Fotla, but her dark suspicions had been true. Finn *had* known who she was all along. And that was the reason why he had pursued her that first night when she had gazed at the moon.

Her masquerade had not fooled the Scots for a moment. Finn had always known MacAlpin's plans. Yet how sincere he had sounded when they'd spoken of a future they could never share.

We could wed in secret. I'd carry you away in the dead of night to a remote hillfort and keep you all to myself.

His passionate confession had melted her heart. Stolen her senses. When in truth all he had told her was the fate that awaited her.

The sharp grip of Briana's hand squeezing hers brought her brutally back to the present. The queen gave a smile that didn't reach her eyes.

"This would not be too terrible. You find Braeson agreeable. And do not forget, Bride herself approves of this union. Why else would she have given you the visions?"

Goddess, forgive her. Surely, Bride had been warning her to stay away from the Scot. Not find every opportunity she could to cross his path. Mairi had allowed her infatuation for Finn to blind her to the truth.

Bride had not intended for them to become lovers at all.

She stiffened her spine and caught the queen's reluctance eyes. "Am I to understand that the Scots have been informed of my presence in Fotla-eviot?"

"There was no need. MacAllister appeared to be privy to this knowledge already. Mairi, I gave you my word to protect you, and I would never have given you up. But our strategy has been uncovered."

Panic swirled through her, making her dizzy. She had begged Bride for more time with Finn. And her goddess, rightly irked by Mairi's inability to grasp the danger she was in, had granted her wish.

A lifetime shackled to the only man she had ever wanted. The man who shared a bloodline with her greatest enemy.

"Mae." Her cousin's urgent voice penetrated the fog threatening to pull her under and she sucked in a sharp breath. Briana turned to the queen. "We shall throw a great feast tonight and ply the Scots with drugged wine. Once they're insensible, we can smuggle Mae to safety."

For a brief moment, she wallowed in the picture her cousin painted before it faded like the mirage it was. It was an impossible plan. The repercussions would be too great.

"Pray, do not make this more difficult than it already is." The queen drew in a deep breath. "Briana, bring my ladies into the chamber. I must send word to MacAllister."

Mairi felt the shudder that ran through her cousin. "Forgive me, Mamma. I will be no part of this betrayal of my beloved Mae."

A stricken expression flashed over the queen's face, gone in an instant.

"Very well." The queen tilted her head in a regal manner, before sweeping from the chamber. When the door shut behind her, Briana turned to face Mairi.

"This is my fault. If I hadn't persuaded you to come to Fotla-eviot, you would still be safe."

"No. You followed the word of the goddess." It would do no good to tell Briana that she feared they had both misunderstood Bride. Her cousin would never forgive herself. "I fear that sooner or later, the Scots would have hunted me down, no matter where I fled."

"Nevertheless, I shall never forgive Mamma for this. We are kin. You don't give up your own blood."

Mairi's squeezed Briana's hand. How odd, that she should comfort her cousin, when it was her own life that was about to shatter around her. Yet, oddly, now the first shock had sunk into her, she didn't bear any malice against the queen, the woman who had been her own mother's dearest friend.

The queen had her kingdom to think of.

But as for Finn…

Her blood burned and heart raced within her breast. Oh, how she had fallen for his sweet lies and flawless deception. How amused he must have been by her gullibility.

At how she had so willingly given him her maidenhead.

It was galling, but she had spoken the truth to Briana. The Scots would never have given up searching for her. She had kept her promise to Nechtan, but it hadn't been enough to keep her safe.

The time for fleeing was over. Now, she had to face the reality of her future.

CHAPTER 20

Finn stood by the narrow window in the chamber adjacent to the palace's kitchens where Constantine had been taken, his arms crossed, watching as the Pict healer finally left. Constantine eyed his bandaged shoulder and gave a suspicious snort.

"Do these Pictish savages know anything of the healing arts? The man didn't even consider bleeding me."

"He appeared competent." Finn strode to the prince's side. "How do you feel?"

"Enraged."

Finn took that as a good sign. Constantine spent half his life enraged. "Doubtless the culprit will be found and dealt with."

"I will deal with him personally."

Finn shrugged. He wasn't going to argue the point. It had been hours since Constantine had been attacked, and he was tired of listening to the prince's endless threats of retribution. "I'll find MacAllister."

It would give him the opportunity to escape this chamber and find Mae. Somehow, he was determined to speak with her. Even if he had to manufacture an excuse for her to consent to see him.

He couldn't leave Fotla with her thinking he had deliberately lied to her. Even if, in effect, he had. Surely, she would understand why, when he explained the full truth to her?

Before he had the chance to leave, there was a knock on the door and MacAllister entered. He shut the door behind him before giving a bow that clearly encompassed Finn as well as Constantine.

He bit back his impatience. It was obvious the man had something of importance to convey, given the satisfied gleam in his eye and smirk on his face.

MacAllister approached Constantine and enquired after his health, which gave the prince another opportunity to vent his spleen. Finn edged closer to the door. He had been mistaken. MacAllister had no news, he merely wished to ensure his master's son was still alive.

He eased open the door, before giving a perfunctory bow in Constantine's general direction. "My lord."

MacAllister swung around. "I have uncovered the information we seek."

Finn froze, his fingers clenched around the iron door ring, as MacAllister's words thundered through his head.

He could mean only one thing. The elusive princess had been found.

Or evidence had been provided of her death. But if that were the case, the king's man would not look nearly so pleased with himself.

A sick sensation settled deep in his gut, and he pushed the heavy wooden door closed once again. Its dull thud as it slammed shut echoed in his chest like a death knell.

Mae would never consent to seeing him again once the true purpose of the Scots visit to Fotla was announced.

Once she discovered he was to be shackled to the Princess of Fortriu.

"You found the princess?" Constantine apparently forgot

about his injury as he leaned forward on his stool, his attention focused on MacAllister. "Where is she?"

MacAllister spared the prince a glance, before returning his attention to Finn. "The princess has been in front of our eyes this entire time, my lord."

With difficulty, Finn released his death grip on the door ring and folded his arms. An answer was expected from him, but what was there to say?

"Has she, indeed?" Constantine leaned back against the wall. "A bold plan. Where was she hiding? Is she one of the queen's ladies?"

Finn exhaled a ragged breath through his teeth. The chamber was too small, and the air had vanished. He needed to get outside, find his horse. Ride into the mountains, or the glens. Hell, anywhere would do but here, in this chamber, where his chest was being crushed and he was slowly suffocating.

"She is one of the ladies of the court, my lord. I'm instructed to bring my lord Finn to the King of Fotla's inner sanctum immediately."

"I shall accompany you." Constantine pushed himself to his feet.

It was bad enough the princess had been found and Finn was trapped. But to have Constantine by his side when he faced the king, and his future bride, curdled his blood.

"My lord, you must rest and regain your strength for our imminent journey back to Dunadd," MacAllister said. "The king is eager to ensure you have every comfort while you recover from this outrage. If it pleases you, he has arranged a private feast and entertainment as a small recompense for your suffering."

Constantine frowned, clearly considering the matter. "Very well. Doubtless I shall meet with the king later, to finalize this matter to our satisfaction."

Finn swung on his heel and pulled open the door. Two servants were there and MacAllister instructed them to wait upon the prince. In silence, he and the king's man left the kitchens through a side entrance, and the brisk highland wind whipped through him, the tinge of ice in the air clearing the paralyzing fog in his brain.

How had the elusive Princess of Fortriu so suddenly been discovered? He turned to MacAllister.

"How can we be certain that the king is not lying to us? This lady he's presented could be any Pictish noblewoman."

"Your skepticism is well placed, my lord. However, I'm certain we have found the missing princess."

"You may be certain of it, MacAllister, but that doesn't make it true."

The palace loomed by his side, separated from the kitchens by a short stone passageway, and they were rapidly approaching the main entrance. He halted, and turned his back on the palace, fixing his gaze on the snow-capped mountains in the distance. MacAllister came to his side, but remained two steps behind, an acknowledgment of Finn's royal bloodline even though they were alone.

"I've had my suspicions since the day after we arrived. The king merely confirmed them when, in the name of the King of the Scots, I pressed him for an answer."

Bitterness burned through his chest. "An answer he was willing to divulge, to avert repercussions for the attack on Constantine."

"It's true this new loyalty to our king goes greatly in Fotla's favor."

A dark suspicion of his own stirred. "One might think the attempted assassination came at a most fortuitous time."

"It helped our cause, there is no doubt."

Finn turned until his gaze met the unblinking stare of MacAllister's. "Do you know any more of this attempt on the prince's life than you're sharing?"

MacAllister's countenance might have been made of stone. "That would be treason, my lord."

Aye, it would. It was treason to even think such a thing. But his birthright had been acknowledged by the king. He was now a prince of that cursed bloodline, and as such he would not remain silent. "Yet the fact remains, this discovery is remarkably convenient."

"It was an unexpected turn of events, but it's always wise to make use of any situation to our advantage."

Finn had no doubt MacAllister had used all his considerable talents for persuasion when it came to showing the Fotla king how much his kingdom could gain by aligning with MacAlpin.

And how much he could lose, if MacAlpin chose to take offense at the attack on his eldest son.

"If I might be so bold?" MacAllister indicated they should continue onto the palace. And unless he planned on storming the walls in a futile effort to hunt down the whereabouts of Mae, there was not much else he could do but fall into step beside the other man. "I believe you'll find the princess to be a most agreeable royal wife."

Finn clenched his teeth to keep his scathing response from escaping. MacAllister already saw too much, knew too much. He'd not give the other man any more ammunition with unwary replies.

But by God, it was hard. This political marriage would be anything but agreeable, and MacAllister knew it.

At least the older man kept his mouth shut until they were greeted by the King of Fotla's men and escorted to the inner sanctum. With every step he took as they went deep inside the ancient stone palace, his future closed in on him like a deadly mantle.

As they stood before the double doors that led to the king's inner sanctum, he threw back his shoulders and set his face into a mask.

He cared nothing for the dignity of the House of Alpin, but he would not disgrace his mother's name by presenting as anything less than a warrior who was sworn to undertake his king's command.

The doors swung open. The chamber was small and filled with a disorientating fusion of vibrantly attired members of the royal family, and the queen's ladies, and a contingent of warriors flanked the walls.

But his gaze arrowed onto the only one who mattered. Mae, seated on the queen's throne.

His heart slammed against his ribs. Christ, no. This entire farce was bad enough, but for her to witness it was a nightmare he had never imagined. She didn't meet his agonized gaze but appeared focused on the empty nothingness above his left shoulder.

Before he could stop himself, he took a couple of strides towards the dais. Instantly, two Pict warriors blocked his path by clashing their swords together to form a cross. A ceremonial display of force, maybe, but it was enough to stop him in his tracks.

The king raised his hand, the warriors stepped back, and Finn reluctantly tore his eyes from Mae to acknowledge the king. But confusion thudded through his brain as finally the incomprehensible tableau penetrated his tangled thoughts.

Everyone in the chamber was standing. Everyone but Mae.

The strangeness prickled through his mind, glimmers of something just out of reach, but he had no time to push through the encroaching shadows and find the answer. The king stepped forward and Finn dragged his attention back to the present.

"You, then, are the favored bastard son of Kenneth MacAlpin." The king spoke in Gaelic and the note of contempt in his voice was palpable. Finn didn't care what the king called him. He'd been called worse. But he'd never been referred to as MacAlpin's favored son before.

Every sense he possessed demanded he glance Mae's way. To

reassure her that in this, at least, he hadn't lied. He was no favored son, merely a valuable tool now the king had use for him. But to look at another when the King of Fotla was addressing him would be an insult of the highest order.

He bowed his head. The king was waiting for his reply, and he knew full well the answer expected of him. But here, when it mattered the most, he would not forsake the honor of the woman who had given up everything for him.

"My name is Finn Braeson, sire."

It seemed an intangible breeze rippled through the court, as glances were exchanged. From the corner of his eye, he could just see Mae. In the glow from the many lamps in this windowless chamber, she seemed to sparkle, a disorientating mirage. But she, alone, appeared immune to the fact he had failed to push his blood connection to the royal House of Alpin.

"We have considered the proposal to join the royal lineage of the Supreme Kingdom of Pictland with that of Dal Riada."

Finn understood the pronouncement. The king acknowledged the kingdom of Dal Riada but refused to recognize MacAlpin's claim to the throne of Fortriu.

Every damn thing was political. He exhaled a shallow breath, and his hungry gaze stole to Mae. She looked so alone. He ached to fall at her feet and beg her forgiveness for this sickening travesty.

Why is she seated on the queen's throne?

"The details of the Princess of Fortriu's dowry need to be addressed," the king said, severing his thoughts. "But in essence, subject to a satisfactory contract, Mairi, Princess Annella of Fortriu accepts this alliance with Finn Braeson, Prince of the House of Alpin."

The queen and Lady Briana held out their hands to Mae, who accepted them as she rose from the throne. A mighty fist punched his gut, sucking the air from his lungs and he stared, bewitched, as Mae finally met his eyes.

There was no trace of the warmth he had grown familiar with over the last few days. They were cold, like the ice of a loch in midwinter. But he barely registered the chill that shivered along his arms. His brain was still reeling.

God in heaven.

Mae was the princess they'd been searching for. The princess he had hoped so fervently never to find.

Mae was his intended bride.

The king was still speaking. MacAllister responded. He had no idea what they were saying. His heart thundered and blood burned, and it took every last shred of self-control he possessed not to stride to Mae and wrap her in his arms.

Her sea-green gown glinted with delicate threads of sapphire and a matching, translucent veil covered her head and draped elegantly over her shoulder. Bejeweled bracelets encircled the tight-fitting sleeves of her gown, from wrist to elbow, and a golden circlet, encrusted with gems, rested upon her head.

The breath caught in his throat. She was not merely a vision whom he had dreamed of since the night they'd met.

She was the woman destined to share his life.

"My lord." MacAllister's low voice invaded his thoughts, but he couldn't drag his gaze from Mae. From the princess. *My bride-to-be.* "We must withdraw, so negotiations may proceed."

Fuck the negotiations. There was something far more important than that. He turned to the king. "Sire, I beg leave to speak with the princess alone."

Another ripple radiated around the court. Clearly, he had breached protocol. But the king didn't have him escorted from the chamber. He turned to Mae, instead, and spoke to her in Pictish.

"Madam, what is your wish in this matter?"

Shock jolted through him. The King of Fotla deferred to her. But then, she was the last living Princess of the Supreme Kingdom of Pictland.

The kingdom that MacAlpin had annexed for Dal Riada.

A sliver of unease chased along his spine. No wonder Mae had been so dismissive of his king. It had been more than a natural disdain for an invading foreigner. It had been personal.

"I will speak with Lord Finn." There was no hint of warmth in her voice, and her use of his royal title scraped his senses. The king waved his hand, and the chamber emptied. Except he and Mae weren't alone as the royal family remained, and so did Bhaic.

She walked to the center of the chamber, looking so regal and untouchable, and nothing like the teasing noblewoman he'd thought he had known. He followed her, since it seemed that was the only privacy they were allowed.

He stopped before her, and suddenly had no idea what to say. And it wasn't because of their audience, whose disapproving eyes he could feel burning into his back.

It was because he didn't know this aloof princess, with her priceless jewels and disdainful air. He needed to find his Mae again.

"It's good to see you." He kept his voice low. The last thing he wanted was to be overheard. "Mae, I had no idea you were the princess."

"You weren't meant to." Her swift retort sent a shaft through his chest. Even though no one could hear their conversation, her voice was like ice. "You were hunting me like a deer, were you not?"

Denial burned through him, but his repudiation lodged in his throat. Because uncovering the whereabouts of the Princess of Fortriu had been the sole purpose of MacAlpin's expedition into Fotla.

But it had never been his. Even before he had met her.

"It's true MacAlpin wanted to find you. But I wasn't hunting you, Mae. You must believe me."

"Must I?" Her eyes glittered like sapphires and although her voice was low like his, venom dripped from each word. "I must believe the word of Lord Finn, Prince of the royal House of Alpin, favored bastard son of Kenneth MacAlpin? Forgive me if I find that beyond my capabilities."

"I'm the same man I was yesterday. Nothing has changed." As soon as the words left his mouth, he regretted them. He hadn't changed, that was true, but in Mae's eyes everything had.

Although that went both ways. He was still reeling from the knowledge she was the elusive Princess of Fortriu.

She tilted her head, as though he had just emitted a foul odor. "Indeed. You are correct. I was a fool to trust my enemy. You have done your father proud."

Her accusation stung, a poisoned barb that dug deep into his heart. Before he could stop himself, he growled, "My father is undeserving of the word."

For a fleeting moment, her mask of icy contempt cracked, and her startled glance was an aching reminder of the Mae he knew. But the glimpse was gone too soon. She narrowed her eyes at him. "Your father is the king of the Scots."

"Aye." To hell with it. They were to be wed, and even if he wanted her to believe MacAlpin cared for him as a son—and he didn't want Mae thinking that, in any case—she would learn the truth soon enough. "But I am my mother's son. I did not lie to you about that, my lady."

She pressed her lips together and he saw a battle rage behind her beautiful eyes. "I am coerced into marrying the son of my bitterest enemy. How can I believe anything you tell me, when you concealed such a thing from me?"

"I swore an oath. I could not break it." *Not even for you.*

"As did I." She bowed her head. "I want to believe you, Finn."

Her words were so soft and filled with anguish, his chest contracted in reflected pain. Unheeding of their audience, or the countless protocols he would undoubtedly break, he took her hand. She didn't pull free.

"You can," he whispered. "I'll never lie to you again. Not even by omission."

She shook her head, a small gesture, and despair replaced the glimmer of hope that had ignited.

"I will always put the good of my people before yours. And you will do the same. There will always be secrets between us, Finn. You know this as well as I."

He understood her concern. But he had to make her see that in this, at least, her worries were unfounded.

"I'm a warrior. Not an adviser to the king. I'm not privy to his political maneuvers. Until he decided I should wed the Princess of Fortriu, I was not acknowledged in the court of Dunadd."

Uncertainty flickered over her face. "You were not brought up in the court of Dunadd?"

He allowed a grim smile to escape. What he was about to say was likely treason, but it was also the truth. "My lady mother was not welcomed at court. Until the day before we left for Fotla, the king did not even recognize my bloodline as his own."

Mae gazed at him, and the last trace of ice melted from her eyes. "You did not help plan this."

It wasn't a question. But he would answer her, nevertheless.

"The missing princess was the last woman in the world I wanted to marry, Mae. Until I saw she was you."

CHAPTER 21

*M*airi stood in the center of Briana's bedchamber, as her ladies carefully removed the jewels she'd worn. News of her status had spread like a plague throughout the palace, and it seemed all the ladies of the court had wanted to assist her, most likely in the hope of gleaning firsthand gossip.

She had dismissed them all, save for her two faithful companions who had accompanied her from Fortriu.

As they packed the priceless Fortriu jewelry, that she had inherited from her foremothers, into their caskets, before placing them into the sturdy chest, Briana finally paused in her agitated pacing of the chamber and stood before her.

"I cannot think of a plan to save you, Mae. I brought you here because I craved your company, but I led you into a trap."

"The trap was not of your making. You must promise me not to blame yourself for anything that happens."

"You're so calm." Briana hitched in a ragged breath. "What did MacAlpin's bastard say to you? You cannot believe a word he says. You must always keep your wits about you."

She knew that. Only too well. The dreams she'd woven of an impossible future with Finn could never be. But perhaps it was possible to forge another kind of future together. One that wouldn't be so terrible, after all.

"He was bound by an oath not to reveal his true identity, just as I was. I cannot blame him for that."

Briana's gaze became incredulous. "He came here with the sole purpose of hunting you down and forcing you into this barbarous marriage."

It was true. Her heart hurt at how she'd been so easily blinded. If she had asked for Bride's wisdom on the matter, instead of foolishly wishing she could spend more time with Finn, would her goddess have helped her to escape this trap before the jaws snapped shut around her?

A tiny flicker of rebellion burned deep within her breast. It was madness. She acknowledged that. But a despicable part of her wanted this marriage to Finn. To the man she had fallen for, not the prince he had turned out to be.

She would die before she shared that with Briana. It was a betrayal of everything she had ever believed in.

But when he'd spoken to her earlier, when he'd told her he meant nothing more to his father than a pawn in the upstart king's game, her defenses had crumbled.

It was true this marriage would never be everything she secretly craved. But if she wished to maintain peace between the Kingdom of Fotla—all of Pictland—and Dal Riada, she had little choice but to agree to MacAlpin's proposal.

It could have been so much worse, after all. They might have wanted her to wed Constantine.

She shuddered at the prospect and took her cousin's hand. "Since there is no diplomatic way out of this, I need to make this marriage work. For Pictland. And Finn is just as trapped in this arrangement as I."

Briana's smile was sad. "A man is never as trapped as a woman when it comes to matrimony."

~

AFTER THEY HAD DINED in the queen's private chamber—a tortuous affair, where the conversation had been stilted and eye contact avoided—they returned to Briana's antechamber. They sat by the fire, along with Mairi's two ladies who were going through her gowns and discussing which ones should be enhanced with new embroidery before her marriage, and Bhaic paced the chamber, a look of thunder on his face.

During her marriage to Nechtan, she had sometimes resented his presence in their lives. But how grateful she was for him now. She knew she could trust him with any secret, and he would sooner cut his own throat than betray her.

How she longed to believe the same of Finn. But it was no use wishing for girlish fantasies. They had shared a wondrous night, but their marriage was based on political stratagems, and she could not afford to forget it.

"Madam." Struana was by her side. She blinked and looked up. Bhaic stood by the door and clearly her lady had a message to convey. She hadn't even been aware anyone had knocked upon the door and that was unforgiveable. No matter what her thoughts, she could never afford to lose herself within them, to the exclusion of what was happening around her.

Hastily, she composed herself. "What is it?"

Struana appeared troubled. "My lord Finn wishes to speak with you."

Her foolish heart leaped at the sound of his name, at the knowledge he had sought her out. Ruthlessly, she crushed the sense of longing. She couldn't allow her feelings to guide her actions, no matter how tempting the notion was.

"Very well." She stood, and Briana stood with her.

"Are you certain this is a good idea?" Her cousin sounded as though it was a terrible one.

"We are betrothed. I will be quite safe with you and my ladies in the adjoining chamber and my lord Bhaic guarding the door."

Finn entered the chamber and she barely noticed when Briana and the ladies withdrew. Bhaic's black glower grazed her for a fleeing moment before he left the antechamber and pulled the door shut behind him and then she was alone with Finn.

He bowed, so formal, and so respectful of her status. She inclined her head and offered him her hand. He strode to her and kissed her bare knuckles, the touch of his fingers igniting slivers of pleasure along her flesh.

"I had to see you." His voice was low, intense, and how easy it would be to drown in the depths of his beautiful eyes. "There are things I need to tell you, Mae, without an audience trying to eavesdrop."

She should correct his use of her name. *Mae* was the one only Briana had used since they were young children. And the one she was known by in Fotla-eviot as part of her subterfuge.

But she liked how he called her Mae. And, after all, he would only use it when they were alone. Irrational or not, it would always remind her of the time they'd shared before their royal duties had encroached into their lives.

She glanced over her shoulder. The door to the bedchamber was slightly ajar, but here, by the fire, there was no likelihood of their conversation being overheard.

By rights, she should retrieve her hand and sit upon the stool, while Finn stood and conveyed his message. But she remained standing, embracing the bittersweet sensation of his fingers clasped around hers.

"What must you tell me?" Thankfully, she sounded calm. It would not do for him to know how his slightest gesture could touch her so deeply. Not now, when their futures were irrevocably entwined.

His grip on her hand tightened, as though he feared she might belatedly attempt to pull free. "I must know if you're agreeable to this marriage or not."

She forced a laugh, to hide the hurt. How could she ever explain to him the turmoil of her thoughts on that matter?

"That is a question, Finn. You said you had something to tell me."

A frown slashed his brow. He appeared tortured by this situation they found themselves in. "Aye. But first I must know what you feel about our intended marriage."

"We scarcely have a choice in it."

He dragged in a jagged breath. "But if we did? Would it please you?"

"You mean if I were merely a Pictish noblewoman, and you nothing more than a Scots warrior?"

"And I asked for your hand. Would you accept?"

Goddess, did he want to break her? It was a future that shimmered on the horizon, forever beyond their reach. But how she wished, deep in her heart, it could be more than an elusive dream.

She gazed at their entwined hands. They were destined to be linked in a political marriage by virtue of their bloodlines. It did not mean they had to hate each other as enemies.

But she could not quite risk opening her heart to him. "Perhaps."

He exhaled a long breath, as though he'd been holding it. "If I hadn't been bound to the unknown Princess of Fortriu, I would have asked, Mae. You're the only woman I've ever wanted as my bride. Yet I have so little to offer a gently born noblewoman, let alone a princess."

"Oh." She smiled. She could risk that much, surely. "I believe you have a lot to offer, Finn. Are you seeking compliments?"

Some of the tension seemed to seep from him at her teasing response. Maybe they could make this work. She *wanted* to make this work, between them, at least.

But what of my vow to destroy the upstart king?

She pushed the unpleasant reminder to the back of her mind. There would be time enough to form strategies once they were in Dunadd. Devising a way to bring about the downfall of MacAlpin and hoping for a congenial marriage with his son were not necessarily mutually exclusive, after all.

A sword through the heart was not the only way to destroy a king.

"I'm serious." He pressed her hand against his heart and despite her best intentions, another layer of her ice melted. "My hillfort, Duncarn, is in a remote corner of Dal Riada. It doesn't possess the luxuries of a Pictish palace."

She recalled their conversation in the church. "The hillfort where your mother and sisters reside?"

"Aye." He sounded reluctant to admit it. "They cannot leave, Mae."

She wouldn't expect them to. But then, she had never expected she would share her household with another mistress.

The status of her birth ensured she would always outrank any royal Pictish woman. But the mother of her husband had her own standing. And besides, his mother and sisters were Scots and therefore who knew how they would react to her presence?

Uncertainty and a slither of fear curled through her. She buried them deep before they could take hold and crack her composure.

In truth, the fortune in jewels she had taken from Forteviot could purchase a magnificent palace, and that wasn't counting the strategic stronghold in Fib that she'd inherited from Nechtan. But her fortune was the heritage handed down from generations of her foremothers.

It was the heritage of the Royal House of Fortriu.

Fortriu, which was now occupied by MacAlpin and his Scots.

"I see." She wasn't sure what else she could say, or even what Finn expected from her.

"It's not grand," Finn said. "But my mother and sisters will welcome you, Mae. And I swear to you, I'll find a way to build you the palace you deserve."

Warmth flooded her heart, easing the pain that had taken up residence since she'd discovered who he really was. "I was not aware that the Scots were capable of building a palace."

He smiled and for the first time since the revelation of his identity, it reached his eyes, and she was lost. "You shall be the architect, and it will be built to your specifications." He paused and pressed her hand a little tighter to his chest. "It might take me years to fund this project, but I shall make it a priority."

She didn't need a palace, but it was true that the people of Pictland needed to see she was being given the respect due to the Princess of Fortriu, even if she had been displaced from the Supreme Kingdom.

"You will not have to fund it alone, Finn. I am not a penniless bride."

A dark cloud chased across his features as though her words, meant to reassure, had instead the opposite effect. "I won't touch your dowry."

"I know that." Her grandfather had ensured she understood the machinations involved when it came to politics, and she'd attended many assemblies with him, even after her marriage. But although she wouldn't be invited into the negotiations for this alliance, one thing was certain. Her fortune was her own and could not be ceded to a husband upon her marriage. Equally, she had the right to do what she wished with it. But now was not the time to argue this point with him. "We shall see."

He cradled her face with one big hand, his thumb gently caressing her cheek. The breath stalled in her breast and longing bloomed between her thighs, as his intense gaze captured her very soul.

"I don't know what grand plan MacAlpin has for when we

enter Dunadd. But, if it pleases you, our true marriage will take place at Duncarn, with my mother and sisters in attendance. That, at least, will mean something."

"I'm sure that will be preferable to anything MacAlpin might have planned in Dunadd."

Perhaps she should guard her tongue, now she knew of the connection between Finn and his king. But Finn was already aware of how she despised MacAlpin, and he'd given no indication they shared a congenial relationship. Quite the opposite, in fact.

But still, she should take care. Her heart ached at the knowledge she needed to curb her responses to the man who would soon be her husband, but it could not be helped. Ultimately, their bloodlines would always stand between them.

"My sweet Mae." He lowered his head, his intent clear, and illicit sparks of desire danced through her blood. She should pull back. Push him away. Too much had changed since yesterday for her to allow him such liberties.

He was a prince, and they were to be wed. Propriety demanded she be mindful of her status, but her virtuous principles melted when his lips captured hers.

She wound her arm around his powerful shoulders, and he deepened the kiss, his tongue invading her mouth in delicious conquest. Her eyes fluttered shut and she surrendered to the flames that licked through her. How easy it was to pretend the events of today had never happened. All that mattered was this man in her arms. The man she was pledged to spend the rest of her life with.

His fingers threaded through her hair, cradling the back of her head in his palm and she dug her nails into his shoulder. Her shawl tumbled to the floor, but she scarcely noticed as he unlaced the ties at her bodice and teased her aching nipples.

With a harsh gasp, he tore his mouth from hers, and for a

heart-stealing moment, his passion-glazed gaze ensnared her before he trailed burning kisses along her throat. His hair caressed her cheek, and his hot breath scorched her skin as he circled her nipple with his tongue.

She clutched his head, pressing him tight against her, as lightning spiraled from the touch of his mouth at her breast to her sensitized core. His searching fingers teased her breast before gliding over her waist and hips, and even through her gown, his touch ignited her like an ethereal fire.

Panting, he pulled back, and a chill whispered across her exposed, damp flesh. She kept her fingers tangled in his hair, urging him back, but he resisted.

"Mae." His voice was hoarse with need and primitive hunger coursed through her. "God help me. I didn't come here tonight to ravish you."

"I do not want you to go." The confession slipped out before she could prevent it. But she couldn't regret it. She wanted him, despite everything.

With fingers that shook, he attempted to straighten her bodice. It was hard to clear her mind when the sight of his fierce concentration on such a simple task was utterly bewitching.

"When we are wed, nothing will keep me from your bed." Tenderly, he brushed errant strands of her hair from her face. "I'm counting the hours until you are mine."

She smiled, how could she not, when he was so impassioned, but disquiet threaded through her, nonetheless. Scots were not Picts, and she had heard fearful tales of how wives were treated in Dal Riada.

He bent and retrieved her shawl, before carefully placing it about her shoulders. Then he gave a formal bow and strode to the door where he turned, and his smile caused the breath to catch in her throat.

But as he left the chamber, that insidious thread of unease

would not be stilled, and an unpalatable truth raised its ugly head.

It did not matter how dearly she wished things could be different. Finn was the son of MacAlpin, and she could never afford to forget it.

Her very life might depend upon it.

CHAPTER 22

$\mathcal{F}$inn made his way to the other side of the palace, where Constantine had been given a small chamber, due to his injury. Much to his irritation, he had also been expected to share the prince's chamber, but it could not be avoided without causing comment. Especially since Constantine himself appeared agreeable to the arrangement.

He gave a nod in greeting to the two Scots' warriors who stood guard outside the door. They nodded in return, their expressions wary. Obviously, they had no idea how to treat him now his royal bloodline had been acknowledged.

That wasn't his problem. As he'd told Mae, he was still the same man he had been yesterday, or last month. The only positive outcome from MacAlpin's acknowledgement was the fact it had brought him to Mae.

God, he could still scarcely believe the good fortune that had been handed to him. He paused, his hand on the iron door ring, and sucked in a deep breath. He had long ago stopped believing in the existence of miracles but discovering that Mae was the Princess of Fortriu certainly came close.

Fuck that. It *was* a miracle.

She was his miracle.

Briefly, he pressed his forehead against the timber door, willing his unruly cock to obey his silent command. Leaving her just now had been the hardest thing he'd ever done. But unlike last night, his chest didn't throb with futile anger at how the fates were intent on tearing them apart.

A few more days. He could wait that long.

He entered the chamber. A fire burned in the hearth and two torches blazed in their sconces, giving ample light to see Constantine had claimed the bed. Not that he minded sleeping on the floor. And at least the chamber offered more protection from the bitter elements than his tent.

Unfortunately, the prince wasn't asleep.

"How is your bride, brother?" Constantine massaged his shoulder, and a grimace of pain flashed over his face. "She's a beauty, that's for certain. Fucking her will be a pleasure, and to hell with duty."

Finn swung on his heel and glared at the prince. "You'll not speak of the princess in such a disrespectful manner."

Constantine grinned. "Despite her status, she is still merely a woman. Or, should I say, her *former* status."

"Former be damned. She's still the Princess of Fortriu, and the reason our king wishes to unite the House of Alpin with her lineage."

Aye, he cared nothing for the House of Alpin, but Constantine did. And if by using that connection was the only way to shut him up, then by God, Finn would use it.

Constantine shrugged his uninjured shoulder. "She has you by the balls already, I see. Doubtless that is what happens when a man is brought up solely by his mother."

It was intended as an insult, but it was insignificant compared to the ones the prince had leveled against his mother when they'd been boys. Finn gave a snort of mirthless laughter.

"Do you wish to continue slandering my lady mother, now I

am acknowledged?" It was merely a question. But his threat was clear. Any disparagement against Lady Brae would from now on reflect not only on Finn, but also MacAlpin himself.

"A lifetime's animosity cannot be wiped out overnight, Braeson. Your existence grieved my gentle mother greatly."

Finn barely managed to hide his shock at the prince's words. He'd never considered how the queen might feel about it. But then, she still had the privilege of her rank and her reputation remained untarnished, unlike his own *gentle mother*, who had never deserved any of the cruelty she had endured.

"My existence is not of my own doing. Should I return to camp?" He was damned if he'd stay here while Constantine dragged up the past.

Constantine exhaled an irritated breath. "We are half-brothers now. I still don't like it, but you saved my life and proved the ties of blood between us are unbroken. The House of Alpin cannot be seen to be fractured."

Finn kept his mouth shut. They had always been half-brothers, but he was as disinclined to claim the kinship now as he had been from the day his mother had wed the tavernkeeper.

Yet his own feelings were irrelevant. He knew only too well the House of Alpin needed a united front to keep the alliance between the Scots and Picts. It was the only way they'd defeat the cursed Norsemen.

But those weren't Constantine's words coming out of his mouth. They were MacAllister's, the diplomat, the one who had managed to find the Princess of Fortriu without any blood being spilled.

If Constantine had finally discovered the art of statecraft, Finn wasn't going to argue the point with him.

He had the far more important issue of his bride on his mind.

~

EARLY THE FOLLOWING MORNING, after Finn had returned from a ride and was tending to his horse in the camp, Ewan strolled to his side and folded his arms.

"It's Lord Finn, now, then." It wasn't a question.

Finn straightened and caught the other man's steady gaze. Ewan was the first one who had directly confronted him with his new status. "So it would seem."

"Now we know the true reason for our journey to Fotla." A dark frown slashed Ewan's brow. "You were under oath. Yet you knew you were destined to wed the princess."

He knew what Ewan referred to. Their conversation, when they had discussed how MacAlpin was using political marriages to strengthen his claim on Pictland. But Ewan was a friend, and he wanted to share the truth.

"Forget MacAlpin's orders. If I had the choice of any woman in the land, the princess is the only one I'd want."

"Then I'm happy for you. It seems the princesses of Pictland have a magical talent for ensnaring the regard of their chosen husbands."

Finn laughed, and slapped Ewan on the shoulder. "If Connor and Cam are half as fortunate as I in their choice of wives, then there is no need of magic." He drew in a deep breath and glanced at the palace. "I must go. My presence is required at the marriage negotiations."

"Good luck," Ewan said with feeling. "The Picts are ferocious in those matters."

Which suited him. He had no intention of Mae being cheated out of any of her inheritance.

THE NEGOTIATIONS HAD BEEN TRAVELING around in circles for what seemed like hours. The lack of fresh air in the king's inner sanctum was oppressive, but Finn appeared to be the only one affected by the overpowering urge to fling open the doors and clear his head.

He gritted his teeth and tensed his muscles. MacAlpin had given him and Constantine strict orders to leave the negotiating to MacAllister. He and the prince were present merely for show.

The King of Fotla sat behind his desk, flanked by high-ranking nobles and Bhaic. Who most likely was a high ranking noble himself, but no introductions had been made.

He'd learned one thing, though. Mae was far wealthier than he had imagined. And MacAlpin wanted to grasp as much of it as possible for himself.

Through Finn.

Injustice burned through him. It was bad enough she had lost her kingdom. He wouldn't sit silently by while they attempted to loot her fortune.

They were back to the subject of the royal jewels of Fortriu. Fuck this.

"Perhaps we might reach a mutually satisfactory compromise," MacAllister said. "There is a certain broach which holds significant sentimental value for my king. In exchange for possession of this broach, he may be willing to—"

"Enough." Finn surged up from his chair and only just stopped himself from banging his fist on the desk for good measure. "Everything the Princess of Fortriu brings into this marriage will remain hers after we are wed. I lay claim to none of her fortune. Sire," he added, bowing his head to the Fotla king who, despite the unforgiveable outburst, did not appear offended. Finn turned to MacAllister, whose lips were thinned and eyes icy as they met his. "Ensure this contract is ironclad so we may return to Dunadd forthwith."

IT HAD BEEN two weeks since Finn had ended the marriage negotiations and preparations for their departure of Fotla had begun.
Messengers had been sent on ahead to inform MacAlpin, and
Finn had assumed they'd leave within a day or so, but he'd
discovered a princess required time before she was ready to
travel.

But finally, they now approached the western coast of Dal
Riada, where the royal stronghold of Dunadd could be glimpsed
through the early morning mist. His chest constricted and he
tightened his grip on the reins. For two weeks, he and Mae had
scarcely seen each other, never mind shared a word. When he
had attempted to speak with her, the way he had on the night
he'd discovered who she really was, he hadn't even been allowed
into her antechamber.

But soon, Mae would be his wife, and no one would have the
right to keep her from him. He only wished they could have gone
direct to Duncarn, but Mae deserved a royal welcome, and for
that he would stomach whatever show MacAlpin planned for
their arrival.

He glanced over his shoulder but couldn't catch sight of her
among the Pict warriors who had accompanied them and whose
primary function was to protect the princess. Not that he
minded. He was glad for their loyalty to their princess, but a frustrated sigh escaped, and he shifted on his horse.

It didn't ease the discomfort. Nothing would, until he once
again held Mae, his bride, in his arms.

Tonight?

God, he hoped so. Leashed need burned through his blood,
and it took all his willpower to concentrate on the most
mundane of tasks. If he had to wait much longer, he feared for
his sanity.

The sun was high in the sky when they finally entered the
forecourt. Warriors were in ceremonial formation and a canopy,

in the colors of Fortriu, had been erected in front of the entrance, where the king stood with his trusted advisors.

He and Constantine dismounted and approached the king, who gripped first the prince's uninjured shoulder, and then his, in an exhibit of royal approval.

"You have done well," MacAlpin said. "The marriage is arranged for the tenth hour, and tonight we shall display our treasure to the court of Dunadd."

Rebellion kicked hard in his gut. Mae wasn't MacAlpin's treasure, and he had no right to refer to her as such. But for once, he kept his mouth shut. He'd do nothing to spoil this moment for Mae by creating a disturbance.

He and Constantine stepped back as Mae approached, Bhaic one step behind her, her ladies and personal guard in her wake. Her cloak and hood were a deep blue, edged with fur, fit for a queen, and more magnificent than anything he'd seen a royal woman wear in Dunadd.

She didn't glance at him as she paused by his side. Neither did she extend her hand to MacAlpin. Not that he had offered her his. Instead, he bowed, and so did all his advisers.

Mae remained ramrod straight.

"Mairi, Princess Annella of Fortriu, Supreme Kingdom of Pictland." MacAlpin spoke in Pictish and extended his hand in greeting. After a heartbeat, Mae accepted. The king kissed her gloved fingers. "Welcome to the Kingdom of Dunadd. We are honored by your presence, Madam, and your gracious acceptance to join the House of Alpin."

For a fleeting moment Mae's expression tightened, before she regained her serene composure. But it was enough. Finn recognized that look on her face and alarm slammed through his chest.

Her candid words were one of the reasons why she so enchanted him. But MacAlpin wouldn't take kindly to Mae's strong opinions. Before he could shatter every protocol in existence and interrupt this dangerous exchange, Mae spoke.

"Indeed." Her voice was cool, and she responded in Gaelic. "It is imperative Pictland and Dal Riada unite against the threat of the Vikings."

Some of the coiled tension eased. Mae was no fool when it came to politics. Hadn't she told him as much?

Only when Constantine shifted by his side and shot him a guarded glance did Mae's response fully penetrate.

She'd agreed Dal Riada and Pictland needed a strong alliance. But she hadn't reciprocated MacAlpin's welcome to join their bloodlines.

"You are correct, Madam." If MacAlpin was irked by her reply, he didn't show it. "That is why we must seal this alliance between our royal houses without delay. The marriage will be undertaken in three hours' time. I trust this gives you ample opportunity to prepare."

"Certainly."

The king offered her his arm and led the way into the great hall. Finn and Constantine followed, with Aedh taking his place not beside his brother, but beside Finn.

It was a silent recognition of his new status, in deference to their birth order.

They entered the great hall, where in front of the dais the queen and his half-brothers' wives waited, flanked by their attendants. He sucked in a shocked breath, his gaze riveted on the noblewoman who stood next to the queen.

His mother.

Standing in the place where, due to her rank, Constantine's wife should be.

His heart hammered, drowning out the sound of the king's voice as he presented the queen to Mae, acknowledging the princess' senior status. What the hell was MacAlpin doing, forcing his mother to the court from where she'd been ostracized so many years ago?

He ignored the poisoned glower Constantine gave him. There

was a fixed smile on his mother's face, but he saw the strain she was under. She had never enjoyed being the center of attention, and here she was, with all eyes of the court upon her. He gritted his teeth and attempted to hide the renewed surge of resentment against the king for forcing her to Dunadd, just to stroke his inflated sense of self-worth.

"Mairi, Princess Annella, may I present the esteemed Lady Brae?" MacAlpin glanced at the still figure of Mae. "Lady Brae is the mother of Lord Finn, Prince of the House of Alpin."

CHAPTER 23

*M*airi entered the antechamber where she and her
ladies had been taken to refresh themselves after
their journey, and to ready herself for the unseemly haste of the
wedding, but they were not alone.

The wives of Constantine and his younger brother, Aedh,
accompanied them. And so did Lady Brae.

As a servant took her cloak, her ladies flanked her, as though
to protect her from the Scotswomen. Aedh's wife appeared
barely fifteen, Constantine's perhaps a little younger than herself,
and neither of them seemed to know quite how to handle this
situation.

One thing was certain. They could not be trusted.

But what of Lady Brae?

She caught the older woman's eyes and her breath caught in
her throat. Her eyes were the same green as her son's and a wave
of longing washed through her.

Goddess, she missed Finn so. Only replaying their conversations in her head during the journey from Fotla had kept her
calm façade intact.

225

Their conversation when he'd told her that his mother was not welcomed at court.

Unease threaded through the longing. Why would he have said such a thing if it wasn't true? But perhaps Lady Brae was only here to greet her. Finn, after all, was not privy to the upstart king's schemes.

If only she could talk to him, but they had scarcely seen each other since the day she'd discovered who he was.

Her personal guard had been increased as befit her revealed status, and her days had been spent sequestered with the queen and her ladies, touching up the embroidery on Mairi's gowns, and ensuring her possessions were accounted for and securely readied for the journey.

But at night, Finn had haunted her dreams.

She desperately wished to speak with him again. For him to wrap his arms around her and hold her close. It had been unbearable to stand beside him but not acknowledge him, while she was forced to accept the foul, insincere greeting from MacAlpin.

Let him imagine he had won a great victory in securing her hand for his son. But when she had established herself in this new life, when the time was right, he would pay for his betrayal of her people.

He would pay in his blood. But Finn would not answer for the sins of his father.

Despite being a foreigner in this land, she was the senior royal and it appeared no one was willing to break the silence. She smothered the loathing for their king that burned in her breast and forced a smile.

"It is kind of you to welcome me, Lady Brae." She spoke in Gaelic since she had no idea if they understood her own language. "Lord Finn speaks warmly of you."

"Thank you, Madam. It is an honor to welcome you into our family."

Lady Brae was respectful, and the two princesses remained

silent, but nevertheless, nerves rolled through Mairi's stomach. All she wanted was to be left alone with the ladies who knew her, so they could begin the preparations for her wedding, but that luxury would need to wait. She would allow no Scots to have reason to level the accusation against her that she was discourteous.

Servants arrived, bringing refreshments, and she sat on one of the chairs by the fire as stools were brought for Lady Brae and the princesses. It seemed some etiquettes were the same as in Pictland, but as Lady Brae carefully seated herself, Mairi caught a glimpse of discomfort flash over her face.

"Please, Lady Brae," she said. "Take the other chair."

Lady Brae froze, clearly astonished by the offer, before she cast a quick glance in the two princesses' direction. Then she sat on the chair opposite Mairi.

"Thank you."

"It is only right." Mairi accepted a cup of herbal tea from Struana. "You are to be my mother-by marriage, after all."

"Indeed." Finn's mother kept her gaze lowered.

Mairi glanced at the princesses. They both avoided her eyes. Goddess, she would be glad to leave Dunadd, even if her future home was tiny in comparison. Surely it could not be more oppressive than here.

She returned her attention to Lady Brae. "You will be glad to return home to Duncarn, I am sure."

"Duncarn?" There was a strangely wary note in Lady Brae's voice, as though she had no idea what Mairi was talking about.

She pushed the troubling thought aside. What was she thinking? Perhaps Lady Brae assumed that Mairi was suggesting she hoped they would soon no longer see each other. Hastily, she attempted to correct that misconception. "I am eager to see Duncarn myself. Lord Finn has told me much about it."

Not quite the truth. He hadn't told her very much at all, but she hoped it helped to ease Lady Brae's mind. She would not wish to offend his mother for anything.

"Indeed, Madam. Finn—the prince secured Duncarn himself. My daughter and stepdaughters currently reside there."

She hadn't realized Finn had stepsisters. And although she intended to help Finn in acquiring a suitable property for their future together, she didn't want his mother to think she was slighting her. Lady Brae would know there could only ever be one true mistress of a household, and Mairi had no wish to usurp her position. "I trust my presence will not unduly inconvenience you all."

Lady Brae's smile appeared strained. "Forgive me, Madam. After the wedding, I will leave for Duncarn, but the Princess of Fortriu and Lord Finn will reside in Dunclach, just north of Dunadd. It is a quite magnificent stronghold, and far more fitting than Duncarn."

Finn had never mentioned such a place to her. "Is this a recently acquired stronghold?"

"No, Madam. It is the prince's heritage."

She took a sip of the aromatic tea, but barely tasted it as jagged thoughts whirled through her mind. This did not make sense. If Finn was wealthy in his own right, why had he given her the impression he was not?

Something was amiss. It was unseemly to question Lady Brae in such a manner, but she couldn't help herself. "I was unaware Lord Finn had this inheritance. Does he not make his home at Duncarn?"

"The king thinks very highly of him, Madam." Was it her imagination, or did Lady Brae sound a little defensive? "Duncarn is too far from the political sphere of Dunadd. The strategic position of Dunclach ensures the prince is always available should the king summon him."

"Of course." Mairi managed to smile before taking another sip of her tea, even though the herbal concoction tasted like ashes on her tongue. She ignored the frantic hammer of her heart and the way her stomach churned in distress. She would die before she allowed her feelings to show to any Scot, let alone the woman who would soon be her mother-by-marriage.

But her shock could not be brushed aside so easily.

It had never occurred to her to disbelieve Finn when he'd told her of his relationship with MacAlpin. Except what had he told her, really?

"I don't know what grand plan MacAlpin has for when we enter Dunadd. But, if it pleases you, our true marriage will take place in Duncarn, with my mother and sisters in attendance. That, at least, will mean something."

Nothing of import. She had put her own interpretation upon his words, tainted by her own disdain of his king. But what else should she have thought? Why had he said their true marriage would mean something only when they were in Duncarn, with his mother and sisters?

Relentlessly, another memory spilled through her mind.

"I'm proud of the noble blood of my lady mother. But of my father, I cannot speak."

She had imagined him the product of an illicit affair. And she'd been right. But she had also been so wrong. Finn hadn't spoken of his father because he despised him or didn't know who he was. It was because he'd been on an undercover mission for his king.

For his father.

There could be only one reason why he'd woven such a web of deceit. He had played on her emotions, using her disdain for his king for his own purposes. How readily she had fallen for his story that until he had been ordered to ride into Fotla, MacAlpin hadn't even recognized his royal bloodline.

Finn hadn't known her long, but he knew her too well. Why risk transporting a hostile princess to Dunadd, when with a few choice words he could have a willing bride instead?

Shame burned through her at how she had believed his whispered confession.

"The missing princess was the last woman in the world I wanted to marry, Mae. Until I saw she was you."

Now she was in Dal Riada, she was trapped. In Fotla, she might still have escaped the Scots' treacherous grasp.

Briana had been right when she'd warned her that she couldn't believe a word Finn said. But even in the midst of danger, she hadn't heeded her cousin's words.

But she would heed them now.

"You must always keep your wits about you."

As Mae departed the great hall, accompanied by his mother and his half-brothers' wives, disquiet ate through Finn's guts. Not just because of his mother's unexpected appearance at court, but by the fact Mae hadn't so much as glanced in his direction since they'd arrived. Not even when the king had announced their imminent marriage. And although he was eager to make her his bride as soon as possible, MacAlpin had given them no choice in the matter. How did Mae feel about it? Did she need more time to prepare?

Not that he was going to question MacAlpin about it. The sooner he and Mae were wed, the sooner he could take her to Duncarn.

"Come." MacAlpin indicated he and Constantine should accompany him, and they followed him to his inner sanctum. It was no surprise that both Aedh and MacAllister came with them, too.

Once the door was shut, MacAlpin stood in front of his desk and leveled his gaze on Constantine. "Was the would-be assassin caught?"

"No, sire. The Picts assured us they would continue with the search." It was obvious Constantine didn't believe the Picts would do any such thing.

"The messenger assured us you will suffer no ill effects from this injury. Is this true?"

"The wound is healing."

"Your life was saved by your brother." It wasn't a question. And judging by the swift glance Constantine threw Finn, he wasn't the only one to notice MacAlpin had not prefixed their brotherhood by *half*.

"Aye." Reluctance dripped from Constantine's admission.

"We will address justice for this when the time is right." MacAlpin then focused his piercing gaze on Finn and the ghost of a smile touched his lips. "As promised, you will not go empty-handed into this illustrious marriage, Finn. Your maternal grandparents have graciously bestowed Dunclach upon you and your bride, together with its entire contents."

For all he cared, his mother's parents could throw themselves off the cliff upon which Dunclach had been built more than two hundred years ago. There was no way in hell he would accept the property from which his mother had been banished because of his own birth.

"I have no need of Dunclach."

"Perhaps not." Amusement threaded through MacAlpin's words. "But your royal wife most assuredly deserves more than an insignificant hillfort in a remote backwater of Dal Riada."

Finn clamped his jaw shut on the denials that threatened to escape. Because the king was right. Mae did deserve more than Duncarn. But Duncarn was all he could offer her.

Should he deny her more luxury, just to save his pride?

"Good. That is settled." MacAlpin nodded, as though the result had never been in question. "Aodhan MacDonnell and his lady wife were only too willing to give up their ancestral seat once the situation was explained to them. Their relationship through marriage to both the King of Dal Riada and Fortriu and the Princess of Fortriu will gain them much prestige."

Aye, prestige was all MacDonnell cared about, and he hoped they all choked on it.

"As long as the princess doesn't have to share the household with MacDonnell's wife." Not that he believed Mae would raise any objections. She was too well-versed in the tangled threads of politics. But there was no chance he'd remain civil to the two people who had caused their only daughter such heartache.

Mirth glinted in the king's eyes. He was clearly relishing this conversation. "Dunclach and all its lands have been unequivocally signed over to you, Finn. It is unthinkable that my fair cousin-once-removed should share her household with anyone."

He knew of the blood connection between Kenneth MacAlpin and the Princess of Fortriu. It was, after all, what linked MacAlpin to the Pictish throne.

Yet from the moment he'd discovered who Mae was, he'd failed to acknowledge the matrilineal ties between her and his king.

He had to remember Mae and the princess were one. And their lineages were interwoven by virtue of their forebears.

Apparently satisfied by his silence, the king turned to MacAllister. "The messenger informing us of the success of our mission imparted no indication regarding the great seal of Fortriu. A necessary precaution for security, no doubt."

MacAllister bowed his head. "My liege, the Picts are, indeed, ruthless negotiators."

"Hard bargaining always increases perceived value." The king shrugged, and Finn fisted his hands, seething at how Mae's worth was so summarily dismissed. "There was only one thing we required from the princess' dowry."

"My liege, I deeply regret the great seal remains within the Princess of Fortriu's possession."

This time the silence thundered around the chamber, raising

the hairs on the back of Finn's neck. What great seal were they speaking of? It was the first he'd heard of it.

"Explain." The king's voice was low, but menace pulsed from that single word.

"The negotiations were cut prematurely short, sire, after which there was no further room for discussion."

Understanding pierced the fog. He had been the one to end the incessant bargaining. Why didn't MacAllister tell the king that?

"Cut short?" MacAlpin turned to Constantine.

"Aye." Surprisingly, Constantine appeared reluctant to drop Finn in the shit. Fuck this. He had nothing to hide.

"I ended the negotiations, sire."

MacAlpin turned icy eyes to him. "Indeed. By whose authority?"

"Nothing had been gained in hours of negotiations. If my liege only wanted the Princess of Fortriu's great seal, why not simply tell the King of Fotla that at the start?"

The king's lips thinned, before he drew in a deep breath. "We will make allowances for your rashness, Finn. You've not had the advantage of learning diplomacy. All is not lost. In a few hours, the princess will be your wife and despite the marriage contract, under our laws all that is hers, will be yours. Whether you take advantage of that or not is up to you. But you will secure the great seal of Fortriu and deliver it to us."

CHAPTER 24

*T*he monastery was but a short walk from Dunadd and had been built soon after the construction of the royal stronghold. Flanked by Constantine and Aedh, Finn made his way to where a monk stood by the altar. The king had decreed this wedding to be of such significance it warranted an extravagant display of ceremonial power.

It appeared every noble was in attendance, eager to witness this marriage between the Princess of Fortriu and the bastard son of MacAlpin. He ignored all the speculative glances aimed his way, from those who now deigned to acknowledge his existence. The same nobles who had frozen his mother from their ranks when the king had turned his back on her.

He drew in a deep breath. None of them mattered. He knew who his friends were, and they were the only ones he'd ever trust.

Incense wafted in the air and the choir chanted in Latin as the monk stood before the altar. Unease twisted in Finn's gut. MacAlpin had spared nothing to give Mae a royal celebration as befit her status, but it was steeped in Christianity, inspired from Rome. There was nothing here that celebrated her own faith.

Was MacAlpin even aware that she still worshipped the old ways?

A ripple moved through the congregation and from the corner of his eye he saw heads turn. He swallowed, his mouth suddenly dry, as he glanced over his shoulder and his heart damn near stalled in his chest.

Mae glided up the aisle, a vision in vibrant forest green, jewels glittering in the flickering light of a thousand candles. Bhaic was by her side, and his half-brothers' wives followed in her wake, but everything faded into a muted blur when Mae caught his gaze.

She didn't smile, but neither did she look away as she reached his side. For an eternal moment it was just the two of them, suspended in a fractured sliver of time, and he ached to pull her into his arms and to hell with this cursed ceremony. But he couldn't even take her hand, as she clutched a sprig of reddish-brown twigs, with deep purple berries nestled between the needle-like green leaves. Only when the monk began the liturgy did she break the spell and level her gaze ahead.

He still couldn't tear his gaze from her. She held her head at a proud angle and wore the same gem-encrusted gold circlet as she had on the day he'd discovered who she was.

She looked every inch a royal princess. Hell, she looked like a queen.

She would always be a queen in his heart.

The ceremony was interminable. He'd never known anything like it. Then again, he'd never attended a wedding within the sacred chamber of the monastery before, either. If MacAlpin was hoping to impress Mae, he had failed. She appeared supremely indifferent to it all.

Finally, it was over, and he offered Mae his arm. She rested the tips of her fingers against his wrist, the touch feather light, but his blood heated, and cock stirred, regardless. He should have known better than to have hoped she'd link arms with him or thread her fingers through his. Whatever MacAlpin had done, she was still the Princess of the Supreme Kingdom of Pictland, and it was clear she intended to remain regal and aloof while his fellow Scots devoured her with their mistrustful eyes.

At the doors, her ladies wrapped her cloak around her before they left the monastery. Dusk had fallen, and warriors holding blazing torches lit the way back to the stronghold. Despite the canopy that servants held over them, to protect them from the elements, the wind was bitter and before he could stop himself, he wrapped his arm around her shoulders and tugged her close.

She didn't melt against him. Her body was rigid, but at least she didn't pull away. Frustration clawed through him. All he wanted was to sweep her away from this farcical performance and into her chamber where they could at last be alone. But there was a damn feast to get through first, and God alone knew what meaningless shit MacAlpin planned for his inevitable speech.

He bent his head, his lips brushing her chilled cheek, and breathed in the tantalizing scent of leather and raindrops that would always remind him of her. His mind filled with images of Mae on the night they'd spent together, of her hair tumbling over her naked shoulders, and the way she had whispered his name in the heat of passion. How desperately he'd wanted to find a way to keep her in his life. And now, she would forever be a part of his life.

He couldn't explain the tangled thoughts. They were too raw, and they didn't need words between them in any case. Mae knew how he felt, despite the circumstances. She was the only one he'd ever confided in. But although he might not be able to tell her how he felt, he needed to say something to melt just a little of the ice she'd wrapped around herself.

Pride surged through him at her quiet dignity in the face of MacAlpin's display. Pride, aye, but something else, too. Something deeper and all-encompassing, and it was too big to confront right now, as they entered the royal stronghold. There would be time enough later, when they were alone, after she had thawed and was sated in his arms, to confess the secret within his heart.

There was only one thing to say to her now and his voice was husky with need as he breathed the words against her ear. "My beautiful bride."

She stiffened, but as they'd just entered the great hall, where the high table had been lavishly decorated for the wedding feast, she was likely reacting to that, rather than his confession. His arm tightened around her in blatant possession, before he reluctantly released her so they could take their places beside the king.

MacAlpin stood and launched into a speech extolling the virtues of the Scot/Pict alliance and how this marriage strengthened all of Pictland. Under cover of the table, he found Mae's hand and squeezed her icy fingers.

She didn't respond in kind.

He exhaled a measured breath. She still clutched her sprig of berries and spiky leaves in her other hand, and the twigs scratched his knuckles. God damn it, how much longer was the king going to speak?

MacAlpin raised his goblet. *Finally.* And then he turned to them.

"The Royal House of Alpin has come full circle. Our Scots and Pict blood merge at last, to unite this proud land. May the union of Lord Finn, Prince of the House of Alpin and Mairi, Princess Annella of Fortriu, bring peace to the Kingdom of Pictland and be a warning to our enemies that we shall never succumb to their barbarism."

Everyone followed the king by raising their goblets and finally Mae turned to look at him. Her face was a mask, and he had no idea what she was thinking, but he could guess.

Under cover of the ensuing rumble of conversation that spread through the hall he leaned in close so there was no chance of anyone overhearing him.

"We both know this was a political alliance, Mae. But that's not why I'm so proud to call you my bride. Let MacAlpin claim what he wishes. You and I are the only ones who matter here, and we know the truth."

A fleeting tremble of her lips was the only sign she understood him. And then she spoke. "I once lamented the fact that you possessed no Pictish blood in your veins. How wrong I was. And how convenient that you forgot to correct my assumption. It is that very blood that wove the trap we now find ourselves in."

This wasn't what he'd expected or wanted to hear from her. Not that he could blame her distrustful mood. MacAlpin's presence was enough to sour anyone's countenance.

"This is no trap. And forgive me for not telling you of my Pictish heritage. In truth, I've never considered it mine. It belongs to MacAlpin, and it's been many years since I coveted anything he possessed."

"Indeed." The word dripped ice and she turned her head, so their gazes clashed. "I understand your king wishes to display me to his people as a sign of his assumed greatness. But when this show is over, will you take me to your hillfort, Duncarn, as you once promised me?"

Shit. The last thing he wanted to discuss here, at their wedding feast, was how MacAlpin had manipulated the future Finn had imagined with Mae. But he could scarcely lie to her.

"I'll take you there one day soon, Mae. But my maternal grandparents have seen fit to bequeath me their stronghold, Dunclach." The king's mocking words echoed in his ears, reminding him just how basic his own hillfort was, when compared with what Mae was used to. It went against the grain, but he forced himself to smile. "It isn't a palace, but it's far grander than Duncarn. More suitable for a royal princess."

Her smile was tight and didn't reach her eyes. "This day is a continual revelation."

"Aye." He knew she didn't mean it in a complimentary way. "For me, also."

With reluctance he straightened, as the feast began, but he was acutely aware that Mae ate none of the fine delicacies placed before her. And while he was no expert when it came to brides and their choice of flowers, Mae's twigs and berries, and the way she'd placed the sprig across her lap, instead of upon the table, struck him as incomprehensibly significant.

Was it a pagan rite? If so, he could hardly complain, even if it made him strangely uncomfortable.

When the last dish had been cleared away, the tables and benches where the nobles and warriors sat were pushed back to the walls and the musicians tuned their instruments. The king, who had insisted Mae sit beside him in the place of honor, leaned in front of her and gave Finn a knowing smile.

"Doubtless you are eager to begin married life with your beautiful wife, Finn. But first you and the princess will lead the dancing. Let them all see the magnificent prize we have acquired for the continued freedom of Pictland."

Before he could take issue with referring to Mae as a prize, she gave a frosty smile. "I *am* Pictland. Our freedom and bondage are intertwined."

It was clear to him her remark was not intended as a compliment. He hoped MacAlpin was oblivious. He didn't much care what the king thought of him, but no way in hell did he want Mae on the wrong side of MacAlpin.

If the king understood her scathing response, he decided to ignore it, as his smile merely grew broader. "How refreshing you are, cousin. Your Pictish charms will invigorate my court, once your husband allows you to leave Dunclach. Perhaps after you have provided him with an heir or two."

Finn surged to his feet and held out his hand for Mae. The sooner he got her away from MacAlpin the better. He couldn't allow Mae to tell the king exactly what she thought of him, even if their thoughts were in agreement.

Except they're not.

Brutally, he shoved the denial to the back of his mind, but as she placed her sprig of leaves and berries on the table and took his hand, the thought lingered, like the sting of a bee.

Mae didn't want children.

Damn it, why was he thinking of this now?

The king's distasteful banter was normal wedding fare. If this were a normal wedding, Finn wouldn't give a shit. But it wasn't. And in one careless remark, MacAlpin hadn't simply overturned his previous assertion that it didn't matter whether this union produced *issue*.

It had reminded Finn that just because he had won the wife of his dreams, it didn't mean he might also one day have the family he craved.

He led her to the floor. Every eye was upon them or, more accurately, on Mae. It wasn't simply because her gown was nothing like a Scotswoman's. The richness of the color put even the queen herself in the shade.

Neither was it the vibrant hue of her beautiful hair, or even the precious gems that cast a glittering shower of rainbow shards around them.

It was the aura of exotic *otherness* that was as much a part of her as the blue of her eyes. The regal way she held herself, reinforcing to anyone with eyes in their head that her legacy in Pictland stretched back for a thousand years, unlike the Dal Riadan interlopers.

As she'd told the king, she was Pictland herself. And no stolen heritage could take that from her.

Instinctively, his grip on her tightened. She was his bride. But this time, it wasn't pride that seared him at how he'd secured such a perfect match. Instead, a hollow ache filled his chest, at the knowledge she was more of a stranger to him now, than the night he had met her beneath the moon.

She tilted her chin, and he could not tear his gaze away. "Is Dunclach to be my prison, Finn, unless you allow me to leave?"

Silently, he cursed MacAlpin to hell. "You're my wife, Mae, not my prisoner. Once we are installed in Dunclach, you're free to visit Dunadd as often as you please." Although why she would want to, was beyond him.

"Your king sees me as nothing more than a brood mare." Bitterness tinged the words, and she no longer held his gaze.

He gritted his teeth as the dance pulled them apart, and his mood didn't improve as high-ranking nobles joined them on the floor. When they were once again close enough to speak without being overheard, he growled against her ear. "Since when do you care what MacAlpin thinks?"

"Is it not what you think, also?"

Her question pierced him like an arrow. "Why would you say that?"

"It seems you believe that is all a woman is fit for."

Before his scrambled mind could summon up a suitable response to her outrageous accusation, the dance once again tore them apart.

When had he ever said such a thing? He barely noticed the young noblewoman who had taken Mae's place as his partner, his glare fixed on his wife as she danced with the king himself.

Until Mae had told him she wasn't certain if she wanted a child of her own, he'd never even considered a woman might possess such a thought. With marriage, came bairns. It was the way things were and would always be.

Unease shifted through his chest and settled somewhere in the region of his heart. Before MacAlpin had acknowledged him and before Mae had come into his life, he'd been so certain that the lass he chose as his bride would happily provide him with a brood of bairns. But would he have thought to even ask if that was what she wanted?

Even after Mae's earlier confession, it hadn't occurred to him to ask her if she'd changed her mind, now they were wed. He'd given no thought of the coming night, save for a raw hunger that at long last he'd possess her once again.

Heat blasted through him as realization struck. He'd been so consumed by knowing Mae would be his, he'd missed the true reason for her chilled responses. Did she imagine he would force her to bear heirs for the House of Alpin?

Fuck it, he had no burning desire to sire offspring that would continue MacAlpin's bloodline. All he wanted were bairns of his own, to cherish, not use as political pawns. It was something they could talk of later. But for now, he wanted the carefree noble-woman Lady Mae in his bed, not Mairi, a princess with the weight of Pictland on her shoulders.

A small lie would put her mind at rest. And if that lie became their truth, he'd live with it. A future with Mae trusting him exceeded any than one with a dozen bairns and where she could not bear the sight of him.

MacAlpin returned Mae, and slapped Finn on the shoulder, a knowing grin on his face. Ignoring how he disrupted the dance, the king spoke. "You have my leave to make your departure, Finn. We do not wish to overtire the princess on such an auspicious night."

It was a dismissal, and he was glad of it. He gave the king a stiff bow and watched as MacAlpin took Mae's hand and kissed her knuckles. She did not curtsey, as any other woman in the land would, but why should she?

She outranked his king, for all that she was a woman.

And MacAlpin knew it.

Formally, Finn took her hand and led her from the floor. Although the musicians continued to play, the dancing stalled as everyone watched their progression. At the high table, Mae's ladies joined them, one of them clutching her wedding sprig. As they left the hall, four warriors followed, two Scots, appointed by the king, and two Picts who had accompanied them from Fotla.

He'd have to get used to it. As the Princess of the Supreme Kingdom, she was valuable, not only to Pictland but to Dal Riada, too. Her every action would be watched, by the Picts to protect her interests, and by the Scots to, doubtless, report back to MacAlpin.

How differently he'd envisaged their life, if only he could have taken her home to Duncarn.

CHAPTER 25

*B*haic opened the door to her chamber, and Mairi and Finn entered, her ladies following. The warriors remained in the corridor, but Bhaic entered also, closing the door with a resounding thud before standing before it with his arms crossed.

She took a deep breath in a futile attempt to slow her racing heart. She couldn't dwell on Bhiac's silent fury, or his tortured confession, before the wedding, that he had failed both her and Nechtan. She could scarcely think of anything but the man who clasped her hand in a possessive grasp, the man who was now her husband.

Struana placed her sprig of jasmine on a small table, and Mairi's stomach churned. It had seemed so daring to use it for her wedding, as a secret symbol that she refused to be used to produce offspring for MacAlpin's continued violation of her land. But what if Scotswomen weren't ignorant of the old ways, as she had always believed? What if the queen, or one of the princesses, saw fit to tell their king that the Princess of Fortriu blatantly proclaimed she would rather remain barren then bear an heir for the House of Alpin?

It had been a mistake. It might cost her dearly. Such knowledge was for women only to use and understand. Not flaunt in a foreign court, where enemies lurked in every corner.

"Mae." Finn's concerned voice cut through her rising panic, and threads of illicit desire warmed her chilled blood. Would it always be this way when he spoke to her? "Are you unwell? I'll have the servants bring you some food. You ate nothing at the feast."

Goddess, she would vomit if she tried to eat. But even though Finn could not be trusted, a treacherous sliver of her heart was warmed by his concern. Surely, it meant something that he had noticed such a thing?

Keep your wits about you.

He might show concern, but she had to remember that all she was to him, bride or not, was a valuable hostage. She could not afford to let her guard down for a moment. However much she wished she could.

"I am not hungry."

"Some wine, then?"

Why did he gaze at her as though she meant the world to him? But then, maybe she did. It just wasn't the world she wanted.

Her head throbbed, and the caress of his thumb against her skin was dangerously addictive. How easy it would be to agree, and allow her fears to drown, but she had already drunk too much wine at the feast. "I thank you, but no."

Was this the way of their life from now on? To be excruciatingly polite to each other, in case they inadvertently said something that could be used against them?

Her heart would wither. How much kinder it would have been to have had only one night with Finn, after all.

A frown slashed his brow. He appeared as unable as her to navigate the desolate chasm that now separated them.

Struana came to their side, her head bowed. With difficulty,

Mairi tore her gaze from Finn's and acknowledged her faithful lady.

"Madam." That was all Struana said, but it was enough. She needed to be prepared for her wedding night, and the precious jewels of Fortriu locked away. Ever since she'd agreed to this alliance, she'd tried not to think of her wedding night. Not because it repelled her. But because she craved it with every particle of her being.

And she should not. The Finn in her heart was not the Finn she had married, but how hard it was to constantly remind herself of that fact.

Yet if she did not, it could be her undoing.

Reluctantly, she tugged her hand free from him.

"I must retire to the bedchamber. My ladies will bid you to enter when I am ready."

"Mae, there's no need for such formalities. You don't need to get ready for me."

He sounded so much like the Finn Braeson who had enchanted her, it was hard to remind herself he was Lord Finn, Prince of the House of Alpin. And always had been.

"It would not be seemly." Goddess, could she sound any haughtier if she tried? What did it matter if he saw the jewels put away? Between the night they'd been betrothed and her wedding day, she had worn many of the precious pieces and the chest in which they were secured was scarcely insignificant. It wasn't as if Finn was unaware of Fortriu's legacy.

It was the reason he had married her.

"Mae." His voice was low. It was clear he didn't want anyone overhearing, and she nodded at Struana who retreated. "If this is what you want, I'll heed your wishes. But if the only reason is because of royal protocol, then I have no use for it. Do you?"

Royal protocol was all she had left. But perhaps she could bend it, just a little.

At her bidding, Bhaic brought the chest from the bedchamber. It was elaborately engraved, with several levels of security besides the most obvious lock and key, to protect the treasures it had housed for hundreds of years. In Forteviot, it had been locked away in its own fortified chamber, as befit its priceless contents. But since she had fled Fortriu, it had been hidden amongst her personal possessions.

Bhaic remained by her side, but Finn didn't appear particularly interested in the chest's contents, as her ladies carefully removed the precious bracelets, earrings, and the coronation circlet from her. Not that it mattered even if he had shown an interest. The most invaluable item, the sacred broach of Fortriu, was concealed within a secret compartment in her medicine casket and she was the only one who knew it.

The broach that only the true king of the Supreme Kingdom could possess.

As Bhaic oversaw the elaborate locking of the chest, Finn took her hand and tugged her close. "Send your ladies away," he whispered, and his warm breath against her cheek sent tremors of need burning through her blood. "You have no need of them when I am here."

It was so tempting. For a brief moment she closed her eyes and allowed his touch to sink into her soul. They were married, and Finn would claim his rights, as would any husband. The only question was would she pretend an aloof indifference, simply to appease her wounded pride that she had been so utterly deceived?

It wasn't her pride. But she wouldn't demean herself to name the truth.

She sighed in defeat. Despite everything, she still wanted him. Perhaps she always would. She'd gain nothing by feigning a frosty façade when they were alone, in their bed. All she would achieve would be to alienate Finn.

And lose any chance of wielding what little power she had secured by accepting this alliance.

Pain squeezed her heart. Procuring information through seduction was a tactic as old as time. The queen had expected nothing less of her back in Fotla, and so too had even Briana. But she hadn't been able to do it then, and wasn't sure she could do it now, either.

Except in Fotla, she'd foolishly believed Finn's pretty words. Now, she was wiser.

Now, she had to be ruthless if she wanted to help her people.

She inclined her head and led Finn into the bedchamber, avoiding the concerned glances from her ladies. He shut the door with a resounding thud and strode to where she stood beside the fire. Before she realized his intention, he pulled her close, his powerful arms wrapped around her, crushing her against his hard body. His chest expanded as he inhaled the scent of her hair, and why was that notion so heartbreakingly arousing?

"You're wrong." His lips brushed her earlobe and his hoarse accusation, far from alarming her, sent shivers of need across her exposed flesh. "I don't think you are fit only to bear heirs, Mae."

"Then you are a rare Scotsman, indeed."

What was she *saying*? Just as they had while they'd been dancing earlier, the words had tumbled out before she could consider them. The way they had before she'd known who he was.

But she couldn't afford that luxury anymore. Especially when they spoke of such sensitive matters. There were plenty of rumors that swirled in the royal courts of Pictland, of how the Scots forbade their women to regulate their own fertility.

Goddess, she had to learn to curb her tongue.

His laugh caught her off-guard and she looked up at him. The breath caught in her throat at the bone-melting smile he aimed her way. "Aye. I am the luckiest of all men to have snared you as my bride."

You snared me only because of your bloodline.

She kept the unvarnished response locked deep inside her mind. But not because she had to play political games with him. It was because his smile illuminated the shadow-filled chamber, like the sun emerging through rain clouds, and it warmed her wounded heart.

Do not fall beneath his charm. Yet it was impossible not to smile back.

"Mae." His smile faded and tension radiated from him. "There is no need to fear. I—" He bit off his words and for a fleeting moment she was certain despair flashed in his eyes. But then he shook his head, and offered her another smile, and the strange sensation that something significant simmered beneath the surface evaporated. It was her imagination. Nothing more. "You should know that bairns have no place in my plans. Do you understand?"

Her heart slammed against her breast. Of everything he might have said to her, she had never imagined it would be this. MacAlpin had made it clear he expected Finn to produce an heir. She was sure that must have been at least part of the reason why they had hunted her down so ruthlessly. So that any child she bore would have Scots' blood in its veins, in an attempt to obliterate its Pict heritage. "You do not?"

"I don't want you to scorn our marriage, Mae. I didn't take *you* as my bride to appease MacAlpin's thirst for conquest."

Yet again, she couldn't stop herself from responding. "You were always destined to wed the Princess of Fortriu. And doubtless, to sire heirs."

"I told you. MacAlpin only acknowledged me the day before we left for Fotla. That was when he told me who my future bride would be. There was no talk of heirs then."

So he was clinging to that lie. But why? Surely he knew someone would tell her the truth. And although she wouldn't have believed anything any Scots told her about Finn, she couldn't dishonor his mother by doubting her word.

But she wasn't going to ask him about it tonight. Not when there was something of far greater importance she needed to clarify. She leaned back against his encircling arms and pressed her palm against his chest. Even through the thickness of his plaid, she fancied she could feel the strong beat of his heart. "You won't care if I am barren?"

His face tightened, as though she had struck him. "You've taken things to extremes, there."

"Indeed. But it is always the woman who bears that stigma, whatever the truth of the matter." Goddess, could she not simply be *quiet*?

"The truth?" He sounded scandalized. And while she'd enjoyed teasing him in Fotla, she couldn't do that now. It wasn't simply her own future at stake. She had to be an agreeable bride if she wanted Finn to feed her information. It was her duty to discover all she could about the Pictish hostages held at Dunadd.

She should gracefully acquiesce with his views. Defer to him in all matters. Let him imagine she was nothing but an empty-headed vessel with no opinions of her own.

Maybe, with any other man, she might have been able to do it. But this was Finn. He already knew she spoke her mind and he wasn't a fool. She couldn't pretend to be a submissive female and expect him to believe it.

Her fingers slipped beneath his plaid, and she gripped his fine linen shirt. "Yes, Finn. The truth. Your people will call me barren because the alternative is to cast doubt on your manhood. And goddess forbid any *man* should be found so lacking."

"No one will dare question any such thing."

"Within your hearing."

"Or yours," he countered.

She played a perilous game. Even in Pictland, such things were not discussed with men. And Scots were savages when compared to Picts. If Finn discovered she had ancient wisdom of recipes that regulated a woman's moon cycle, he could find ways to destroy her supplies. And she could not allow that to happen. Bride's relentless warnings of her fate should she conceive were seared into the very fabric of her being.

Yet despite the danger, this confrontation was too exhilarating. For the first time since she'd discovered his heritage, she felt alive inside—the way she had after meeting him beneath the moon.

"What are you proposing?" she said. Their gazes clashed, and his eyes were dark with passion. She hitched in a ragged breath and his heady scent of wild forests and hidden glens seduced whatever remained of her good sense. "That we do not consummate our union?"

Goddess, surely not. Even though she could no longer trust him, her body burned for his.

His smile glowed feral in the firelight. "That is not an option. This *union*," he spat the word as though it offended him, "will be true in every sense of the word."

Her grip on his shirt tightened and in response he cupped her bottom with one strong hand and tugged her close until there was no space between them. She gasped as the heat from his palm sank into her flesh, a brand of possession, and she tilted her head so she could see his face. Her veil, no longer secured by her circlet, slipped to her shoulders, and she speared her fingers through his glorious hair.

"For the good of Pictland," she breathed against his lips, even though, deep in her heart, she wasn't doing this for her beloved country at all.

"No." His hot gaze roved over her face before settling on her mouth. "For the good of us."

His lips claimed hers in a kiss that incinerated every thought in her head save for the man in her arms. This was no chaste, duty-bound gesture. It was wild, savage, an unmistakable demand for surrender.

A primitive groan tore her throat and Finn's commanding grip on her tightened, crushing her against him until she could scarcely breathe. She tangled his hair around her fingers, a silent demand for more, for everything that only he could offer.

He pulled her veil from her shoulders and dropped it to the floor, before wrapping his hand around the back of her neck. Raw need shivered through her, and it was only his unyielding strength as he clasped her in a possessive embrace that kept her upright when his tongue plundered her willing mouth.

Liquid heat bloomed deep inside, and she shifted restlessly within his relentless grasp. She wanted him naked, wanted to explore his wonderful, warrior-hard body, but she seemed incapable of doing anything but cling to him as though her life depended upon it.

His teeth nipped her lip and she gasped, shock spearing through her, as the pleasurable pain arrowed straight to her sensitized clit. She dug her nails into his head and his rumble of laughter caused quivers to race over her with reckless abandonment.

"Do not be alarmed." His deep voice, thick with lust, was another arousing caress for her senses. "I would sooner cut off my arm than cause you any injury."

She panted into his face. "Do I appear alarmed to you, Finn Braeson?"

The name slipped out, unintentional. He wasn't Braeson, yet in her heart he always would be. But even though passion fogged her responses, she should beware. She could not allow him to see through the fragile defenses she was still desperately trying to construct.

A strange expression flashed over his face as though, far from irritation that she had called him by a name that tied him to his bastardy, he welcomed it.

"Aye," he whispered, and his fingers caressed her neck with mind swirling promise. "Never forget who I truly am, Mae."

"You're my husband." In a sane sliver of her mind, she knew that wasn't what he meant, but she needed a barrier between them, no matter how flimsy, before she spilled secrets that could never be shared. Just because she wished things were different between them, did not make it so. "I am unlikely to forget that."

"I shall make sure of it." His growled response was barbaric, and she should not find it so alluring, but needle-sharp thrills cascaded low in her belly and her breath caught in her throat.

Heady desire throbbed in the charged air as he tugged with barely concealed frustration at the ties at her bodice. She was tempted to assist, but it was too entrancing to feel his strong fingers graze her skin as he struggled with so simple a task.

"Your elaborate Pictish gown conspires to defeat me," he said, as he finally loosened the ribbons and shot her a triumphant grin.

Her heart melted, no matter how hard she tried not to let his teasing words affect her.

"Perhaps you should have allowed my ladies to prepare me for you tonight, as is only right and proper."

"And deny myself this torturous entertainment?"

"It seems the strangest things amuse you."

"You amuse me." He offered her a leering grin as he tugged her gown over her shoulders.

"Should I be offended?"

"Why should it offend you that I can't get you out of my mind? That every time I think of you, I want to hold you in my arms?"

Her gown slithered to the floor in a pool of green, and she had the absurd desire to follow it. His words shouldn't affect her so. They were, after all, merely words, and she had discovered to her cost that they meant little.

But here, in the shadows of night when there were only the two of them, she could pretend all was well. A poor substitute for the dreams she'd held, but if they helped get her through the days, it was all she could ask for.

He unwound his plaid and stripped off his shirt, standing before her in all his masculine glory. She drew in a ragged breath and traced her fingers over his hard, chiseled, muscles, and in response he tugged her hair loose from its green ribbons.

She pressed her lips against his chest, teasing with her teeth and tongue, and his groan of pleasure was exhilarating. Daringly, she nipped his flesh, savoring his taste and how her touch caused him to shudder in her arms.

With a harsh intake of breath, he stripped her under-gown from her.

"My bride." His gaze raked over her, a searing flame of possession. He scooped her into his arms and laid her on the bed, towering over her like a shadowy warrior from ages past.

He lavished kisses across her flesh, teasing the inside of her thighs and her hips, until she writhed, mindlessly, beneath his searing caresses. Finally, his mouth captured hers and he speared his fingers through her hair, pinning her to the pillows. It was barbaric and thrilling, and she clawed his biceps, relishing how his muscles flexed beneath her fingers.

But still he resisted taking her, and the intoxicating caress of his hard body against hers was sweet torture. Desperate need burned through her, and she hooked her legs around his hips. His rigid length branded her swollen clitoris, and a needy gasp escaped, as her last coherent thoughts unraveled.

With a savage groan that vibrated his body he surrendered to her unspoken demand and pushed into her, filling her completely. She clung onto him, her only thread of sanity, as exquisite pleasure spiraled through her with every glorious thrust. The frenzied beat of her heart filled her head, his hot breath caressed her cheek, and the primal scent of passion flung her over the transcendent edge.

With a smothered curse he pulled out of her and grabbed his

shirt. Sated and dazed, she clung onto him until he had spilled his seed and his rigid body relaxed. With a deep sigh of satisfaction, he rolled over and pulled her into his arms. All she could hear was the ragged mingling of their breath, and the thunder of their hearts, as he pressed his lips against her brow in a kiss that meant so much more to her than it should.

inn stretched in the bed, a sense of deep contentment flowing through his body. Mae was curled beside him, her hand on his chest, her breath a sensual caress across his skin.

Instinctively, he tightened his arm around her, and she gave a soft sigh.

My wife.

In more than name. No one, not even the king himself, could part them now.

He opened his eyes. Light filtered through the shutters at the windows and the fire had all but died, yet he knew the hour was late to still be in bed. For him, at least. Not that he was inclined to move. Not when his enticing bride was naked in his arms.

His cock stirred and graphic fragments of the previous night simmered through his mind. He should let her sleep, but he couldn't stop himself from pressing his lips on the top of her head and inhaling the evocative scent of her hair.

Slowly, she awoke, and tipped back her head so their gazes meshed. "Good morning, my lady."

"Is it morning already? I feel I scarcely slept for a moment."

"My fault," he conceded. "You are too tempting a bride for me to resist."

"You misunderstand. I wasn't complaining."

"Nevertheless, you should rest. I will arrange for your ladies to attend to you here in the bedchamber." But not until he had taken his delightful wife once again.

She arched her back, and her breasts pressed against him in a teasing caress. "I have never woken with a man in my bed before."

Lust speared through him. "You had best get used to it, Mae."

"I will do my best."

Her prim response, when her hair was tangled across the pillows and her lips swollen from his kisses, made him laugh. "Tell me what you wish me to do."

Anticipation thrummed through him as she blinked sleepily, clearly considering his command. Then she wriggled up his body, an unbearable torture, until they were eye-to-eye.

"There is one thing." Her voice had dropped to a whisper, and he glided his hand along her back until she shivered with need.

"Name it."

"Could you grant me access to speak with the royal hostages held in Dunadd?"

Her question was like a bucket of iced water thrown at his head. It took longer than it should to grasp back his staggered senses.

But fuck. He'd imagined she was still in a fog of newly wed bliss. Not that she was already devising political strategies.

While they were still in *bed*.

"Finn?" There was a trace of wariness in her voice, and he forced a smile before she guessed how she had rocked him. Why wouldn't she ask about such a thing? This was, after all, a political marriage.

Except, for them both, it was so much more than that.

He sucked in a deep breath. Unlike him, she saw things more clearly. Soon, they'd move to the cursed stronghold of Dunclach.

It was natural she should make the best use of her time before they left Dunadd.

Aye. That was all this was. It had nothing to do with her wanting him out of her bed.

"That's a matter for the king to decide. But I can speak to him on your behalf, if you wish."

"I could speak to him myself."

Unease shifted through him. He didn't want her speaking to MacAlpin. He didn't want the king to say something that might jeopardize the fragile trust he was trying so hard to build with Mae once again.

And then something else erupted in his brain, and the lingering tendrils of lust in his blood turned to ash.

Talargan was a royal hostage. And he was in love with the Princess of Fortriu.

～

WITH GRIM DETERMINATION, Finn marched to the southern face of Dunadd where the hostages were held. It was likely Talargan had heard of Finn's elevation in rank, and his marriage, and it would be far easier to leave Dunadd without speaking to him.

But he couldn't do it. He owed it to their previous friendship to face the prince, for perhaps the last time, and at least try to explain what had happened.

Talargan accompanied him in a chilling silence as they left the shadow of the stronghold behind them. After they'd marched for some distance, and the prince still hadn't spoken, Finn took a deep breath and halted.

He faced the prince. "My lord," he said, and didn't get any further as Talargan punched him in the face, sending him reeling. Before the prince could follow up his attack, the two guards who had accompanied them lunged forward and grabbed Talargan's arms, dragging his back.

"Snake tongued bastard," Talargan snarled, venom dripping from each word.

Finn spat blood on the ground, before glowering at the guards. "Release him."

The guards glowered back but did as they were bid. He was now, after all, MacAlpin's son.

Talargan stamped ahead before coming to an abrupt stop. Finn heaved a sigh and joined the prince. After several moments of strained silence, he spoke. "MacAlpin ordered me to wed the princess after we last spoke, my lord. I've never lied to you about this."

Talargan's jaw flexed. "So you are now wed to the Princess of Fortriu."

"Aye. And if it means anything, I would die for her."

"Easy words to speak."

"Aye." He acknowledged that truth. "But she is my light. I'll let no man harm her."

"Because she is now your property."

"No." He grabbed Talargan's arm and swung him around. "That's not why. I didn't plan this. But it happened. And I swear to God I'll do everything in my power to ensure her happiness."

"Except grant her freedom."

Finn released his grip on the prince's arm and stepped back. He'd spoken the truth. He'd do anything for Mae.

But in this, the prince was right. Because he would never let her go.

FINN HAD LEFT Mae in bed, with instructions she should catch up on her sleep. As he passed through the great hall and climbed the stone stairs, he inhaled deeply but couldn't get Talargan's tortured expression from his mind.

He felt for the prince. If Mae were with another man, he'd be eaten up inside at the thought of it. But he couldn't change what had happened and even if he did possess that power, there was no way he would.

She was the only woman he wanted.

As he entered the corridor that led to their chambers, his senses went on full alert as two of the king's personal guard greeted him. He pushed by them and as he reached the door, it opened, and the king himself stepped out, followed by MacAllister.

"Finn." MacAlpin grasped his shoulder. "How remiss of you to leave your bride alone so soon after the wedding. We trust you will take better care of her forthwith."

"Sire," he ground between his teeth, as he attempted to process the fact the king had been with *his wife*. "You wished to see me?"

Except MacAlpin never went looking for anyone. He had messengers who brought people to the king. It was inconceivable MacAlpin was in this part of the stronghold. And yet, he was.

MacAlpin gave a short laugh. "No. Our gracious cousin was kind enough to speak with us. All is well." His gaze dropped to Finn's split lip. "Fighting for the honor of your wife already? We are impressed."

With that parting shot, he swept down the corridor, his guards following.

What the fuck? Had Mae sent her own messenger to the king, requesting an audience? Why would she do that, when he had told her he would deal with it?

She wasn't to know that he'd had no intention of procuring a meeting between them.

He marched into the antechamber. Mae sat on one of the chairs, in another of her splendid, foreign gowns, her ladies beside her, and on the far side of the chamber Bhaic stood, his face its usual impassive mask.

She was a princess and royalty were always surrounded by

their attendants, but he didn't like it. It reminded him of the reason why they had wed, when all he wanted was the noble-woman who had enchanted him beneath the moon in Fotla.

He went to her, but she didn't greet him with a smile. With a jolt, he realized she was silently furious. What the hell had MacAlpin said to her?

She was his bride, but she was also the senior royal in the land, and she had been ousted from her kingdom by his father. They weren't in public, but neither were they alone. Maybe by acknowledging her rank, he could ease her wounded pride.

"Madam." He inclined his head and held out his hand. "May we speak?"

Shock flashed across her face, as if she found his deference suspicious, but at least she took his hand.

"Of course." Her voice was icy.

He led her to the bedchamber and shut the door behind them. "What happened?"

She swung about and held her hands to the flames that now roared in the fireplace.

"Forgive me if I do not swoon with delight when your king chooses to descend upon me."

"What?" He came to her side. "You didn't summon him?"

She shot him a scandalized glance. "I did not." She exhaled a long breath and it seemed some of the tension seeped from her body. "I confess, I was going to send a message to request an audience with him. But he preempted me. Fortunately, I was suit-ably attired for the occasion."

So she hadn't planned on waiting for him to speak to MacAlpin on her behalf. It was galling, but he wasn't surprised. "What was so important that he could not wait to see us both together?"

Her glance was guarded. "It was me he wished to speak with. I assumed you knew of it."

"I assure you I did not."

"It is of no consequence." She focused on her outstretched hands, where precious heirlooms of Pictland adorned her fingers. "A standard greeting he bestows upon all Pictish royals wives, I am sure."

Finn doubted it. "That was all? A greeting?"

"Indeed."

There was something she wasn't telling him. "What was his response when you requested leave to visit the hostages?"

Acid churned in his gut. Was the real reason she wanted permission so that she could see Talargan? Just because she had been forced to marry an old man, did not mean she had forgotten her first love.

Had the prince been her first love? Or had it all been in Talargan's mind? Since discovering Mae's true heritage, the possibility hadn't even occurred to him.

But it did now. And it clawed into him with poisoned talons of doubt.

"Your king made it very clear it would not be seemly for the Princess of Fortriu to concern herself with such manly political issues." Her voice dripped venom. "Alas, we achieved nothing but an impasse."

Damn MacAlpin to hell. "It's true women hold no political power in Dal Riada, Mae. But if it eases your mind, I can assure you the hostages are being accorded all rights due to their status."

"Except for their freedom."

Her words punched through his chest like rocks from a slingshot. It was the same accusation Talargan had leveled against him so recently.

"I can't deny it." His response was harsh. What else could he say to her? There was nothing he could do to change the situation.

She sighed and shook her head, and then frowned as she focused on his lip as though she'd only just noticed his injury. "Were you in a fight?"

Crows would peck out his tongue before he admitted the truth of what had just occurred. "A minor skirmish. A hazard of being a warrior."

"Goddess," she muttered, as though he were a willful child, and she spun about and opened one of her mighty trunks. Frowning, he watched as she pulled out an intricately carved casket and placed it on the table beside the fire. She gave him a regal look. "Come. Sit on the stool so I might attend to your wound."

He sat on the stool, but only because it appeared his injury had helped dampen her ire against the king.

"It's not life-threatening," he was compelled to say, as she withdrew a small glass jar and examined the contents. "Merely a scratch."

"This will prevent any noxious substance from manifesting."

That silenced him. Although the possibility was remote, he had no wish to fall victim to such an ignoble end.

As Mae administered to him, her luscious cleavage was at eye level, and her irresistible scent teased his senses. His cock throbbed with need, and it was hard not to wind his arms around her and pull her onto his lap. But the firm set of her mouth assured him she wouldn't appreciate it.

"There." She tilted her head and scrutinized her handiwork. Whatever she had used stung like angry bees, but she nodded, clearly satisfied, before packing her jar and other implements she had used back in the casket.

He threaded his fingers through hers, stilling her actions. "Do princesses usually know such medical arts?"

"This one does." She glanced at him. "All Pictish women do. It is a fearful thing to imagine Scotswomen are ignorant of such basic arts."

Before he could stop himself, he brushed his fingers over the scar that slashed his temple. Scotswomen did possess medical knowledge. If not for his mother's swift intervention, on that dark night so long ago, he could have bled to death from his injury.

But noblewomen were not royal princesses. Yet what did he know of princesses, beside Mae?

His gaze roved over the casket. It was a beautiful piece of art itself, with compartments for all her jars and pots. As she hastily closed it and pressed her palm against the lid, a thread of disquiet edged through his mind.

Were the contents of this casket what she had referred to when she'd told him not all women were at the mercy of a man's seed?

The question hovered on his tongue. But he would never utter it. The knowledge was hers, to share or not. And in truth, it still gave him uneasy visions of witchcraft and he had no wish to delve further down such dark pathways.

He hauled his thoughts back in line and gave her a smile. "Thank you, my lady."

Was it his imagination, or did relief glow for one endless moment in her eyes?

"You are quite welcome." And then she smiled, and warmth flooded through his chest.

He couldn't wait to take her from this place. Dunclach wasn't Duncarn, to be sure, but at least they would no longer be under the same roof as his king.

CHAPTER 27

*B*efore he left her, Finn had told her they were leaving Dunadd as soon as possible and she was certainly ready to depart at the earliest opportunity. Except, after she had changed from the magnificent gown her mother had worn for her wedding day, into something more practical, the two princesses and their entourage descended, along with a great assortment of refreshments.

Ostensibly, it was a friendly gathering of royal ladies, to wish her well before she left for her new home. But she trusted neither of them. They were likely here on their cursed king's orders, in the hope she might let something of consequence slip.

And that would never happen.

Constantine's wife, Orla, ventured to admire Mairi's gown, and for a few moments the conversation centered on the points of difference between Pictish and Scottish cloth and decorative practices.

But it was all superficial, and inside she was still seething over MacAlpin's visit earlier.

She hadn't shared everything with Finn. It hurt, not knowing for sure whether he was privy to the king's actions or not, but regardless, she had to take care. For her own safety.

MacAlpin *had* dismissed her concerns for the welfare of the Picts he still held hostage, and he'd told her such things were men's business. But then he'd revealed the real reason why he had wanted to speak with her.

He wanted the sacred broach of Fortriu, to consolidate his power over Pictland. And in return, she would be granted access to certain high-ranking hostages.

She would sooner see the broach destroyed by her own hand, than have it fall into that upstart's ruthless clutches.

"If I might be so bold, Madam," Orla said, as a servant poured her a third cup of wine, "as to wish you such great happiness in your marriage as I have found with my lord Constantine."

Constantine was an unfaithful oaf. Mairi kept a serene smile on her face. "Thank you."

Orla smiled, clearly relieved she hadn't caused offense. "I shall pray for God to bless you with a son, as He saw fit to bless me."

"Indeed." She couldn't help the hint of ice in her voice, but Orla appeared oblivious, as she held out her cup to be refilled once again.

Orla proceeded to speak at length about her young son, and Mairi sipped her herbal tea in silence. She knew, of course, Orla was a grand princess from across the sea, from the land where the Dal Riadan Scots had originated. MacAlpin had secured that marriage for his eldest son years before he had turned his sights to the princesses of Pictland.

But of Aedh's bride, she knew nothing.

When Orla paused for breath, and another sip of her wine, Mairi turned to the younger woman. "Have you been in Dal Riada long, my lady?"

Margery dropped her gaze to her lap. "Eight months, Madam," she whispered, and Mairi could not instantly place her accent.

"Margery is the youngest daughter of a minor Northumbrian royal house," Orla said, giving Margery's clasped hands a comforting pat. "Alas, the alliance was not enough to ensure peace, but I have told her many times, once she bears an heir for her lord, her status in the House of Alpin will be assured."

Goddess. Unexpected sympathy stirred in her breast for the young woman, a minor princess in a foreign land, and she was compelled to respond. "Eight months is nothing."

"Aye." Orla nodded sagely, and her hand shook as she placed her empty cup upon the table. "Nothing at all. Not even a hint of quickening."

Orla had entirely misunderstood her, but Mairi was in no mind to correct her. If only she could speak to Margery alone and discover whether she truly desired a child or not. There were ways to assist. But she did not dare share such knowledge with so many foreign ears listening.

"I am certain all will be well," she said to the younger princess, who gave her a shy smile.

"We are fortunate with our husbands," Orla said. "My lord Constantine holds me in the highest esteem since I birthed our son, and Lord Aedh is honorable, and never lays a hand in anger upon Margery. I am sure the same is true for Lord Finn, despite his disturbing reputation."

Her acidic thoughts regarding Constantine's behavior, and the fact Aedh's restraint from beating his wife was somehow quite remarkable, splintered at Orla's final remark. "What?"

"My lady Orla," whispered Margery, clearly horrified, but Orla ignored her and leaned closer to Mairi. Unable to help herself, Mairi mirrored her action.

"Only this morn," she breathed dramatically, "he attacked a royal hostage without provocation. Warriors had to drag them apart."

No. She did not believe it. Finn would never attack without

provocation. And why would he attack a royal hostage in any case?

What of his injury?

To be sure, it could easily have been caused by a fist. Unease threaded through her. It still didn't mean he had attacked a Pict.

"My lady," Margery said again, twisting her fingers together in clear agitation.

Orla spared her a fleeting glance. "Hush, Margery. It is no great secret. Half the stronghold bore witness to the attack on the Pictish prince."

Her unease magnified. *Do not ask.* She would not lower herself to listen to gossip. But gossip was often the only way one learned what was happening beyond one's web of spies.

And she had not even established her faithful network in this new land, yet.

She took a sip of tea so the princess would not see her disquiet. As she replaced the cup on the table she said, "Pictish prince?'

"The Prince of Ce," Orla said. "Perhaps the princess is acquainted with him?"

Talargan. Once, when she was a carefree girl, she had imagined she was in love with him. But she had never told Finn, she was sure of it. Was it mere coincidence that Finn and Talargan had fought?

Her stomach knotted in distress. Why had they fought? Was it because she had asked to speak to the hostages?

"Of course," she replied, thankful her voice remained even, as though Orla's disclosure was no great revelation. "I am acquainted with everyone in the royal houses of Pictland." And then she couldn't stop herself. "One skirmish with a royal hostage hardly warrants a prince to bear the stigma of a disturbing reputation."

"No, Madam." Once again, Orla leaned closer, and her voice dropped to a whisper. "But it is said the prince murdered his own stepfather in cold blood and would have hung, if not for the king's intervention."

How dare Orla say such things about Finn? He was a warrior, and she had no doubt he had slain his enemies in battle. Such was the life of a warrior.

But what Orla suggested was outrageous. She would not believe such lies.

Without warning, the scathing words Constantine had uttered in the stables, when he had disclosed Finn's true heritage, echoed through her mind.

Douse your temper before it lands you in more trouble than even our father would be willing to extract you from.

She hadn't paid the comment any attention at the time and had forgotten it until this moment. What had he meant by the cryptic remark?

I don't care.

Finn had kept the truth from her, but he was not a violent man. He was caring and just, and she would not allow Orla's scandalous gossip or Constantine's spiteful accusations to tarnish the future she was determined to carve out with her husband, however superficial it inevitably would be.

But the disquiet lingered, all the same.

As his lady mother led Finn and Mae through the great hall of Dunclach, he attempted not to scowl at the wealth that was evident in the tapestries that adorned the walls. He'd never been inside the stronghold before and the very air suffocated him, but he would suffer it.

For the sake of Mae.

His mother turned and spoke to Mae. "Madam, before I show you to your chambers, would it please you to see the magnificent views from the tower? I used to spend many hours there when I was a young girl."

"I should be delighted," Mae said, before glancing at him. "Did you also spend hours there when you were a boy, Finn?"

He grunted. Why was she determined to believe he had grown up here? "I did not."

In single file they navigated the stairs within the tower, Mae's ladies trailing behind him, and Bhaic at the rear. Would it always be this way now? He smothered a sigh as he joined his bride and sucked in the chilled, winter air.

Grudgingly, he had to admit the tower's view was, indeed, magnificent. Not only was the surrounding countryside laid out below them, but it also gave an unparalleled outlook across the sea. Even though mist hung low over the water, he could just see the Isle of Mull, beyond which lay the sacred Isle of Iona.

He glanced over his shoulder, to where Mae had remained close to the stairs, hugging her cloak around her. He went back to her and only just refrained from winding his arm around her. Curse all the damn royal protocols. "Are you well?"

Maybe she was afraid of heights. It had never occurred to him. His Mae was not afraid of anything.

"Of course." She caught his gaze, and the blue of her eyes stole his breath. "I have never seen the sea before. Fortriu is land-locked, and my first husband's stronghold in Fib was nowhere near the coast."

"It's not the best time of year for your first sight of the sea." He smiled, hoping to coax a likewise response from her. She had been strangely quiet since they'd left Dunadd as though she had inexplicably withdrawn from him. But why would she, when they were leaving the oppressive royal stronghold behind?

"No." She shivered, and to hell with royal protocols. He wrapped his arm around her shoulders and tugged her close.

"Let's get out of here."

∿

IT WAS LATER that evening when they were finally alone in the bedchamber that had been allocated to Mae. Apparently, his bedchamber was at the other end of the corridor.

That was another royal protocol that could go to hell. He intended sharing the same bed as his wife, not visit her in the dead of night with the sole objective of begetting an heir from her.

He shoved the thought to the back of his mind. He wasn't going to think of bairns and Mae when she had made her own views on the matter very clear.

She stood by the fire, warming her hands, and despite how charming and how perfectly she had played her role as the lady—the princess—of Dunclach at the feast to welcome her, something was still amiss.

He went to her, and she didn't move away, but it felt as though she was a thousand miles from him in her mind.

"Mae." He grasped her shoulders and gently turned her to face him. "What is wrong? Has someone offended you?"

Even as he asked the question, he knew her response. Mae was not the kind of woman who took offense at the slightest thing.

"Certainly not." For a moment, he thought a smile hovered on her lips before she sighed, instead. "Very well. Is it true that you and the Prince of Ce fought this morning?"

Shit. He had hoped to keep that from her, but he should have known better. Anything done in public at Dunadd soon became fodder for gossip.

"It was not a fight," he was compelled to correct her. "Merely a blow or two. The prince does not approve of our marriage."

She took a shuddering breath. "I imagine he does not."

He didn't want to ask her. Didn't want his darkest suspicions confirmed. But in the end, he couldn't help himself. "Is he the prince you would rather have wed, had you been given the choice all those years ago?"

She was silent for so long that the knot which had been lodged in his chest since his confrontation with Talargan expanded, digging into his heart, and making it hurt to even draw breath. God damn it, why hadn't he kept his mouth shut? He didn't need to know. It would make no difference to their situation.

Mae was his bride, and she would always be his wife.

Finally, she spoke. "It was a girlish dream. Nothing more. He is distant kin, and I grieve that he is held hostage by your king, but I'm not in love with him, Finn."

Her words should have reassured him. But she had reminded him, as though he needed it, of how MacAlpin held so many of her royal relations, as insurance for the Picts' compliance with his ambitions.

It wasn't his doing, but guilt ate deep, and all the half-buried suspicions of what had really occurred at the gathering of the Pictish royals at Dunadd seven months ago reared their ugly heads once again.

But he could never speak of that with Mae. He cradled her face, his thumbs stroking the soft skin of her cheeks, and desperate need flared through him. Her kiss reached a dark place deep inside him, her touch ignited a raw possessiveness that consumed him, and her sweet sighs as he claimed her for his own was a balm on his wounded soul.

No. He could never raise his suspicions with her and risk shattering the fragile trust she placed in him; and destroying all the hopes he held for their future together.

CHAPTER 28

*F*inn had been master of Dunclach for three days, and despite its prestige, impressive location, and the wealth generated by the land and local village, he missed Duncarn.

But Duncarn could never provide the kind of lifestyle the Princess of Fortriu was used to. And while MacAlpin thought nothing of disregarding the marriage contract and expected Finn to claim everything that Mae owned, the very idea infuriated him. Did the king have no honor when it came to the Picts?

Even thinking such a thing was treason. But then, many of the things he'd harbored against MacAlpin over the years could be considered treason. It was lucky no one could get inside his head and hear his thoughts.

As he approached the stronghold, after another day spent learning the vast inventory of Dunclach's surrounds with the steward, his heart lightened. What did it matter if he lived at Duncarn or Dunclach, so long as Mae was waiting for him there?

A warrior galloped towards him, pulling to a halt by his side. "My lord, the Norsemen have been sighted."

Fuck it, would those savages never cease their invasions?

"Has a message been sent to the king?"

"Aye. We await instructions."

He already knew what the instructions would be. To set sail to Iona and repel the Norsemen once again.

~

DUNCLACH MIGHT NOT BE a Pictish palace, but it was certainly grand, and beside the bed and antechambers Mairi now possessed, she also had a separate chamber on the ground floor for her own personal use. She was in there now, with her ladies, Lady Brae, and two Scots noblewoman who MacAlpin had assigned to her.

Spies, doubtless. They would learn nothing from her. Nor would the small contingent of Scots warriors the king had also assigned to protect her glean any information from her own loyal men.

She paused in her needlework and briefly closed her eyes. As mistress of her own stronghold, she answered to no one but Finn. And he'd told her he didn't mind what she did all day, as long as she was happy.

It was clear he hadn't the slightest idea what was involved in running a household such as Dunclach. Not that she was concerned. She was well trained in such things, and Lady Brae had handed over the keys as soon as they had arrived.

It was... odd. She could not quite put her finger on it, but it seemed the servants did not show Finn's mother the respect she deserved. And as for Finn himself, he always smiled and laughed when they were together, and showed her such attention that it was easy to imagine all was well between them.

On the surface, it was. But that was all their marriage could ever be, and she was not sure how much longer her heart could take it.

She took a deep breath. Perhaps she should ask him about his stepfather, but what good would it do? Whatever he said wouldn't change her loyalty to her countrymen, or his loyalty to his king. This was her life, and it was irrelevant that she wanted so much more with Finn. She wanted *everything*. But that was nothing but a broken dream.

She lay down her needle and flexed her fingers. Yesterday afternoon, and for half of this morning, she and her entourage had gone riding. Certainly, she had wanted to spend time with her beloved Audra, and ostensibly she had been learning about the extent of her new home.

But mainly, she had needed to get away from the foreboding stone walls of Dunclach.

There was nothing welcoming in this place. From the moment she had stepped over the threshold, an eerie sense of oppression had swirled around her. An unsettling sensation of wrongness.

I shouldn't be here.

The conviction thudded through her constantly, and only dissolved when Finn held her in his arms.

It was madness. This was her destiny. She needed to stop wishing for an impossible future and focus on weaving a web of intrigue in the court of Dunadd, by those loyal to her.

Yes, that was what she needed to do. There would be no more procrastination. But she still couldn't shift the disquiet that intertwined with every beat of her heart and every breath she took. Something was deeply amiss, and she couldn't fathom how to right it, no matter how fervently she prayed to her goddess.

Without warning, the door swung open, and Finn strode in, big and vital and her heart leaped in her breast, the way it always did when she caught sight of him. Her ladies rose from their stools and curtseyed, but she barely noticed as her husband came to her side and took her hand.

"Madam," he said. He had taken to addressing her this way

since their marriage and while she appreciated that he acknowledged her rank in public, every time he did, a hidden piece of her heart ached. How dearly she wished they could go back to the time when all she had been to him was Lady Mae.

Except those rose-tinted days had never existed anywhere outside of her beguiled mind.

And then she saw the frown on his brow, and the tense set of his mouth, and her senses sharpened. "What has happened?"

Finn glanced at his mother, who sat beside her, and bowed his head in greeting, before turning back to her. "The Norsemen were sighted from the tower."

Alarm raced through her, and she stood, her needlework tumbling from her lap onto the floor. "You have been summoned into battle?"

Dear goddess, she didn't want Finn fighting the Vikings. Even though he was a warrior, and that was what warriors did. Her stomach churned and she gripped his hand, willing him to refute her words.

Knowing that he would not.

He gave a resigned smile, and cradled her face, as if they were alone. It was foolish to take such pleasure from so small a gesture, yet her body craved his touch in the same way the earth herself needed the sun.

"I await the king's command." His gaze turned intense. "But do not fear, Mae. Dunclach is well protected, and a strong contingent of warriors will remain here at all times."

"I do not fear for myself. The Vikings head for Iona, do they not?"

"Aye. The bastards won't rest until they've stripped the sacred Isle bare." He shook his head. "Forgive me. I did not mean—"

"Oh. I have heard far worse."

This time, his smile reached his eyes. How could he look at her with such warmth and caring, if he did not mean it, even a little? But even if he did care, it could never be enough. She had to harden her heart, for her own sake, or she could never find peace in this marriage.

"My sweet Mae." His voice was low, for her ears only, and for a scandalous moment she was certain he was about to kiss her. But he straightened before their lips met, leaving her breathless and with her heart hammering with frustrated need. "I shall return to you as soon as I am able."

"Indeed. I am counting on it." And she wouldn't allow herself to dwell on the unthinkable. Finn *would* return to her. She would countenance nothing less. "Now I must be an attentive wife, and ensure you have everything you require for the journey."

He laughed and brushed his lips against her ear. "In that case, we must hasten to the bedchamber so you may fulfil your promise."

Heat flooded her cheeks as, still holding her hand, he led her from the chamber. Hastily, she shook her head when her ladies made to follow her and bit her lip so she would not smile like a besotted maid as he marched through the great hall with her by his side.

"This is most irregular," she whispered, as they reached the stairs and he indicated she should go before him. As she clutched her skirts and went up the stairs, he wrapped his hand around her waist, and she stumbled. Goddess, what was wrong with her? One false move and she would plunge to her death. Instead of that prospect rightly alarming her, the only thing that filled her head was how arousing Finn's possessiveness was.

"Be careful." His hoarse command was a rough caress against her heated skin and as she entered the corridor, she spun around to face him.

"I am not the one making improper suggestions, my lord."

"I haven't made any improper suggestions to you, my lady." Then he leaned in close, and his hot breath scorched her ear. "*Not yet.*"

"I cannot wait until you do." It was no use trying to hold her tongue when Finn ravished her with his eyes. All her inhibitions unraveled, and she welcomed it. In his arms, it was easy to pretend their world was as perfect as she had once dreamed.

He wound his arms around her and walked her backwards to her chambers. So far, he hadn't taken advantage of sleeping in his own bedchamber and she certainly wasn't complaining. Her foolish heart adored waking up next to him each morning, and the inevitable lovemaking that followed.

Liquid heat pulsed between her thighs and a delicious shudder coursed through her body. She tangled her fingers in Finn's hair as they stumbled into the antechamber, and he kicked the door shut behind them.

"Your wait is over." His wicked grin stole her breath as he tore her shawl from her shoulders and tossed it onto the floor. "I am nothing if not an attentive husband."

"It is true I have no complaints when it comes to the marriage bed."

He laughed. "I shall take that as a compliment, my love, even if I feel there is a hint of disparagement in your remark."

My love. Ah, if only. She pushed her impossible wishes to the furthest corners of her mind. "You may take it any way you desire, I am sure."

"Good." His voice was rough as he tugged her close. "I intend to take you so thoroughly, you will think of nothing else while I am gone."

"Your confidence astounds me." *Do not think of the reason why he is leaving.* "How gratifying that I know you can live up to your promise."

"I trust you will never have cause to lose faith in me."

"Rest assured, I shall tell you if I do."

He pushed her veil from her head and speared his fingers through her hair, holding her still as his mouth captured hers. His tongue teased and explored, and before she had more than a taste, he left her gasping, as his lips glided over her jaw and along her exposed throat.

Her breasts were heavy, and her nipples ached for his touch. She arched her back, pressing against his rock-hard body, but it wasn't enough. Not nearly enough.

With a low growl, he scooped her into his arms and marched into the bedchamber. She wound her arms around his shoulders and dusted kisses along his strong jaw. His uneven breath rasped against her, a delightful counterpoint to her own erratic pulses, and when he lowered her to the floor she clung onto him, not wanting to ever let him go.

He cupped her breasts, his thumb teasing her nipples through her bodice, before he grasped her gown and hauled the material up her legs. "You tempt me beyond all reason, my lady Mae."

Feverishly, she pulled up his plaid, her fingers gliding over his magnificent thighs. His groan rumbled in his chest, thrilling her soul, and when her searching fingers found his thick cock, she let out a ragged gasp.

"Likewise, Finn Braeson," she managed to pant, before she lost the use of her voice altogether. His hot, hard, erection filled her palm, and she stroked his taut flesh with her thumb.

He sucked in a sharp breath, but before she could bask in the power she held over him, his fingers found her wet slit and a choked cry escaped her throat. He teased her swollen clitoris, before he pushed inside her slick channel, using his fingers like a foretaste of his glorious cock. Her legs shook, and she could scarcely stand upright, and still he relentlessly spun her closer to the edge.

Fiery pleasure spiraled, wiping everything from her mind but this moment. He abandoned her breasts to crush her in a harsh embrace, and thank the goddess, for her legs had turned to water.

Her head fell back, one hand grasping his cock and the other clutching his biceps as he coaxed every last exquisite convulsion from her trembling body.

Gasping, she opened her eyes, and Finn gazed at her with an intensity that wrung another uncontrollable shudder through her sensitized folds. She dragged back her scattered senses and croaked out a single word. "Yes."

He leaned so close their breath mingled. "Yes, what?"

"Yes, you are a most attentive husband."

"Aye. But I've yet to make an improper suggestion."

She licked her lips and tried to steady her shaking legs. "This was quite improper, I believe."

His grin was feral, and renewed sparks of desire flickered through her.

"There are many ways I intend to take you, my sweet wife. But for now, this will suffice."

Before she could guess his intention, he swung her around in his arms before pushing her down on the bed, with her feet still upon the floor. Stunned by that unexpected maneuver she craned her neck, to see what he was doing.

Anything she might have said died in her throat when he hoisted her gown above her waist, baring her naked bottom to his hot gaze.

"Finn *Braeson*," she managed to gasp, but it wasn't outrage that burned through her blood or sent quivers racing along her exposed flesh.

His growled response was unintelligible, as he shoved a pillow under her, which undoubtedly gave him an even better view of her unclad behind.

His big hands cupped her cheeks, in a sensual, circular massage that sent illicit thrills cascading through her tender slit... and other places.

Raw lust gripped her vitals and instinctively she clawed the bedcover. "Goddess, this is *most* improper."

"I'm glad you approve." His voice was hoarse with need. "Your arse is so pretty, Mae. So soft and untouched."

"Not so untouched *now*." Despite her best endeavors, she could not stop from shifting restlessly on the bed, but it did nothing to alleviate the throbbing desire that teased her clitoris.

Roughly, he shoved her feet further apart, his thighs pressing against hers as his hands cradled her hips. With one mighty thrust he filled her slick, welcoming heat and she sucked in a ragged breath at his masterful possession.

"Mae." He sounded tortured. "You're so tight around me. Fire and silk." He leaned over her, his body covering hers, and dropped a hot kiss on her neck. "Tell me how I feel inside you."

You feel like we belong together.

But she could not say that. Not even now, when they were as one, because it was too close to what her heart most wanted.

"I do not have the words."

He pulled back, before pushing into her so fully she saw stars dance before her eyes. "Try."

"You fill me utterly," she gasped. "It is strange and wonderful, and I feel I might shatter."

His hand slid over her hip, and he cupped her sex, his finger pressing against her swollen bud. "Aye. Shatter around me, Mae. Let me feel you come as I ride you, my sweet bride."

The last threads that anchored her to reality unraveled, and she met him thrust for thrust, as his rasping breath echoed through her head. The glorious pressure built, but in the last sane sliver of her mind, urgency thundered.

"It's safe," she panted, barely aware she even spoke aloud. "Finn, *it is safe*."

He didn't ask what she meant. Finn was the most considerate of husbands, but there was no need for him to take care today. In truth, not ever, when she could protect herself against conception. But dear goddess, she wanted to once again feel him inside her when he reached his climax.

He pounded into her, restraint gone, a frenzy of harsh breaths and slick flesh. As she tumbled over the edge of the world he was there, with her, holding her tight. His big body shuddered as he pumped his hot seed inside her, flooding her, touching the very essence of her being. His voice filled her mind, his face filled her heart, and nothing existed except for this man.

My love.

CHAPTER 29

*F*inn held Mae close as they lay on the bed, her head on his chest. He'd pulled a bedcover over her, but without a fire in the grate, the chamber was all but freezing. He smothered a sigh and briefly closed his eyes.

He was merely delaying the inevitable. Soon, he would have to rise and prepare himself and his warriors for the battle that loomed. But here, in Mae's arms, political mandates and bloodied killing fields seemed so far away.

If only that was the truth.

She stirred, and his hold on her tightened. He wasn't prepared to leave her just yet. Not until he had no alternative.

As if in response to his thought, there was a knock on the antechamber door, and he bit back a curse as Mae pushed herself up onto her elbow.

"Remain here," he ordered her, before leaving the bed. He couldn't resist glancing back at her, and his gut clenched. She looked utterly ravished, with her hair loosened from its usual braids and it took all his willpower to turn his back on her and close the door between the chambers, before he marched to the outer door and flung it open.

Bhaic stood there, along with the ladies who had accompanied Mae from Fotla. They dropped him a curtsey, but the older man merely gave him a cold look, before he spoke.

"Your king's man is here to see you."

~

MACALLISTER WAS WAITING for him outside Dunclach's inner sanctum, and bowed his head when Finn arrived, before they both entered the chamber.

"My lord. I'm here as a matter of great urgency on behalf of the king."

"Aye." He could not hide the tinge of bitterness in his voice. He'd been in countless battles for his king, but never had he been so reluctant to undertake his duty. Because never before had he possessed an enchanting bride. And God damn it, he did not want to risk leaving her a widow. "I am ready."

"The king commands you leave Dunclach instantly, and escort the Princess of Fortriu to your hillfort, Duncarn."

He frowned. "What?"

"The Norsemen are set to invade our shores. The Princess' safety is paramount, and she must be taken inland."

What the fuck?

"The Norse do not head to Iona?"

"It appears they have changed tactics. The king sent a contingent of warriors to accompany you. It is his command you leave now with the princess and her entourage. There is no time to waste. We will ensure her possessions follow as swiftly as possible."

He couldn't fathom what, but something was amiss. He took a step towards MacAllister. "Surely, if the Norse are invading, the king requires all his warriors to protect our land."

MacAllister took a deep breath. "My lord, I did not wish to share this with you. But the king received word that the

Norsemen are intent on abducting the Princess of Fortriu for their own despicable ends. Therefore, it's of—"

"Mae is in danger?" He glowered at MacAllister. "Why didn't you tell me this at once?"

MacAllister inclined his head. "You see now the necessity for ensuring the princess leaves Dunclach."

"We'll leave at once." He marched from the chamber, and after giving orders for the horses to be readied, he made his way back to the bedchamber.

Mae turned to greet him with a smile that did not quite reach her eyes. "Are you summoned, my lord?"

He took her hands. The very notion that the northern barbarians dared to even contemplate harming her, made his blood boil. "Aye. But not to battle. We are to depart for Duncarn immediately."

"Your hillfort?"

He didn't want to alarm her, but Mae deserved the truth. Besides, he knew her well enough. She would not swoon in terror, as he imagined many princesses or noblewomen might do.

"The Norsemen plan to invade Dal Riada. They won't succeed. Our shores are heavily fortified. But you are a prize they would dare much to procure and Duncarn is far from here."

"I see." That was all she said, and he knew she understood what he had not explicitly stated. "Then I shall arrange for our departure forthwith."

"There is no time, Mae. We must leave now. The wagons will slow us down. Your possessions will follow, I promise you, but there is no time to waste."

She bit her lip, clearly considering his words and he attempted to smother his impatience. She was the Princess of Fortriu and was not used to obeying orders without question. But God damn it, this was her life that was at stake.

"Very well. But I must take my medicine casket with me, Finn.

It has been handed down through generations of my foremothers and I cannot leave without it."

"Of course." He'd carry it himself.

THE FOLLOWING MORNING, through the mist and rain that had plagued them for the last hour, Finn caught sight of Duncarn and despite everything, his heart lifted. Last night, when it had become too dark to travel safely, and to rest their horses, they had stayed in a minor noble's hillfort, but they had left as dawn broke.

And now he was home. Where he had wanted to take Mae from the moment he had met her.

Just not under these circumstances.

He had sent one of his warriors on ahead, to let his stepsisters know of their arrival, so they could ensure the fires were set in the bedchambers. He glanced at Mae, who rode by his side. She was drenched, but not a word of complaint had passed her lips.

His steward, Norval, greeted him at the entrance, and Finn dismounted before helping Mae from her mare, and then his mother. Norval bowed. "Welcome home, my lord."

Finn gripped his shoulder in greeting, before taking Mae's hand and leading her inside. His first priority was to get her warm and dry again. She pushed back the hood of her cloak and shivered as she glanced around, and his good mood deflated.

Duncarn was not fit for a princess such as she.

In the great hall, his family awaited, their gazes fixed upon Mae as though she was a vision from another world. And she was. He had always known it. But now she was here, in his world, and despite the modest surroundings of his hillfort, pride surged through him as he saw her smile.

"Mairi, Princess Annella of Fortriu," he glanced at Mae, "may I present Annis and Glenna, my stepsisters, and my half-sister, Rhona."

His sisters dropped respectful curtsies, but even Rhona appeared to have lost the power of speech. Mae inclined her head.

"I am delighted to meet you." Her gaze slipped to the bairns, who were clinging to Annis' skirts, their eyes wide as they took in this mystical creature who had appeared in their midst.

"Nessa and Iver," he told her. He squeezed her fingers before releasing her hand and dropping to his knees. Carefully, he placed her precious casket on the floor before turning to the bairns and holding out his arms. "Do you not have a hug for your uncle?"

CHILLED to the bone and dripping water onto the stone floor, Mairi barely noticed the discomfort as she gazed, spellbound, as Finn embraced the wee children, yet what care he took to ensure they did not become soaked by his wet garments.

He had not mentioned his nephew or niece. Or the fact one of his stepsister's was heavy with child.

It was obvious the children adored him. They patted his face and tugged on his hair, laughing as the water dripped to the floor. She had never imagined a Scots warrior—a prince—could be so gentle with little ones.

Deep in her breast, a despairing longing unfurled. She caught her breath, but the elusive sensation of loss, of something that would always be just beyond her reach, shivered through her like the touch of a thistledown on the breeze.

Goddess, she scarcely knew what she was thinking. The prospect of never holding her own babe in her arms had never affected her so profoundly before, and there could be only one reason for her flustered senses.

She was still reeling from the sense of *knowing* that had rushed through her the moment Duncarn had emerged from the swirling mist.

As though here, in an obscure corner of Dal Riada, lay her destiny.

Annis approached. "Madam, if it does not offend, may we welcome you to Duncarn and extend our best wishes upon the marriage to our dear brother, Lord Finn."

She hauled her spinning thoughts back into line. "Thank you."

"May I show you to your chamber?" Annis cast an anxious glance in Finn's direction. He picked up her medicine casket, that he had tried so hard to shield from the elements during their journey, and for which she would be forever grateful, and stood.

"My thanks, Annis," he said. "I'll take the princess to our chamber, if you could attend to our lady mother."

Finn led her across the great hall, and although it was the smallest hall she had ever seen, it emanated a strange sense of comfort, in a way the grand hall in Dunclach never had.

She resisted the urge to glance over her shoulder, although she could hear the low murmur of voices of his mother and sisters as, no doubt, they discussed her rushed arrival.

They went up the stairs, her ladies following behind Finn, and when they reached the corridor, he paused outside a door and took a deep breath.

"I told you once I had little to offer a princess. I fear none of the bedchambers possess their own antechambers, but this is the grandest one we possess in Duncarn."

"It is quite all right." She had only been here for a few moments, and already preferred it to Dunclach. But she knew where their duty lay. And besides, she could not establish a web of spies in the Dunadd court when she was so far away from it. "This is but a temporary measure, after all. Once the Viking menace has been crushed, we shall doubtless return to your stronghold, Dunclach."

"Aye."

Was it her imagination, or did he sound despondent at the knowledge?

She entered the chamber and blinked. Finn sighed. "It is not what you're used to."

Her bedraggled ladies huddled by the fire, warming their hands, and she turned to Finn and grasped his arm. "Its compact size will ensure we are kept warm and dry during these cold winter months."

Except she doubted they would be staying here for the winter. She pushed the thought aside.

He laughed and shook his head. "Its only advantage, I think."

"Finn. My ladies are I need dry gowns. We brought nothing with us."

His expression turned serious. "Forgive me. I shall ask my stepsister to attend to you instantly." He placed her medicine casket, with its priceless heirloom hidden safely within, on a small table, before kissing her hand and leaving the chamber.

AT LEAST MAIRI and her ladies were now clean and dry, and although it was kind of Finn's stepsisters to lend them gowns, she did not feel at all comfortable in the strange, Scots' fashion. Still, it would not be long before their belongings arrived.

There was a knock on the door, and her heart leaped in her breast, even though she knew Finn was too busy with the influx of warriors who had accompanied them here to visit her yet. Struana opened the door, and Rhona stood there, holding a huge platter of cold meats and delicacies. Struana took the platter from the young girl, and invited her in.

Rhona bobbed a curtsey. "Mamma said you and your ladies must be famished by the journey."

"We are, thank you." Mairi smiled at Rhona, as Struana placed the platter on a table by the fire and her ladies gathered round. "Will you join us?"

"Oh." Rhona's eyes widened in astonishment. "If you are certain? I should be honored."

Her ladies brought over some stools and for a few moments they ate in companionable silence, punctuated only by her ladies complimenting the flavorsome food. Then Rhona sighed. "You are not nearly as terrifying as I had imagined."

"I'm gratified to hear it." She couldn't help smiling at the girl's honesty. "We Pics are not so very different from Scots."

Silently, she qualified her statement. *Some Scots, at least.*

"Indeed," Rhona said. "But it was more that you are a grand princess, rather than a foreigner. We thought Finn would marry a local lass."

Something sharp dug through her heart but she managed to keep the smile on her face, for the sake of Rhona. "Finn wished to marry a local noblewoman?"

He had never indicated anything that suggested he had been planning to wed. But then, why would he say that to her? Once MacAlpin had decreed his fate was to marry the Princess of Fortriu, he had no choice but to go through with it.

Except, even now, she had foolishly imagined he had not given his heart to any other woman. Because despite everything, she wanted his heart for herself.

"Oh no, Madam. Finn never wanted to wed a noblewoman." Rhona drew in a sharp breath and pressed her lips together. "I should not have said that."

It was right and proper that she did not encourage Rhona to gossip, but she could not help herself. "Why didn't he?"

"Because..." Rhona's voice tailed away, before she straightened her spine and sucked in a great breath. "Because a noblewoman would expect her own hillfort, and Finn promised us we would always live here, together. But my mother assures me a grand princess of Pictland has many strongholds and palaces of her own, and would have no need to be mistress of Duncarn." Rhona leaned forward on her stool, and there was no mistaking the worry in her eyes. "I know there can only ever be one mistress of a hillfort, Madam."

But what of Dunclach? Why would Rhona imagine Finn would expect his bride to live here, when he owned such a great stronghold close to Dunadd?

Yet Finn had only ever mentioned this hillfort to her. The hill-fort where his mother and sisters lived.

She gave Rhona's hand a brief squeeze. Whatever the truth of the matter, Finn's sister needed to be reassured.

"Your lady mother is correct, Rhona. And rest assured I should never wish to take her place as mistress of Duncarn."

Rhona's relief was palpable. "Thank you, Madam. Oh, not that I *want* you to leave," she added hastily. "I am certain Finn will spend more time at home, if you're here. But I am glad you have your own household. Although I hope it's not too far away. I cannot *wait* until Finn has bairns of his own who I can love as dearly as Nessa and Iver, and Glenna's new wee babe when they arrive."

"I... see." Goddess, sweet Rhona was making her head spin. But there was no need for unease. Children invariably arrived after marriage. No one need know neither she nor Finn planned on having any.

Rhona pressed her hand against her mouth and her eyes widened in dismay. "Forgive me," she whispered, through her fingers. "I am too forward. Mamma will be grieved if I have offended you."

Ruthlessly, she pulled her scattered senses back into line. "You have not offended me."

Rhona gave a heartfelt sigh. "Mamma says it is unseemly to speak of such things, but we are sisters-by-marriage now, are we not? And you are wed to my beloved brother." She smiled and shook her head. "We both know how dearly he longs for a bairn of his own, although he thinks no one has guessed this."

Finn wanted a child? But he had specifically told her children had no place in his plans. Why would he say that?

She tried to ignore it, but despair washed through her, nevertheless. *He lied to me again.*

Rhona stood and bobbed a curtsey, pulling her from her confused thoughts. "I must go, Madam," Then she leaned close and whispered in Mari's ear. "I'm glad you are here."

She gathered the platters and as she left the chamber, Bhaic entered.

"Madam." He took her hand and bowed. "May we speak?"

Her head throbbed with all that Rhona had disclosed. *Finn wanted children.* But now was not the time to brood upon why Finn had deliberately misled her. With difficulty, she pulled her focus back to the present, and her ladies, who had been gathered around the fire with her, retired to the other side of the chamber. It was not very private, but it would have to do.

"Any sign yet?" She kept her voice low.

Bhaic sat on a stool and leaned towards her so he would not be overheard. "No. Your scouts returned and reported there was no sight of the wagons. There is no reason for such a delay."

Unless the wagons containing all her possessions had been attacked. But that was scarcely likely. Ten of her most trusted men had remained at Dunclach, to accompany the wagons and MacAlpin would certainly have sent a contingent of warriors to protect such a precious cargo.

"Perhaps they were delayed by the weather."

"It is possible." It was clear he thought no such thing.

She sighed. Although the delay was inconvenient, she was not too concerned. But Bhaic was troubled, and she had the conviction it was not all connected to the late arrival of the wagons. "Is there something else of which I should be informed, my lord?"

He bowed his head. "There is something, Madam. Word

reached me before we left Dunclach that the steward of my lord Nechtan's stronghold in Fib is ill and not expected to live. Without his steady hand, I fear the property and lands will fall into disrepair."

"I see." She understood what Bhaic did not say. Nechtan had no surviving matrilineal relatives to claim his stronghold. But through the lineage of her foremothers, and as his widow, she had inherited everything, and it was her responsibility to ensure the land was tended and village prospered. She squeezed Bhaic's fingers. "We will not allow that to happen."

CHAPTER 30

Finn surveyed the site a short distance from his hillfort that he'd set aside for the Scots and Pict warriors. He understood the need to protect Mae at all costs. But although the village prospered and his land was well maintained, it was not equipped to supply the needs of an additional four dozen warriors in the middle of winter.

Yet there was no alternative. They would remain here until summoned back to Dunadd by MacAlpin.

It was late afternoon when he finally made his way back to the hillfort. The camp was set up, a muddy quagmire, but warriors were used to such conditions. He'd endured it himself many times over the years. Besides, there simply wasn't room in Duncarn. Hell, there was barely enough room to accommodate Mae and her ladies.

He rubbed his hand over his face and sighed. It was one thing he didn't need to concern himself with. They were, after all, returning to Dunclach when the danger had passed.

Through the pelting rain, he saw riders' approach. Finally, Mae's wagons had arrived. But it was MacAllister who galloped up first and dismounted. Finn nodded in greeting before the wagons rolled up and he organized the trunks to be taken to his and Mae's chamber.

He led MacAllister and his men inside and they stood before the fire in the great hall. He turned to the older man.

"What news of the Norsemen? Did they land?"

"The king sent our ships to head them off. That is all I know."

Finn grunted. A battle at sea in winter was hell.

"My lord." MacAllister glanced at his men and without a word they retreated, leaving him alone with the king's man. "I regret to inform you that we were ambushed on the way and one of the princess' trunks damaged."

"How the fuck did that happen with the number of warriors guarding the wagons?"

"I was riding ahead and not part of the skirmish. By the time I returned, the trunk had been retrieved and the thieves dealt with. Please convey my apologies to the princess."

Although it was not his fault, the damage to her property had been sustained by his countrymen and for that he shouldered the blame. "I trust none of her possessions were stolen."

"I cannot say, my lord."

At least Mae would tell him if she discovered anything was missing.

"There is one more thing," MacAllister said. "With this new Norse threat, the king intends to bring forward his plans to relocate to the royal stronghold of Fortriu and requests your presence."

"The king wants me to return to Dunadd now?"

"He does. He requests you return with me this day."

Finn exhaled a frustrated breath. What the hell was MacAlpin playing at? "We have just arrived here, MacAllister. And now we are to return?"

"Only you, my lord. The princess is to remain here, with a smaller contingent of warriors to ensure her continued safety."

Something did not add up. "Why does the king need me? To fight the Norse?"

"No. He requires the presence of his royal sons to ensure safe passage of the Stone of Destiny to Forteviot."

The Stone of Destiny, the seat of power for all true Scots kings, going back so many generations its origin was obscured by the mists of time.

"If that is the king's command." He did not even try to hide the irritation in his voice. It wasn't as though he had any choice.

"The king also requests you bring the great seal of Fortriu as a matter of utmost urgency."

He recalled the marriage negotiations, and MacAlpin's displeasure when he discovered Finn had interfered. And the king's insistence that Finn acquire it for him.

In truth, it hadn't crossed his mind since. No way in hell would he ask Mae to give up anything she possessed just to appease MacAlpin's insatiable thirst for power.

"The great seal that is part of the princess' personal fortune?"

"I believe it is somewhat more than that, my lord."

Finn bit back his response. He didn't need to share anything with MacAllister. "I shall take my leave of the princess."

THERE WAS scarcely room to move with all the trunks in the chamber, but before Mairi could change into one of her own gowns, Bhaic indicated he wished to speak with her. The only place for privacy, now the chamber was so crowded, was in the corridor, and she tugged her shawl around her to keep out the chill.

"I've spoken briefly to our men who accompanied the wagons." His voice was low. "It appears the Vikings were heading to Iona, after all."

She frowned. "Why would MacAlpin say they were intending to invade Dunadd?"

"For his own nefarious purposes, I have no doubt."

"Perhaps he was misinformed."

"Doubtful."

She doubted it, too. But the alternative was he had deliberately misled them. Why would he do that? The Vikings, after all, were their common enemy. He had nothing to gain by lying in this matter.

"There were no problems transporting our possessions from Dunadd?"

"Our men tell me the journey was uneventful, Madam."

"Very good." Then she sighed. "I had best make certain the jewels of Fortriu are secure."

He bowed his head and accompanied her back into the chamber, and she led him to the trunk which held the chest. Her ladies surrounded her and while the two who had accompanied her from Fortriu were aware of the intricate locks that protected the treasure, the two noblewomen MacAlpin had assigned to her did not.

She had no intention of allowing them to witness it, either.

One glance at Struana was enough for her dear friend to understand her wishes, and usher the ladies to the other side of the chamber. Bhaic lifted the top of the trunk and reached inside for the sturdy chest.

In silence, he placed it on the floor.

Her heart hammered in denial, and she pressed a shaking hand to her breast as her gaze fixed upon the destroyed carvings around the lid, that had once concealed the intricate locking mechanisms.

She sank to her knees and ran a trembling finger over the ancient wood. Bhaic kneeled by her side, and she could only be thankful that the bed was between them and her ladies, so they could not see what had happened.

"We were betrayed," she whispered. How could she have been so foolish, so blind to MacAlpin's ploy? The only way he could steal the jewels of Fortriu was by ensuring they were left in Dunclach. And the only way to do that was to make sure she left the stronghold in haste.

Grimly, Bhaic opened the chest. But it was not empty, as she had imagined. Frowning, she reached for the nearest casket and opened it, and drew in a sharp breath. Gems sparkled, all in their allotted places.

She glanced at Bhaic, and he opened another casket. The jewels appeared untouched.

"What trickery is this?" she breathed. In silence, they went through every casket until she was finally satisfied.

Nothing had been taken.

Because the one thing MacAlpin had wanted, was hidden within her medicine casket.

"Did they take what they were searching for?" Bhaic's gaze was steady. He knew of the powerful broach, of course. But even he did not know where she had hidden it, after the death of Nechtan.

"They did not." She closed the lid of the casket on her lap and replaced it in the chest. Fury burned within her breast at the despicable depths to which MacAlpin had sunk, and her own stupidity for not foreseeing this.

But it was more than that. So much more.

Yesterday, when Finn had hurried her from Dunclach, had he known this was his king's plan?

No. She could not believe it of him. *Would* not. She gripped her fingers together and took a deep breath. She had to believe he was ignorant of this act, or the flimsy façade she clung onto that their marriage could somehow survive, would crumble to dust.

There was a knock on the door, and Bhaic helped her to her feet as Finn entered the chamber. Even wet through, he was a commanding presence, and when his green gaze caught hers, her breath caught in her throat and pulses raced in pitiful need.

"Mae. Madam," he corrected himself. "I must speak with you."

"Leave us," she said, and her ladies and Bhaic dutifully obeyed. Self-consciously, she smoothed down her gown. While Finn looked magnificent as always in his plaid, she felt awkward and ill at ease in the strange Scots attire. But it did not matter what she wore. She was the Princess of Fortriu, and the Supreme Kingdom's legacy had been violated.

He came to her and took her hand. Why did his touch always affect her so? It took all her willpower not to curl her fingers around him and rest her head against his shoulder.

"The king has summoned me back to Dunadd." Frustration threaded through his statement, and she tried not to acknowledge the forlorn sense of abandonment his words evoked. "I'm sorry, Mae. I'm to leave directly."

"One cannot go against the word of one's king." Goddess, she had not meant to sound so scathing. But even the merest mention of MacAlpin turned her stomach.

Finn's gaze turned calculating. Or was she imagining it?

"When the Norsemen have been defeated, I shall request leave. You and I shall have time together, just the two of us. I swear."

She swallowed. She could say nothing. It might even be better to hold her tongue. But she could not. "How goes the battle with the Vikings, Finn? Do you know?"

He sighed heavily and released her hand, before dragging his fingers through his wet hair. "MacAlpin sent ships to accost them at sea. It seems their plans to invade Dal Riada have failed."

Because they never intended to invade Dal Riada.

She flattened her palms against her thighs before she betrayed her disquiet by twisting her fingers together. It was possible, after all, that Finn did not know the Vikings had been heading to Iona.

"Why does your king need you so suddenly?" She tried to

keep her voice light but wasn't sure she succeeded. Not when the rock lodged within her chest grew bigger with every tortured breath she took.

This time there was no mistaking the wary expression that flashed across his face. "He intends to move the royal court from Dunadd."

Her chest tightened and involuntarily, her fingers flexed. *Remain calm.* But it was so hard to keep her fury, her sense of *betrayal*, from escaping. "To Forteviot."

"Aye." He sounded reluctant to admit it. "I believe the Norse threat hastened his decision."

She believed no such thing. And if her own men had not confirmed that the Vikings had been sighted heading to Iona, she'd think MacAlpin had fabricated the entire danger.

So he could get his hands on the sacred broach of Fortriu. But in that, at least, he had failed.

"How convenient." The words were out before she could stop them. Why could she not curb her tongue whenever she was with Finn?

"Ah, Mae." His sigh drove a pain so acute into her heart, she could scarcely breathe. "I don't know what to say. MacAlpin set his sights on Forteviot and is determined to move his court there. If not this day, then some other. There's no stopping him now."

She took a jagged breath. "He will never be the true king of Pictland. And he knows it."

"Why are we discussing this? There's nothing we can do to change his course. I don't want to leave with bad blood between us, Mae, due to MacAlpin's actions."

Of course he didn't. He wanted to leave Duncarn safe in the knowledge his wife believed every word he said to her. A bride bedazzled by her husband's attentiveness and charm. The loyalty and unquestioning obedience of the Princess of Fortriu, who gave legitimacy to his father's claim to the Supreme Kingdom's throne.

Because if she questioned him, the masquerade of their marriage would be torn asunder. There would be no need for him to maintain a courteous pretense, and any small hopes she'd harbored for happiness with him would be nothing more than ash at their feet.

Finn is not trying to delude me.

But he had lied to her before.

Yet that did not mean he had been party to the indefensible ransack of the treasure of Fortriu. She clung onto that flimsy thread. Her lifeline.

"One of my chests was broken into." Somehow, she managed to keep her voice neutral. Finn was innocent of that outrage. She was sure of it.

"Aye. Hell, I should have said, Mae. Thieves attacked the wagons and tried to steal one of your trunks. Is anything missing? I'll have the area searched if so."

Her mouth dried and heart thudded erratically at his confession. Dear goddess. He knew of the damage to her trunk. And had concocted a despicable story to appease her outrage.

"Thieves?" It was all she could manage. Yet he was right. The Scots who had broken the locks on the chest were nothing less than common thieves.

"I'm told they didn't get away with anything. Was anything damaged?"

He looked so concerned. Her stomach churned with distress at how easily he could twist the truth while gazing so intently into her eyes.

"Perhaps you would like to see for yourself." Her voice was icy as she swung about and indicated the chest that was on the floor behind her.

He bit out a curse and crouched before it, running one finger along the ruined carvings. "Isn't this the chest that contains your jewels?"

As if he did not know. He had witnessed Bhaic opening the chest on her wedding night.

"It is."

He remained crouching but didn't attempt to look inside the chest. Nor did he look at her. "Are you certain nothing is missing?"

"Quite certain."

"Is this the only chest that was damaged?" There was an odd note in his voice that she couldn't place.

"It is. Strange, do you not think, that these thieves knew exactly which chest to steal?"

He stood. A frown carved his brow. "Aye."

Was that all the answer she deserved? Did he think her so enamored of him that she would not question anything he said?

Why was she trying so hard to absolve him of any blame in deceiving her? If he had not so thoroughly undermined her defenses with his chivalrous façade, she would see his culpability as clearly as she saw the aristocratic nose on his face.

There was no happy future in this marriage. There never had been.

Something broke deep inside her, and the last shreds of self-preservation withered in defeat. This latest insult to the dignity of Pictland could not be swept aside, simply because she so desperately wished to preserve an illusion. "Don't treat me like a fool, Finn. I know there was no attack on the journey."

His gaze sharpened. Clearly, he had not expected her to dispute his account of events. "How would you know that?"

She would not lower herself to answer such a question. Did he believe her utterly isolated in Dal Riada?

"Why did you ensure we left Dunclach in such haste that we could not take our belongings with us, unless it was imperative I leave behind the chest containing the fortune of Fortriu?"

"Damn it, Mae. The Norse planned to attack. We had to get you to safety."

"You know as well as I that the Vikings were heading to Iona."

His jaw tensed. "That's not the information I received."

So even in the face of the truth, he refused to admit it. Because that would mean going against his king's word.

She had never expected anything less from him. But how she had secretly hoped for so much more.

"Alas." Her throat was thick with unshed tears, but she would never allow Finn to see her weep. "We shall never see events from the same perspective."

"How can you say that?" His glare was fierce, and he made to take her hands before obviously thinking better of it and folding his arms across his chest instead. "We are wed, Mae. We see things as one."

Grief squeezed her heart at how, even with her eyes wide open, she had been so blind. "I'm not a meek Scotswoman who agrees with everything her husband utters, Finn. I do not see things the way you do, and I never shall. Any hope for reconciling Pictland died the night your king massacred the nine nobles of royal blood who contested his claim to the throne of Fortriu."

Raw pain flashed across his face, but she would not fall for his deceptions. Not again.

"I was fighting the Northumbrians." The words throbbed with suppressed anger. At her refusal to comply with his constraints for what passed as the truth, perhaps? "You know enough about me that I wouldn't lie to you about such a thing."

"I know nothing about you." The truth of her statement pierced her heart. She couldn't blame this all on Finn. She had always known but had chosen to believe in deception and lies.

The last threads of caution unraveled. It didn't matter what she said to him now. Any possible influence she may have held in this new life had surely died. "A man rumored to have killed his own stepfather?"

How did that make him any different from MacAlpin?

"You listen to rumors, now?" His voice was harsh and there was no mistaking that her allegation had hit home. And proved the rumor as truth.

"I have no choice when it's the only way to learn information."

"You could try asking me, Mae. I'd tell you anything you want to know."

How degrading that, even now, she so desperately wished to trust him. "Alas, there's nothing you could say to me that I would be willing to believe."

Had she imagined the pain that flashed in his eyes? Most likely. She appeared incapable of hardening her heart against Finn, yet to survive, she had to.

"Do you really think so little of me?"

His quiet accusation thrust through her breast like a freshly forged sword. How much easier it would be to disregard his words if he had flung them at her in anger.

But he was too cunning for that. He knew how to manipulate her foolish senses, but she could no longer allow her heart to lead the way.

She tilted her head in a regal manner and focused on his shoulder. Goddess help her, if she looked into his eyes again, she would be forever lost. "I think nothing of you, Finn. If not for the bloodied ambition of your king, we would never have met, nor been plunged into this disastrous alliance. I may not condemn you for your bloodline, but I cannot admire you for it."

Every barbed word shredded her wounded soul, and unable to help herself, she caught his gaze. His face was a mask. She scarcely recognized the man who had once held her close and whispered such sweet promises of a life together that could never be. How despicable that she longed to return to that imaginary existence.

A deathly silence echoed around the chamber, a tangible, suffocating, presence, and she had the wild need to scream, to run. To do anything but stand here serenely, as though her world wasn't shattering around her feet. But one thousand years of Pictish pride stiffened her spine and kept her silent, as once again he glanced at the broken chest.

Finally, he inhaled a great breath. It sounded eerily like a deathly portent. "What is the significance of the great seal of Fortriu?"

And there it was. The reason for all the subterfuge. She refused to lower herself to explain something he could not help but know already.

"If you truly do not understand the power of the sacred broach of Fortriu, then I suggest you ask your king. It is very clear he will stop at nothing to acquire it."

ae's condemnation flayed him like ice and her beautiful blue eyes were as cold as the deepest loch in the depths of winter. But her words were poisoned daggers, tearing through his heart and ripping out his guts.

This, then, was all she thought of him. All she had ever thought of him. Denial burned through him, to justify or explain, but the excuses locked in his throat. It made no difference. In her eyes, he was guilty by virtue of his tainted blood. Because everything she accused MacAlpin of was true.

She stood before him, and even in the Scots gown, so unlike her own, there was no mistaking her regal bearing or the fact she was so far above him their paths should never have crossed. And as she'd so eloquently reminded him, they never would have, but for MacAlpin's ambitions.

His bride. How proud he had been to call her that. How easily he'd assumed she was as invested in their marriage as he.

Not because it was a political alliance. But because she wanted it.

Wanted to be with him.

But it had all been inside his bewitched mind. Nothing more.

"I think nothing of you."

Her scathing words would haunt him forever. All the times they had spoken, before cursed duty had come between them, meant nothing to her. She had formed her opinion before they had even met, and nothing had changed it.

Deep in his heart, he couldn't even blame her. His king had taken everything she most cherished from her. Her heritage. Her freedom.

Her choice of husband.

He had to get out of here before he said something he'd regret. Something that showed her how great her power was over him. Because even now, when the façade had cracked wide open, revealing the sordid underbelly of how she viewed their union, the truth was he'd do anything to ensure her happiness.

He gave a stiff bow and marched out of the chamber, avoiding her ladies who clustered at the door, before making his way down the stairs and through the great hall.

It was empty. He should seek out his lady mother and take his leave, but he would need to pretend all was well, and he couldn't stomach it.

She would understand.

He took a deep breath before leaving his hillfort. MacAllister and his men waited, along with most of the Scots warriors who had accompanied him and Mae earlier today. At least she still had her own contingent of Pict warriors. And they were loyal to her.

They would protect her and for that he was grateful. But it was a hollow comfort, when he had to face the fact Mae had never trusted him, no matter how he had imagined otherwise.

"Is all well, my lord?" MacAllister said. The damn man always saw far too much.

"Aye." It was hard to be civil to the one who was likely responsible for breaking into Mae's trunk. But MacAllister would not have done such a thing without a direct order from the king.

Dull rage rolled through him once again at how MacAlpin

had disregarded the most basic construct of respect by violating Mae's property. It was obvious she thought he had been involved in the deception to hasten her away from Dunclach. Obvious she had never believed him when he had told her MacAlpin did not confide in him.

As he rode off with the others, he couldn't help glancing over his shoulder at Duncarn. Already it had been all but swallowed up in the mist that accompanied the constant rain, and only a dark shadow remained.

A stark manifestation of the despair consuming the void that had once been his heart.

FINN CLOSED the door behind him, and the pride that had sustained Mairi throughout the torturous confrontation fled her bones. She collapsed onto the edge of the bed and buried her face in her hands.

He hadn't denied anything. Not even a little. The pain in her heart was like a fiery serpent, spreading throughout her breast, crippling her ability to breathe, or think.

It was over. Everything. There was no coming back from this. Every foolish dream she'd ever woven around a future with Finn lay in tatters, beyond repair.

So much for imagining that here, in Duncarn, lay her destiny.

She sucked in a shaky breath and forced her hands to her lap. There was no doubt in her mind that next time, MacAlpin would rip apart everything she owned in his quest to secure the sacred broach.

If she couldn't keep it safe, she had to destroy it. For the sake of Pictland.

Grimly, she focused on that thought, banishing all others from her mind, as she stood and found her medicine casket. She pressed her hand against the lid and briefly closed her eyes. Finn's smiling face confronted her, his infectious laugh echoing through her head. How hard it was to push through the bittersweet memories of his touch and concentrate on the only thing that mattered.

And once that was done, she would leave this hollow marriage behind. She feared she'd lose her mind if she had to pretend an aloof disinterest in her husband every time he was near. How could she bear his cold glances and the naked distrust that now hung like a specter between them?

He had married her for one reason only. To find the sacred broach for MacAlpin.

It was better the illusion had cracked open, revealing the tawdry reality. At least now she had no more excuses to pretend a union with the son of MacAlpin could possibly work. But nevertheless, a shameful part of her wished desperately to return to the faithless masquerade of yesterday.

There was a knock on the door, and she swung around, as Struana entered the chamber and dropped a curtsey. Mairi forced a smile, although it seemed her face might crack with the effort.

Struana came to her side. "Madam, I understand my lord Finn's sister has taken to her chamber."

Her scattered thoughts sharpened. "She is gone into confinement?"

"I thought you should know." Struana hesitated. "It is a strange situation to be in, to be sure."

Mairi took Struana's hand. It was, indeed. Should she offer her support and assistance, the way she would if Glenna were a beloved cousin? They were, after all, related by marriage. In any other circumstance, a sister-by-marriage under the same roof would naturally be in the birthing chamber.

But they did not know each other. And she was hindered by her rank.

A princess could not attend the birth of a commoner. It was too scandalous.

She bit her lip, and her glance fell upon her medicine casket. She had attended only two births of royal relatives, some years ago before she had wed Nechtan, and although she had been little more than an observer, she had learned a great deal.

If Scotswomen truly were as ignorant of the gifts of Bride as she feared—as she had always been taught—then how could she not help Glenna through this trial of childbirth as best she could?

Finn had betrayed her, but that was not his stepsister's fault.

She picked up her casket. The destruction of the sacred broach would have to wait.

In the early hours of the following morning, Glenna was finally safely delivered of her son. Mairi stood at the end of the bed, while Glenna's sisters and Lady Brae made her comfortable and fussed over the babe, and she sent a silent prayer of thanks to her goddess.

She had been welcomed, but the Scotswomen had been far from ignorant in the ways of the goddess, for all that they worshipped the new god who had no time for the old.

Another long-held conviction of Pictland's enemies crumbled to dust. The Scots might not allow their women the same political freedom as the Picts, but it didn't mean they were entirely at the mercy of their menfolk.

Any woman who understood how to use Bride's gifts during childbirth, would know of the power the plants of the earth gave them over their moon cycles.

We could have been friends. Desolation echoed through her as she smothered the ember of kinship that flared deep inside. Finn had made it perfectly clear by his actions that he didn't really want her.

She was an outsider, here. She always would be. How pitiful that she wished it could be different.

Silently, she left, and returned to her chamber. Her ladies, now asleep on their makeshift beds, had kept the fire burning bright and the warmth was welcome after the chill of the corridor.

For long moments she gazed into the flames. It didn't matter how hard she tried to ignore it. Even now, despite the devastating confrontation with Finn, the otherworldly flicker of *knowing* that had assailed her when she had first seen Duncarn yesterday, continued to haunt her.

It was nothing like the grand stronghold of Dunclach, where centuries of bloodied secrets seemed to cling to the very walls themselves. Here, in Duncarn, even the betrayal of the broken chest seemed oddly disconnected to the reality of this small hillfort.

But it meant nothing. It wasn't a sign from her goddess that all would be well. It was her own foolish heart wishing for something that could never be.

How she longed to sink to her knees and surrender to the nameless grief that squeezed her breast in a merciless vise.

But she feared if she did, she might never find the strength to do what had to be done.

She picked up her medicine casket and took it to the far side of the bed, where none of her ladies, if they were awake, might see what she was doing.

Moments later, she held the sacred broach in her hand. It was as large as her palm and had been passed through the female line and worn only by the true High Kings of Pictland for countless years.

Sorrow gripped her heart. There would be no more Pictish High Kings, but at least the upstart would never wear this revered relic.

She secured it in one of the leather pouches that hung from

her girdle and swung her cloak around her shoulders. First, she would ensure the broach was dismantled, its jewels scattered and buried where no one would find any traces.

Then she would leave this place and never return.

Bhaic had replaced one of the guards outside her door, and in silence he followed her down the stairs and into the kitchen. No one was about, and by the light of the lantern he carried, she found a sharp knife.

It would do. She secured it to her girdle and made her way into the great hall. But instead of slipping out of the hillfort unseen, she came face to face with Annis.

"Madam." Annis dropped a curtsey. "I wish to thank you for your kindness in helping my sister."

Mairi forced a smile, even though she had the forlorn urge to weep at the beautiful bond between Finn's sisters. "I was honored to attend. It warms my heart to see how close you and Glenna are with Lady Brae."

How dearly she would cherish such a loving link with her mother-by-marriage. Much as she'd adored her father and grandfather, there had always been a wistful yearning deep inside for her mamma whom she had never known.

But she would never have the chance to forge anything with Lady Brae.

Annis' face transformed from a polite stranger to one that glowed with love. "Truly, our lady mother is the greatest of gifts. Glenna and I are so grateful for the day she and Finn entered our lives." She hitched a sharp breath. "I mean, of course, Lord Finn."

Yet Finn was rumored to have killed her father. And although she had her doubts, he hadn't denied it when she had flung the accusation in his face.

"I am certain he feels the same." He had spoken so warmly of his sisters, that day in the Christian church. She had no doubt of his love for them. But if he had been brought up as a beloved son of MacAlpin's, surely he had not lived with his mother and step-sisters. It was all so… strange. What was she missing?

"He is truly the best of brothers." Annis hesitated. "He would never say it, Madam, but he is the reason we are all here, now. He saved our lives, of that we are in no doubt."

Was Annis implying that Finn had killed their father in self-defense? She could scarcely ask her outright, yet she had to know.

"I have heard… whispers," she began, but before she could say anymore, Annis took her hand.

"The whispers lie," she said fiercely, before appearing to realize her breach in etiquette as she hastily released Mairi's hand. "Forgive me, Madam. I mean no disrespect. I know it is a sin to say so, but our father was a brute. When Finn confronted him the last time he laid hands on our lady mother, our father smashed a tankard on his head. We thought… we thought our beloved brother was dead, there was so much blood."

Dear goddess. The scar upon Finn's temple. She had imagined he had received it during a battle.

He had.

"I understand," she whispered.

Annis took a shuddering breath. "I should not speak so freely, Madam. But I cannot bear that anyone should think badly of him. The king intervened, to save him from the gallows, but he should never have been accused of murder in the first place."

Instinctively, she took Annis' hand, but her mind was whirling. Why would a royal prince be accused of the murder of a commoner under such circumstances in any case?

Without warning, Finn's words from the feast at Fotla-eviot echoed through her head.

"I'm proud of the noble blood of my lady mother. But of my father, I cannot speak."

Had she been wrong to doubt his word? Had Finn, after all,

313

not been raised as a royal son of MacAlpin until recently, just as he had told her?

But why would Lady Brae tell her otherwise if it was not true?

She squeezed Annis' fingers, and before she could stop herself, a buried truth spilled from her lips. "I do not think badly of him."

"Thank you, Madam." Then she smiled. "I should return to my sister."

"Of course."

As she watched the other woman leave, a terrible possibility gnawed through her. After discovering Finn's true heritage, she had been so certain she could no longer trust him.

He had lied to her from the night they had met.

Had he, though?

She took a deep breath, disorientated by the force of her errant doubt. She tried to wipe it from her mind, but instead, an insidious conviction that nothing was as it seemed slithered through her senses.

Just as she had given her word to Nechtan to conceal her identity, Finn had also given his word to MacAlpin. She could not continue to blame him for that.

A shudder crawled along her spine as fragments of the scathing words she had flung at him scorched her mind and she squeezed her eyes shut. But it didn't prevent her from seeing, once again, the hurt that had flared in his eyes.

Why, though, had he assured her he didn't want children? It didn't seem to be part of MacAlpin's plans, so what had Finn hoped to gain by it?

He did want a family. And to be sure, a man could lie about such things, and still plan to impregnate his unknowing wife. But Finn had been careful. Every time, except when she had told him it was safe. Why would he do that, if it went against his own wishes?

Because he knows I did not wish it.

She pressed her fingers against her throbbing temples and tried to still her racing thoughts. There were things she didn't understand, but how could she accuse him of lying to her if she did not even try to find the truth?

And the only way to uncover that truth was if she saw him again.

Indecision warred within her breast, but there was no time to dwell upon it. Soon it would be light, and she had a mission to accomplish before then.

With Bhaic by her side, she left the hillfort. But already time had escaped her. Dawn had broken, and bronze and yellow streaked the sky as they hurried to the stables where Audra greeted her with a soft whicker. Quickly, she readied her mare and led her outside. In the distance, to the west of the hillfort, there was a forest. The perfect place to hide the broach.

The sun burst upon the eastern horizon, a vivid splash of red and orange, illuminating the landscape. Mairi gasped, and pressed her hand against her breast, her mind momentarily stunned by the visage before her.

Majestic standing stones stood in a perfect circle, and the sunrise glowed between the ancient monoliths, throwing stark shadows across the land. A wondrous sight at any time. But it was so much more than that.

This is the stone circle from my dream.

CHAPTER 32

For endless moments Mairi gazed at the sacred circle, as tangled questions thundered through her mind. For weeks she had beseeched her goddess for a sign that she was on the right path, but Bride's presence had remained elusive.

She had feared her goddess had turned her back on her, for seeking out Finn's company instead of avoiding him.

For making the wrong choice on the night of the Blood Moon.

But here, in Duncarn, was the answer. It could be nothing else.

Except she did not understand the message.

In silence, she handed Bhaic Audra's reins, and made her way to the nearest stone. It towered above her, and she let out a shaky breath as the power from the earth, the power from suppressed gods, sparked in the air like lightning.

Loose tendrils of her hair floated around her face, although there was no wind, and goosebumps chased across her skin, even though she was far from cold. She lifted her hand, as if in a daze, and pressed her palm against the ancient stone.

A crimson mist clouded the sky, ancient stone walls crowded in on her, and whispers echoed, terrifyingly familiar.

There is no hope for the poor lady.

Raw pain ripped through her, and her head tipped back as a silent scream locked in her throat. No. *No.* She was back in the nightmares that had haunted her as a maid. That had visited her again, after the Blood Moon. The visions she had once thought were warnings from her foremothers, but now knew were from Bride herself.

But why? Why did she have to relive the deaths of her mother and grandmother, over and over again, when there was nothing she could do about it? She had already learned its harsh lesson. If she had a babe, she would die.

What are you trying to show me, Bride?

The walls tumbled around her, and once again the stone circle filled her vision. She braced herself, knowing what was to come, and as in her dream, the earth shuddered, and cracks split the mighty stones.

Terror hammered through her. She should tear her hand away and return to the mortal realm.

She gritted her teeth and pressed harder against the standing stone. Bride had led her here for a reason. She had to see this vision through to its end, no matter how distressing.

Battle cries rent the air, and spectral warriors from the seven clans of Pictland fought through the ages, a thousand years of her heritage flashing before her eyes in an instant.

From the golden sunrise that spilled between the stones, a dark figure emerged, walking towards her, and the Pictish warriors faded into the earth. A dry gasp tore her throat. It was Finn, his black hair whipping against his aristocratic cheekbones from a nonexistent breeze, his green eyes bedazzling her, and his beautiful, beloved, voice filled her mind.

Trust me.

Before she could take his outstretched hand, the crimson mist descended, swirling about him, and he disappeared, leaving a wretched chill within her breast. *Do not leave me...*

The sunrise vanished, the world darkened, and the Blood Moon filled the sky, throwing the sacred circle into stark relief.

Dread understanding flooded through her. A hoarse sob flayed her as she sank to the ground, her hand dragging down the stone.

It wasn't her grandmamma or her mamma she had witnessed perishing, time after time. It was Pictland herself.

There was no hope for her precious, beloved land to survive the inexorable advance of the Scots. MacAlpin would achieve his aim of eradicating her people from the annals of time.

An icy wind whipped through the circle, banishing the darkness and the lingering remnants of the Blood Moon. The sunrise balanced on the horizon. A new day, after the long, blood-soaked night. The wind dropped as suddenly as it had started, and in the fragile stillness, an ethereal whisper echoed down the ages.

Goddess willing, we must save the babe, at least.

And finally, she saw the truth.

Pictland would not die. She would be reshaped, perhaps, but she would survive.

And so would her people.

Rebirth.

Pict and Scot. Together. A new beginning.

For so long she had refused to accept MacAlpin had a legitimate claim on the Kingdom of Fortriu. But just because her great-grandfather had forbidden anyone to speak of his headstrong daughter's elopement with the Scot, Alpin, didn't mean it had not happened.

Her hand fell from the stone, and she pressed her palms into the damp earth. This, then, had been her destiny all along. Not to fight the upstart. But to help safely deliver Pictland into her future.

A future where they could stand, together, against the threat of the Vikings.

She pushed herself to her feet and briefly touched the pouch that held the broach. Her heart ached for everything that would never be, but she knew what she had to do. The time had come when she had to face MacAlpin, and it would be on her terms, not his.

She turned to Bhaic, who had extinguished the lantern and hadn't moved from his position.

He bowed his head as she approached.

"We must leave for Dunadd. Ensure our warriors are ready within the hour."

As one, they turned towards the hillfort, and Lady Brae was standing not a stone's throw from them, wariness carved into her beautiful face. Mairi took a deep breath. Scots did not believe in the old ways, but she would not hide her faith in her goddess in this new life.

"My lady," she said, and Lady Brae inclined her head in greeting.

"Madam." She glanced at the standing stones. "I have always believed it wrong of me, yet I find great comfort within the circle."

"It is a sacred place, to be sure."

"Aye."

Their eyes met and understanding glimmered between them. They might believe in different gods, but they both felt the ancient power of this place.

She needed to get to Dunadd, but there was something she had to know.

"My lady, why would Finn tell me the king has only recently acknowledged him as his son?"

Lady Brae looked aghast. "Madam, I beseech you not to hold this against him. The king has now granted my son all he is due.

There was no reason for Finn to trouble you with this, now you are wed."

"Finn told me the truth before we were wed." Guilt twisted through her at how she had assumed he'd lied. But he never had. He had only withheld parts of the truth, and only then because his king had demanded it.

Never forget who I truly am.

How badly she had misjudged her husband in everything. She prayed she was not too late to repair the damage between them.

"I..." Lady Brae faltered, before inhaling a great breath and squaring her shoulders. "Forgive me for misleading you, Madam. The king assured me that the Princess of the Supreme Kingdom could wed only a beloved royal prince of the House of Alpin." She swallowed, and pain flashed across her face. "He requested that I refrained from enlightening the princess as to Finn's true upbringing."

Renewed anger against MacAlpin tightened her chest. She could imagine how such a request had been framed.

It had been a royal command. And no one could disobey their king.

Finn hadn't lived a life of privilege as a favored royal son. His position was as precarious as hers. Honored, for as long as they were useful to MacAlpin's purpose.

She took a step closer to Lady Brae. She had broken Finn's trust in her, and she would do whatever she could to win it back.

But there was something else she wanted, too. She wanted to belong to his family. "There is nothing to forgive. But there is something I request. I would be honored if, when we are alone, you and your daughters would be kind enough to address me by my given name, Mairi."

～

FINN and the other warriors had camped overnight and arrived in Dunadd the following morning. Heavy clouds obscured the tops of the mountains and the royal stronghold loomed on its mighty hill, a menacing silhouette of deceit and betrayal.

When Finn finished tending to his horse, he left the stables and marched into the stronghold. He had avoided being alone with MacAllister during the journey, since he could barely look at the other man's face without wanting to punch it. Which, although satisfying, would hardly give him any answers.

Besides, it wasn't MacAllister he wanted to confront. It was the king.

In the great hall, Ewan came over to him, and they gripped arms in greeting. Just as they always had.

"Are you accompanying the king when we leave for Fortriu?" Finn kept his voice low so he wouldn't be overheard by any of the other warriors who were in the great hall.

"No." Tension radiated from Ewan and Finn gave him a sharp look. "I am to return to Fotla as part of the contingent to investigate the attack on Constantine."

"I thought MacAlpin had entrusted the King of Fotla to deal with that."

"Aye. But MacAlpin wants his own men there. We're under strict orders not to implicate the royal family in any way." Ewan gave him a sideways glance. "For the Princess of Fortriu's sake."

Finn folded his arms and couldn't meet his friend's eyes. He knew well enough the terms of the marriage contract. Mae's hand, and in return the Fotla king would not be held responsible for the attack on Constantine.

He didn't know why she hadn't reminded him of that, also, yesterday. It was, after all, more scathing evidence of how MacAlpin was willing to do anything to get his own way.

~

IT WAS late afternoon before he had the chance to speak to MacAlpin, who, for all his insistence that Finn returned immediately to Dunadd, had not summoned him into his presence.

Not that Finn had been idle during those hours. He'd discovered many of their warriors had, indeed, been dispatched in ships to confront the Norse, but there was confusion as to whether their enemy had been heading for Iona, or the coast of Dal Riada.

Strange, how he gave Mae's word more credence than that of his own king. Yet it had not even crossed his mind to disbelieve her, when she'd told him the Norse had been heading for the sacred isle.

Or that there hadn't been an attack on the wagons during the journey to Duncarn.

He was leaving the camp to return to the stronghold when he spied MacAlpin and his close confidents returning from a ride. As MacAlpin dismounted, he approached.

"Sire, a word if I may?"

MacAlpin gave him a piercing look before deciding to grant his request. He waved his confidents aside and wrapped his arm around Finn's shoulders in a display of fatherly affection. He wasn't sure he'd ever get used to that. Or enjoy it.

But for now, he'd suffer it.

"I trust married life is to your liking?"

He'd cut his own throat before allowing MacAlpin to guess how the dreams he'd harbored for his marriage had smoldered to ashes beneath his feet.

"Aye." His response was harsher than he had intended, but he couldn't help it. And he had accosted his king for answers, not meaningless banter. "There is a matter I must bring to my liege's attention. The princess' treasure chest was broken into before it arrived at Duncarn."

The king was silent, as he surveyed the stronghold. Did he intend to ignore the question?

He released Finn, which was welcome, but then gripped his

shoulder instead. Another display to show anyone who might observe them of the blood bond that was now acknowledged between them.

"Did the princess say anything was stolen?"

He wasn't here to play word games. "I believe the great seal of Fortriu was the only reason the chest was forced open."

MacAlpin's fingers bit into his shoulder, before his grip relaxed once again. "You protect your wife's interests. I admire that, Finn. That is how it should be. The princess is our shining star, and her importance will never be diminished."

Somehow, he managed to keep his mouth shut, but his mind seethed. Mae's perceived importance had already been diminished, the moment MacAlpin had seized the Kingdom of Fortriu.

"I take it," MacAlpin continued, "that you do not have the great seal in your possession?"

"I would not dishonor the princess by asking for it, after her possessions had been ransacked." Mae's parting shot echoed in his ears. Much as it went against the grain to ask MacAlpin anything, he had to know. "Why is it so important?"

Finally, the king released him, and folded his arms. "Possessing the great seal will silence any remaining opposition to my right to the Supreme Kingdom. But alas, we can wait no longer before moving the royal court to Fortriu. The Norsemen grow bolder with every passing year."

"Was there a threat of abduction against the princess? I heard the Norsemen were heading to Iona."

MacAlpin's jaw flexed, and in the twilight, Finn saw annoyance flash across the king's face. "You know as well as I that they have their sights set on Dal Riada. We will protect Dunadd, but the court will relocate. You will accompany us when we transport the Stone of Destiny in the morning."

It was true he believed the Norse would not rest until they had taken Dunadd, but it was also true that MacAlpin had avoided directly answering his question.

His accusation.

It didn't matter. Nothing the king said had changed Finn's mind. MacAlpin had ordered the ransacking of Mae's possessions.

"Aye, sire."

MacAlpin drew in a deep breath. "Know this, Finn. We will take all of Pictland. It is the destiny of the House of Alpin. Honor your royal wife, as befits her status, but when it counts, always remember to whom you owe ultimate loyalty."

With that warning—threat—he gave a nod of dismissal before marching away.

Finn swung away and glared at the mountains that loomed as dusk spread across the land. MacAlpin wasn't merely his father. He was his king. Six years ago, he had saved Finn from the gallows, and ensured he was trained as a warrior. His word was law.

"One cannot go against the word of one's king."

Mae's response, when he'd told her he was needed at Dunadd, thudded through his head. At the time, he'd imagined she was regretful that the king's command meant he had to leave her.

They both knew a royal command could not be ignored.

But she hadn't meant that at all. For Mae, their marriage was nothing more than a political alliance. She was his bride because of duty, not because of any other foolish notion he might secretly have harbored.

She was too good for him. He had always known it. His blood was contaminated by the House of Alpin, and every time Mae looked at him, all she saw was her enemy. If her possessions had not been ransacked, would she ever have revealed the depths of her contempt for him? Or would she have continued to play the part of a dutiful royal wife, while he lived his life believing they shared something so much more?

It was better he knew the truth. But it was a hollow assertion.

Because given the choice, would he rather have continued in ignorance, just to keep her by his side?

A futile wish. Sooner or later, the past would have overtaken them and forced a confrontation. The suspicions that had haunted him since the massacre of the Pictish nobles in the spring would not be silenced. He'd only ever voiced them to Ewan, that day in the tavern when they'd first arrived in Fotla, but even then they hadn't spoken of them openly.

That blood-soaked night was the reason there was no hope of a future for him with Mae. In her eyes, he was as guilty as MacAlpin. It made no difference that he had been in Northumbria and had returned to Dunadd only after the outrage had been committed.

Mae believed, if ordered by his king, he would have slain her countrymen in cold blood.

Because no one could go against the word of their king.

But she was wrong.

His fist curled around the hilt of his sword. He wasn't the only one who had refused to assist in the aftermath, when the Pict warriors who had accompanied them into Northumbria had been taken hostage. Yet their subversion had never been confronted. It was as though that ugly scene had never happened.

With difficulty, he released his death grip on his sword. The last shards of light from the sun vanished beyond the horizon and in the distance, thunder rumbled an ominous warning of the oncoming storm.

It was true he'd never see things from Mae's perspective. It wasn't his people who had been betrayed. But that didn't mean he couldn't understand her anger at the injustice.

He'd spoken from his wretched heart when he'd assured her they saw things as one, but they were only words, and easily dismissed. She had no reason to believe him.

Why did he even care anymore? The pretense was over. Their

marriage was dead. Yet he knew why, even if the reason would remain locked deep inside until the last breath left his body.

Slowly, he turned to face the stronghold. He could never win her back but there was something he could do, to prove he believed in her, to prove that when it came to a choice between her and his king, she would always be first.

Even if she never knew it.

CHAPTER 33

*I*t was dark, it had started to rain, and thunder rolled across the moonless sky by the time Mairi arrived at Dunadd. A messenger had ridden ahead to announce her arrival, and servants ushered her and Bhaic into a small chamber near the great hall. A fire burned in the hearth, and she warmed her hands, grateful for her thick cloak that had protected her from the worst of the weather.

Refreshments had been set upon the table and as Bhaic poured her a warm drink, she took off her cloak and placed it over a stool. She might be windswept, which was not how she wished to faced MacAlpin, but at least she was in one of her Pictish gowns.

Although perhaps she should have brought Struana, to help her look more presentable. But her dear, loyal friend deserved some time to rest, and it wasn't as though Mairi expected to stay in Dunadd for any length of time.

Just long enough to negotiate terms with MacAlpin and, goddess willing, ask Finn to give her a second chance.

There was a knock on the door and when Bhaic opened it,

MacAlpin marched in, accompanied by MacAllister and another two men she did not recognize.

"Madam." MacAlpin bowed his head before coming over to her and taking her proffered hand. He gave her knuckles a perfunctory kiss. "We believed you to be safely ensconced at Duncarn."

Disapproval tinged his voice. He was obviously not accustomed to his orders being disobeyed. She bit back the temptation to question him on her broken chest and the true destination of the latest Viking incursion, but that was not why she was here.

Her purpose was to unite Pictland. And alas, confronting MacAlpin with his deceptions was not the path to peace.

"There are matters we must discuss."

He glanced around the chamber, and a frown slashed his brow. "Where are your ladies?"

"They remained in Duncarn."

"You rode here unaccompanied?"

She knew exactly what he meant, but she was the Princess of Fortriu, and would not have her remaining freedoms dictated to by this Scots king.

"Indeed, I did not. My warriors ensured our safe passage."

"We shall assign suitable noblewomen for your entourage." It was clear he was uncomfortable with the notion of speaking with her while she was unchaperoned, and it irked her greatly. Somehow, she managed to give him a regal smile.

"There is no need. My words are for your ears only, and my lord Bhaic and your man MacAllister will remain to bear witness."

After a heartbeat, MacAlpin gave a nod, and his men joined the two of hers who stood on guard outside the door.

Once they were alone, Bhaic and MacAllister stood in front of the closed door, their arms crossed.

So many times she had dreamed of being alone with MacAlpin, when she could take vengeance for the wrongs he had inflicted upon her people. Had she requested the dismissal of MacAllister at this meeting, it was possible the king would acquiesce.

But it had always been a fantasy. She was no highly trained warrior and a king ensured he was never alone with his enemies. But the thirst for revenge had been her constant companion during her exile, the elusive flicker of light she had focused on, in the darkness.

And now, for the future of Pictland, she had to give MacAlpin the one thing she had pledged to keep from him.

But it was not only for Pictland. She did this for Finn, also, to protect him against the fickleness of an unscrupulous king.

"What do you wish to discuss, cousin, that was of such importance you braved a risky return to danger?"

It did not escape her notice how he called attention to their blood connection. She didn't like it, but she could no longer ignore the truth. Pictish blood ran through MacAlpin's veins and for that, he had the right to claim the Fortriu throne.

But only because he had eliminated all other contenders.

"Our beloved land is in peril." Pictland had been in peril before and prevailed. But this time, the goddess had allowed her a glimpse of what might be. And she could not allow that dark future to come to pass.

Her pride was a small price to pay to ensure her people survived.

"It is. This alliance between Scot and Pict is the only defense we have against our common enemy."

Unlike the last time they'd spoken, he was not dismissing her with pretty, empty words. He knew why she had come here and what she was prepared to offer. And for that, he appeared willing to overlook the fact she was a woman.

"Before my husband, Lord Finn, left Duncarn, we spoke at length."

The scathing words she'd flung at Finn pierced her heart.

"I know nothing about you."

But she did. He was the most honorable man she had ever known. He had not wed her for the sacred broach of Fortriu. He was unaware of its significance, and he hadn't demanded she surrender it before he left for Dunadd. A command she was certain his king had expected him to obey.

"Indeed." MacAlpin inclined his head, but sharp interest gleamed in his eyes.

"We discussed the circumstances that brought us together and considered how best we might help forge a new destiny for the sacred broach of Fortriu."

It was almost the truth. She had no qualms twisting what had really happened at Duncarn to MacAlpin now that her eyes had been opened.

"I do not see things the way you do, and I never shall."

Her accusations haunted her. To be sure, Finn owed the king his life, but he was not the indulged son she had once imagined. He likely saw the events that had bloodied Dunadd's walls far clearer than she gave him credit for.

Even if he could never forgive her, she would ensure that MacAlpin was in no doubt that to bring the clans of Pictland together, Finn's presence was as essential as hers.

"We are in agreement, Madam. The destinies of Pictland and the great seal are inextricably entwined."

"You recall, no doubt, our earlier conversation on this subject."

He bowed his head. "In return for your gracious legacy, we will establish generous protocols for the Princess of Fortriu to visit with our esteemed royal guests."

They were hostages. But she was not about to argue semantics.

"As a gesture to commemorate recognition of our entwined destinies, cousin, we request half the royal and noble born Picts currently residing in Dunadd be returned to their kingdoms."

"Alas, Madam, this request cannot be accommodated."

She remained silent. She had attended many political assemblies with her grandfather, King Wrad, and knew the value of such a tactic.

After a long moment, MacAlpin drew in a deep breath. "Nevertheless, such an auspicious occasion does merit great concession. We will allow five Pictish nobles to return to their kingdoms."

"This is most gracious." It wasn't, and she longed to tell him what she thought of his miserly offer, but such was politics. "We propose in addition to the five noblemen, five of royal blood are also permitted to return to their kingdoms."

MacAlpin studied her in silence. She refused to stir beneath his gaze. If he thought he could intimidate her by such a strategy, he was sadly mistaken.

Finally, he glanced at MacAllister, who bowed and went to the desk on the far side of the chamber, where he procured ink and parchment. Bhaic followed and stood by the king's man's side, to ensure no trickery threaded through the binding document.

Good. The sooner the formalities had been completed, the sooner she could reunite with Finn.

Her stomach churned with nerves. She wanted to ask MacAlpin about Finn but didn't trust herself not to show her anxiety. And if there was one thing she knew, it was that MacAlpin believed she and Finn were as one.

Without warning, Talargan's face replaced Finn's in her mind and she sucked in a sharp breath. Why was she thinking of the Prince of Ce at a time like this?

Foreboding crawled along her spine and no matter how she tried to ignore it, the sense of dread seeped into her bones.

This was madness. To be sure, she wanted Talargan's freedom, but now was not the time. There were, after all, Pictish kings who were still held hostage.

Dark shadows spread across the chamber, swallowing the air.

Her heart thundered and head throbbed, and it took every shred of willpower she possessed to keep the apprehension from her face.

The lantern on the table took on an eerie, red glow, and for one breath stealing moment, she saw the Blood Moon reflected in its flame.

It was a message from Bride. She did not understand why, but she knew what she had to do.

"We request that Talargan mac Bredei, royal prince of the Kingdom of Ce, is one of the princes returned to his kingdom."

Surprise flashed across MacAlpin's face. Clearly, he had expected her to suggest a more senior royal, but he merely nodded. "As you wish."

Time slowed, and she battled the terrible urge to flee this chamber.

To find Finn.

Before it's too late.

Finally, it was done. Bhaic was by her side as she scrutinized the document and approved the names selected. And now she had to fulfil her part.

She took the broach from her pouch and in her mind, she saw her grandfather, the great High King Wrad. How proudly he had worn this symbol of Pictland on his plaid. But she was doing this for Pictland. It was Bride's will.

With the broach on her palm, she offered it to MacAlpin, and he took it with due reverence. When he had finished scrutinizing it, he looked at her.

"We will invite the ten Pictish guests you have selected to the feast this night. They shall return to their kingdoms in the morning. But tonight, will the Princess of the Supreme Kingdom do us the honor of affixing the great seal—the sacred broach of Pictland—on her new king?"

How dearly she longed to plunge a dagger through his corrupt heart. But they were childish fantasies, and had she ever succeeded in such a rash action, her beloved land would have suffered the consequences.

And so would Finn.

She breathed in deep. Witnesses to the ceremonial handing over of the sacred broach were imperative and how better to spread the word than by using the high-ranking Picts this treaty had released?

"Very well." She inclined her head in acceptance, but it was not as though she had a choice. And now that her duty here was completed, she needed to escape.

To find Finn.

After the king assured her he would have noblewomen sent to the bedchamber she had used before her marriage, she swung her cloak around her shoulders and took her leave. Bhaic remained, to ensure the treaty remained intact, but instead of making her way to the stairs, she hesitated.

Outside.

It was an implacable command. She glanced at her men who flanked her, who had accompanied her from Fortriu, all those months ago, and had never by word nor deed betrayed her.

"The goddess calls me," she said, and without a word they followed her to the main double doors, barred against the storm that raged outside. From the great hall, another dozen of her men fell into formation behind her.

One of her warriors opened the doors. Wind billowed, and she pulled her hood over her head before stepping outside. Rain lashed down, blinding her, but even without that hindrance it was impossible to see anything. The torches that normally illuminated the stronghold were drenched.

What am I doing here?

Bride had called her, and Finn needed her. But the night was black, and she had no idea which direction she should take.

Great goddess, I beg you for a sign.

Lightning speared across the sky, a flash of white and violet that lit up the heavy clouds. The afterglow lingered, imprinting on her eyelids, a fiery arrow shot straight from the bow of Bride herself.

The answer could not be clearer.

Follow the light.

CHAPTER 34

"My lord, I swear to you on my honor, this is no trick." Finn couldn't keep the frustration from his voice as he and Talargan stood at the door that led outside.

It had been easy enough releasing the prince. There were no warriors guarding the entrance to the stronghold where the hostages were held. Too many had been sent to fight the Norse or were engaged elsewhere. And Dunadd's strategic position ensured that, even in this foul weather, enemies would be seen approaching from any direction.

No one would expect a Scots warrior to release a valuable Pict. Or be looking for a lone rider departing the stronghold.

"Fuck it, Finn, why should I trust you?"

"Because we fought side by side against the Northumbrians."

"Your upstart king is also your father."

"Aye." There was no getting away from that fact. "But what happened here was wrong. I can't change it, but I can do what I can to ensure you return to your kingdom."

In the flickering light from the torches in their sconces, indecision flared across Talargan's face. "I'm not the only Pict here that went to Northumbria. Why me?"

"I can't release everyone. It's too risky. But a single rider can escape undetected in this storm."

And I wed the woman you love.

Guilt stabbed through him. But even now, when his wife had told him exactly how little she thought of him, he would change nothing. For a short, shining, moment, Mae had been his. And even if it had been an illusion, she'd shown him a life that he had scarcely dreamed possible.

They stepped outside and Finn unhitched the horse he'd taken from the stables and handed Talargan the reins.

After a moment's hesitation, the prince took the reins. "I won't forget this, Finn. You've put your life in danger for me."

He was committing high treason. But he hadn't put his life on the line for Talargan. It was so he could feel worthy enough to look into Mae's eyes again, even if all he saw was scorn.

She would forever remain unaware of his actions. But he had crossed the line and there was no going back. Now and forever, when it came to Mae, he would always see the world as she did.

Lightning split the sky, illuminating a dozen or so warriors heading their way.

His heart slammed against his chest. It was unlikely he'd been recognized, but there was no time to waste. Thunder rocked the heavens as he grabbed Talargan's arm. "Get out of here."

As the prince mounted the horse, an unnatural silence fell, punctuated only by the incessant rain pelting onto the ground. Blackness covered the land, and it would be easy enough for both Talargan and him to evade the warriors.

From the dark, an achingly familiar voice froze him in his tracks.

"Finn Braeson, is that you?"

Mae. How could she be here? Was his addled mind taunting him, now? Beside him, Talargan dismounted and gripped his shoulder. Proof, as though he needed it, that however improbable, Mae was indeed here.

"What in the name of all the gods…" Talargan's low growl was swept away in the wind, and Finn stepped forward, leaving the prince in his wake.

"Mae?" His voice was harsh. Had MacAlpin captured her, after he had left Duncarn, and brought her to Dunadd? Did the king think to incarcerate her, like he had the other Pictish hostages?

Outrage burned through his blood. He would never allow his wife to suffer such indignity, no matter how many warriors guarded her. He drew his sword, even though he could scarcely see his own hand in front of his face. "Are you harmed?"

"I am not." She sounded so much closer than before. Another flash of lightning lit up the sky, and she was standing less than an arm's length from him. "My men protect me."

Her men? Instinctively, he tightened his grip on his sword, even though there was no need to defend her against her loyal warriors. His head throbbed, and he could make no sense of her appearance. "What are you doing here?"

"I came to speak with MacAlpin."

She was in Dunadd voluntarily. Thank God for whatever strange twist of fate had caused her to cross his path before she'd had the chance to demand an audience with the king.

With a smothered curse, he sheathed his sword before he swung about and opened the door behind him. Mae entered, and pushed back her hood. Her beautiful hair glowed in the torch-light and raindrops glittered on her eyelashes. Just like the time he'd met her outside the farrier's, in Fotla.

When he had lost his wretched heart.

Brutally, he shoved the past back where it belonged. He had to get Mae to safety and ensure she did not speak her mind to the king.

"MacAlpin is unavailable. He's committed to moving his court at first light."

"We have already spoken."

Her quiet words slammed into his brain with the force of a battle ax. Horror clawed through his chest. "What?"

"My business with MacAlpin is done."

Her business? Raw fear collided with the horror. He knew her opinion of the king. Knew, also, she was not afraid to say exactly what she thought.

Yet if she'd told MacAlpin how deeply she despised him, would she be free to wander as she pleased?

Maybe his feelings showed on his face, as she added, "I told you once that I don't speak my mind so freely to everyone, Finn. I'm capable of diplomacy, should the occasion warrant it."

"Nothing warrants you traveling here from Duncarn in treacherous weather." His guts clenched. A multitude of dangers lurked in the mountains and glens. Anything could have happened to her.

"This matter could not wait." She hesitated before drawing in a deep breath. "I bestowed the sacred broach of Fortriu to the House of Alpin."

Speechless, he gazed at her. Even wrapped in her cloak, there was an air of fragility about her that made him want to pull her into his arms and never let her go. To protect her from the king's machinations and ensure no harm ever befell her.

But, as she had once confided in him, her fragility was an illusion.

She was not a delicate flower unable to face the realities of life. Her strength of will was formidable and, somehow, she had kept the broach MacAlpin had so coveted safe from his clutches, until she had decided its fate.

"Why?" He could not help the thread of awe in his voice. MacAlpin had all but resigned himself to the fact he would never possess the broach. But then, Mae didn't know that.

She caught his gaze, and once again he lost his soul in the beautiful blue of her eyes. It was surely a trick of the flickering flames, but he imagined he saw no condemnation in their flaw-less depths.

"I did not relinquish it for MacAlpin's sake. I did for the future of Pictland."

Aye, he should have known. Because everything she did was for the good of her beloved land. Before he could respond, Talargan, who had kept his distance outside the door, marched in. Mae gasped and Finn clenched his fists as something raw and ugly tore through his chest.

"Talargan," she said, as though she could not believe her eyes. "What are you—how are you—"

"Mairi." Talargan's familiar use of her name burned, but not nearly as much as when the prince went to her and pressed his lips against her gloved fingers. Finn barely stopped himself from grabbing the prince and hurling him to the ground. It would do no good. Certainly, it wouldn't change Mae's opinion of the man she had been forced to wed. "By all the gods, it's good to see you again. I grieve for all that you have suffered these last years."

Talargan still held her hand. Mae didn't appear to mind. Had she told him the truth when she'd said she had never loved the prince? Or had that been a rare display of diplomacy on her part?

Mae inclined her head. "Thank you." She pulled her hand free and glanced at him, wariness etched upon her face. "Finn—"

"Madam." Urgency throbbed in Talargan's voice, and Finn's glare at the interruption went unnoticed. "Come with me to Ce. I'll protect you with my life."

Rage seethed through Finn's blood at the prince's presumption. "No one protects my wife but me."

Mae and Talargan both turned to him, as though they'd forgotten he was even there. He refused to acknowledge how right—how regal—they looked together. A royal born prince, worthy of the Princess of the Supreme Kingdom.

God damn it. He would do anything, give anything, to make Mae happy. But he couldn't let her go.

"Your king has what he wants," Talargan said. "The sacred broach is enough. He no longer needs the princess."

I need her.

For a terrible moment, he thought he'd roared his confession aloud.

"MacAlpin will never allow his shining star to escape." What the fuck was he saying? He didn't give a damn what MacAlpin would or would not do. *He* was the one who didn't want Mae to escape this marriage. Even if it was nothing more than broken dreams crushed into the mud.

Once again, Talargan gripped his shoulder. "If you care for her at all, allow her to leave with me. Let her live among her own people, instead of foreigners who will never show her the respect she deserves."

Every word drove another dagger into his heart. Mae deserved all that, and so much more. She deserved everything that he could never offer her.

Mae curled her fingers around Talargan's forearm, and a deadly weight settled deep in Finn's chest. She had made her choice. How could he force her to stay, when her heart beat only for the good of Pictland?

"My lord." There was a quiet authority in her voice and Talargan turned to her. Finn dragged in a deep, ragged breath. This then, was how it ended. "I will not accompany you to the Kingdom of Ce."

Wild hope hammered through him. Mae had chosen to stay. With him.

"You can't stay here." A thread of desperation heated Talargan's voice. "Madam, I implore you to consider this matter."

"There is nothing to consider. I pledged an oath to protect Pictland and made a vow to wed my lord Finn. I won't tarnish my honor, or the honor of our beloved land, by breaking my word."

The hope died an inglorious death. She stayed because of duty. Not because she didn't want to leave him.

But it was all he had. It would be enough. "Madam, allow me to escort you to the great hall." Where he would demand a suitable chamber be made available for her. He glanced at Talargan, who appeared unable to drag his tortured gaze from Mae. "My lord, you must leave."

"Wait." Mae didn't raise her voice. She didn't need to. Regal power radiated from her, yet it was more than that. An intangible aura he could not instantly place.

Pagan.

"My lord, may I ask that you do not depart Dunadd yet? I wish to speak with my husband."

Talargan gave a stiff bow before leaving them alone. Finn raked his fingers through his wet hair and couldn't drag his bewitched gaze from her. He couldn't imagine what she wanted to say to him, but there was something he needed to tell her.

"I'm sorry you had to relinquish your sacred broach, Mae. It was wrong of MacAlpin to attempt to steal it from you."

She licked her lips, and he had the uncanny notion she was nervous. But Mae was never unsure of herself. Certainly, not with him.

"I know you had nothing to do with that, Finn. Please accept my apologies for doubting you."

He hadn't expected an apology. He wasn't even sure what to do with it. "How could you do anything but doubt me? MacAlpin's blood runs through my veins."

"Yet you are not your father's son."

God, he hadn't expected that response, either. "I take that as a compliment, my lady."

"As you should, my lord."

Mae wasn't cold and haughty, the way she had been the last time he'd seen her. He feared he was deluding himself, but it seemed she wanted to repair the tenuous bridge between them.

Give him a second chance to prove himself worthy of her. He should simply take what she offered, and get her out of here.

But something still did not fit.

"Why were you in the storm, Mae? Didn't MacAlpin offer you hospitality?"

"I care nothing for his hospitality. I traveled to Dunadd for two reasons, Finn. To confront MacAlpin and..." she hesitated before taking a deep breath. "And to find you."

He took a step closer to her. Couldn't help himself. "What was so urgent that couldn't wait until I returned to Duncarn?"

Her gaze slipped and she focused on his chest. "I told you. To apologize for doubting you."

The wild hope that there was something left to salvage in their marriage rose from the ashes once again. "Mae," he said, but before he could continue, she raised her hand.

"Forgive me." Her arm dropped and she gripped her fingers together. "But I must know. How is my lord Talargan free?"

Shit. This wasn't something he wanted to discuss. He didn't want Mae involved in this act of treason at all. In fact, they needed to get the hell away from here, before they were all discovered, and she was condemned along with him.

He cleared his throat, but no inspiration hit him. "I must return you to safety."

She frowned. "But I do not understand. How did MacAlpin convey his command to you, when I left him in the chamber? Bride guided me to you directly. I cannot fathom how you arrived here before me."

He had no idea what she was talking about, or which issue he should comment on first. He picked the most obscure. "Bride led you to me?"

"Indeed. I'm not certain why her message was so urgent, but I could not ignore her sign."

He still didn't understand, and shook his head. "We must go, Mae."

She ignored his outstretched hand. "What of the others? Has MacAlpin reneged on our treaty?"

His gaze sharpened. "What treaty?"

She tilted her head. "You are not here on MacAlpin's orders?"

His senses went onto full alert. "What?"

Wariness clouded her eyes. "In exchange for the sacred broach, MacAlpin will release five Pict nobles, and five of royal blood including Lord Talargan."

He exhaled a long breath. His grand plan to show the uncaring fates that he believed in Mae above his king, crumbled to dust. It meant nothing, for the king had already granted Talargan his freedom.

Yet he had still committed treason, and for her own safety, he could not allow Mae to guess the truth.

"The king will honor his word, my lady." His statement sounded hollow, and he couldn't blame her for not believing it. But in this, at least, Finn believed MacAlpin would follow through. Why wouldn't he? He now had possession of the broach he'd coveted for so long.

"Finn." Her whisper was drowned out by the thunder over-heard, but he still heard her. Or maybe it was his heart that heard. "Did you release Talargan yourself?"

Why did she question everything? Why could she not just accept there were things that could not be spoken of?

Yet that very trait was one of the reasons why he was standing here, risking his neck.

Lightning split the sky, throwing an eerie glow around them. She gasped and pressed her hand to her throat. "*Bride.*" Then she swung around to Talargan, who stood outside the open door. "My lord Finn and I request your assistance."

It did not matter how much he wanted to prolong this encounter with Mae, even though he feared it might be the last time they were together. Every moment they stayed here put her in danger.

"You're coming with me, Mae," he said. "You can't be discovered here, do you understand?"

She turned to him and for a surreal moment he thought she was going to take his hand. But instead, she clasped her hands together at her breast.

"I beg you to trust me, Finn. Bride has shown me the way, but I was blind for so long. This is the vision I shared with you, when I thought you had entered my dreamworld."

Shivers skated along his arms. He recalled that conversation but had considered they spoke of no more than a dream. Yet standing here now with Mae, as lightning flashed outside and the torches flickered against the ancient stone walls, he could easily believe her goddess had a hand in their destinies.

She gave names to Talargan, clearly those whose freedom she had negotiated with MacAlpin. Finn unlocked the doors and stood by her side as the men swore fealty to her.

"There is not much time, my lords," she said. "But know this. Your freedom today, and the chance of peace for our beloved Pictland, is possible only because of the chosen one of Bride herself—Lord Finn, Prince of the House of Alpin."

The Picts shot him glances of varying degrees of hostility. He glared back. What was he meant to say? The *chosen* one?

He didn't even believe in their gods.

There was a commotion at the door and MacAllister strode in, accompanied by two dozen of the king's most trusted warriors. They came to an abrupt halt and MacAllister swept his gaze over them, his expression inscrutable.

By his side, Mae took a breath, obviously with the intent of addressing the king's man herself. Silently, he cursed, and stepped forward, protecting her not only from the Scots' curious glances, but from whatever fallout might occur from his rash decision to assist her.

"The Picts," he said. "Released, as commanded by the king."

For a heartbeat, MacAllister's far too shrewd gaze met his,

before he bowed, accepting Finn's statement without question despite what might be going through his head. "We shall escort our honored guests to the great hall, my lord."

When they were finally alone, silence wrapped around them like a suffocating fog. She wouldn't catch his gaze, and instead seemed intent on smoothing the leather of her gloves.

"Mae." He wasn't even sure what he wanted to say. Only knew he had to find out how she truly felt, even if the truth destroyed the last glimmer of hope in his heart. "Why did you change your mind?"

She didn't ask him what he meant. For which he was grateful. He scarcely knew what he meant himself.

"The standing stones at Duncarn. It's the place my goddess has been leading me to for all these years." There was a hushed, reverential tone to her voice and when she looked at him it took every shred of willpower he possessed to keep the despair from his eyes.

The reason she had traveled to Dunadd to speak with him, and present MacAlpin with the broach, was because her goddess had decreed it must be so.

Mae hadn't come here to see him because she wanted to repair the remnants of their marriage. Why did he keep wishing for the impossible? Yet he knew why.

The prospect of a future without her in it, was an unending, bleak existence.

"Then I am glad Duncarn was of assistance to you, my lady."

"The stones at Duncarn are most powerful."

"If you say so." He hadn't acquired the hillfort because of the stones. He'd acquired it because it was all he could afford. But pagan or not, he'd found a strange comfort by walking in that ancient circle.

She gripped her fingers together. "Bride called you to Duncarn, Finn. I am sure of it."

What did it matter whether it was her heathen goddess, the

God he had been taught to worship since birth, or some unknown Fate who had compelled him to buy Duncarn? In the end, all it had done was impel Mae to relinquish her beloved broach.

"I don't believe in the old ways." Didn't he, though? He believed in Mae. Maybe that was enough.

"But Bride believes in you," she said softly. "And while it grieves me that MacAlpin did have the right to contest the throne of Fortriu, it means royal Pictish blood from the Supreme Kingdom flows through your veins, also. You are all that is best in both Pict and Scot."

He folded his arms, a pitiful defense against her captivating allure. God help him, but he would rather hear her scathing words than have her make believe all was well between them. "There's no need to sweet talk to me because of your goddess. I know you were forced into this marriage. I thought—I hoped— you might come to care for me enough to make this work. But I see now that was nothing but a delusion."

"Finn." There was a pleading note in her voice that he hated. He should free her from this contract now, allow her to live her life away from the intrigues of the House of Alpin. But the words locked in his throat. How could he say farewell to the woman who was his life?

She took a small step closer to him. The evocative scent of raindrops and leather swirled around him, mocking his resolutions. He would never see rain again without thinking of his beautiful Mae.

"Finn," she said again. "I was resolved to travel to Dunadd to speak with you before I ever saw your standing stones."

"Because your goddess told you to."

"No. Because I could not bear you might think I meant my unkind words to you. I *do* know you, Finn. And I feel… that there are many things we see in the same way."

"Mae." He gave a heavy sigh. "You were right. You will always put the good of your people first. And there will always be secrets between us."

"I was wrong," she whispered. "I only accused you because I was afraid that if I had to make a choice, I would choose you above my beloved land."

The heavy beat of rainfall faded. All he could hear was the thunder of his heart in his ears as the defeated hope slammed once again into life.

Had he misunderstood? "You would choose me?"

"I understand you swore an oath to your king. You could not break it."

He remembered telling her that the night they were betrothed. But the truth was, that oath was only a small part of why he hadn't told her he was the son of MacAlpin. It was because MacAlpin's son was bound to the mysterious Princess of Fortriu, and Finn Braeson had wanted only the elusive Lady Mae.

"MacAlpin is my king. But he doesn't own my heart." The words escaped, unbidden, and there was no taking them back. Yet he wouldn't even if he could. Surely, she had to know. He had given her his heart the day they had spoken in the rain.

"Please," she said softly. "Why did you release Talargan?"

He had once told her he'd never lie to her again. Not even by omission. And while he had never wanted her to know about his actions tonight, events had escalated in a way he could never have foreseen.

He was certain that, in her heart, Mae knew why. But maybe he needed to tell her, regardless.

"Something's not right about what we've been told of the massacre of the Pictish nobles. I don't know what happened here in the spring. But I do know that no Pict should be held hostage because of it."

"Dear goddess." Horror flashed across her face, and she clutched his forearm. "Your king would have your head if he heard you utter such treason."

He gave a grim smile. "Aye. But I have no intention of telling him this to his face."

"Yet you were prepared to help a prized hostage escape."

"It's a small thing. But I hoped it would help ease my conscience."

"Your conscience is clear, Finn Braeson. There was no need to risk your life for this noble act."

He had feared she would never call him by his true name again. He took her hand from his arm and pressed it against his heart.

No more secrets between us.

"My life is yours, Mae. I would risk all that I am to be worthy of your esteem."

She shook her head, and it seemed tears glittered in her beautiful blue eyes. "I would not have you sacrifice so precious a thing as your life on my behalf."

"You once told me one can never go against the word of one's king. If my honor is worth anything, I had to."

"Do not throw my uncaring words back in my face, I beg you."

He had to make her see. "I'm not. But you must know. When it matters, it's not my king who has my loyalty. It's you. It will always be you."

Her bottom lip trembled. It was his undoing. "I followed you to Dunadd to ask for another chance to win your regard. To tell you I trusted you." Her voice was husky, and he tightened his hold on her hand. "I did not expect you to have already chosen me over your king."

He bowed his head and rested his forehead against hers. She was as vital to him as the air he breathed, the very blood that filled his veins. He thought he'd lost her, but she had returned to him. He would spend the rest of his life ensuring she never regretted it.

"You have more than my regard, sweet Mae. You have my

heart." He drew in a shuddering breath. "I love you. More than you will ever know."

She tilted her head so he could see her face, and her smile illuminated all the dark corners of his soul. "I love you, Finn Braeson. With all my heart."

He held her tight, savoring the feel of her in his arms once more, and the way she clung to him as though he was her everything. A ragged breath tore from his throat, and he buried his face in her soft hair.

His wife.

He pulled back and gazed into her beloved face. "I haven't forgotten. I shall build you a palace as I once promised."

"Oh." She gave a small laugh. "I do not need a palace, my love. I'm proud that Duncarn is the hillfort of the House of Braeson."

My love. He had never thought to hear such an endearment on her lips.

"House of Braeson has a certain ring to it," he said.

"Indeed. And I dearly hope we shall spend many happy times there with your family. But," she hesitated and then took a quick breath. "Your inheritance of Dunclach will require a good deal of your time."

Aye, damn it. He knew that, but although the idea of living there didn't appeal, if that was what Mae wanted, it was not that much of a hardship. "If you wish to make our home there, we shall return as soon as the Norse threat has passed."

"Dunclach is not our home. Merely your responsibility. But Nechtan's stronghold in Fib is now mine and is in sore need of our presence. I know it is in Pictland, but would it please you to call this home?"

Fib was some distance from Dal Riada, the kingdom beyond Fortriu. He'd never thought of making his permanent home in Pictland, but then, he had never envisioned loving the Princess of Fortriu, either. "It doesn't matter where we live, Mae. If you are there, it is my home."

"I'm glad. Your lady mother is the rightful mistress of Duncarn, and I would not wish to intrude. Oh." Her eyes widened and she cupped his jaw in a tender gesture. "Finn, I should tell you. Glenna was safely delivered of her son early this morn."

"A son?" He gave a laugh of relief that all was well. "That is grand news."

For a moment he imagined the bairns he had once longed to fill his home with, and regret pierced him. But it was a fleeting thing, when compared to the happiness of the woman in his arms.

"It is." Mae traced her fingertips along his jaw, a featherlight touch, that warmed him to the depths of his soul. "I told you once that I was not certain I ever wanted children."

"Ah, Mae. Don't concern yourself with this. We have each other. It will be enough."

She shook her head, as though in wonder. "You are all I want. But I must tell you. I didn't understand the visions Bride sent me. For seven years I thought I was foreseeing my death should I conceive, but it was the rebirth of Pictland herself my goddess was showing me. If you do not mind waiting, I believe my fear will fade in time. The warning was not for me, and I should so dearly love to have your child, Finn."

A fierce wave of love, devotion, and bone deep protectiveness swept through him, and a future filled with all he had ever secretly dreamed of glowed with promise. "Sweet Mae. I'll wait forever and whatever happens, our life together is all I want."

She wound her arms around him, his courageous, Pictish princess, and sealed their future with a kiss.

~

HER SAVAGE SCOT

THE HIGHLAND WARRIOR CHRONICLES
BOOK 1

Scots warrior Connor will do anything to protect Aila from the Vikings. But to save her he must defy his king, betray his country, and forsake his honor

When tough Scot warrior Connor Mackenzie rides into the barbaric lands of the Picts on a mission for his king, he never expects to be captivated by a beautiful Pictish widow. Drawn under her spell, yet unaware of her true identity, he risks everything for one passionate night in her arms.

Aila, princess of Pictland, swore long ago she would do anything within her power to help defeat the Vikings who invaded her land and murdered her husband. But after meeting Connor, her frozen heart thaws and once again she imagines a future filled with love and passion.

Connor delivers the message from his king and Aila becomes a pawn in a deadly game of politics. Her heart belongs to Connor, but she must marry the prince of Dal Riada—Connor's half-brother.

But as dangerous secrets unravel, both Connor and Aila must find a way to outwit their enemies if they want a chance of surviving, together, in this fractured new world.

HER VENGEFUL SCOT

THE HIGHLAND WARRIOR CHRONICLES
BOOK 2

My enemies will pay for what they've done

The only reason Scots warrior Cameron MacNeil agrees to go to Pictland is so he can have vengeance on the Pict noble who killed his sister. He has no intention of falling for anyone, especially not a pagan princess who is married to his enemy. But when fate throws them together, he struggles to contain his attraction.

Caught in a loveless marriage, Elise has no means of escape. But as a fragile friendship forms between her and the tough Scots warrior, she knows if they want to survive this alliance between their people, they must trust each other. As she opens her heart to her taciturn warrior, she imagines a life together, even if it's an impossible dream. And then her husband turns up dead, releasing her from the vows she's come to dread.

When danger threatens her life, Cam risks everything to keep her safe from his king's machinations. He should be happy now his enemy is dead, but guilt cripples him at the secrets he must keep, for if Elise ever discovers the truth, he'll lose her forever.

But Elise has a secret of her own, one she is blood bound never to reveal. Even if keeping it means she'll lose the only man she's ever loved.

ABOUT THE AUTHOR

Christina Phillips is an ex-pat Brit who now lives in sunny Western Australia with her high school sweetheart and their family. She enjoys writing historical romance with a touch of fantasy, paranormal romance and contemporary romance, where the stories sizzle and the heroine brings her hero to his knees.

She is addicted to good coffee, expensive chocolate, and bad boy heroes. She is also owned by three gorgeous cats who are convinced the universe revolves around their needs. They are not wrong.

ACKNOWLEDGMENTS

I'd like to give a big thank you to all my readers for your support and patience while I've been deep in the cave with Finn and Mairi, and a special thanks to those of you who have waited so long for me to return to 9th century Pictland! It's good to be back :-)

Eternal gratitude as always to Amanda Ashby and Sally Rigby. Amanda, for your incredible insights when I'm rocking in the corner, and Sally for your straight talking when I'm teetering on the edge! Long may our tiaras sparkle!

And for my amazing family, Mark and our children, our sons-in-law, and beautiful grandsons. Biggest hugs ever!

AUTHOR'S NOTE

Although Kenneth MacAlpin, King of the Scots of Dal Riada, became King of Pictland in 843 AD or thereabouts, this is a work of fiction based on myths, legends, and my own imagination.

Forged in blood, United by Passion
The Highland Warrior Chronicles

Her Savage Scot
Her Vengeful Scot
Her Baseborn Scot
Her Wicked Scot - coming in 2022
Her Rebel Scot - Prequel coming in December 2021